RAMLEAJ CHRONICLES

1. HIGH MASTER

2. DEMON LORD (FORTHCOMING 2025)

OTHER BOOKS BY AUTHOR

RIGHT LOVE, WRONG TIME (COMING NOVEMBER 2024)

GHOST WITNESS

1. LITTLE MISS JANE (FORTHCOMING)

STAR OF ATHENA SERIES

Rising Star Arc

1. HER CHAMPION

2. NOTHINGS FOR SURE

3. AN ARMY OF SHADOWS

4. FROM THE ASHES

HIGH MASTER

Robin Rhoden

Content Warnings
(please be aware if any of these things may disturb you)

- fantasy racism
- death and body mutilation
- captivity
- torture

Copyright © 2024 Robin Rhoden

All rights reserved.

ISBN:
ISBN-13:

For all of the 'gifted' children:

Too smart for your peers
Too immature for the adults
Too much pressure to live up to

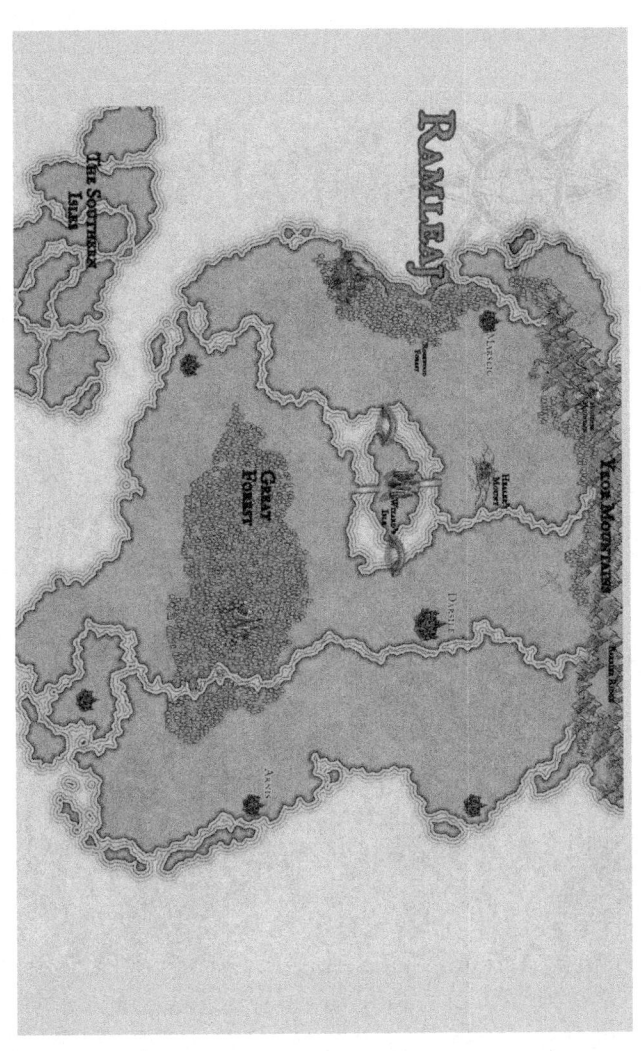

1

Dworkin raced down the stairs, the stones cold under his bare feet. Rain pelted the walls of the castle and splashed in a window where the shutters had been ripped open by the wind. He thanked the Twins his people were safe inside the castle as he paused to yank the shutters closed. Pushing the latch back in place with fumbling fingers felt like it took forever. He needed to return to his task. His wife's words still echoed in his mind and made his heart pound. He wouldn't be able to relax until he knew his foster brother was safe.

Lightning flashed, followed immediately by a rumble of thunder that felt like it would shake the whole earth. He braced himself against the wall as he finally reached the door to his study. He rushed past the reports and to do lists he'd left spread out on the desk to unlock the large chest behind it. Buried under the blankets and books, he found the box he'd been searching for.

His hands shook as he set it on the desk and pushed the ornately carved top open. The hinges inside creaked from lack of use, but the square of glass slid into place just as Darian had shown him it should, years before. He felt around the back of the box until finding the small slip of paper tucked into the edging.

"This better work, Darian." He sighed, unfolding the paper and scanning over the word. He swallowed hard then spoke the word, hoping he got the pronunciation right.

For a second he thought nothing was happening, then the glass started to sparkle. Tiny lights like floating gemstones swirled across it's surface, twinkling and shifting until they settled into a pattern and flashed brightly. He blinked the light from his eyes then found himself looking at the face of a very annoyed Darian. Gray eyes peered out from under his sopping wet purple hood, lightning flashing in the sky behind him.

"Dworkin? What's wrong?"

"Everything here is fine." Just blasted cold, he thought as he pulled a blanket from the chest around his shoulders and glanced longingly to the fireplace. "Wait, why are you out in this miserable weather?"

"I was called to a last minute meeting with the council, the message said it couldn't wait." Darian sighed and rolled his eyes. "What is it, Dworkin? I told you this spell was for emergencies."

Dworkin hesitated, suddenly feeling sheepish and silly. "I had to know that you were okay. Leslien had a vision and-"

"I'm fine, Dworkin. Just cold and wet and already late." The image shifted and Dworkin found himself looking at the sky for a second. Darian growled and tugged on the reigns of his stallion until the image stilled again. "I think this might be another case like the veal."

Heat rushed to Dworkin's cheeks remembering the time he had ridden to the capital city after his wife had been certain the king and queen were being poisoned. When he got there he found the whole court sick from some veal that hadn't been cooked properly. Leslien's visions were unpredictable and uncontrollable, a last remnant of her rumored Wythelm heritage. Still, sometimes they were right, and he wasn't willing to take any chances with his brother's life.

"She saw you teetering between darkness and light, with all of Ramleaj depending on you." Dworkin dropped his eyes and his voice, fear and embarrassment warring inside him. "I had to check."

Darian's face softened even as he shook rain from his hood. "I appreciate your concern, brother, it's just not a good time. Get some rest and I'll go to this blasted meeting. Have the box open in the morning and I'll contact you then."

"Of course. Safe travels, Darian."

He waited as the image faded into the tiny lights and then back to clear glass before closing the box again. The chair creaked as he leaned back, rubbing at his burning eyes. He wasn't a fool, there was no way he was going to get any sleep this night. He hadn't told Darian about the way Leslien's eyes had glazed over, or the dreamy quality her voice had taken. Mostly, he hadn't told him everything she had said.

"All should beware," he muttered again to himself, the words burned into his mind. "He teeters on a knife's edge, the wizard with the world on his shoulders. Should he fall, purple fades to black and all is lost."

2

Darian grinned as he slid away the seeing glass. He loved Dworkin for being worried about him, but the man couldn't have picked a worse time to decide to use the spell after letting it sit dormant for all these years. The soft flashing and beeping had nearly given him a heart attack imagining what could possibly be so wrong at Darsile for the duke to be reaching out to him in the middle of the night. Dworkin wasn't the kind to ask for help if he could avoid it, hence why the spell had gone unused for so long. Then he chooses to use it basically because his lovely wife had had a bad dream? They would both have a good laugh in the morning, then next time he was able to make his way to Darsile, he would recharge the spell. Just in case it was ever actually needed.

He pulled the large hood of his purple robe further over his face and let Ebony have his head. With the rain pelting down and the only light being the intermittent flashes of lightning, he could barely see the horse's alert ears in front of him but he didn't really want to use a spell light if he could avoid it. The massive black stallion knew the way to Wizards' Isle and would probably get them there safer without his help.

Hoof beats changed to the sharp staccato of stone that must mean they had made it to the bridge that spanned to the center of the lake where the wizards had set up their school and headquarters. He squinted through the rain to try and make out the soaring towers. As lightning filled the sky with thunder rumbling right after, he could just make out the multilevel buildings with their peaked towers and sodden flags flapping in the harsh wind.

Why weren't there any lights? No candles burning, no spell lights adding their odd glow to a window. Sure, it was past curfew for the students but there seemed to always be Masters up working on one thing or another. Having the place completely dark was an eerie sight that set his teeth on edge. The slight buzzing in his ears as he passed through the protective barrier that kept uninvited guests off the island did little to settle his nerves.

"Horrible night for travel."

Ebony jerked to a halt and Darian spun in the saddle. At first he couldn't see anything and thought he must have been imagining things, but he called up a spell light and could just make out a man on the other side of the bridge.

Dark hair and eyes seemed almost a part of the night and stark contrast to the pure white suit he wore. His large hat seemed to repel the rain somehow, the fluffy white feather still standing at attention. The white lace at his neck and the end of each sleeve still looked perfectly starched and even his white shoes were pristine.

"Did you need shelter, friend?" Darian called over the thunder and wind.

The man grinned and pulled a cloak as white as the snow on the Ykor mountains around his shoulders. "Oh, no. I just couldn't pass up the opportunity to speak to the great High Master. You're a legend in your own time after all."

"All I am right now is very wet and very late." He tried to laugh but there were chills tracing down his spine that had nothing to do with the rain trying to slide under his cloak. "So if there is nothing you need, I really should be going."

"Of course, High Master. I'd hate to keep you from the Council. They would be absolutely lost without you, wouldn't they?"

"They got along just fine for hundreds of years before I came along." Darian laughed, trying to ignore the fact that the man had no way of knowing he was headed to a meeting with the Wizard's Council. It was a pretty fair guess after all. "We should both get out of the weather. Good evening, sir."

"Yes, good evening."

Darian nodded and let the spell light fade as he turned Ebony's head back towards the buildings. As if his nerves weren't already high from an emergency call back to the Island, and Dworkin's cryptic worries, now this strange man to top it all off. He could practically feel his blood racing through his veins, singing with worry and anticipation. He shook his head and tried to write it off as the storm making a normal encounter seem even more odd.

"Half breed," the man's voice seemed to snarl right in his ear.

He spun back, mouthing the words to flare the spell light back to life, but the bridge and the land beyond were completely empty. There was no where the man could have gone that fast, no shelter or buildings close to the Isle. It was as if he had never been there to begin with.

"I'm losing it, Ebony." He growled and released the spell light, surrounding them in darkness again.

The massive horse just snorted and shook the rain from his mane before setting off for the stables.

Darian pushed through the massive doors to the central building, gripping his long staff with one hand while shaking out his soaked cloak with the other. He considered a heat spell to dry it but that would be a waste of energy and he was already feeling tired. He'd just have to deal with being cold and wet through the meeting.

He'd done his best for Ebony as quickly as possible since the night stable hand seemed to be slacking off. He'd rubbed the big stallion down with straw then tossed a wool blanket over him and promised to come back for a proper grooming and feeding as quick as he could.

The silence made him uneasy as he jogged up the grand staircase past the formal portraits of all the Head Masters who had ever lead the council as well as a few other Masters who had done something noteworthy. Reaching the top of the stairs, he averted his eyes. While done well, he hated looking at his own portrait. It was just weird.

Out of breath, he skidded to a stop in front of the grand doors to the Council Chambers. He took a moment to straighten his clothes and catch his breath. He was thirty five years old and had already surpassed all the levels of Master to the point where they had to create one for him, still he felt like a boy being brought to task any time he was called before the council. He took another deep breath before pressing the purple gem at the top of his staff to the indentation in the doors and muttering the spell that would allow him entrance.

As soon as the doors swung inward, a familiar voice called from inside. "Darian, my boy, do stop dallying at the door and come in."

He blinked and swallowed the retort on his tongue, fighting to remain calm as he strode into the room. A shiver traced over him even though flames danced in the large fireplaces on the two long walls, tracing patterns of light across the black marble floor. No breeze stirred the long tapestries lining the walls but he swore he could almost hear the wind, or maybe whispers just beyond comprehension.

The center of the room was dominated by a long table made of Karmak wood, the hardest tree in Ramleaj and the same wood that made up every wizard's staff. As always the table was surrounded by fourteen chairs, six on either side and then one at either end. Most were filled by the Master Wizards who made up the Wizards Council, all with their bright red cloaks pulled around their shoulders or draped over the chair behind them.

Three chairs stood empty, the guest chair closest to him and one of the six on the far side. Once again, Master Clesum must have ignored the Head Master's call to council. How he remained the King's Wizard with all of his antics, Darian would never understand.

The final empty chair belonged to the Head Master himself who stood staring at Darian. Frencis smiled kindly and motioned to the guest chair.

"Glad you could finally make it. We waited as long as we could but you will understand we eventually had to start without you."

"Of course," Darian said, sliding his staff into the holder in the arm of the chair then sitting on the edge of the seat. "My apologies, Head Master, the weather made for difficult travel."

"Yes, yes." Frencis sighed with the wave of his hand. "Now, where were we?"

Darian swallowed hard. Had he done something, or insulted the council in some way without realizing it? He couldn't remember Frencis ever being so short with him, even when he was a young boy constantly sticking his nose where it didn't really belong.

Frencis paced in front of one of the fireplaces, his red cape floating in his wake. "As I was saying, it has been way too long that the wizards have sat back and watched the three races of Ramleaj try to kill each other. The Cregas deep in their mountain, the Wythlem hiding away in their forest, and worst of all, the humans spreading like wildfire everywhere else. If we do not step in and use our might to get them all under control, they will destroy all of Ramleaj and take us down with them."

Darian's head jerked up. He glanced to the other Masters but they were all just nodding their heads and muttering in agreement. Had he seriously been called here to discuss a hostile takeover of Ramleaj? That's certainly what it sounded like but he couldn't bring himself to believe it. Or believe that they had thought for even a moment that he would go along with it.

"Excuse me, Head Master, but don't you think that's being a little harsh?"

Frencis turned to him again, just grinning and staring like he knew a secret that Darian wasn't privy too. The longer the Head Master stared at him the more his brain began to swim. A fog kept creeping into his mind and making it hard to think or even focus. He shook his head trying to clear it but that only made Frencis smile grow larger.

A loud thump echoed through the room making them all jump. Darian listened and thought he heard it again, followed by a muffled voice. Frencis looked about the room with a scowl, there was a slight surge of power in the room and the sound was gone again.

"Missed one it seems," Frencis muttered as if to himself.

Darian cocked his head. "One what?"

"A window, of course. Must seal the shutters tight against a storm like this, right?" Frencis smiled and moved to lean against the back on his chair. "But back to matters at hand. You said I was harsh? You have commented much the same many times, High Master. You have practically devoted your life to trying to solve all the problems that their petty squabbles cause."

Darian leaned his arms against the table with a sigh. "I've dedicated my life to trying to get them to work together, not to take them over."

"Not all of us look at things as sympathetically as you do." The small Master to his left laughed as he turned to smile at Darian, his thick beard and mustache parting to reveal two rows of tiny, pointed teeth.

Darian jerked back, chair and staff clattering to the floor behind him. His heart pounded in his chest and his mind raced, pushing against the fog that had such a tight hold on him. He shook his head and pressed the heels of his hands to his eyes. It wasn't possible he had seen what he thought. It couldn't be. He'd known these men basically his whole life.

There was the sound of shuffling as his chair was retrieved and he was gently pushed back into it. When he opened his eyes again, Frencis hovered over him, gray eyes full of concern.

"Is there a problem, my boy?"

He blinked, looking first to Frencis then around the table to the other Masters. They were all talking but it was as if they were far away and he couldn't make out what they were saying. The same small Master turned to him to speak, lips parting to show a perfectly normal set of teeth.

He gulped a couple of breaths and tried to bring his heart back under control. "What's happening to me?"

Frencis rose with a laugh and squeezed his shoulder a little too tight. "What do you think is happening?"

All of the other Masters leaned in as if waiting for his answer. Darian wet his lips and tried to swim through the fog to get his mind to work but it was getting worse. The whole room seemed to swim, or was it his own head? Out of the the corner of his eyes he would catch a glimpse of green skin or long claws but when he turned to look, it would be gone. If he tried to look up at Frencis, the world tilted more and felt he might drown. Those gray eyes locked with his again and for a moment he was falling into them to be lost forever.

Frencis looked away and he jerked back into his own mind. He leaned back and closed his eyes for a moment, reciting a quick calming mantra he had learned from Miramel. He had to get control of himself. Whatever was happening to him, he couldn't let them see before he understood it himself.

"I guess I'm more tired than I thought," he muttered, opening his eyes again. "Sorry for the interruption."

Frencis patted his shoulder and returned to his seat at the other end of the table to continue the insane discussion of how they would conquer Ramleaj and force the three great races into submission. Darian only half listened to what was being said and watched those around him. Even though Frencis led the conversation, the Masters' eyes kept drifting to him then quickly looking away if he caught them. The more and more it happened, the more he started to wonder what they were seeing.

He began to whisper a spell under his breath, moving his lips as little as possible. The others would feel the gathering of power but it was a fairly small spell so hopefully they wouldn't pay much attention. For all they knew it could be another wizard on the Isle practicing.

No one seemed to notice as he brought together the final strands of the spell and spoke the words to release it into the air. The power welled inside him then burst, settling over him like a fine gauze. His vision shifted to that of the next Master who turned to look his way.

He had fully expected to not like what he saw. He would understand if he looked young, cocky, or even a little crazy at this point. He certainly hadn't expected for everything to take on an odd yellow haze. Through the spell he looked so small and frightened, huddled down in his chair. Dark blood coursed just below his skin and throbbed at the pulse point just below his jaw. Darian shook himself and dropped out of the spell, even more confused than ever before.

He dropped his eyes to his shaking hands as his vision returned to normal. As the Master's babbled on, all of it sounding like complete nonsense to Darian, Frencis' eyes kept drifting to him. Those gray eyes held him, almost pleading him, but for what? To understand? To say that he agreed? Or something else? What if all of this was an elaborate plan by Francis to tell Darian that he was in danger?

Taking a deep breath, he pulled on his tiring power once more and whispered the words of the spell again but made a few slight changes on the fly. He'd never tried it this way so he was just hoping it would work. Instead of focusing on himself, he adjusted the spell, hoping to see the way the Masters saw Frencis. If they looked to Frencis like a juicy meal the same as they had him, well, then either something was very wrong with his spell or with the Council.

His vision fought to shift into the spell but that same fog kept pushing back at him, growing thicker and darker every time he tried to fight against it. The room still took on a yellowish tint but any time he tried to look at Frencis, his vision swam and he was nearly pushed out of the spell. He caught flashes of black clothing and sinister smiles but couldn't focus on anything for more than a second. Suddenly, a strange face smile at him through the fog, teeth bared and gray eyes practically glowing before morphing into Frences' concerned gaze as he was forced out of the spell.

He couldn't help but think of the first time he'd seen Frencis looking down at him that way. He'd been six years old, following the former Duke of Marslic as one of the Masters showed them around the Isle. Darian had been frightened and lost. His mother had passed only a couple years before and Marslic had become his new home, Dworkin his brother. But his out of control magic had caused one too many problems around the keep and no matter how much the former Duke wanted to act as a father, something had to be done. They had encountered Frencis outside one of the classrooms and he had bent down kindly to assure tiny Darian that this really was the place for him and that everything was going to be all right. There had been many times in his life he had called back on that moment with the Head Master's kind green eyes shining at him to remind himself that this is what he was supposed to be doing.

He rolled the ring he always wore on his right hand, a habit he often did when thinking. Something about the memory stirred in his mind, telling him things weren't right.

The fog lifted a little and Darian jumped to his feet, grabbing his staff to hold out in front of him. "Imposter."

"What are you talking about, High Master?"

He backed away as Frencis tried to come closer. He gripped his staff so hard the grooves of the wood bit into his hand and the stones spiraling up it's length, the deep purple amethyst at the stop started to glow from sheer, undirected power seeping out of him.

"I don't know how you've done it, but you're not the Head Master," he motioned to the rest of the Masters staring at him from their seats, "and these probably aren't the real council either."

"I fear our High Master may have caught an illness traveling in this weather and it is messing with his mind." One of the Masters sighed with the click of his tongue.

Another half rose from his chair. "Or perhaps it is a spell making him see threats everywhere."

"Or maybe he fell from that giant horse and hit his head."

Darian hesitated just a moment, the staff in his hands lowering slightly. All the strange things that had happened, from the man on the bridge to this insanity, what if it was something wrong with him?

No, he couldn't take that chance. He couldn't risk the Wizards Guild and school falling into the hands of someone powerful enough to replace the whole council.

"Stop it," he yelled, jerking up the staff again to point directly at Frencis. "As High Master and highest ranking guild member present I am placing you all under arrest."

Frencis stared at him for a moment then started to laugh. It was a deep maniacal laugh that rumbled in Nate's gut and and filled the room.

"Well done, my boy," a new voice spoke through Frencis. It was deeper with a dark undertone. "I was starting to worry but you did it."

"Did what?"

"Passed the test. Unfortunately that will not change your fate much."

The man that wasn't Frencis stepped back and spread his arms. The illusion fell away like fog clearing. The man who now stood in front of him looked vaguely familiar but the shock wouldn't let his brain place just where from. He was tall and willowy with surprisingly graceful features. His dark eyes were slit like a cat's and his ears were delicately pointed. A Wylthem, yet not like any that Darian had ever met. Long black robes billowed around him from a wind Darian didn't feel, his hands stretched out almost as if to reach for Darian.

He tried to back away from the man. If he could just get out of this room and to Ebony, he could ride until he reached Marslic or Darsile. Surely Dworkin or the King would have some idea of what to do. But his foot slid on something thick and moist, nearly making him fall.

Bile filled his throat as the rest of the illusion fell away. The Council room was bathed in blood. Twelve of the world's greatest wizards were strewn about like broken dolls, Master Frencis nearly in pieces where he had come to rest near a wall, his hand still reaching upwards as if to grab something. Twelve creatures stared down at him with hunger in their eyes and sharp teeth bared. They stood a full head or more taller than him, with hunched shoulders and arms that hung to their knees. Green skin stretched tight over thick muscles and flat, hairless heads with protruding yellow eyes and high pointed ears.

Darian swallowed the contents of his stomach back where they belonged and raised his staff again. He quickly chanted the most powerful attack spell he could think of and sent it flying out of his staff directly towards the dark leader of this nightmare troupe. The man didn't even flinch. With a light wave of his hand, the spell was knocked aside to bounce into the fireplace, making it flair purple for a second and then collapse upon itself.

"Let us not play that game. You will just tire yourself out and waste our time. We have places to be after all."

At a nod from their leader, two of the creatures stepped towards him. He was able to sidestep the first but the other grabbed him from behind and squeezed his arms together until he couldn't move and his feet were dangling above the ground. He lost his grip on his staff and heard it clatter to the ground, far out of reach.

"Who are you?" He gasped, struggling to catch his breath with his ribs being constricted.

"Me?" The dark man smiled with a small shrug. "I am the one who never was."

3

The rain drummed against the tiles of the roof, clattering through the thick forest to reach them.

Miramel hesitated as another roll of thunder echoed over the land. Adjusting the tray in her hands, she continued on with a small laugh. Why was she acting like a scared child? The Lady of the Forest would protect them as she always did.

The quarters she was headed to were at the far edge of the compound. Her feet padded silently over the stone floors and through the arched walkways, cool air flowing through the open compound. Awnings kept the rain from getting inside so no one had bothered pulling the shutters or closing the doors. The sturdy building had stood for thousands of years. A little rain would not hurt anything, she reminded herself as she reached the very end of the hallway.

Reilan liked her privacy and stayed out there with her little pond, preferring the company of her fish over other Wylthem. Miramel did not understand it but maybe it had to do with being a water born, or with being centuries old.

"Reilan," She called as she pushed back the curtain of strung sea shells and slipped into the chambers, "Mother says you have not eaten in a while. She asked me to bring you something."

The rooms were quiet and dark. Miramel placed the tray on the central table, next to the small bubbling fountain made of river rocks. She doubted Reilan would be asleep already but there were not any lights or any signs of the elder Wylthem.

"Reilan?" She called a little louder, moving through the space.

"Come dance with me, child."

She followed the call to the archway leading outside. Wrapping her shawl tighter around her shoulders, she stepped under the awning to scan the small garden. It was odd for so much rain to reach the ground through the thick trees that surrounded and covered their secret city.

Another flash of lightning illuminated the garden. Reilan spun in the rain with her head tilted back and arms raised high. Her long white hair was plastered to her, clothes soaked through. Miramel had never seen the elder Wylthem so happy as she held out a hand.

"Come on, do not tell me a princess is too high and mighty to dance in the rain with an old friend."

Miramel grinned and started to step out but immediately stepped back. The rain slithered over her skin, feeling oily and unnatural against her bare arm. She used the edge of her shawl to swipe it off then sniffed at the fabric. There was a faint smell that made her think of burning wood and heavy smoke.

"I think you should come in, Reilan," she called over the thunder. "This rain is unnatural."

Reilan turned to her and grinned broadly, her eyes holding a wild glint. "It is rain, child, pure water. Just because we do not get much in the forest doesn't make it unnatural."

Miramel shuddered. She could not shake the feeling of the water on her skin or the flash of fear that it stirred inside her. How could

Railan not feel it? Being water born must mean she knew more than a forest born like Miramel but something just did not feel right.

Another bright flash of lightning felt way too close, the rumbling of thunder following a mere breath behind. Over the loud thunder, a sharp crack broke the night air sounding as if it came from somewhere at the center of the complex. Miramel's eyes went wide as her heart plummeted to her stomach. Reilan stopped dancing and turned to Miramel, face filled with the same fear rushing through Miramel.

Miramel tossed her shawl over her head and gritted her teeth before dashing out into the rain. They circled the building together, looping back through another passageway and dashing in and out of the interconnected buildings until they reached the central courtyard. Other Wylthem were already gathering around the massive fountain that dominated the courtyard.

The stone tree towered above them, carved in such detail that every tiny leaf had even tinier veins and texture. No one knew who had carved it, it just seemed to have always been. Normally, water bubbled and slid it's way down the branches and leaves to drip into the large pool below. The rain poured alongside the fountain water, leaving burning black trails everywhere it touched. Her stomach clenched. There were those who said this fountain was directly connected to the World Tree, the central life force that fed all dimensions.

Miramel pushed her way through the crowd, trying to reach where her father stood at the far edge of the fountain.

He pulled the hood of his silver cloak over his dark hair and delicately pointed ears, the fabric immediately shifting and adjusting to the darkness and colors of the land around them until his figure almost disappeared. His shoulders shuddered as dark eyes flashed to the falling rain then back to the fountain.

"Father," she gasped, sliding to a stop at his side, "I heard a crack. What happened?"

He sighed and motioned to the fountain. From this side, she could see that a large branch had broken off and lay half in, half out of the pool at the bottom. The jagged edge where it had broken off was black and charred, the black spreading quickly up the branch until it was completely consumed.

"Come, let us get back inside, my inonym." He wrapped and arm around her shoulders. just as the old term of endearment wrapped around her heart, and turned her towards the nearest entryway. "I do not like the feel of this rain."

She swallowed, glancing back over her shoulder at the fountain and the dead branch at its feet. "What is happening, Father?"

He paused a moment under the awning and closed his eyes. "I do not know yet, but I doubt it is anything good."

She shuddered as he hugged her shoulders and kissed her temple, then strode off down the hall towards his study. She could already imagine all the parchments he would pull from the shelves to consult and pour over for the rest of the night. She watched until he disappeared around a corner then turned back to the courtyard, muttering whatever little words she could think of as comfort to the Wylthem that streamed past her back inside.

Shortly she was alone, watching the dead branch through the rain sheeting off the awning. Lightning flashed again, further away this time but still close enough to blind her with its light. As she tried to blink away the flash, her vision shifted for a second and she was standing in a fancy room surrounded by men wearing red cloaks and staring hungrily at one man draped in purple. Another blink and she was back in her home, surrounded by the rain and darkness.

"Darian?" she whispered, her breath catching in her throat. "Do you have something to do with this? Or know something?"

She searched herself, trying to bring back up the vision but nothing would work. No matter what she tried, all she had was the memory. Thunder rumbled through the air and this time it may as well have been in her own mind. Pain flared from the back of her head and spread quickly, make her sway where she stood and turning her stomach upside down. She leaned against a nearby column, gasping for breath.

"What is happening, Carame? Are you all right, my friend?"

4

Braslic

Braslic kept a dagger in one hand and the head of the creature in the other. He was covered in mine dust, blood, and the mountain only knew what else. Behind him, four of his men carried the bodies of the other two that had left with them for patrol.

    He moved quickly through the maze of turns without having to stop and think. He had probably traveled the whole mountain up and down more times than anyone else and never got lost. As he paced, the blood of the creature left a burnt groove in the stone, the soft plops and hissing the only sound of the little band.

    Caves grew larger and tunnels more refined and in little time he burst forth into the central hall. All activity stopped and a hush fell over the underground city as people caught sight of their Aegis and his prize. Wails broke out behind him as the payment for that prize was revealed. Still, he kept walking.

People moved out of his way as he stormed up the massive steps to the Hall of Heroes and kicked the door open. The tables had been pushed back to the sides long ago, remnants of the last meal swept away and replaced by one central table covered in maps and papers, held down by thick and dusty books. Gerent Selick and his head city planner conferred over the maps, their pale heads bent together as they pointed and discussed.

Braslic tossed the head so that it hit the floor with a sickening mix of a thud and splat then rolled to land just short of the table. Sharp teeth and beady eyes stared up at the two shocked Cregas. His men moved forward and gently laid the bodies of their fallen brother and sister on the stone floor as well then hastily left the room. They knew all too well not to be caught in the crossfire that was about to explode.

"You stand here planning an expansion when our people can't even mine without being attacked by these nightmare beasts."

He shuddered as images of the battle raced through his mind. Sharp claws against the rock, trying to swing ax and dagger without hitting one of your own in the tight quarters. Rats larger than you with claws as long as your dagger rushing at you from every direction.

Selick leaned his arms against the table to make a face at the head as it seeped black blood across the stone. "Protection of our people is your responsibility, Aegis Braslic, and it looks like you've done your job once again."

"At the cost of two lives."

"I know, brother, I'm sorry. I don't have an answer for these beasts that aren't supposed exist out of fables and nightmares."

Braslic slid his dagger away with a grunt. "There is no shame in asking for help. You get help from the Head Planner, from me, from all of our people. We survive by working together, there can be no harm in asking the humans for assistance. The High Master may know what to do against such strange creatures, or at the least approach the human king for us."

"I'm not sure they'll have any interest in helping us after the last encounter between Cregas and Humans but we have to try something." Selick ran a hand over his face and sighed. "Send Denlin in search of your friend and see what he can do."

Braslic shook his head. "Denlin has never been outside the mountain by himself. He would be lost before the pass or eaten by the dragons. Besides, if the High Master is on the Isle, I am the only Cregas with permission to cross the bridge."

"I can't spare you just yet, brother." Selick motioned him forward then pointed to a couple places on the map. "The high tunnels are flooding from this nonstop rain. We have to move the people in deeper and block off the tunnels to keep the water from going any further. I'll need your help with that. Sometimes I fear our people respect you more than they do me. They will open their homes to the displaced if you ask it."

Braslic scrubbed a hand over his chin, pressing his tongue to his teeth. Now was not the time to have the same argument again. How many times had he told Selick he had lost focus, that the people didn't see him enough, especially in battle. You couldn't be a warlord if you didn't fight.

"Plus," Selick sighed and shrugged his shoulders, "there is the caravan to think of. If you don't trust Denlin out of the caves alone, do you really trust him to lead them to market?"

"I will do what I can, brother, but I must leave as soon as the caravan is safe at market. It is a long journey to the humans and everyday lost is another that lives are in danger."

"Yes, of course. We will get you on your way as soon as possible. For now rest and prepare the rights for your fallen soldiers." Selick wrinkled his nose at the head and the goo eating into the rock floor around it. "And get someone to clean up that disgusting thing."

His back groaned as he placed another slat of wood on the pyre then stepped back so the families could place their offerings before the bodies were brought in. He stretched and watched as his soldier's parents and loved ones spread blankets across the piles of wood then tucked tiny notes and mementos into the pile for the dead to take to the afterlife with them. Their quiet sobs filled the domed cave as his eyes drifted to the multitude of niches carved into the wall, each filled with a tiny jar to hold a small portion of the ashes of someone lost. The rest of the ashes would be carried to the top of Mother Mountain as soon as the rain stopped to be carried away by the wind.

He couldn't help but think of the three pyres he had had to build on a distant mountain, unable to carry the bodies so far home. He'd brought as much of the ashes back with him as he could but it just wasn't the same. The battle had been brutal, killing not just his men, but his hopes of expanding their community to a sister mountain. A mountain the humans weren't even using but guarded so zealously.

He gritted his teeth as he realized his hand had reached for dagger and ax. There was no one here to use them against, no matter how his blood still boiled. High Master Darian had talked them into peace, and he knew it was the right thing. They weren't strong enough for a war right now, but he still hated having given up that mountain so easily.

He took a seat on the white circle that followed the edge of the room, with the families of the warriors on either side of him, the rest of the attendants spreading out to complete the circle. At his nod, a gong sounded and echoed through the tunnels. A procession carried the bodies in, laying them gently on their respective pyre, followed by Gerent Sectic dressed his finest war regalia. Braslic had to hold back a snort at how tight the bracings had become and the dull, unsharpened edge of the ax that swung from a stretched belt.

The mother of his youngest soldier leaned over and patted his leg. "You should say a few words."

"It is not my place," he whispered back, giving her hand a soft squeeze.

The old woman adjusted her shawl and sat up a little straighter, giving a small sniff as she blinked rapidly. "Maybe it should be. My Denma always said if you were in charge-"

"Stop," he hissed under his breath, adjusting his ax in its holster, "Denma was a great warrior and I was honored to serve with her but she should not have spoken of such things and neither should you.

Selick is Gerent and I will not challenge him."

She grew silent and just stared at her daughter's body as Selick intoned the traditional words and lit the ceremonial torch. Light danced on the mourners faces and the walls of the cave, only growing brighter as he touched the torch to each pyre.

Braslic forced himself not to look away as the flames grew higher and engulfed the bodies of Cregas he had called friends and comrades. Smoke hung heavy in the room, filled with the herbs they had tucked into the wood, and the essence of those that fueled the flames. Even as his eyes started to burn and his lungs protested, he breathed in the smoke in shallow breaths, as did those around him. With each breath, they took in the essence of the fallen and added the best of them back into the community, allowing them to fight another day within the hearts of their compatriots.

5

Dworkin

Dworkin was still shrugging into his coat as he strode into the office. Leslien was already waiting for him, leaning against his desk with her hands bunched in a dark green dress that matched her eyes as they stared up at him. He placed a kiss on the top of her blond braids before moving around her to sit in front of the box again.

"It isn't like him not to keep his word," she whispered.

"No, it isn't."

A dark fear had settled over them both just as surely as the clouds hung over the land. Dworkin had stayed in front of the blasted box the whole night and well into the morning without Darian's face ever appearing in the glass. He had spent a whole day trying to go about his usual duties as the rain continued to pour, but kept finding himself back at the box. He'd tried saying the word again and again but nothing would happen. He seemed remember Darian having said the spell would need to be updated after each use but couldn't be certain.

"But it's possible it's just something wrong with the box." He tried to offer a smile but knew it looked forced and weak. "Maybe he tried to and I wasn't here or it wouldn't come through properly."

Her hand brushed his shoulder, fiddling with the collar on his coat. "If you believed that, you wouldn't already be dressed to ride."

"I just have to check," he said, pulling her hand to his lips for a kiss. "I'll ride over to the Isle and have a good laugh with him, then be back in time for the Festival. Maybe he'll even come back with me and we can all ride to Darsile together for the festivities."

"The children would love that."

He reached out and pulled her into his lap, burying his face in her neck to breath in her warm scent. Every day he got to wake up with her in his arms, he wondered what he had ever done for the Twins to bless him so. His first wife had been for duty, the girl that his father had wanted, the one that was a good match for the land and politics. It hadn't been a bad marriage and when she had died young from a fever, he had mourned the loss of a dear friend. But when the Queen had introduced him to the daughter of a knight from one of the southern dukedoms, he knew what his first marriage had been missing. She had quickly brought love and light like he'd never known to his life and blessed him with the two beautiful children that looked just like her.

She shifted a little and unclasped the necklace that she always wore, letting the chain and stone pool into her hand. She turned his hand over and let the pile slide into his palm, closing his fingers over it. He let his thumb run over the green stone a couple of times before looking up into her eyes. The necklace had been in her family for generations, supposedly handed down from the however many greats grandmother who had been full blooded Wylthem. He'd never seen her take it off for anything before.

"My mother always said this was magic but she didn't know how it worked. I would feel better if you took it with you. You can give it back to me when you return."

"It'll be back around your neck before you know it." He slid the bauble into the pouch on his belt then pulled her tight for a kiss. "Tell the children I love them and will see them soon."

"Be careful, my love. Something is not right in this world, and I fear you are riding right into the thick of it."

He tried to laugh and wink at her but it sounded hollow. "Just how dangerous can the Wizard's Isle be? They're on our side, remember? Worst that could happen is I get turned into a toad or something."

There was a sharp rap at the door and then the sound of a page boy clearing his throat. "Apologies, your grace, but the men are wondering if you still plan to ride out or if they could go back to bed."

"Yes, I'm coming." He called through the door as Leslien hopped to her feet and straightened her skirts. He leaned down to kiss her cheek again and then whispered in her ear, "I highly doubt Bartol meant for the boy to repeat what he said word for word."

They followed the page down the stairs and into the great hall of their castle. Dworkin squeezed her hand lightly before they moved to the altars on either side of the door. He kneeled in front of the altar to the god as his wife mimicked his motions at the altar of the goddess. With his head bowed he said a quick prayer that the god would protect his people in his stead and speed his journey home. Carefully, he reached out and snuffed the single candle before rising to his feet. Leslien lit a stick of incense from the goddess candle and placed it in the holder before rising to her feet as well.

Before he could change his mind, he forced himself to walk outside the keep where his personal retinue had already gathered in the courtyard. He had warned them the day before that they would probably be riding out as soon as the weather cleared but didn't say why. When the rain had finally stopped late the night before, he had told them to saddle up at first light and, as usual, they had listened.

His gray mare, Mist, was already saddled and ready to go, tugging anxiously against the grip of a young stable boy. The jangle of metal and slap of leather, mixed with a few grumbles about it being too early in the morning, was all that broke the chill silence. Dworkin's breath puffed in the air and his leather gloves did little to keep his fingers from aching. The heavy rains spoke of spring's arrival but Marslic was Ramleaj's northernmost Dukedom where winter didn't release her hold easily.

Bartol moved his chestnut gelding close as Dworkin checked the straps then swung into the saddle. The head of his personal guard, and a close friend for many years, Bartol watched him with that look that said he saw more than he ever said. A large stocky man, his deep brown skin accented by black hair and thick beard gave away his southern heritage and his rough hands told of a hard soldier's life. A deep scar traced its way down the side of his face, disappearing into his beard. The man never spoke of how he got the scar or his life before coming to serve at Marslic so Dworkin didn't ask.

"The men be asking which direction we ride." Bartol glanced around at the small group as they finished their final preparations then pitched his voice low so that only Dworkin would hear. "And complaining a bit about not knowing why we be riding."

Dworkin shifted his jaw and tried not sigh. "We ride towards Wizard's Isle, but we'll take the route through Rosewood Forest. It's quicker and it's been too long since I've checked in with Frodrick."

Bartol held his restless horse in check for another moment but when Dworkin offered no other information, he just nodded and rode off to get the men in order. It wasn't normal for Dworkin to withhold information like this but Bartol was too good a soldier to question his superior, and Dworkin too careful of a husband to reveal his wife's secret. People might look at her as exotic and beautiful for her Wythelm heritage, but that didn't mean they would trust anything else that might come along with it.

With a grunt he motioned his men around him and then up to the parapets for the gate to be opened. Mist felt his unease and jumped to a gallop at the slightest touch, her hooves flying over the ground with the others close behind.

6

She spent most of the next day and night in bed with her head pounding and crazed dreams disturbing her sleep. Visions of large green creatures with arms stretching to the ground and the Wylthem with gray eyes that led them. When she finally woke, the morning shown bright and clear but her mood was anything but.

Restless, she donned her favorite forest gear. Soft leggings that felt like a second skin, a simple shirt and lightweight jacket over the top then braided her long red hair up around her head and the silver crown that rested against her forehead. Her fingers brushed over the delicate hilt of her silver sword but she passed it up for her bow and spear, laying them across her bed while sliding into her silver robe and strapping on her quiver. With spear in her hand and bow slung over her shoulder, she strode from her rooms and out towards the forest.

She tried not to look at the fountain as she passed through the central courtyard. Someone had removed the broken branch but you could still see the jagged black edge where it had snapped off and the trickle of the water had taken on a slight discordant note.

"Mira, you are up," her mother called, jogging down a hallway to catch up with her. "I was beginning to worry."

Queen Piala rose on her tiptoes to kiss her taller daughter and brush a stray hair back under Miramel's crown. A rock born, she was slightly smaller and darker skinned than the forest born with deep black hair braided to her hip and eyes that shone like sapphires. The golden crown that rested on her own brow had once been worn by her mother in the great city of Fandrel, long before all of the Wylthem left had retreated to share Melcader.

Miramel forced a smile for her mother even though she ached to be out amongst the trees and animals. "Just a headache, Mother. I am fine now."

"And where are you going?" Piala took in the weapons with a raised eyebrow. "To the training yards or the treetops?"

She smiled and shook her head. Mother knew her way to well. "I need to get out amongst the trees and move about. I thought I would head to the north quarter. There is a mother puma in that area I would not mind checking on."

"That is also the area closest to the the Wizard's Isle." Piala's face grew dark as she crossed her arms. "You are not planning on leaving the forest without permission to see your friend, the High Master, are you?"

The thought had crossed her mind but she shook her head. Her people needed her here for now. Perhaps she would send out her messenger dove, just to check in with Darian and see if he had any idea what was going on.

"No, mother." She pushed her smile brighter than she felt before kissing the top of her mother's head. "I will be back for evening meal. I promise."

She did not wait for a response but slipped out the closest archway and melded into the woods. For a while, she just walked along the small deer path that ran nearby. With a few long breaths, she opened her deeper senses to the land around her. The life force of the trees and plants, plus the very animals living within them from the high soaring birds to the tiny ant crawling across her boot, flowed through her and strengthened her. She wondered briefly if this was the same exhilarating feeling that Reilan got from wading in her pond, or mother when digging for crystals. Her mind just could not make the connection. She was her father's daughter through and through, a forest born tied to the trees and shadows, the deep wild places one dare not tread if they did not know what they were doing.

When she reached the edge of a small stream, she jumped up to grab a low hanging branch and pulled herself into the trees, scrambling a little higher with a chipmunk racing beside her. She smiled and passed him a nut from her pocket before continuing on to the next tree, moving from branch to branch and trunk to trunk through the canopy just as easily as she could have walked along the ground.

Something buzzed at the edge of her awareness, distracting and unsettling. She settled on a branch and laid her hand against the rough bark, closing her eyes and opening her mind even more. Sifting through the chatter of animals, the sigh of the wind, and the happy dapples of sunlight, she found the buzzing. The trees were whispering to each other. They waved and sighed, hushed sounds rushing through roots and branches just under her awareness. When she tried to reach deeper, to send out little prods of curiosity, the trees shuddered and quieted. Whatever had them so upset, they did not want to talk to even her about it.

A flash of white appeared on the ground ahead of her, moving fast down the path. Curious, she dropped from the trees and followed as quickly as she dared but it was just out of her reach. She couldn't ever seem to get a good look at it, just a bit of white leading her this way or that through the paths until it disappeared all together.

Searching the area for any sign, she almost missed the sound of other large lifeforms moving nearby. She listened for a moment and could tell that one moved on four padded and furry feet while the other wore similar soft soled boots as she did. With a grin she turned and moved their direction as quietly as she could.

Reaching the edge of a small clearing she first saw the large black cat she had told her mother about. Mottled fur moved over her lean body, long tail high and friendly. She lowered her head and butted against the leg of the Wylthem who reached out to run a hand down her silky fur. He flipped back the hood of his robe, mottled browns and greens fading to the usual silver, as brown hair spilled out around his shoulder. Brown eyes remained on the large cat but a small smile pulled at the sides of his mouth.

"Glad you are back up and about, princess."

"You caught me as usual, Larsle." She laughed and rose from her hiding spot to wave to him. "I should have known better than to try and sneak up on the best scout in my father's service. I did not know you were assigned this quadrant today."

He tipped his head towards her and started to speak but turned to look over his shoulder instead. Miramel heard it too. Something crashing towards them through the forest and coming closer quickly. With a hiss, the cat jumped into the tree above Miramel just as the massive creature burst through the foliage on the other side of the clearing.

The bear roared, showing off a mouthful of teeth meant for biting and shredding. It pawed the air with claws as long as the knife strapped to her leg, then dropped back to all fours and charged forward again. Larsle squared his feet and raised his spear but she was faster. In a blink she had an arrow notched in her bow and sent it flying into the broad side of the bear. The arrow buried itself deep, only the fletching showing through the thick fur. It stumbled a couple more steps before falling to the side to not move again.

Larsle crept forward and stabbed at the bear a couple of times to be sure it was dead before looking to her. She pressed a foot against the animal's shoulder and grasped the fletching of her arrow, working it side to side and pulling until she was able to get it free without breaking off the tip.

Larsle squatted down to investigate the bear's mouth and eyes then shook his head. "He does not seem ill and I know we did not startle him. Why would he charge like that?"

"It does not make any sense," she whispered with a shake of her head. "Then again, not much does lately."

He cast one more look at the bear before pulling her aside a little. "My patrol and I will be sure the meat and carcass are handled properly, Carame, but you look pale. Is there something you wish to tell me? Why did you really stay in your quarters for a full day?"

"Are you really on patrol or did Father send you out here to check on me?" She snapped, pulling her arm from his. As his eyes narrowed in pain she sighed and softened her tone. He'd always been such a good friend, there was no reason to take her frustrations out on him. "I had a headache, just like I told Mother, and strange dreams. Nothing I can remember but I know they had to do with Darian and I know they weren't good."

Larsle rolled his eyes and moved a few steps away. "Your pet human again? Do you not think that we have enough problems here instead of worrying about him?"

"I can not control what I dream about, Larsle. Besides, he may have answers that could help us figure out what is happening to our forest. That storm covered all of Ramleaj. I doubt we were the only ones affected."

Larsle turned his back on her to move back to the bear, his shoulders tight and angry. "That storm was a storm, nothing more. It was pure accident what the lightning did, and it is not like it hit the real Tree, just a stone facsimile."

"You know what they say."

"What the old and superstitious say, yes. They say a lot of things. That does not make them all true." He placed a hand to the side of his mouth and trilled a bird call of the northern pike wing, a bird not native to this area. "Thank you for the assistance, Princess. I can handle it from here. Enjoy your walk but please, do not stray too far while my troupe are too busy with this to watch you."

Her eyebrow shot up but she bit back the words. To watch her? He knew very well that she could outmatch every one of his troupe except possibly himself. She was one of her father's best solo scouts and an accomplished hunter though she found no enjoyment in the act. He knew all these things, which made his statement hurt all the more, because that was exactly what it was supposed to do.

High Master

Miramel found her mother and father in his personal study. She stood in the doorway watching them for a moment. Books and parchments were spread everywhere, a glass of berry wine for each sitting untouched on the desk. Mother played with the crystals on her necklace in jerky, nervous movements while Father stared out the window, not even bothering to move the lock of red hair that had fallen over his face.

"Did you need something, daughter?" he said without turning around.

She wet her lips and stepped into the room. She had not really thought about what she would say, just that she wanted to see them.

"Idilm Larsle and I were forced to kill a bear in the north quarter. It charged us for no reason with another predator present."

"That is the third such attack since the solstice," Mother whispered with a shake of her head. "Something has the whole forest on edge. Even the rocks tremble."

"The trees whisper to each other but do not want me to hear what they say."

Father turned to face them, tucking the stray hair behind his crown. "I have felt a darkness building for some time now. Something familiar that I can not name yet. It seems as if the storm has blown that door wide open and I fear what it will take to shut it again."

Her mouth went dry and she could feel the headache trying to return. Sliding off her bow and quiver, she left them at the door then moved to perch on the edge of the desk. Her fingers ran over the delicate edging of her jacket until she forced herself to stop and fold her hands in her lap.

"Larsle believes there was nothing unusual about the storm, and that the fountain is just stone and not connected to the real Tree."

"As I want them to believe." Father leaned forward and rubbed a hand over his face. "I do not want the people panicking before we even understand what is happening."

Her lip slid between her teeth and she cleared her throat. "Perhaps it is time we consult with the High Master. I have a deep feeling that he is connected to all of this somehow."

"Inonym," Father sighed and pinched the bridge of his nose, "I have humored your friendship with the human wizard because it is of little harm and he has done well at keeping our secrets. That does not mean I am prepared to include him in decisions that have nothing to do with him."

She jumped to her feet, throwing her hands in the air. "Nothing to do with him? The Life Tree fuels the whole of Ramleaj, by the Lady, all the dimensions. If something is wrong with it-"

"Then it is the responsibility of the Wylthem to care for it," Father snapped, slamming his hand against the table. "Our secrecy and separation is what keeps us safe, Miramel. I will not have some human putting our people at risk and that is final."

Her teeth clenched and hands shook at her sides. Her mother tried to reach out to her but she did not want to be comforted. She turned and stormed from the room, pacing quickly through the halls and courtyards with no mind to the Wylthem who called out to her or quickly jumped out of her way. She did not stop until she reached the pasture deep within the trees and even then continued to pace in the high grass.

A soft nicker drew her attention as a tall white creature stepped from the brush. Like a horse but leaner and more graceful, with a solid white coat and silver mane, Arilla crept closer. From her forelock sprouted a single long horn that sparkled with colors in the light like the most perfect opal.

"You have scared away the whole herd, my friend."

She stopped pacing and forced herself to take a few deep breaths, running her hand down Arilla's long neck. "Apologies. Father just makes me so angry sometimes. I do not understand why he is so insistent that there is no way the Wizards could help just because they are not Wylthem."

"Well, humans and Wylthem do not exactly have the best history." Arilla wrapped her neck around to rest her large head against Miramel's back. "You and I know Darian well enough to know he is not like those ones but your father has to be cautious. It is his job as king."

Miramel sighed and relaxed into her mount's neck. "It should be his job as father to trust my judgment a little more."

7

Dworkin

A day and a half of riding hadn't helped his mood any. He held the reigns loosely and let Mist have her head, knowing that she would follow the horse ahead of her as they picked their way along the forest path.

They had camped for an uneventful night at the edge of the forest, the night watch reporting nothing unusual, and rose to a warm day without a cloud in the sky. Still, nothing could purge the dark feeling that clung to Dworkin's back and made his travel rations sit heavy in his stomach.

A familiar scent tickled his nose. He had just raised his head to look around when the rider at the front of the line called for a halt.

"Is that smoke?" Bartol pulled his horse forward a bit, sniffing at the air.

"Fire at the homestead," one of the men called from the front.

They all kicked their horses to a gallop, leaning low over the animals' necks to avoid any tree branches. Dworkin could hear the snap and crackle of flames on wood long before he felt the heat or saw the fire itself. The whole garden and shed were already consumed, the flames now licking at the small cabin. The children huddled off to the side as Froderick and his wife carried buckets of water from the stream.

The men dismounted, tossing their reigns to Duntiel, the youngest member of the group. The boy was already struggling to hold the frightened steeds but just nodded and added Mist's reigns to his grip. Her calm energy and superb training helped to quiet the others and they stopped pulling even though their eyes were wide with fear.

"Your grace," Froderick called without stopping, "I have never been happier to see you."

Dworkin just waved and moved to join the others. They grabbed anything they could find that would hold water and quickly set up two lines that moved the water from the creek to the fire in half the time. It seemed to take forever but finally the fire was out and the forest safe.

Dworkin collapsed on the ground next to Froderick. They were both breathing heavy and covered in soot. Froderick stared almost unseeing as the soldiers poked about, being certain that none of the smoking ashes were going to flare back into flames. Dworkin couldn't even imagine the loss he must be feeling. The man's family had lived out in the forest for as long as Dworkin's family had held Marslic, maybe longer. All they ever asked for was to be left alone to live how they chose.

"What happened?" Dworkin grunted and nodded his thanks as Bartol passed a full water skin to him.

Froderick sighed and shook his head. "I don't know. Everything was fine when we turned in but the smoke woke us this morning. Started at the edge of the garden and moved like it had a life of its own."

"It's them, I say," his wife snapped, the children huddling around her skirts. "They been pestering us for weeks, now this?"

"Nema." Froderick gave her a look that had her closing her mouth but not backing down.

Dworkin's shoulders tensed and the lump in his stomach grew harder. "They who?"

Froderick glared at his wife before looking back to Dworkin. "Someone has been harassing us for a while now. They pester or steal the chickens and rabbits, steal our tools and vegetables. Some nights they make so much noise they keep us up all night but all you can see is shadows at best. Nema is convinced it's the Wylthem trying to take their land back."

"It's not their land." Nema straightened, regal as any lady of court despite her simple dress being covered in filth. "They abandoned it long before your ancestors even came here."

Bartol raised an eyebrow and crossed his arms. "What makes you think the Wylthem used to live in this area? I've only ever heard of them in the great forest."

"The ruins." Dworkin pushed to his feet, smiling at the memory. "Froderick, Darian, and I found them when we were boys. They're out to the west a bit more, where the forest nearly meets the ocean."

He didn't add that Darian had run off to tell his friend in Melcader all about it. Dworkin still wasn't sure how his brother had gained entrance into the legendary city, much less call an actual Wylthem a friend. Nema would probably take that as further proof that the secretive race was behind this.

Bartol rubbed at his dark beard with a mischievous look in his eyes. "Doesn't really sound like the Wylthem your friend talks so about, Your Grace. Sounds more like a Tikole."

"A what?" Dworkin raised an eyebrow.

"A Tikole," Bartol said with a shrug. "Nasty little creatures. No bigger than a dog and covered in hair with sharp razor like teeth and even sharper minds. The priests would always warn us children that if we angered the wrong people, they might send a Tikole after us to teach us a lesson."

Frodrick and his wife stared at each other and then at Bartol with their mouths open before turning to Dworkin. Dworkin rubbed a hand over his face to hide a smile before clearing his throat and standing.

"We will figure out what's going on and help you rebuild." Dworkin sighed and glanced to the sun, already on its downward arc through the sky. "For now, my men will take you back to Melcader.

Leslien will make sure you are fed and safe. Bartol, Duntiel, and Cantiem, you'll continue on with me."

Even as Froderick was saying his thank yous, Dworkin nodded and turned away. His mind ran in circles as he walked back to retrieve Mist. Everything seemed to be getting more odd by the minute and all roads seemed to lead back to Darian no matter what way he looked at it. He had a feeling this tightness in his gut wasn't going to go away until he and a certain wizard could sit down for a long chat.

He glanced up as Bartol swung into the saddle next to him. With a shake of his head, he reached out and tapped the man's leg.

"What was that? You really think these Tikole creatures set the fire?"

Bartol grinned with a shrug. "Of course not. There's no one this far North that would know how to summon one. Seemed like if they were going to throw out crazy and unfounded ideas, I might as add one just as far fetched for them to consider."

8

Braslic

The hum of the llama's was taking on a different sound. Braslic moved a little closer to the leader and listened. They were upset, worried about something. His teeth clenched as he stepped off to the side a little bit so he could study the little caravan without halting the progress. He hadn't noticed anything and the other Cregas still chattered happily amongst themselves as they made their way down the mountain path. Still, if the animals were upset, there was probably something to it. He studied the surroundings. On one side the mountain rose like a sheer wall reaching to the clouds with her sacred peak hidden above. The other side was open air, the tops of trees from below nearly eye level with him as he stood on a rock to oversee the path. Nothing looked amiss but the llama's continued to hum agitatedly as they ambled by with their heavy packs safely tied to their backs.

He hopped from the rock and fell into step with the last Cregas in the line, growling as he adjusted the wide brimmed hat that he despised wearing. How did anyone live out here all the time with the varying temperatures and blinding light? It wasn't even summer yet and the sun was already too intense for his liking. He longed to just be back in the cool darkness of the caves, but he wouldn't be returning with the caravan. Who knew how long it would be before he saw home again?

"What has the animals all stirred up?" Denlin whispered, leaning in close.

Braslic's eyes kept scanning the area as the front of the line reached a bend in the path. "I'm not sure yet, but keep your eyes open."

Denlin nodded, his eyes falling on the heavy packs of the nearest llama. Braslic started moving back towards the head of the line. He patted their necks and checked straps, speaking calming words to animal and Cregas alike as he passed. He tried to tell himself that anything from a leaf to a passing animal could have upset them and him being nervous wouldn't help anything.

Then all hell broke loose.

The lead animal, still just out of his sight around the bend, let out a scream that could wake the mountain herself. Braslic picked up his pace and tried to squeeze his way to the front as Cregas started to yell and other animals joined the scream.

Dark figures had swarmed the front of the caravan. One was already holding the lead llama while others rushed the Cregas with swords drawn.

He took stock as he pulled dagger and ax. Two leggars, about twice his height. Black scarves were wrapped around their head and faces but left their eyes exposed. Big round pupils confirmed what he'd already suspected. Humans.

With a battle cry, he jumped into the fray. The humans were taller and stronger but also slower. He ducked under one's legs and pulled the sword out of the hands of another with his ax, trying to make his way to the one attempting to lead the reluctant llama away.

His men joined the fray and it was hard to move in the small mountain pass. He heard a scream and glanced over his shoulder just long enough to see a human tumbling over the side of the mountain. There was a sharp clank right next to his ear. He turned back to see Denlin holding a human's sword just inches from his head in the hook of his ax. With a nod of thanks he moved on towards the screaming llama again.

The man was struggling against the kicking and angry llama with one hand, his sword in the other. With a laugh, he pointed the sword at Braslic and gave another yank on the reigns of the llama.

"You may as well just give up. You're the size of a child, what do you think you could do against me?"

Braslic grinned and feigned right before diving left. He swung his ax towards the human's stomach, bracing his arm for the block he knew would come. As the sword scraped against the ax handle, he twisted it to catch the sword then lashed out with his dagger. In quick jabs he stabbed the man twice in the gut and slashed sharply across his sword arm. The man dropped the llama's reigns and fell back with a yelp.

"You blasted little cretins! If you knew your place there wouldn't be a problem." He snapped before blowing on a horn from his belt. "Retreat!"

As the humans scrambled through the rocks and down a side path, Braslic caught his breath and grabbed the reigns of the llama. Scratching the animal's neck to calm it down, he glanced around at his people. They were frightened and had a few scratches and scrapes, but everyone was accounted for and no one seemed seriously harmed.

"How are the goods?"

There was chatter amongst the group before Denlin walked up to him with a broken bottle in his hand. "Lost about a third of the Marsim gel when a bag ripped open, but everything else seems to be here."

"That's going to really cut into our payment," Braslic sighed, thinking about the dwindling food stores back home, "but there isn't anything we can do now. Get the llama's calmed down and back in line so that we can get to market before anything else goes wrong."

He paced amongst the tables just waiting for more trouble to happen. Nothing seemed to go right for them anymore so why should a simple day at the market? It still bothered him that the humans on the trail had given up so easily. Even though there had been no more disturbances as they made the way to the bottom of the mountain and outside the small forest to the agreed meeting point, the animals remained on edge and so did he.

He watched as Denlin accompanied a couple of their people who had been trusted with the small amount of coin they had to spare. They moved from table to table on the human side of the meadow where the market had been set up. The amount of goods they carried as the coin pouch got lighter and lighter didn't seem near as large as it should be.

He circled back to their tables, hearing raised voices as he moved closer. The hair on the back of his neck stood up and he picked up his pace. One of those voices sounded more familiar than it should.

"That's ridiculous. It was half that price last month."

The Cregas selling the ore sighed and shook her head before speaking in Common. "No, sir. The ore was cheaper last month but not half price. We have never sold our ore that cheap."

"Are you calling me a liar?" The human roared as Bartol stepped behind the table next to his young seller.

He looked the man up and down with a feigned disinterest. He was dressed in fine clothes, with a bird in flight wrapped in flames emblazoned on the short cloak he had pinned at one shoulder. More for show than to actually keep someone warm or protect from the blasted sun. Braslic guessed he must be a lord of some sort, probably a minor one to be out here haggling himself instead of sending someone to do it for him.

"No one is calling you a liar, sir. Merely stating a fact. The price of ore has gone up fifteen percent in the last month, but it did not double.

Unfortunately, we have had a very poor month between animals attacking in our tunnels and the rains flooding our best deposits so they are unreachable right now. A smaller turnout means higher prices. If you are not willing to pay, then I am sure someone else will."

"And then what are our blacksmiths supposed to use? We need horseshoes, and tools, and weapons." The man snarled as he crossed his arms in a huff then gave a sharp wince. As he did, the sleeve of his shirt inched up a bit to show the edge of a rather bloody bandage.

Braslic's eyes narrowed as it all clicked together. The familiar voice, the flippant attitude, even the wound on his right arm. He couldn't prove anything, but he was fairly certain this young lord had been the leader of the group that attacked them. He thought about saying something but they needed the sale. Right or wrong, if he accused the man then that definitely wouldn't happen.

"Why Lord Ranklus, where ever did you get that horrible looking wound?" A woman's voice interjected softly.

Ranklus bristled and straightened, pulling his sleeve down tight. "In the training yards, Great Mother. 'Tis barely more than a scratch, really."

Braslic snorted at the young human's answer but turned to smile and incline his head to the older woman. The Healers were their best customers and it was always nice when the Great Mother came out herself. She was a tall thin woman, who stood ramrod straight and kept her chin high but there was a kindness and warmth about her. She reminded Braslic of a Cregas mother, loving of all her children but not afraid to put them in their place as needed either.

"Still," she said, trying to catch a glimpse of the arm Ranklus was hiding from her, "it wouldn't hurt for you to get it looked at by one of my girls. They can be certain there won't be any infection and even help reduce the scarring."

"Thank you, Great Mother, but really it's fine." Ranklus grinned with his teeth clenched as he pulled a bag of coins from his belt and tossed it on the table then grabbed the bag of ore to toss to his men.

As he stormed away, Braslic glanced to his companion who was looking through the bag of coin. The way she grinned, he figured the young lord had been so flustered, he'd paid more than their asking price. With a slight chuckle, he turned to the human woman and motioned further down the table.

"It's an honor to see you again, Great Mother, though I am afraid I have some bad news."

She lifted the skirt of her long white dress to follow him, the jeweled belt at her waist shifting so that the ruby caught the sun. Braslic's smile deepened. Pride filled his stomach with warmth as he thought of the neighboring mountains around Mother Mountain that provided all of the Wizard's and Healer's Guilds the gems that they so liked to play with.

They reached the table he'd indicated, with it's measly amount of bottles and powders laid out, already packaged for the Healers to take back to the Mount with them. She sighed and shook her head, picking up one of the bottles to carefully inspect the contents.

"Another bad harvest, Braslic?"

He growled and shifted his hat again. "For the Dulung powder, yes. The mushrooms just don't seem to be growing like they used to. We had quite a bit more of the Marsim gel but it was damaged in an attack on our way down the mountain."

"I do hope none of your people were injured." The Great Mother gasped, looking at him over the bottle then letting her eyes drift back to where Ranklus and his men were loading up a carriage and preparing to leave.

Braslic held back the laugh that filled his stomach, but just barely. "Nothing we can't handle. Still, I don't have the amount that I promised you. I can cut the price by twenty percent and we'll get you the rest just as soon as we can. More cocoons should be opening up before the next moon and we'll be able to extract more gel from the new herd. They may even have some made up by the time the caravan returns to the city."

Great Mother placed the jar back in the box and waved a couple of her girls over. "No, need. We'll pay full price as long as you promise to get the next batch to us as soon as you possibly can. This is the only medicine we have found that seems to help with the Withering."

Braslic hesitated as he glanced around to his people. He hadn't planned on returning to the caves with the caravan but they couldn't spare anyone else leaving the community to deliver the supplies to the Healers. It would slow him way down, but they desperately needed the money. There were certain things that they just couldn't come by in the caves that they had to get from the humans. Mushrooms and fungus, llama meat and milk, could get them through in a pinch but they had found a long time ago that bread made from human wheat could fill you up more and feed the masses, as well as clothes made from the plants the humans grew allowed the yarn made from llamas to go further.

"I will bring everything that they have prepared to you personally, Great Mother."

9

Dworkin

Dworkin pulled Mist to a halt on the hill overlooking the Wizards' Isle. The lake surrounding it glistening blue in the morning light, the pennants that topped each soaring tower flapping lazily in the breeze. From his perch he couldn't see any movement which felt odd but he couldn't say for sure that was true. The last time he'd been to the isle was nearly five years earlier for the ceremony to make Darian High Master. Of course that day had been a bustle of activity but that didn't mean every day was. If all the children were in class it was likely you might not see anyone outside. Right?

"So?" Bartol laughed nervously as Dworkin just stared at the silent island. "Are we going to go down and say hello or is he supposed to meet us out here?"

Dworkin sighed and shook himself. "We go down, but slowly. I don't want to cause a ruckus if we can avoid it."

Their horses picked their way down the hill and towards the large bridge that joined the island to the main land. Duntiel rose in his stirrups at the edge of the stone bridge, looking around as if something was going to jump out at him.

"Is it true what they say? That there's a barrier that will kill anyone who tries to enter uninvited?"

"It won't kill you," Dworkin laughed as the kid relaxed back in the saddle, "just a hard shock to knock you back."

Bartol grinned at the shocked expression on Duntiel's face but leaned towards Dworkin. "I assume there is a reason you're not concerned?"

Dworkin reached into his pouch, rummaging past Leslien's necklace and a few coins to pull out a small silver medal connected to a purple ribbon. "Because, when you're family of the High Master, he gives you a permanent invitation."

"That includes anyone traveling with you, right?" Cantiem moved his horse a little closer, gaining a warning whinny from Mist.

Dworkin just grinned over his should as he pushed through the shimmering wall. "Guess we'll find out."

The others all gave each other hesitant looks but pushed on quickly, not wanting to get to far from Dworkin for fear of the magic not working. Dworkin tried to hide his grin. Darian had specifically explained to him that it was more intent than proximity that made the charm work. If Dworkin wanted he could bring a whole caravan full of people through, but someone could be right on Dworkin's heels and not make it if he didn't want them to follow.

He shoved the medal back into his pouch and hopped off of Mist. She pranced and tossed her head, eyes rolling to check their surroundings. He patted her neck and tried to see what had upset her, but couldn't pick anything out. Nothing seemed out of order. The doors to the school were closed up tight, the large trees that dotted the lawn swaying slightly in the breeze.

There was a slight buzzing noise he couldn't quite place that made it hard to focus. He wondered how the Wizards got anything done with that constant annoyance. Maybe after a while they just didn't hear it.

No stable boy came out to take the horses for them but maybe that was because they were unexpected, or that was just the way things worked on the Isle.

"Duntiel and Cantiem, take the horses to the stables and see that they're cared for. Bartol and I will see if we can find someone who might know where Darian is."

As the boys led all the horses off, Dworkin took a deep breath and looked around. The only real place to start was the main doors. Together they climbed the small set of stone stairs up to the large double doors and Dworkin banged the heavy knocker three times. When no one answered, he pounded his fist against the wood with a growl.

"Dworkin," Bartol whispered, tapping his arm, "what's that?"

He glanced to his man then down where Bartol pointed. Spreading from under the door and across the stone at their feet was an all too familiar red-brown stain.

"It could be anything," he said, even though his stomach was trying to clench.

Swallowing hard, he raised his hand to pound on the door again.

"Your grace," Duntiel yelled, running across the grass towards them, "you should see this."

He glanced back to the door and then to Bartol before they all set out back across the lawn towards the stables. Cantiem stood outside, his face white as he gripped the horses' reigns.

Dworkin looked to him before moving inside. The first thing he noticed were smears of the same red brown on the floor and walls. His stomach twisted. It was getting harder and harder to deny what those stains looked like.

Before he could process anything, a large black blur came barreling towards him. He jumped back out the door and to the side just as the massive black head pushed out of the barn and into the sunlight. Dworkin gasped as he lunged forward and grabbed the horse's halter, cooing and muttering as the stallion tried to free himself.

"Hey, hey, Ebony, it's okay. Hey, calm down, big boy."

Big brown eyes rolled to him and blinked a couple of times before relaxing under his touch. Ebony turned and started nudging around his clothes and into all of his pockets, searching for a snack. He grinned and pulled out one of the sugar cubes he kept handy for Mist and held it out for the large stallion.

"What are you doing out? Huh, boy?"

Dworkin ran his hand over the horse, growing more concerned as he went. A woolen blanket had been tossed over the horses back but it was twisted and trying to fall off. There was dried sweat stuck to Ebony's back and his lower legs were covered in old, dried mud. His mane and tail were both in knots with twigs and hay stuck inside. It looked like the last time he had been ridden was probably in that massive rain storm and then he'd never been cared for after that. Darian would never leave his horse in such a state willingly. He'd sooner make sure Ebony was dry and warm than even worry about himself.

With a slow breath, he turned and glanced inside the barn again. Just as he had feared, all of Darian's tack was merely tossed to the side and not cared for either. Unmistakable with it's black and purple designs and specialty holder for his staff, the saddle was tipped to the side and the saddle blanket a wet bunch underneath.

"Duntiel," he had to take a few breaths before he could continue calmly so as not to upset the men, "you're going to stay here with the horses. This big guy won't give you any more trouble if you get him something to eat then see if he'll let you give him a brush down. Bartol and Cantiem, we're going inside."

He didn't wait for acknowledgment of his orders, just patted Ebony and started striding across the lawn. He pulled his sword and stopped in front of the massive main doors, glancing once again at the stain at his feet, then turned to the others. Bartol and Duntiel exchanged a look before pulling their own swords. They didn't know Darian as well as he did, didn't understand that Ebony not being cared for told him so much more than anything they'd encountered so far.

He motioned his head towards the door and Bartol took the hint to move closer. He held up three fingers then slowly put each one down. When he held up a clenched fist, they both leaned back to kick the door as close to the fancy doorknobs as they could. The first kick delivered a cracking noise but didn't quite open so they leaned back and tried again.

As soon as the doors burst open, they were overwhelmed by a scent Dworkin knew all too well from battle but never expected to find in such a quiet and tranquil place. Bartol placed his free arm over his mouth but kept his sword at the ready as Cantiem gagged quietly behind them. Dworkin took one last breath of fresh air then forced himself to step inside.

The buzzing they had heard earlier was the swarms of flies that filled the grand hall. Bodies lay everywhere in different mangled states and all in advanced stages of decomposition. Items of daily life lay scattered, books and papers and bits of wood strewn about as if simply dropped to never be picked up.

"They were attacked blitz style," Bartol grunted, arm still over his face. "Killed quickly and just left to lay there as whoever it was moved on to the next target."

"Who, or what?" Duntiel bent down and ran his fingers over four deep grooves in the marble floor then motioned to several other such sets all around them.

"They've been here at least a week but that doesn't mean there isn't any danger left." Dworkin gripped his sword and angled towards one side of the wide double staircase. "Stay alert and cautious. You see even a hint of purple, call it out."

Bartol hissed as he nearly tripped then kicked at the item that had rolled under his foot. "What is this?"

Dworkin bent down to look. At first it seemed like just a random chunk of wood with colored glass embedded into it, but then he grew cold as he realized they were surrounded by similar wood.

"It's a wizard's staff, or what remains of it. They took the time to smash each and every one," Dworkin whispered. Someone had been very angry and known exactly what they were doing. Darian always said a wizard's staff was like an extension of himself, to have them smashed like this was like adding insult to injury.

His mind tried to go in a thousand different directions as they slowly climbed the stairs past shredded portraits and more gouges on the walls in sets of four. Had Darian been in the middle of this battle, or had it already been like this when he showed up? It would be just like Darian to proceed the same way they were instead of stepping out and calling for help. But he would have been alone, and armed only with his magic.

Everywhere they went was filled with the same level of destruction and death but no signs of whatever had caused it. He moved forward cautiously until he found what he guessed to be the doors to the Council Room. Darian had said he'd been called for a meeting so surely this is where he'd been headed before he noticed the destruction below.

One of the doors stood slightly ajar so they slid inside. His eyes swam in a sea of red so pervasive he couldn't tell how much was from the Master's red cloaks or the massive amounts of blood covering everything. The central table was broken and lay on it's side, only the chair closest to them still standing upright.

"Dworkin," Bartol whispered and touched his arm, then motioned to the floor.

Laying on top of the blood and gore, was a single length of wood not smashed like the others. His hand shook as he sheathed his sword then reached down to pick it up. The familiar purple stone winked at him and was like a stab to the heart. No more could he try to tell himself that maybe Darian hadn't been here at all, or that he left of his own accord. This staff being here, alone, meant that his friend had stood in this very spot and something bad had happened. He only hoped that having it still in one piece meant that Darian was as well.

A loud banging noise made them all jump and look around. The banging continued, along with a muffled voice yelling. Dworkin listened and was sure that it was somewhere nearby but couldn't see anyone.

"Over there."

Duntiel pushed past him, stepping over and around bodies to the far corner of the room. His face twisted in disgust as he tugged at a body that was leaning against the wall. There was a squelching and squishing noise as it slid to the floor and out of the way. Almost immediately, a portion of the wall flung open and something wrapped in brown fell out. Only when it started to scream did Dworkin realize it wasn't a what, but a who. A young teen wrapped in a brown cloak, who shortly stopped screaming and turned to vomit in the corner of the room.

Dworkin cursed and rushed to the boy's side. The young man glanced up with large brown eyes filled with fear, gripping his staff until his knuckles were white under skin nearly as brown as his cloak.

In one fluid movement, Dworkin pulled the staff from the boy's hand and tossed both it and Darian's back to Bartol then pulled the thick hood over the boy's head. He wrapped an arm around thin shoulders and pulled the boy in tight to his side.

"It's okay, we're friends," he said quietly, starting to guide the boy towards the door. "We're going to get you out of here but I need you to do me a favor. You keep that hood on and focus on my boots, nothing else. Understand?"

The boy nodded and leaned in to him with a shiver. "Who are you?"

"My name is Dworkin, Duke of Marslic and Knight of the First Order to King Mathias," and about a thousand other useless titles he thought to himself, "these are my men Bartol and Duntiel."

The boy's head jerked up to look at him, their surroundings forgotten for just a moment. "High Master Darian's friend? He was here, I tried to warn him but..."

The sentence trailed off as he started to turn his head. Dworkin could feel the tension building in the boy's shoulders and knew that whatever happened in these moments would possibly shape the boy for life.

"Yes, he is my friend and foster brother." He carefully pulled the hood back into place and started forward again. "I'm sure you did everything you could but we'll talk about it outside. Right now, you only care about my boots. They're pretty nice boots after all."

※

It took everything Dworkin had not to bombard the kid with questions as they sat on the grass. The warm sun gave a semblance of normalcy to the whole crazy scene as the boy scarfed down all the travel rations they could offer. The horses quietly munched on the grass, the only sounds Duntiel's soft mutterings as Ebony danced around while the soldier tried to brush his coat out.

"Thank the Twins," the boy sighed around a mouthful of food, "I thought I was going to starve to death in there. If I hadn't hidden a some biscuits in my pocket from dinner, I probably would have."

Dworkin smiled but his heart was too filled with worry to really feel it. He nodded to the cloak puddling in the grass around the boy. "Brown makes you, what, a student?"

"Apprentice, sir," he blushed as he chewed on a strip of dried meat, "your grace, I mean. Apprentice Keslar. I was in the council room to take my exams to move up to Student."

He grew quiet and set the food down. Dworkin took a deep breath and leaned forward as the boy's face grew dark. There had been too many times of seeing that exact same look on young soldiers after a battle. How this moment went could shape the rest of Keslar's life and how he handled death from here on. It wasn't a responsibility Dworkin had ever relished having.

"Do you think you could tell us what happened?" He asked quietly, moving a little closer. "Feel free to stop any time it gets to be too much."

Keslar pushed the remaining food away and wrapped the cloak tighter around himself. "As I said, I was taking my test to become a Student. The Masters do it late at night so that other kids couldn't try to spy and know what to expect. Things were going really well and I was sure I was going to pass when we heard a scuffle and yelling outside the door. I don't know how they got past the border spell and the guard to get on the Island."

Dworkin grunted, thinking of the tingling feeling as they had passed over the bridge. The spell was definitely still in place and should have kept out anyone who wasn't invited. How could whatever monsters that could do this get themselves invited onto an island full of wizards?

"Maybe he used his magic to make them look like someone that the guards would invite over," Keslar muttered, picking at the edge of his cloak, eyes on the two staffs laying side by side in the grass between them.

"He had magic? Just like a wizard?" Bartol walked over and sat on a rock nearby, his back against a tree.

Keslar shrugged. "Like a wizard but not exactly. It felt different when he used it."

"What do you mean?" Dworkin prodded as the boy grew quiet again, trying not to push too hard but anxious to know how Darian fit into all of this. "Did he fight the wizards with his magic?"

"No, there was no need for that. His creatures took them out before it could even come to magic. It was Master Frencis who shoved me inside that hidden door, just before they burst into the council room. I could see everything through the peep hole, but didn't really want to."

Dworkin and Bartol shared a look, remembering the decimation that they had seen. It was enough to make a seasoned soldier's stomach turn and not something a young boy should ever have been exposed to.

"What about Darian?" Dworkin prodded, trying not to let the boy spiral into thoughts of the destruction he'd seen. "Was he there at the time?"

Keslar shook his head and took a long swig from the water skin Bartol had given him. "No, but he was definitely the man's focus. As soon as the council was dead, the man said they had to get ready for Darian. He put a spell over the whole island to make it look like nothing was wrong when Darian got there. I've never felt someone call on so much power. It fooled even the High Master for a little bit, but he used some kind of spell too and figured it out. I've felt his power before, when he would guest lecture in a class or give presentations, so I noticed it underneath the constant thrum of the other guy's."

"What happened to Darian after he figured it out?"

Keslar gave a small shrug. "I tried to warn him, I really did. I was banging and yelling, but the guy covered it up somehow."

"Don't beat yourself up about not being able to help them." Bartol grunted from the rock, methodically cleaning something out of his boot tread. Dworkin didn't even want to think about what it might be that he was scraping off with the tip of his knife. "You would have been killed too and then we would have no idea what happened here and be of no help to the High Master."

Dworkin forced himself to nod calmly. "What happened to the High Master, Keslar?"

"He didn't even have a chance to fight," Keslar whispered. "They grabbed him right away and when he still tried to use his magic, one of the creatures hit him over the head and knocked him out. That was when the man said they had what they had come for and they all left, one of the creatures carrying the High Master over its shoulder like a child."

Dworkin jumped to his feet and walked a little ways away. Mist wandered up and nudged his shoulder, Ebony not far behind. He gave them the last two sugar cubes left in his pockets then absently rubbed at their velvety noses. He should be happy that Darian was alive the last time he was seen, even if that was around a week before. If whoever this was had wanted Darian dead, he could have just done it right away after having taken out a whole island full of wizards. But how much did it really mean to know your friend was alive, when they were in the hands of someone that powerful? And when you had no idea where to even start looking for them.

Bartol walked over and gripped his shoulder for a moment then grunted as the horses started to inspect his pockets for treats. He pushed the inquiring noses away and they just stood there for a long moment in the companionable silence.

"Should we tell the king? I know you're worried about your friend, but taking out all of the Wizards could be an attempt to weaken us so they can attack further."

Dworkin could see the man's logic, could accept that he was probably right, but still shook his head. "He's not just a friend, Bartol. He's my foster brother. We were raised together since he was four and I was five. I have to at least try to find my him before the trail gets even colder."

"Understood, your grace." Bartol grunted and crossed his arms. Dworkin looked up but there was no judgment or anger in the man's face. "I'll have the men start cleaning up here so that we can leave as soon as possible. Take all the time you need, sir."

Dworkin turned and looked around at the grounds, his mind not fully functioning. "Cleaning up?"

"The bodies, your grace. We can't just leave them."

A rock fell into Dworkin's stomach and made him want to curl into a ball to disappear. "Yes, of course. I'll help you in just a moment."

10

The dark figure crept through the forest on silent feet, her steed as black as the night next to her. With her senses open she knew where every animal was, every member of the night watch as they passed overhead in the trees. They would not be expecting her, wouldn't even notice. A dark shiver might run down their spine but they would write it off to the cool breeze or all the odd things happening lately. If they even bothered to look, with their eyes or senses, they would assume she was another Wylthem out for a late night stroll amongst the trees. Zarentle had given her that one gift.

She had had to see it. It had been so long, locked on the other side of the barrier. At first she had dreamed of this place. She had held on to the thought of tall trees and peaceful rivers to hold onto hope. Hope that she would return home someday and go back to being herself. Then she had found herself, her true self. Once she had opened herself to the darkness, she had known that was were she had always been meant to be.

The building sprouted from the land as if a part of it. The pale stone that made up the walls came from the cliffs that bordered the ocean to the south, the rust colored roof tiles had been made from a mud that could only be found at the edge of the great lake long before the wizards had claimed it for their own. As always, the windows were wide open so that the wind and animals could play in and out as they chose, plants growing around and up the walls until it nearly swallowed the building whole.

She slipped inside, checking around every corner before moving on. The residents may not sense her with Zarentle's spell over her, but if they saw her here in the soft light they would know what she was. She could still hear the word on her mother's lips in the stories meant to scare little Wylthem children.

Leranti. Mind your parents and your teachings, little ones, or the Leranti will take you in the night and make you one of them. They will twist you until you are unrecognizable and only evil will live in your heart.

Not fully accurate, but close enough.

She reached the central courtyard and stood under the Tree, watching the water splash over it and into the pool at her feet. Dark lines trailed down the metal bark, the broken and charred stump of a branch standing out in stark relief. Her hands itched with the magic she had been given in her transformation, the magic that could destroy the Tree once and for all and plummet this land into the darkness she had been living for years. Only the promise of her dark lords that all the waiting would be worth it in the end stayed her hand.

"Hello?" A voice called sleepily through the night as footsteps approached. "Who is out there? Larsle?"

A sneer crossed her face. It was the little princess, though not so little any longer. She had grown into a tough warrior of her own right and would be a worthy opponent when the time came. But it was not time yet.

She opened a portal and, glancing to the Tree one last time, stepped through. She turned back, closing the rift with a word just before the princess stepped into the empty courtyard.

11

Miramel searched the courtyard but could not find anything. She could have sworn she had heard someone out here. Then again she had only been half awake and still reeling from another crazy dream. Even fully awake, crazy images of never ending hallways and dark smiles filled her thoughts.

"Princess? Is that you?"

She spun as new steps shuffled into the courtyard. For a second she did not recognize the Wylthem hanging onto a doorway as if were the only thing keeping her standing. Her white hair was thinner, patches of scalp showing through. Her skin had a translucent quality with blue veins showing prominently. It was as if she had aged centuries since Miramel had watched her dance in the rain.

"Reilin?"

A weak grin crossed the Wylthem's face. "Yes, of course it is you. Who else would come see me at this hour?"

Miramel cocked her head and moved closer cautiously. "Reilan, I did not come see you. You are in the courtyard. See, the tree is right there."

Reilan's face dropped as Miramel moved closer but her head did not turn, not towards Miramel or the tree. Miramel hesitated then passed a hand in front of Reilan's face with no reaction. This close she could see that blue eyes now had a milky white film covering them so that only the vertically slit pupil showed through.

Reilan was blind.

The image passed through Miramel's mind in a flash. Reilan dancing in the rain with her head thrown back and hair soaking. The acrid smell still lingered on the shawl she had worn that night and not touched since.

"I," Reilan's hands released the doorway to flutter in front of her, "I was following the sound of the water. I thought it my fountain."

Miramel swallowed the sob that built in her throat. She didn't want to upset her elder even more than she already was.

"How about we go see Father? I am sure he would love to spend some time with you."

"No, no, dear. Do not wake the king up for me." Reilin protested even as Miramel took her by the arm and started leading her through the halls.

Miramel breathed deep through her nose and let it out through her mouth slowly. "He will not mind at all. I promise."

※

She paced the small office while Mother stared at a book but had not turned a page in ages. Father had been in with Reilan so long the sun was beginning to come up and morning birds starting to call to each other. As they chirped their melody to announce to the world that they had survived another night, Miramel leaned against the window and rubbed at her temple. The headache she'd been battling off and on seemed to be returning with a vengeance.

"You are weakening, love. You can only push so far," Mother seemed to say to her book without looking up.

Miramel smiled briefly but it was a weak one. She adored the connection that her parents shared, the way they always seemed to know how the other was feeling even though they be far apart. She often wondered if she would ever have that deep of a connection with someone. Or at least, someone she was actually allowed to love.

She shivered and wrapped a blanket from the back of a chair around her shoulders. Pulling it tight, she buried her face in it and breathed deep. It still held Mother's sharp, earthy scent from when she had woven it and Father's warm, growing smell from use. Even with its thick weight around her, she could not get warm and curled in a chair to pull her bare feet up inside the blanket.

Mother closed the book with a sigh and looked up at her. "I did not think the night chill was that bad."

"Maybe worry steals my warmth." Miramel sighed, snuggling into the blanket as far as she could. "I can not fight this chill."

"You have reason to worry." Father appeared at the doorway, looking exhausted.

He had tied his hair back at the base of his skull but tendrils escaped to frame his face and his white shirt was soaked to his back with sweat. He crossed the room in quick strides to pour a large glass of berry wine and start drinking in large gulps. Mother sat up a little, wide eyes darting to Miramel then back to her husband.

"How is she, carame?"

He sat in his large chair and leaned his head back. "There is nothing I can do for her. It is as if she ages a decade every few minutes. She will fade before moon's end and I can not figure out how to stop it."

"Was it the rain? She was the only one out in it while all the rest of us tried to stay covered."

Mother rose from her seat and walked over to kiss Father's cheek then sit on the edge of the desk while holding his hand. "It is not your fault, carame. Even you can not heal everything. Poor thing was so desperate for a connection to her homeland she did not stop to notice that rain was unnatural."

"You know who this all reminds me of? When he was young and would get angry."

Father's eyes focused on Mother as if they were sharing the same thoughts. Mother closed her eyes and gave a small nod.

"I have thought the same, but is it possible?"

Miramel wiggled out of the comfort of her blanket to lean against the desk and try to get their attention. It was nearly as if they had forgotten she was even in the room.

"Reminds you of who? What is going on here?"

Father looked to her and shook his head. "Never mind. Your mother is right. That was a very long time ago and it is not possible."

"Then perhaps it is time-"

"We should let your father rest," Mother said suddenly as she rose from the desk and grabbed Miramel by the hand. "Come. It is morning already and there are things to be tended to."

Miramel bit the edge of her tongue and allowed herself to be dragged out of the room. Once in the hall, she yanked her hand from her mother's grasp and started walking the other direction.

"Mira," her mother's voice was quieter, almost pained as she used the old nickname, "do not be so hard on him."

Miramel turned and shrugged. "I am not trying to be. I am just suggesting that if we do not have the answers, someone else might."

"A human." Mother sighed and gently pushed her further from the door. "We tried living in the open with the humans once, child, and it cost us everything. Even as your father took over Melcader from his father we allowed the humans to visit our forest for hunting and recreation. They nearly ruined the last home we have."

"But Darian is not like that."

"So you say, and I have never had an issue with him, but the last time a Wylthem was obsessed with a human man it ended very badly. She was the last of the meadow born and she left us to be with him. We have not seen her since you were barely walking." Mother kissed her cheek and brushed a hand through her hair. "So I hope you can see why he wishes to be even more careful with his own daughter."

Miramel dropped her eyes and cleared her throat. "I have no intentions in leaving, Mother. I just want to do everything possible to keep our people safe."

"So does he."

Miramel pursed her lips to try and hide the frown. She was getting really tired of everyone telling her that she could not understand Father's decisions because he was king. Maybe he could not understand her ideas because he had been isolated here in Melcader for too long.

"I think I am going to try to get a little more sleep then I will help you with the animals in the infirmary."

Mother nodded and stepped back. "Of course, dear."

She forced herself to walk back to her quarters calmly, smiling and nodding at those she passed. Once at her rooms she glanced around to be sure no one was looking before reaching her hand up to the small nest above her door. She made a soft cooing sound in her throat and two black doves poked their heads out of the nest. Rising to her tiptoes she gently picked up the male and cradled him close.

"I know your eggs are young but I have need of you, friend."

She cradled the bird close as she entered her rooms and pulled a small slip of paper from her keepsake box on the shelf. Her thumb ran over the embossed family crest before she rolled it tiny enough to fit in the little tube she had fashioned for the bird's leg. With a kiss on his head she walked him to the window, sending him thoughts of Darian, and of finding, and of purpose. When she opened her hands he hopped on the windowsill for a moment before taking to the air and flying off into the bright spring day.

"I am sorry, Father, but as princess and future leader of our people, I, too, need to do what I think is best."

12

Braslic

Braslic reached back and checked that the pack was still tied tightly to his saddle. Tucked inside were not only his supplies and rations, but the precious bottles he had promised the Healers. It had taken longer to prepare the gel than he had hoped, and he had had to fend off two more animal attacks while waiting, but he was finally on his way.

On a gut feeling, he pulled his llama hard to the left and convinced her to take the smaller, and shorter, path. Lurp, as he had affectionately named the not so bright animal, hummed and grunted, trying to fight her way back to the familiar path but finally gave in and plodded on as directed. The caravans would never fit through these tight rocks and were forced to zig zag down the mountain pass. Besides, it was safer to stay on the face of Mother Mountain. Once away from her, you were right out in the open to be seen by the other inhabitants of the great Ykor Mountains. His fingers caressed the handles of his favorite daggers at his hips and his ax bumped reassuringly against his leg with every step, but they weren't much comfort when the enemy you were keeping an eye out for could snatch you up faster than you could even draw your weapon.

Lurp froze in the middle of the pass and trumpeted her shrill warning call. He sighed, and hopped from the saddle just as a shadow crossed their path. At first he thought a cloud may have covered the sun to give him a slight break, but the shadow had a shape and was moving too quickly. He tried to swallow his heart back into place but it remained firmly lodged in his throat as his eyes rose to the sky.

Giant wings that would easily span the whole central complex of the caves, spread from the massive body high above him. Red scales glistened in the bright light, hurting his eyes even through the dark glasses that he wore. No matter how hard he tried, or how much he reminded himself that he was a brave warrior, he couldn't stop the trembling in his legs as the creature turned and swooped towards him.

With a massive thump that shook the ground under his feet and kicked dust up into the air, the dragon landed on the path in front of Braslic and Lurp, then ambled slowly towards him. Lips curled back to reveal row upon row of sharp teeth, large predator eyes following Braslic's every move.

Lurp tugged and pulled at the reigns, trying desperately to run back home. Or possibly further down the mountain. Anywhere other than the dinner plate they seemed to have been served up on. Braslic pulled the reigns tighter so that her nose was tucked up against his shoulder and held tight.

"What do we have here? A little morsel out in the open, far from his stone protection?" The dragon's words were thick, too much tongue and teeth to make common speech easy. "And he has brought along a bit of desert as well, how kind."

Braslic fought not to back away. "I just be passing through, dragon. The agreement states as long as I don't hunt on your land you are to give me safe passage."

"I made no such agreement, morsel." Steam puffed through the dragon's teeth as it's head lowered. "The elders don't speak for all dragons. Besides, I won't leave even a bone for them to find of you."

"Actually they do," another voice filled the valley.

Braslic gripped his daggers even though he doubted they would do much good as another dragon slithered down the stones towards them. This one was smaller and green with a yellow stomach, yellow eyes focused on the red dragon.

"This has nothing to do with you, Nemclis." The red dragon snapped. "You're barely even a dragon."

Nemclis bared his teeth, moving between Braslic and the other dragon. "I'm dragon enough to take you on, Rundem, and close enough to the elders to know you're supposed to be patrolling the pass right now."

"There hasn't been activity on the pass for weeks. Old Larsma probably imagined the whole thing."

Nemclis lifted a clawed foot as if calmly studying his nails. "Maybe, maybe not. Either way, shirking your duties and breaking a treaty are more then enough to get you banished from the hunting grounds again. Just when you were starting to put back on the weight."

The two dragons stared each other down, teeth bared and wings spread. Braslic tried to search the area for a way out of this confrontation but couldn't see a path that wouldn't put him even more in the middle. After a few moments, Rundem let out a hiss that sent shivers down Braslic's spine then took to the air. The flapping of his massive wings nearly blew Braslic's hat off as he rose then banked sharply to the left to disappear over the Ykor Mountains.

Nemclis watched him fly away before turning his long neck to look at Braslic. "Are you all right, little one?"

Braslic bristled at the comment but gritted his teeth to keep from stating it. "I'm good, thank you, just trying to pass."

"Of course you may, Cregas." Nemclis raised his head and looked around. "Just be careful. Things are not as safe as they once were."

Braslic fought back a laugh. No one had to tell him that. It was the whole reason he had left the comforts of his caves, but something the dragon had said to the other stuck out to him.

"What pass are you dragons watching and why? I didn't think anything could threaten you."

Nemclis hesitated, curling his neck and looking around before laying his head on the ground next to Braslic. "The Barrier Ridge. One of the elders was hunting in the area a while back and swore he saw something passing from the other side."

"Nothing is supposed to be able to pass from that side of the mountains. It's been sealed since the war."

A cold dread filled Braslic's stomach as he started to sweat. He didn't want to think about it but that would explain so much. The creatures they were dealing with in the tunnels hadn't been seen since before the war either. Long enough ago that many thought them just fairy tales to frighten children at night.

"You are right there, little one, and we all hope that he is wrong. But just in case he wasn't, I'm on my way to speak with my friend Darian. He's a wizard and should know a lot more than we do."

Braslic blinked and shook his head with a smile. "Well, don't that beat anything. I'm on my way to find High Master Darian myself. Thought he or his kind might have an answer to the problems we Cregas be facing. Might we search for him together?"

"I'm afraid there are a couple of things I must look into first," Nemclis backed up politely and motioned with a clawed foot to the now cleared path. "How about we make a deal that whoever should find him first, will let him know that the other is looking for him?"

"That is a deal, and thank you."

Braslic tipped his hat and climbed back up in the saddle. As Lurp started down the path, he found his spirits a little lighter even with the heavy news adding another layer of fear to his heart. Who could have ever imagined he would be able to make a deal with a dragon?

13

Everything hurt. Darian lay still and took assessment of himself. His head was pounding, his throat dry and burning. He tried to move and his right shoulder protested sharply, his back asked to lodge complaints as well. He rolled to sit and groaned as his stomach joined the chorus. He just breathed for a long moment then forced his eyes open.

The room was dark with only a bit of light coming in from a window high above him to make a small rectangle on the dirt floor. The walls were of a smooth black rock with a slight curve that told him he was in some sort of tower, the bottom of one judging by the floor.

He sat on an outcropping of the same rock, barely large enough to be considered a cot with no mattress or blankets to soften it. That at least partly explained the complaints of his back and shoulder. Directly across from him was a single wooden door with a panel at the top that looked like it could be slid open.

A dungeon. Just great.

It certainly wasn't the first he'd ever been in. He had the poor habit of angering local lords with his too blunt honesty at times, or his sarcasm, or just being him it seemed. In their younger days it hadn't been unusual to find Dworkin right beside him but that had lessened as his friend married and had children.

As the shock of waking up confined wore off, he started remembering how he had gotten there. The image of the carnage at the Isle slammed into his mind and made his already angry stomach revolt. He gagged but there was nothing left to come up so he doubled over with violent dry heaves. When they finally passed, he sat on the floor, trying to catch his breath and clear the tears from his eyes.

How much time had passed since then? A day? A week? There was no way to know. By all evidence he was the highest ranking member left in the world, and possibly the only one who knew of what had happened. He had find a way out of here quickly and get help.

There was no way he could climb those slick walls, and even if he could, he wouldn't fit through the tiny window. Even if he could break down the door, who knew what kind of guards or challenges waited for him on the other side. At the very least probably more of those creatures that had been in the council room. That left only magic, not his favorite option when he was already this tired and in pain but he couldn't see any other choice.

He used the rock cot to help pull himself to his feet and searched his surroundings. He sighed realizing that his staff was no where to be found. He could work his magic without it, but having the focus and vessel right now would have been a big help. For a second, he wondered if he could use the stone on his ring the same way but that was gone too.

He sighed and closed his eyes, trying to reach past the pain and building fear to find that warm, glowing ball that he imagined in his core to represent his magic.

He decided a simple transport spell was probably his best route. It was the least flashy and might even buy him a little bit of time before his captor realized he was gone. The image of the dark man with gray eyes swam through his mind and sent a shiver down his spine but he pushed it away. That was to be worried about later.

With a deep breath he imagined the great hall of Marslic with it's cozy fire, clean rushes, and worn tapestries. He imagined Dworkin in his great chair, looking over one of the many reports that his staff loved to give him and that he always complained gave him headaches. There would be a couple of hunting dogs chewing on bones at his feet, the lovely Leslien working on needlework at his side while the children ran around laughing and playing. It was the perfect little scene, the quiet life that he often spent late nights alone envying his friend for. Carefully, he added himself to the room. He imagined how surprised Dworkin would be, how the children would run to him wondering if he had sweets or gifts. With a smile on his lips, he finished chanting the words to activate the spell and waited for the flash of light that would initiate the shift.

The flash never came. Instead there was a new, sharp pain, like barbed wire wrapping and tightening around the core of his magic. He screamed, gripping his head and dropping to his knees.

He was still gasping for breath as the panel in the door slid back, two yellow eyes staring in at him.

"Yous stops that," an odd lisping voice snapped. "Puny magic no work in there. Stupid chanting hurt Litsen ears. Stops or Litsen makes you stops."

Shock rolled through him. He sat in the dirt and pulled his knees up to his chest, pain still rolling through him from multiple sources but mostly the assault on his magic. How was that even possible? Of course all of the major cities had wards against evil spells, but that was just the block the effects the spell might have. He had put many of them in place personally. He had never heard of any kind of power that could actually stop another person from using their magic. Not just stop them, but attack their ability if they even tried.

A few moments later, the door opened and two of the massive creatures pushed through. Now that the shock had worn off, he remembered what they were. Nelcant. Twisted monsters from nightmares and fairy tales. They weren't supposed to exist in real life.

"Master glad yous finally awakes. Master been waiting," one of the Nelcant growled as they dragged him to his feet.

It was the same voice as through the door so this must be Litsen. Darian took a notice of his shredded right ear, probably from a previous fight. He wasn't sure if being able to tell his guards apart, but it certainly couldn't hurt. Right now, he had to grasp for any advantage he could find.

Listen pulled out a pair of metal rings connected by a small chain and closed them around Darian's wrists. As the metal clicked tight against his skin, a cold cage wrapped around his magic, not as painful as before but just as confining. He swallowed hard but tried to think positively. If they needed magic canceling bindings, that meant magic could be used outside of his cell. He would just have to figure out how to get out without the bindings.

The Nelcant pushed him forward but his legs protested and didn't want to work. Muttering and growling to each other, they lifted him again and half led, half dragged him between them.

Outside his cell, the tower was massive. He tried to count the turns and then how many flights they traveled up the winding staircase but the pounding in his head was too distracting. Everything after he had been grabbed by the Nelcant in the council room was black until he'd woken up here, so he figured between that and the splitting headache, he must have been knocked out pretty quickly. Whether it had been by a spell or the old fashioned way, he wasn't sure.

He had lost all sense of time or direction by the time they stopped before a large door set into the stone. At twice Darian's height and at least six feet wide, it made even the Nelcant look small. It shone like polished silver and radiated with a powerful magic. Some kind of odd sea creature was etched into metal, a mass of tentacles and dangerous looking teeth. Gemstones studded a starry sky with a single amethyst held at the center by the two largest tentacles.

The purple gem made him miss his staff again but also made him curious. It wasn't just for style that he had chosen an amethyst for the top of his staff or purple for his cloak. Gems were used in the order of difficulty to work with, the red ruby for Master being the best anyone had ever gotten before. He had thought himself the only one to have bent the stubborn purple gem to his will, but here was one staring him plain in the face, the magic practically glowing around it.

Litsen muttered a word that Darian didn't catch and the door swung silently inward. With only a slight hesitation, the Nelcant again hefted him up and dragged him forward.

The room was cavernous, larger than it seemed the areas they had passed through below could support. Rows upon rows of pillars spread out in every direction around him and held up a ceiling so high it hurt Darian's eyes to try to look for it. The floor around was a deep black with silver streaks etching through it but they walked down a black carpeted path thick enough to muffle the Nelcant's shuffling footsteps.

They continued at the same pace but everything around them seemed to speed up. Pillars rushed by at a blinding speed then came to a sudden stop so quickly Darian's head was left spinning. He was starting to feel as if he had somehow entered an alternate dimension where the very rules of existence were suspended.

They stopped in front of steps made of the same black marble that led up to a high dais. Sitting in a massive throne, his captor grinned down at them like a child being presented with a present. His black robes swirled about his ankles as he rose and slowly moved down the steps to stand face to face with Darian.

"Finally. So nice of you to join us."

Darian forced himself a little straighter, fighting not to wince at the pain that twinged through him. "My pleasure, I'm sure."

The man waved the Nelcant away and slowly circled him as if inspecting a piece of furniture. "High Master Darian, the most powerful wizard in the history of Ramleaj. Surpassing all levels at half the age that most reach Master. I am impressed."

"Murderer of the complete Wizard's Council and countless innocent young wizards." Darian growled. "I'm disgusted."

"A little testy this morning, are we?"

Darian just rolled his eyes. His head was pounding much too loudly to keep up this level of banter. "Can we just get to the point? If you plan to kill me, try your best and see what happens. If you're expecting a ransom, my friends know that I would never want them to pay a single coin for me."

"I am sure you underestimate what people would be willing to do to get you back," Zarentle laughed and paced back around to face him, "but money has no meaning to me. No, my boy, what I desire is revenge and you are going to help me get it."

Laughter rolled through him until it turned into a coughing fit that left tiny red droplets on the sleeve he held in front of his mouth. This man was obviously insane, and Darian was starting to feel as if it was contagious.

"And why, by the Twins, would I want to do that?"

"We will get to that, for now, let us go over the details of your stay. Breakfast and lunch will be taken in your quarters but you shall join me for dinner each night. Any time you are out of the cell, you will be cuffed and in the company of a guard. Is this understood?"

Darian grinned and glanced at the metal around his wrists. The man made it seem as if he had a choice. Rolling his shoulders, he blinked a few times as he wavered and nearly felt as if he would fall. He spread his feet slightly wider, refusing to give the satisfaction of his collapse.

"You never answered my question. Who are you?"

The man climbed back up the stairs and settled back in the massive throne, waving for the Neclant to return and lift him up again.

"You may call me Zarentle. We'll talk again soon, Darian. Rest for now."

"They're all dead."

Zarentle calmly cut a piece of meat before looking up with a grin. "What's that, my boy?"

His teeth grit against the term but he chose to ignore it. They were sitting at dinner for the third day since he had been there. Or at least since he had been awake. A large black table had been set up at the bottom of the dais, and a full service spread out between them. Every night, Darian just slumped in his seat and watched Zarentle eat, quietly testing the shackles to try and find a way out and going over the mental map that he was forming of the tower.

That morning he had woken up and it had all been clear. He felt stupid for not having figured it out sooner. With a sigh, he shifted in the hard wooden seat and grinned back.

"The people that you want revenge against, they all died centuries ago."

Zarentle lifted his wine glass, and slowly crossed his legs as he leaned back in his cushioned seat. "I never said who I was in search of."

"It wasn't that hard to figure out once my brain was clear enough to put all the clues together." He wrinkled his nose at the plate and pushed it away without having touched the contents. "I'm just embarrassed it took me so long."

Zarentle sipped at the wine and just stared at Darian as if unsure what he was talking about.

Darian rolled his eyes. "You want me to say it, don't you?" He shrugged. What did he care? He would stroke the man's ego if it bought him a little bit of time to figure a way out of there. "You want to pay back the original Wizard's Council for locking you behind the Barrier Ridge of the Ykor Mountains. Well, you're a few centuries too late, Zarentle, or should I say Demon Lord."

"Very good." Zerentle laughed as set the wine glass down and clapped his hands. "You got most of it right, and so quickly."

Darian sighed and rubbed his hands over his face. "That's the part I can't figure out. You wanted me to know, to put all the pieces together. You knew I would have heard of you and that I can speak Wylthem. Why go to such trouble? Why not just tell me from the start?"

Zarentle wiped his mouth with a black napkin then delicately laid it on the table before crossing his silverware over the plate. He rose from the table and a Nelcant immediately rushed in to refill the wine glass and clear the plates. He paced the room which seem to grow smaller with each time he turned, making Darian's head hurt again. A window appeared in the nearest wall for Zarentle to lean against and stare out dramatically.

"You've heard their version of the story. How the great races of Ramleaj came together to defeat the Demon Lord and restore order to the world. They probably gave it some grand name, too."

"War of the Races," Darian muttered.

Zarentle turned with a grin. "That's it? Well, no matter. They never told you the rest of the story, about how the races were tearing each other and the world apart. About how I tried to bring them together in the type of peace and harmony that you have spent your whole life trying to promote."

"Peace and harmony?" Darian snorted, shaking his dirty and matted hair out of his eyes then motioned to the Nelcant standing nearby. "You summoned creatures from people's nightmares to force them into servitude."

"I did what I had to do," Zarentle snapped. He paced back to the table and leaned across it so that his face was mere inches from Darian's. "You see it too, my boy. Their fighting and squabbling, the effect that it has on them and the land. In all your attempts at diplomacy and care, nothing has changed. Nothing will ever change. Ramleaj needs a firm hand to guide her. I could be that person, and you, boy, could be my heir."

Darian's eyes went wide as those gray eyes stared into his, so expecting and so hopeful. He couldn't help it. Something inside him snapped and he started to laugh. He laughed until his stomach ached and tears poured from his eyes. He laughed so long and hard that he almost fell out of his chair, all while Zarentle watched him with eyes growing darker and darker.

"You kill my mentors and innocent children, kidnap me and threaten the people and land that I care about, then you ask me to join you? Wow. You are the definition of insanity, sir."

Zarentle roared as he leaned back and raised his hands. A ball of pure energy formed between them, spinning and pulsating light into the room. Darian started to mutter a protection spell on instinct before remembering that his magic was locked as tight as his wrists by the bindings.

Then, just as suddenly as the storm had come, Zarentle visibly relaxed. Closing his eyes, he took a couple deep breaths and the light faded, the power dissipating into the air around them. He lowered his hands and opened his eyes, motioning Litsen forward with a smile.

"Rest well, High Master," he said quietly, "and consider my offer. I will have my revenge, you can either be a part of it, or the first victim.

It is your choice and I will only wait so long for you to make it."

14

Zarentle

Zarentle curled his lips and looked at his poor shoes. They had been standing in this muck just watching Darian sleep for what felt like ages now. What could possibly be so interesting? He was the one who had gone to all of this trouble to find and capture the High Master and even he was not this interested.

Not that the dirt and muck was a problem for his companion of course. He could walk through a sand storm and somehow not get a speck on that pristine white suit of his.

"What are you doing here, Tez?"

Cold brown eyes turned to study him without emotion. He hated that name, which was exactly why Zarentle continued to use it.

"I was curious," Tez said quietly, turning back to Darian.

"Couldn't help but wonder what was so important about this one human for you to squander so much of the power that I gave you. He really doesn't look like much."

In his current state, Zarentle could not disagree. Darian was growing pale and thin from refusing to eat and not getting outside. His long purple cloak was dirty and frayed, his fine black clothes reduced nearly to rags and hanging off of him, his black hair dirty and matted where it had come loose from the small ponytail at the base of his neck. Being constantly separated from his magic seemed to be taking the biggest toll. The spark was fading from his pale gray eyes, that strength of presence gone when he entered a room.

"Do not underestimate him. He is much more than he appears."

Tez grinned and walked out of the cell. "Yes, I know. More than even you know. I could see that when we spoke."

"What do you mean, you spoke to him?" Zarentle growled, chasing Tez down the hallway.

Tez glanced over his shoulder with that same bored expression. "Not much, just exchanged a few words. Don't be so worried. I'm not going to mess with your silly little plan, no matter how wrong I think it is."

"It is personal. You would not understand."

Tez spun to glare at him, blocking the path down the hall. "Oh I understand more than you think, more than you do. Heed my words, Zarentle, kill him now or he will be your downfall. I promise you that."

"I do not need your advice, or your help. I will handle this on my own, without you."

"If that's how you want it." Tez shrugged with a grin then turned to walk down the hall. Within five steps, he had disappeared completely.

15

There had been too many bodies for them to bury. They had been forced to build a large pyre and send the Wizards to the afterlife by flame. Dworkin said that was how the Cregas did it, since you couldn't bury people in rock. There had been a sneer to his voice as he talked about it, but Keslar had been too upset to ask why. They said all the normal prayers and asked for the Twins' forgiveness for breaking tradition. He just hoped the Wizards would still find their way to rest, especially Master Frencis. Silently, he had added the prayers of his father's people. Worship of anyone but the Twins was frowned on here but his dad had taught him anyway and he figured all the wizards deserved any help they could get.

He could still see the flames as he lay in his borrowed bedroll that night even though they had traveled a ways from the Isle. He was so exhausted he should have fallen right to sleep but he couldn't stop hearing the strange popping of the fire or smelling the awful stench of burnt flesh. After a few moments of tossing and turning, a large hand rested heavily on his shoulder.

"Think about the happier times with them, not their ending," Dworkin said softly. "It won't make the pain go away, but it'll make it a little easier to carry."

He rolled over onto his back and stared up at the stars. He could barely see the Duke's face in the dancing fire light but it looked pained and distant. "You've probably seen a lot of death."

"Too much." He sighed and tossed a stick into the fire. "But there is one time that has stuck with me more than most. About a year ago, my men were patrolling the mountains just north of Marslic when they came across a whole troupe of Cregas. I don't know what they were doing so far from their mountain but there they were. They attacked immediately, catching my men off guard. I lost four good men that day."

"Why would they do that?"

Dworkin rubbed a hand over his face, mussing up and then smoothing his blond beard. "I don't know. Somehow, Darian convinced me it was all a misunderstanding and not to retaliate. He saved the day, like always."

"He's still alive, your grace." Keslar sat up and hugged his legs to his chest. "If they wanted him dead they would have just killed him on the Isle."

"I know," Dworkin sighed, "that's not what I'm worried about. If it were anyone else that we were trying to rescue, Darian would be the first person that we called for. Who do you turn to when you're trying to rescue the person who rescues everyone else?"

Bartol grunted from his perch on a nearby log as he whittled a stick to a point. "I'm curious as to why? This seems an awful big show of force just to get to the High Master."

Keslar loved the big man's voice. It reminded him a lot of his own dad's. He was tempted to ask where the dark skinned knight might be from but afraid of being rude.

"I guess we'll just have to find the bastard and ask him." Duntiel laughed. He was the youngest of Dworkin's group, only a few years older than Keslar, with dark hair and eyes that always seemed to be laughing at something. "Right before we shove a sword in his belly."

Cantiem rolled over in his bedroll and leaned his head against his hand to look at them, reddish blond hair falling across his face as he glared at Duntiel. "I'm glad you're so confident we can take on someone who was able to best the entire Wizard's Guild and the High Master. I, personally, am not looking forward to facing him."

Duntiel turned in his seat to face the other man, face hard. "You're a knight, Cantiem, start acting like it."

"I'll show you what it means to be a knight, you little-" Cantiem grumbled, half out of his bedroll when Bartol roared.

"If you two don't stop arguing, I'll put you on latrine duty for a month when we get back home. Just the two of you and the muck for hours on end." He growled and jumped to his feet, tossing the stick into the fire. "Now get some damn sleep while your Duke and I take the first watch."

The men grumbled but settled down. Keslar rolled over and stared at Ebony's saddle where it had been placed near a tree, the High Master's staff still in the special holster that he had engineered for it. The swirl of gems twinkled like stars in the moonlight, so many more than the measly two that were on Keslar's as it lay within arms reach like always. He hadn't really stopped to think about it but Cantiem had a point. This man had batted away the a spell from the High Master like it was a fly buzzing around his face. Even if they found him, what did they really expect to do against him?

※

He didn't realize he had fallen asleep until he opened his eyes to find that the fire had died down. Dworkin snored lightly in his bedroll nearby, hand on his sword and looking ready for battle even in sleep. Duntiel and Bartol were on the other side of the fire. Cantiem must be on watch somewhere nearby but Keslar couldn't see him.

He sat up and reflexively checked over the pack that held everything he owned, even though he had just been using it as a pillow. Feeling uprooted and adrift for the second time in his life, he was thankful that Dworkin had insisted they get a few things from his room to bring along. He hadn't really known what to grab so had settled on a few extra clothes, his best spell book, all the snacks he had hidden in a drawer, and a handful of various baubles that didn't really have any worth but had meaning to him.

His heart slowed as he saw that everything was in place and just how he had left it. Satisfied, he rose and moved to one of the logs the men had rolled into a half circle around the fire. He pinned his cloak around his shoulders and tossed more wood into the fire, watching the embers dance back to life.

As the light of the flames grew brighter, he could see the figure of a man walking towards him. At first he thought it was Cantiem and almost waved, but as the man drew closer, it definitely wasn't the young soldier. It was a tall man with dark brown hair and even darker eyes, wearing a fine suit of pure white that almost glowed in the moonlight.

"Are you in need of help, friend?" He kept his voice kind even though he was shaking inside. It was drilled into your head from very early on in a wizard's training that everyone was a friend until they proved otherwise, and that you should offer help any time that you are able. However, he still reached down to be certain his staff was nearby. If nothing else, he could jab Dworkin with the butt end of it to wake the Duke up.

The man smiled and sat down on another one of the logs. "Merely a moment's rest by your fire, young scholar."

"Oh, I'm no scholar," Keslar whispered and pulled his cloak higher around his chin, his cheeks warming, "just an Apprentice Wizard."

The man smiled and held out his hands to the warmth of the fire. "I doubt that. Something tells me you spend more time in the library than just about anyone else on the Isle, that you always know the answer in class but aren't always brave enough to speak up, and that your studies come fairly easily for you so you're constantly looking for more to learn even though you have no idea what to do with all that information just yet."

His jaw nearly fell open. How could this smiling man have spent all of two minutes with him and seemed to see straight through to his soul? He shifted uncomfortably in his seat and threw a log on the fire to not have to look at those dark eyes any longer.

"You seem a little over dressed for travel, my lord," he said in a feeble attempt to change the subject.

The man laughed softly. "I'm about some very important business, Keslar, and now I must be off to it. Thank you for the warmth of your fire."

"Who are you talking to?" Cantiem called from his other side, striding towards the fire with a dramatic yawn.

Keslar cocked his head at the knight then turned back to the man in white. Except there was no one there. The log was as empty as when he sat down. Had he dreamed the whole thing? It wouldn't be the first time he'd fallen asleep sitting up.

"No one," he muttered, rising to return to his bedroll, "just thinking."

Cantiem watched him a moment then shrugged and started nudging Duntiel with his foot. "Wake up, fool. It's your turn for watch."

Keslar lay back down as the two argued over whether it was really time. He pulled his staff under the blanket with him, running his fingers thoughtfully over the brown chunk of amber attached to the top. Could he really have dreamed the strange man in the white suit? It had felt so real. Blinking, the last thing he saw before drifting off again, was Duntiel poking at two logs crackling in the fire.

16

Darian had lost all track of time. He had no idea anymore when it was day or night, or how many days had passed. He couldn't go by how many times he was brought back to the table to dine with Zarentle. Someone that adored illusion so much could easily decide to make it seem like dinner time whenever he wanted.

He passed his time sleeping or trying to find ways to keep his mind busy. It was a trick he used a lot when stuck on a spell or some other problem. Sometimes if you let your mind wander and focus on stupid stuff, the answer you really needed would come to you while you weren't focusing on it. He doubted it would work for a problem such as this, but was ready to try just about anything.

He was just starting the third verse of a rather dirty song he had learned from the Cregas when a dark figure appeared in his little patch of light. He raised his eyes to look back as Zarentle stared down at him, but made a point to finish the verse.

"Come," Zarentle turned, motioning him to his feet, "there is something I wish to show you."

When he didn't move, Litsen pulled him to his feet and slid the bindings around his wrists. The Nelcant was much gentler than usual, probably trying to convince his master that the many bruises lining Darian's body weren't his doing.

Zarentle led the way out of the cell and through the usual hallways, Litsen and another Nelcant following a little way behind them. Darian counted the turns like always, trying to keep the map in his mind fresh and accurate, but when they reached the top of the stairs Zarentle took a sharp right instead of the usual left that would lead to the doorway with the sea creature.

"How are you enjoying your stay with us, High Master?"

Darian leaned against the wall to catch his breath, ashamed at how weak he had become. Litsen caught up and gave him a sharp shove to get him moving again.

"You really know how to treat a guest, I'll give you that."

Down another hallway then one more right and suddenly they were in a large entryway. The first thing Darian noticed was a soft breeze on his face that smelled of trees and flowers and other living things. On the other side of the room, great twin doors had been left wide open so that the sunlight poured in and he could see blue sky and open grasslands beyond. Without even a thought, he gathered up any remaining energy he had and made a mad dash for it. The doors loomed closer and closer and he could practically taste his freedom.

The Nelcant were on him before he had gone ten steps. Zarentle clucked his tongue and closed the large doors with a wave of his hand. The thunderous click of the latch engaging was nearly enough make him want to sit down and die right there.

Zarentle sighed as he was dragged back to his feet. "I prepare a surprise for you and you have to misbehave. What kind of gratitude is that?"

"What surprise?" Darian coughed, trying to catch his breath.

Zarentle just smiled and motioned to a staircase along the side of the room. Darian didn't remember having seen it there before but he had been so focused on the open door he hadn't really noticed anything. Zarentle hummed the same song Darian had been reciting as he climbed the stairs with his robes swishing about his feet. Darian had to be practically carried up the stairs by Litsen, making a mental note to never, ever, sing that song again. After the third time of stumbling, he gave up and just allowed the Nelcant to heft him in one arm and drag him up the rest of the way. He had never felt so tired or weak before and couldn't help but wonder if it had to do, at least in part, with being cut off from his magic.

The stairs leveled out into a short hallway with only one door at the very end. Zarentle took a large silver key from his pocket and carefully fit it in the door before pushing it open and backing away. Litsen moved forward and deposited Darian just inside the door then backed away as well.

Barely able to raise his head, he looked around the room from his knees and nearly cried. The room was large and warm. Heavy tapestries lined the walls and thick rugs covered the floor. He ran his hand over the plush fibers, thinking they were the softest thing he'd ever felt. Straight in front of him was the largest bed he had ever seen with four posts carved of ebony wood and thick velvet curtains tied to them. Three mattresses had been piled up with a mass of blankets and pillows on top.

Off to his right, a large copper basin was filled with water, steam lifting in soft waves from it's surface. He could smell soft herbs that he knew would ease his aching joints and loosen the stiff muscles. Hanging from a rack next to the bath was a suit of fine black silk with a thick black cloak to match.

If he didn't hurt so bad he would have thought he had died in that dark, musty cell and this was his reward in the afterlife. What he wouldn't give to soak in that warm bath and then sleep for a few days in that giant bed.

"It could all be yours," Zarentle whispered in his ear, breaking the magic of the moment, "all you have to do is say you will join me."

Even as his heart sunk into his empty stomach, he was tempted. Anything to be allowed to wash the blood and grime from his skin and have just one good nights rest. To make the nightmare end, if only temporarily. Almost against his will, he opened his mouth to speak but again his eyes fell on the long black cloak.

His mind jerked and he saw himself wearing such a cloak, standing on top of a tall black tower looking out over a desolate land. As his eyes adjusted, he started to make out landmarks that he recognized but only just barely. Piles of ruined stone stood where Darsile and Marslic should be, charred tree trunks all that remained of the Great Forest and its majestic Wythelm city. Even the great Ykor Mountains, home to Cregas and dragon, lay in rubble at his feet.

He closed his eyes against the vision, tears streaking the dirt on his face. Bile rose in his throat at the thought that he had even considered it for a second. He shifted his shoulders and leaned forward until he could grip the tattered remains of his purple cloak, mentally holding on to the vows that it represented, then forced himself to his feet. He shrugged off Zarentle's hand when the man reached out to help him and sent him back a step with a dark look. He turned and took one step out of the room, swayed on his feet, then took another before collapsing back to his knees.

"Litsen," he stopped to wet his lips and try to swallow even though his throat was on fire, "take me back to my cell. Now."

17

Keslar woke the next morning to Dworkin lightly patting his back then setting a few rations next to him.

"Eat up. We need to get moving."

He sat up and stretched with a yawn, blinking in the morning sun. Dworkin nodded and went back to picking up around camp. The rest of the men were no where in sight but their things were already packed and sitting next to the horses. As Dworkin worked, the camp nearly disappeared before his eyes, leaving practically no signs that they had been there. Keslar nibbled at the rations, amazed that a Duke would not only travel just like any other soldier, but also share in the work. Somehow he'd always imagined them riding in fancy carriages with a retinue of staff waiting on them hand and foot.

"Best not to leave any trace behind, never know when you might be being followed." Dworkin grunted as he spread the ashes about and rolled the logs they had found back into random seeming places. "I'm sure it's not on the level of a Wylthem, but I've picked up some tricks over the years."

Keslar nodded and started rolling up his own blankets and checking around for anything he might have dropped. "Have you ever met one? A Wylthem, I mean."

Dworkin hefted one of the packs and started tying it to the packhorse with a grunt. "Darian says he goes to their city all the time, that he's good friends with some of them. My wife's family says they have Wylthem blood in their heritage, but a full blooded one? No, I never have."

"I think I'd like to meet one." He sighed and brushed the leaves from his cloak before shouldering his pack. "Where are your men?"

"We've been searching for clues, lad. Trying to figure out which way to go from here." Bartol stomped back into camp, scratching at his beard. "This is a big countryside, can't just go wandering about with no heading."

Dworkin tugged at the the ties on the packhorse then moved to pick up his saddle. "And did you find anything?"

Bartol just shrugged with a shake of his head but Cantiem and Duntiel came running into camp together, eyes wide and out of breath. Cantiem pushed red hair out of his eyes before pointing off to the East.

"We found some footprints in the mud on the bank of a stream. They aren't human, sir."

"Then that's the way we go." Dworkin nodded with a sigh. "Load up, boys."

Keslar watched the soldiers work together and prepare. He thought about telling Dworkin about the stranger at the fire but still wasn't certain he hadn't dreamed it. After a few moments, Dworkin walked towards him, leading Darian's giant black horse over.

"It was fine for last night but Mist can't carry the both of us for very far. Ebony will take care of you." He gave the horse a stern look and crossed his arms. "Won't you, Ebony?"

The black stallion tossed his head and seemed to roll his eyes but stood still as Dworkin tied Keslar's pack to his saddle then helped him up. Keslar shifted and adjust in the saddle, trying to find a comfortable position when his legs could barely span the large horse's girth. Dworkin gave Ebony one last look before swinging up into Mist's saddle and motioning that it was time to head out.

Hours later, his seat was numb and his legs ached from trying to stay in the saddle. They had lost the trail a ways back and were circling around trying to find some sort of sign. No matter how many times the knights dismounted and checked the ground there didn't seem to be any sign and he was starting to lose hope.

He attempted to shift his weight in the saddle but nearly lost his balance and had to grip the reigns to keep from falling. Ebony snorted as he side stepped then stopped all together. His long neck turned to try and nip at Keslar's leg.

"Sorry," Keslar muttered to the horse, "I'm no High Master, that's for sure."

Ebony snorted again as if in agreement before turning his head back around and walking on. Duntiel pulled his gelding past them, laughing so hard he almost led his horse right into Cantiem's. Cantiem's horse tried to nip at Duntiel's as both knights tossed insults at each other.

"Those latrines are still an option," Bartol yelled from the back of the line.

Both men quieted down and straightened out their horses but still shot dark looks each other's way. Bartol grunted and shook his head.

"You and Ebony doing okay?" Dworkin called back from his place in the lead. Mist picked her way along the path with head high, absolutely intent on ignoring the antics of the boys around her, human or equine. "He could be the pack horse and you could ride Mary if he doesn't want to behave."

Ebony's head shot up to stare at Dworkin. With a soft neigh he picked up his pace and pranced softly to Mist's side, matching her well behaved gait step for step. Dworkin just laughed and shook his head.

Keslar started to say something but he was distracted by movement in the sky. A small green speck was growing steadily larger as it angled directly towards them. Shading his eyes against the sun, he watched until he could make out wide green wings, a long neck and a swishing tail. His breath caught and for a moment he sat just frozen in the saddle.

"Dragon," he yelled. He yanked and tugged on Ebony's reigns but the horse refused to listen. In desperation, he slid from the saddle and ran for the trees.

Dworkin calmly pulled Mist to a halt and leaned over to stop Ebony. With both sets of reigns in one hand, he used the other to shade his eyes and study the sky, Bartol doing the same from behind. Keslar watched them from the trees, torn between his desire to drag them out of harms way and the absolute terror freezing him in place. He breathed heavy thinking it was just like the Council all over again. Was he just going to stand here and watch these men be slaughtered as well?

Bartol raised a hand to point to the sky, calling out to Dworkin. Dworkin turned Mist and nodded. Keslar sighed with relief. Now they saw what he had seen and would get out of sight themselves.

Instead, Dworkin dismounted and calmly walked to the area of the road where dirt and leaves were stirring as the dragon circled lower and lower to the ground. With a loud thump and skid, the dragon impacted with the ground then rose up and shook its head. It was nearly twice as tall as Ebony, possibly three times as long if you counted the swishing tail. It stretched its neck out as if to soak up as much sun as possible, then lowered its stomach to the ground and tucked its wing's against its body.

"Still need some work on those landings, I see." Dworkin laughed as he strode towards the beast.

The fear built up inside Kelsar until it finally sent him running from the trees to pull on Dworkin's arm. "What are you doing? Get away from it."

Dworkin just stared down at him and at the arm he was gripping. A dark disapproving look crossed his face as he pulled his arm away. Bartol also dismounted and jogged up, placing a heavy hand on Keslar's shoulder.

"It?" A deep voice laughed nearby, the sound rumbling through Keslar's stomach. "I've been called a lot of things, but never an it."

Dworkin growled and glared at Keslar again before nodding to the dragon. "My apologies, Nemclis, I guess manners aren't taught at the Isle anymore."

Keslar took a step back but Bartol still held on to his shoulder. Dworkin's disappointment in him stung but he could barely feel it under the deep shock. The Duke was speaking to a dragon the way a person would to a friend, as if it weren't an evil beast that could choose to swallow them whole at any moment.

"My manners are just fine to creatures that deserve it," he snapped, yanking out from under Bartol's hand. "A dragon is no one's friend but his own."

The dragon raised his head and snorted out hot air. "Well, that's quite the greeting. How many dragons have you known, tiny wizard?"

"Only one but that was quite enough. I learned all I needed to know about your kind the day he devoured my family and the rest of our town."

Silence filled the clearing. The knights all studied the ground or the sky while the dragon reared it's head back as if Keslar had smacked him in the nose. He gripped his staff, liking the mental image the thought brought. Only Dworkin reacted, grabbing Keslar by the cloak and pulling him off to the side.

"Look, kid, I'm sorry about your people and I get where you're coming from, but that is a friend of mine and I will not let you insult him."

Keslar tugged his cloak out of the Duke's grasp and glared back. "Really? And what if I were to introduce you to a friend who happened to be a Cregas? Would you be able to trust him, or would you be remembering every one of your men that their people slaughtered for no reason."

"That's different." Dworkin roared then seemed to catch himself and lower his voice. "Okay, maybe it's not so different, but Nemclis is. He wasn't even raised with the rest of the dragons. Darian found his egg before he even hatched and raised him until he was too big to live with humans. He's an orphan, just like you."

Keslar couldn't think of anything to say. Why would the High Master even bother? He could have just destroyed the egg and made sure there was one less monster in their world, but instead he decided to raise it like a pet. He took a few deep breaths and thought about the talks the High Master often gave at the Isle. He was always talking about how every creature of Ramleaj was important and deserved a wizard's protection, of how the races should all work together and make the world a better place. With that in mind, it was less surprising but still didn't make sense to him.

"My deepest apologies about your family, young wizard," Nemclis lowered his head and ambled closer to him, "but I'd hope you could take a chance and get to know me. Not all of my people are man-eating demons. In fact, it's rare enough I have a good idea who it probably was."

Keslar sighed and turned to Dworkin, trying to ignore the beast all together. "We're wasting time when we should be trying to find the trail that will lead us to the High Master."

"You're looking for Darian as well? I was hoping you might be able to tell me where to find him, Dworkin. I need to speak to him, as does a little Cregas I passed a couple of days ago. He tells me they are having some trouble in the caves and would like the High Master's help."

Dworkin sneered at the mention of the Cregas, then crossed his arms and looked off to the side for a moment. When he spoke, his voice was thick with emotion. "Darian's been taken, Nemclis. A mystery man and his monsters killed every wizard at the Isle and kidnapped Darian."

"It has to be connected," Nemclis whispered.

"Speak up, dragon." Bartol laughed as he strode closer. "You know I hate it when you mutter."

Nemclis sighed deeply and raised his head to look around before lowering his head back to them. "My uncle Derlin was flying near the Barrier Ridge and swears that he saw movement. Now, he's an elder and his eyesight isn't what it used to be, but his mind is whole. If he swears he saw something coming from the other side of the Barrier, I believe him."

"That's impossible," Duntiel laughed and shook his head. "There's nothing beyond the Barrier Ridge. You can't pass in and out of nothing."

Keslar's stomach churned and he found himself pacing. Of course he had heard the old stories but so many said they were just exaggeration. Everyone agreed the War of the Races had happened, it was why they would be having the Spring Festival soon. But if the first Wizard's Council actually locked some kind of ultimate evil behind the Barrier Ridge? Most figured it was just propaganda and exaggeration. A spell that strong and meant to last this long just wasn't possible, was it?

Dworkin ran his hands through his hair and stared off into the distance before letting out a long breath. "So Darian was right, it was real."

"You're not saying," Bartol swallowed, shaking his head before continuing, "this, man, that took the High Master, might be the actual Demon Lord?"

Keslar was shaking as he stared from face to face. Duntiel and Cantiem had grown quiet and white, looking to each other and down to the ground. Fear swirled in his gut as he looked to Bartol who was looking wide eyed at Dworkin, practically begging the Duke to tell him he was wrong. He didn't think anything could scare the big man, the thought of it stirring absolute terror in Keslar.

"We have to ride to Darsile," Dworkin snapped, already moving towards Mist. "The King needs to hear about this."

Keslar ran to catch up as the other men jumped into the saddle. "What about the High Master? We can't just abandon him. If it really is the Demon Lord, he needs our help even more."

Dworkin pulled Mist close, holding on to Ebony's halter to keep him still. "Darian would kill me if I rushed to save him without making sure the rest of Ramleaj was safe first. I really should have gone there first but we were on an already cold trail, now we have no other lead to follow. If you don't like my decision, you can turn around and go home. Otherwise, hold on tight and try to keep up."

Keslar didn't bother to remind the Duke that he had no home to go to. He crawled in the saddle and turned Ebony's head in the direction of the capital city. For once, the big stallion didn't fight him. He must agree it was the right decision as well, not that that made Keslar feel much better about it.

Dworkin's face softened as he gave a small nod then kicked Mist into a gallop, Ebony and the others falling into a line behind him. Keslar leaned low over Ebony's neck and held on as tight as he could but let the horse lead the way. A dark shadow passed over them and he glanced up to see Nemclis flying just above them, circling every now and then to not get too far ahead.

Keslar gritted his teeth, focused on Ebony's ears and just hung on. He wasn't prepared and nearly slid from the saddle as Bartol pulled up next to him then reached out to grab Ebony's reigns. Pulling on them as well as his, he slowed both horses so that the rest of the group pulled way ahead of them.

"What are you—"

"We'll catch up well before they stop for the night." Bartol sighed as their horses settled into a calm walk, though Ebony's sides seem to shudder with the urge to run.

Keslar's eyes dropped as he fiddled with the reigns in his hands. "You going to yell at me too? He's a dragon for the Twins' sake, Bartol."

"Are the Twins the only gods that you pray to, malak?"

His breath caught. He hadn't heard that word since the last time he'd spoken to his father. While he didn't really appreciate being called a little boy, the flowing syllables of his dad's language sent a shiver through him.

"You're from the Southern Isles as well? My dad was from there and talked lovingly about it though said he could never go home."

Bartol nodded slowly. "That's why I'm so surprised you would act such a way. Dworkin can hold his prejudices against the Cregas much easier having never felt it himself, but those of us who have been looked down on because of the color of our skin or the way we speak, or the gods we choose to follow? You'd think we'd know better."

"For other humans, yes," Keslar snapped. "I'd never treat a human that way but a dragon is a dangerous animal."

Bartol grunted and raised a dark eyebrow at him. "You know, they called us animals once."

"Why?" Keslar whispered. A sob caught in his throat as he thought about his dad, about how some people would go to the next town to find a carpenter instead of asking him to do the work, or would cross the street to not get too close. It was far from everyone, but enough that even a little boy had noticed.

"Because centuries ago, the kings of the Southern Isles decided to join with the Demon Lord to try and save themselves when it looked like there was no way to win. Was it the right thing to do? Probably not, but they were desperate and hoping to save their people."

"But that has nothing to do with us today."

"Just like how Nemclis had nothing to do with killing your village." Bartol grunted just before kicking his horse back into a gallop.

By the time they pitched camp for the night, Keslar felt no bigger than the beetle crawling across his pack. He still wasn't convinced that a dragon could be trusted, but he had disappointed two men that he deeply respected. As far as his heart was concerned, he may as well have punched his own father or Master Frencis himself.

As soon as camp was taken care of, Dworkin stomped off to the nearby open field where the dragon soaked up the last rays of the sun. The duke's shoulders were tight and his movements tense. Keslar felt like a heel for adding more stress to the man.

Bartol stepped up beside him and together they watched Duke and dragon settle into a quiet conversation. After a moment, Bartol's heavy hand fell on his shoulder.

"We'll let them be. While we might worry about the High Master, he's family to those two. Let them have a moment."

Keslar nodded and turned towards their small fire with the older man. Bartol nodded in approval as Duntiel hung a pot of water above the flames then motioned for Keslar to sit. He pulled a bag of root vegetables and dried meat from a pack to set between them and then produced two knives.

Keslar took the knife he was handed and started to chop the vegetables for the pot. "Wizards aren't supposed to have family. They teach us our allegiances are to the guild and Ramleaj, anything else is a distraction."

"That sounds like a dumb rule." Bartol snorted as he dropped chunks of meat in the pot then started digging through the pack again.

"That's what the High Master always said." Keslar laughed and shook his head. "Very loudly and to anyone who would listen."

Bartol glanced up with a wink. "Good thing. If it weren't for having a brother so worried, no one would be out here looking for him."

Keslar dropped the vegetables in the pot with a sigh. It was a sobering thought to know that if he had died back on the Isle, there wouldn't be a soul to mourn him. He would be just another nameless young wizard that people would cluck their tongues over the sadness of it all but not shed a single tear.

"Blast it." Bartol growled and glanced around at the two young knights. "Which one of you fools forgot to pack the ladle?"

While the two men argued and accused each other, Keslar grinned and lifted his staff. He pointed the amber stone that topped it towards the bubbling pot and said the words of the spell. As he said the release word, he made a slow circular motion with his staff, careful not to go too fast. He'd made that mistake before.

Bartol laughed and slapped him on the back as the soup started to swirl along with the movement of the staff. "Nice trick, kid."

Heat rushed to his cheeks and he ducked his head. It was a really simple spell that all young wizards learned when assigned to kitchen duty but it felt really good to have someone proud of him for once.

They settled into a comfortable silence as the soup simmered and swirled. Bartol leaned back against his pack and shaded his eyes with an arm while chewing on a stick with a sharp, familiar scent that he'd pulled from the pouch on his belt. Keslar tried to just let the man rest but silence had never been something he was good with.

"Bartol?"

The knight didn't move, just made a low sound of question in his throat. Keslar carefully adjusted the swirl of the soup and took a breath before continuing.

"When we were talking earlier, you mentioned gods. Ones other than the twins."

Bartol lifted his arm and looked at Keslar with eyebrows nearly to his hairline. "Your dad didn't teach you about our people? About where you come from?"

"I was still really young when they died. I barely remember them." He dropped his eyes and fiddled with a hole starting to form in the edge of his cloak. "I vaguely remember Dad having a table in the corner with a little figure made out of wheat or something. I wasn't allowed to play with it. I remember some of the prayers he would say he'd often burn something that smelled like that in front of it."

Bartol took the stick out of his mouth with a wink. "Yallo root. It's really not good for you so don't start. If he was burning it, that would be Marken, a trickster who can bring great prosperity but can also cause a lot of trouble if you don't acknowledge him."

"There are others?"

Bartol stretched out his legs and smiled at the darkening sky. "Lots. Dema is spreading her gem encrusted cloak above us now so her sister, Sula, can sleep. There's Ren of the rains and her husband, Tanu, who's great ax makes the thunder and lightning. Pelli swims along the shore, her body made of water as she protects the creatures of the sea and rewards fishermen who pay her proper respects."

Keslar's jaw fell open, his mind swimming with the thoughts of so many gods. He was so busy trying to picture them all that he barely noticed Dworkin wander back into camp and sit down near them.

"Do you think..." Keslar chewed at the inside of his cheek and scrunched his face, trying to put into words the confusion in his mind. "I've grown up going to service and worshiping the Twins. We're supposed to thank them for having blessed us with our power and use it to help Ramleaj in return. Do you think it would anger them if I wanted to learn about these other gods? Might they choose to take my magic away?"

Dworkin leaned forward and scooped out some of the soup with a wooden bowl but didn't start eating right away. He sat watching the steam rise off the soup with his elbows on his knees and a distant look in his eyes.

"I'm no priest, that's for sure," he laughed and shook his head, "but I know that the Twins are supposed to be loving and nurturing. I've never thought of them being vengeful like that."

Bartol shrugged with a laugh. "And none of mine have struck me down yet for adding the Twins to my invocations."

"Put it this way," Dworkin added with sad look, "Darian has studied both the Wylthem and Cregas religions for years now. Tells me about taking part in their traditions and practices any time he visits them. Twins haven't taken his power away yet."

Bartol dipped a bowl of the soup and handed it to Keslar before going back for one himself. "Whether you decide to start worshiping my gods as well as those you already know or not, is very much up to you. I think your dad would have really liked it if you knew about that side of you and where you came from, though. Even if all you have is the knowledge and you don't do anything else with it."

"Yeah, I'm sure he would," Keslar whispered, trying to swallow a piece of meat past the lump in his throat.

He grew quiet as the older men turned the conversation to the road and how long it would take them to reach Darsile and the king. Picking at the stew, he thought of the things other wizards and even some of the teachers had said about him. The way some had even doubted if he had the right to be there if he wasn't fully from Ramleaj even though he had been born on the same soil they had.

Might those jabs about his color, or his parentage, have hurt a bit less had he know more about where he'd come from? Might he been proud instead of crying himself to sleep and dishonoring his father by wishing to be someone else? Those people were all gone, consumed by the funeral pyre he still saw when he closed his eyes and while he found no satisfaction in that, he knew there would be others. Maybe it was too late for them, but he was still here. Maybe this was why the Twins had chosen to spare him, if it had even been the Twins and not one of the other gods Bartol spoke of.

18

She stopped to catch her breath then hefted the stones a little bit higher and continued on. The little fountain was a lot heavier than it looked and it was starting to feel like she would never reach the infirmary without dropping it. Finally, the door was in reach and she swept in, setting the fountain down on the nearest flat surface she could find with a thunk.

"Who is there?" Railin sat up from the bed with a start, the blanket sliding from her lap to puddle on the floor.

A lump caught in Miramel's throat and her eyes burned. The Wylthem who had always been so full of life and adventure looked worse than death. The small bits of hair that she had left hung in limp strands around her head, her bones protruded from paper like skin, and blind eyes darted about the room.

"It is me, Railin," she whispered, bending to retrieve the thick blanket and wrap it back around the Wylthem's legs. "I brought your fountain."

Railin sighed and relaxed back against the thick pillows, allowing Miramel to pull the blanket up to her shoulders. "Thank you, dear. It is much too quiet in here."

Miramel glanced out the window as she pulled the water skin from it's leather strap slung over her shoulder. She could hear the breeze rustling through the leaves, the birds softly calling to each other, and animals wiggling through the brush. With a shrug, she poured the water into the basin at the bottom then dipped her finger inside. Opening her senses she could feel the wild spirit of the water, so akin to the wind. Both longed for movement and change, neither ever truly be contained. Guiding the want for movement, she showed the water how to bubble and dance over the little rocks and then find it's way back up to do it over again. It did not listen to her the way it might a water born, but she was asking something that came natural to it so it decided to comply and in short order the fountain was bubbling as happily as a brook.

"Much better," Railin said with a soft sigh. "Thank you, princess. Will you sit with me for a while?"

"Of course."

She moved to the seat closest to the window, the thorny raspberry bush just outside leaning closer to her. She leaned her arm against the window and lightly stroked the plant, a bit of climbing ivy reaching out a tendril to wrap around her arm. As the plants calmed and soothed her, she could not help but think of those like Railin and her own mother. How would she feel if she had to be out of the forest for too long, away from all things green and growing? Probably desperate enough to do something just as crazy as dance in poisonous rain.

"Princess, I did not expect to find you here."

Her attention jerked back to the room. Larsle stood in the doorway, another Wylthem behind him. She carefully disentangled herself from the plants and stood up, straightening her skirts and finding a smile for her old friend. He did not smile in return, but glanced to his companion then back to her.

"Do you know where your father is?"

"I believe he is in his study, consulting his books again." She circled the bed to move a bit closer, patting Railin's legs as she passed. "What is your need of him?"

Larsle sighed and stepped to the side a little, pulling his companion up next to him. It was one of the young guards. She recognized him from the scouting and arms classes that she taught though she could not pull up his name at the moment. She did remember that he was a decent fighter but was often easily distracted by his curiosity.

"Show her," Larsle whispered.

The young guard hesitated then held up his hand, slowly unwrapping the strip of fabric that had been wrapped around it. He was shaking as she wrapped her hands around his to study his palm. The hand she held looked like that of an ancient Wylthem, though the man standing before her was probably only a couple hundred years old. She grabbed his other hand and held the two together. Where one was smooth and youthful, only marred by the callouses expected from someone who handled weapons regularly, the other was wrinkled and cracked. The fingers were swollen and bent as if plagued with arthritis.

"When did this begin?"

The guard cleared his throat, pulling his hand out of her grasp to tuck into his side. "It started to hurt a bit a day or two after the storm, but I thought it only injured from bow practice. The past few days it has turned into this."

"He hid it from me for a while." Larsle turned to glare at his charge before looking back to Miramel. "I only noticed when he could not hold a sword today in practice."

She pursed her lips and glanced back to Railin who had fallen back to sleep. Carefully, she pushed the others out into the hallway before looking the young guard in the eye. "You mentioned the storm. Did the water touch you? Did it actually get on your skin, not just clothing?"

"I may have held out my hand to try and catch it." He blushed and dropped his eyes to the floor. "It smelled so odd and felt almost like oil. I just wanted to try to understand it."

She sighed and gripped his shoulder. "That is what we are all trying to do. Larsle, please go see if my father is in his study and ask him to come to me. I will get your friend settled into the next room."

Larsle's eyes were full of questions but he took the hint not to ask them right now. With a curt nod, he turned on his heel and took off down the hallway in long strides.

She forced herself to smile as she motioned the young Wylthem into the nearest room where he could comfortably wait for her father. Once back out in the hallway, she forced herself to take a couple slow, deep breaths before pulling up the sleeve of her dress. Snaking up her arm was a short path of dry, cracking skin. As she ran a finger over the patch, she remembered the way the rain had felt on her skin, slick and oily for the brief moment before she had swiped it off.

Footsteps echoed down the hallway, approaching her quickly. She jerked her sleeve back down and took one second to feel mild panic, before tucking it away just as her father and Larsle rounded the corner.

19

Dworkin jumped from the saddle as soon as they were within the courtyard. "Cantiem and Duntiel, go into the city and restock our supplies. Bartol, check in with your contacts here and see if they know anything. Grab the horses and meet me back outside the city where Nemclis is waiting. Kelsar, you're with me."

His men gave quick nods and dashed off in different directions. The well trained stable boys were already leading their horses away to be fully groomed and fed in the royal stables. Dworkin's eyes fell on the tower in the corner of the courtyard and his stomach clenched. Darian's home away from home, his personal residence any time he was in attendance of the court. Just another reminder that Dworkin had no idea where his brother was, or if he was even still alive by that point.

"Where are we going?" Keslar huffed, practically running to fall into step with him.

"To see the king and queen. That's why we came."

Keslar stopped as if he had been glued to the floor then ran to catch up again. "But don't you have to request an audience or something? You can't just walk in on the King."

The guards at the door in front of him seemed to have the same idea as Keslar. He didn't recognize them, probably new recruits thinking they had the most important job ever being assigned to guard the royal family. Really, they were guarding the court, the king and queen's guard's stayed right by their side and out of sight, disguised as friends and lords or ladies. Though they usually really were those things as well. A role Dworkin held anytime he was at court, which gave him the authority and confidence to merely push the soldiers' spears out of his way and continue into the grand hall.

All heads turned as they burst through the doors. Nearly the whole court seemed to be in attendance which was odd. It seemed early for everyone to have ventured out after a long winter in their respective homes. He didn't care which lords or ladies lined the walls of the large room though, his focus was on the man sitting just above them all.

Matthias sat slightly slumped in his throne, large golden crown looking heavy upon his brow. Dworkin knew from experience that his friend was most likely dreaming of being out hunting or swapping war stories with his friends to get himself through the tedium of court. He always said that listening to his people's problems was important, but would be easier to stomach if they would at least try to solve things themselves before coming to him. Having his quiet but loving wife at his side and their small son playing between them helped, but only so much.

The two of them were in contrast to the king in every way but also his pride and joy. Narlise had passed on her dark hair and eyes to their son, but he was a much lighter shade of brown than her thanks to the paleness of his father.

"Your Majesties, I need to speak with you immediately."

Matthias sat up in his chair and leaned forward. His eyes sparkled and he grinned as he started to speak, but it was the young man in the center of the floor that spoke up first.

"With all due respect, your grace, I have the floor at the moment."

Dworkin crossed his arms and looked the young lord up and down. He wore the deep blue of Arnis, Dworkin's uncle's dukedom to the south, in lavish layers including a small caplet slung over one shoulder with the bird in flight of Arnis. On his feet were the same sturdy, black riding boots that Dworkin and the King both wore, but where theirs were scraped and scuffed, his shined pristinely since he wouldn't know the front end of a horse from the arse if guided there.

"I appreciate the respect, Lord Ranklus but what I have to say is much more important. Your majesties-"

"And how would you know? You don't even know what I was talking about."

Dworkin rolled his eyes and fought back a growl. "Because what I have to say is more important than anything. Your majesties, the Wizards have been attacked, the council decimated."

A figure stepped forward next to the King's throne, red cloak pulled tight over a round stomach, hood perched over bald head even though it wasn't cold in the castle.

"We appreciate your concern, Duke, but we've already heard of the attack."

Keslar stepped forward, pointing his staff at the master wizard. "And how would you have heard, Master Clesum? Clearly you weren't there since you're whole and healthy while the rest of the council was slaughtered."

"My heart aches for my brethren." Clesum placed a hand over his heart and tried to look solemn. "I can only think that the Twins must still have a plan for me that I was not able to make it to the meeting."

"How dare-"

Dworkin placed a hand on Keslar's arm and pulled him back a little. He could understand and respect the fire in the young man, but he may as well have been talking to a wall. Everyone knew that Clesum was mostly useless. Many whispered that Head Master Frencis had only assigned him to the position of King's Wizard so that he would rarely come back to the Isle, and that King Matthias put up with it because if he really needed anything Darian was often in residence at his personal tower.

"No, child, how dare you? Even an island boy should know better than to speak to his elders with such a-"

"What did you call him?" Dworkin growled through clenched teeth. He knew very well that Clesum wasn't referring to the Wizard's Isle when he looked at young Keslar's dark skin.

Matthias motioned Clesum back with a dark look and gave Dworkin a quiet sign to stop before leaning forward and looking at Keslar kindly. "We are sincerely sorry for your loss, young wizard, and if we find the party responsible we will hold them accountable in the worst possible way."

"Your Majesty," Dworkin's eyes drifted to the queen who was still quietly working on her embroidery even though he was certain she heard all, "the High Master has been taken as well."

Queen Narlise's hoop fell from her hands to clatter to the floor. An all too thin hand pressed to her throat as wide, dark eyes implored Dworkin. "What do you mean, taken? When?"

"At the attack. Nearly two weeks ago."

Mathias leaned back with a smile and gently patted his wife's knee. "You must be mistaken, Lord Duke. It was the High Master himself who told us about the attack. In fact, he had an injured friend with him that he was taking north to the Healers."

"Your Majesty, I know what I-"

Dworkin again caught Keslar's arm and gave a small shake of his head then bowed low. "My apologies for interrupting your court then, your majesties. If you have no need of me we will ride out and be sure that the High Master was able to get his friend the help needed."

Matthias' eyes darkened slightly as he studied Dworkin. They had known each other nearly as long as he had Darian. Matthias had been a gangly teenage prince when they had first been deemed old enough to travel with his father to court. Now King and close friend, Matthias had certainly picked up on the change in Dworkin's voice and manner but didn't dare mention it in front of the court, or especially his fragile wife.

"Of course, Dworkin," he said quietly, putting emphasis on using Dworkin's given name and not his title. "We would much appreciate you checking in on our friend. Please report back to me what you learn."

"Yes, Matthias. Thank you." He started to turn away but turned back with a small bow. "Might I ask the crown of a favor myself? I have been away from home for longer than I expected. Could a message possibly be sent to Marslic that I shall contact them again as soon as I have spoken to the High Master?"

Narlise smiled softly and patted her child's head as she picked up her needlework again. "It is too long since I have been in contact with the Lady Marslic. I will send the letter personally, your grace."

"Thank you."

Dworkin continued to grip Keslar's arm as he turned and stomped out of the grand hall. Keslar babbled a million questions and objections but Dworkin couldn't hear him over the all the questions of his own or the sick feeling growing in his gut.

20

Keslar

Even though the Duke had released his arm, Keslar practically had to run to keep up with Dworkin as he wound his ways through the city streets. He had never seen so many people squeezed in one place before. They were all yelling and trading and trying to get their own little missions done. Dworkin strode through them with the cool confidence that had people moving out of his way and turned heads as he passed. Keslar jogged at his heels, head down and just trying to go unnoticed.

Dworkin turned suddenly down a side street and out of the crowds. Keslar glanced to the large city gates before jogging to catch up.

"Aren't we supposed to meet the men out by Nemclis?"

Dworkin glanced over his shoulder but kept walking. "We will in just a minute. There's one more person I want to check in with first."

They moved through the quieter part of town, catching glances from the people there. The shops were smaller and made of simpler materials. Most of the walls were white, lacking the bright colors and varying woods of the richer houses and businesses they had just left. The men and women milling about on the streets were dressed in garbs of natural materials and simple shapes, un-dyed and un-ornamented. They had obviously entered the poorer section of Darsile. As they wound their way through the streets, somehow it didn't surprise Keslar anymore that the Duke knew his way around the average person's part of town as he did the palace grounds.

An amazing mix of smells caught Keslar's attention and his stomach rumbled loudly. He realized he hadn't had anything other than travel rations to eat since the dinner before the attack, and he'd barely eaten that from being so nervous about his test.

"It's about time you made your way back here, boy," a voice called over the crowd.

Following the sound, and smells, they came to a stop in front of a modest stand tucked between two small buildings. Dworkin smiled as he leaned over and hugged the elderly woman who sat behind it. Kelsar was practically drooling as his eyes took in the steaming meat pies and other delicacies that filled the stall.

"You boys never come to see me, anymore," she chiding gently, "but at least Darian makes an effort."

Dworkin shrugged with a shy grin. "Darian can travel a lot easier than I can, Marta. I have kids and a dukedom to worry about now."

"This can't be one of those little ones." She laughed and motioned to Keslar. "I may lose track of time but not that much."

Dworkin laughed and smacked Keslar on the shoulder, pulling him a little closer. "No, no. This is Keslar, a new friend. He's rather hungry and I figured he should have the best in Darsile."

Keslar glanced to Dworkin. He had no argument of trying this wonderful smelling food, but was his stomach really a good enough reason to delay meeting up with the men and trying to find High Master Darian?

Marta reached out a wrinkled and age marked hand to shakily wrap her fingers around his wrist, as if measuring it. "Skin and bones, ye be child, skin and bones. Don't this one take care of ye?"

Keslar shrugged and felt the heat rush to his cheeks. He didn't know what to say. He'd never really met anyone like Marta. "He tries, ma'am, but we've been on the road a long time now and I do eat a lot."

"Of course, you be growing, boy. It's what you do. But don't you ma'am me. I'll not be insulted in my own stand."

Dworkin's laugh was so full and strong Keslar couldn't help but join in. A wide, toothless grin lit up Marta's wrinkled face, making her green eyes dance with light. She winked and handed him a large fruit tart while starting to bag up a variety of items for them to take along. Dworkin set a small bag of coins on the counter but leaned his hip against the stand and tapped a finger against the wood.

"Speaking of Darian, I've been trying to catch up with him. You haven't seen him lately have you?"

Marta looked to Dworkin for a moment, passing over the bag of food. "You know, I heard folks say he was in the city the other day so I went down to the main street to try and catch his attention. Wanted to see if he had more of that salve for my joints. But something didn't seem right. He just rode right past everyone without saying a word or even smiling. Wasn't even on that big horse of his that loves my apple tarts."

"Thanks anyway," Dworkin nodded, giving Marta a smile that didn't take the pain out of his eyes, "but we really should be going."

Dworkin shouldered the small bag of treats and steered Keslar back down the street they had come from. He waved to Marta then bit into the tart. The buttery pastry flaked away and his mouth was filled with the juicy sweetness from inside.

"I've never tasted anything so good."

Dworkin nodded but seemed distracted. "Marta's the best."

He finished off the tart as they passed a stand selling portraits of the royal family. He paused and shoved the rest of the tart in his mouth. He couldn't stop studying the portrait even as Dworkin turned back to see why he wasn't following. The royal family had struck him in person but he'd also been distracted by the annoyance of Master Clesum and just the general overwhelm of being in the presence of a king.

Now that all of the extra stuff was gone, he was overcome by the feeling again. The King was exactly what he had expected. With blond hair just a shade darker than his thick crown and heavy beard with hints of red, he was build for strength much like his castle. There was wisdom in his blue eyes and lines of worry around his mouth. His large hands were strong and calloused from sword and spear just like Dworkin's. This was no king to sit in the lap of luxury and let others do the dirty work.

It was his queen and the prince that kept catching Keslar's eye though. They both had thick ebony hair and large brown eyes. The boy had a build that looked like it could grow into the strength of his father, but Narlise was a slight woman with skin just bordering on brown and a tired look about her eyes. He had no idea that someone who shared his heritage sat upon the very throne of Ramleaj.

"The queen seemed really upset to hear something was wrong with the High Master. Are they close?"

Dworkin shrugged. "They are the only actual blood family each other has left. They aren't super close but definitely care about each other."

"Family?" Keslar blinked and shook his head as they started for the city gates again.

"Darian's mother was Narlise's aunt. They're cousins. I thought everyone knew that." Dworkin's face fell and he pulled his coat a little tighter. "I wish there had been time to request a private audience with the king. I hadn't even considered how much it would upset her."

"But Darian isn't from the Southern Isles."

Dworkin just shrugged. "They are related on their mother's side. The queen's foreign blood comes from her father."

Just like me, Keslar thought for a moment.

He pictured again the dark circles under her eyes and the weakness of her movements, the way King Matthias had looked at her like she might break. "Is she ill?"

Dworkin stopped mid-step to stare at him. With a growl he glanced around then pulled Keslar into the church of the god twin that flanked the city gates with its mirror, the church of the goddess twin, on the other side of the broad street.

The Duke smiled and nodded as a couple of men passed them on the way out of the church but never let go of Keslar's arm. Once they were alone he dragged them to one of the benches towards the back and sat down.

"Why would you ask that?"

He shrugged, still reeling from the shock of Dworkin's reaction. "She looked so weak and the king seemed so protective of her and the prince. Even more so than a husband usually is."

"We try to keep it quiet so this doesn't go beyond you and me, but the queen is not in good health. She was weakened by the prince's birth and has never recovered no matter what the healers do. She doesn't seem to be in immediate danger though she did look worse today than last time I saw her. Only the King, myself and a few other people know. And now you. I only tell you because you're too damn observant and it would dangerous for you to draw your own conclusions."

"I understand," Keslar mumbled, thoughts swirling in his mind. He had often seen the High Master dance around answering questions, or hear about how he supposedly in a secret meeting with this person or that one. He'd thought it must be so exciting to be privy to secrets from the highest people of Ramleaj. Now that he was getting a small peak of that world, he realized it wasn't nearly as glamorous or exciting as he thought. In fact, it was rather scary.

"The queen is weak because her faith is weak," a deep voice rumbled nearby. "King Mathias should have known choosing a queen with foreign blood would be frowned upon by the goddess."

Keslar turned to find a priest hovering at the end of the bench. Long yellow robes were embroidered with gold and silver thread, a white and gold vestment around his neck with gold tassels brushing the floor.

Dworkin rose to his feet with a deadly slowness and crossed his arms. "That seems dangerously close to treason, Brother Orin."

"What is said within the church is protected, as you will remember, and free from royal scrutiny. I will admit, I did not recognize you, Duke Marslic. Usually you actually dress for church."

Dworkin glanced at his road worn clothes and shrugged. "When I'm not in the middle of a journey and actually attending a service, yes I usually do. However I was to understand the god would take us as we are, no matter what we wear."

"Very true, Duke Marslic," Brother Orin inclined his head with a small smile, "though it is a sign of respect to be sure we are clean and presentable before entering his presence."

Keslar glanced between the two men as they stared at each other, then cleared his throat nervously. "I look forward to attending one of your services when I am able to spend more time in Darsile, Brother. The church is amazing."

It wasn't just flattery, though he was hoping that would work to ease some of the tension. The stone building was massive with both long walls filled with stained glass windows depicting scenes from the stories about the god and goddess and how they had founded the human race here in Ramleaj. In front of the long rows of benches was a raised alter dominated by the sun disc that represented the god, trails of incense floating up to fill the air with the scents of sandalwood and jasmine.

"Another of foreign blood, I see." Brother Orin sniffed and looked him up and down, tapping the end of his staff with a slippered toe. "Still, you could attend a service every day and live in harmony with our god instead of trying to be one yourself. Our doors are always open for those who wish to leave dark studies behind them and find the light."

"I appreciate the offer," Keslar forced himself to say through clenched teeth as he pushed his way past the priest and towards the door, "but I believe it is time we were on our way. Isn't that right, Duke Marslic?"

Dworkin climbed over the bench so as not to have to pass the priest and joined him by the door. "It certainly is. May the Twins be with you, Brother Orin."

"As if you would even recognize them if they stood right in front of you," Keslar growled under his breath as he pushed open the door and rushed back out into the busy street.

Dworkin followed closely and silently until they were outside the city gates then steered them to the edge of the road where things weren't as crowded. Once they were out of the crowds, the duke wrapped an arm around Keslar's shoulders and pulled him close.

"What was that all about?"

Keslar sighed and gripped his staff until his fingers hurt. "There has been a change in the priesthood over the past few years. They seem to think that magic is a perversion of the natural order of things that the Twins gave us. They keep trying to recruit young boys away from the guild, and have even succeeded with some."

"No wonder Darian hasn't really been attending services as much as he used to." Dworkin snorted and shook his head. "The church definitely is not what it was when I was growing up. I'm not really sure what happened to it."

The walked the rest of the way in silence until they reached the hill where Nemclis and the knights waited. The dragon had spread out his wings and long neck, soaking up every ray of the sun he possibly could. People passing on the road below either stared openly or rushed past as to not risk being in his presence. Keslar still bristled at the thought and didn't blame them one bit.

As they drew closer, the dragon opened one great eye then yawned broadly before sitting up. "So, what is your king to do?"

"Absolutely nothing." Keslar growled.

Nemclis glanced at him then turned to Dworkin who attempted to recount their meeting with the king. Keslar noticed he left out all mention of the queen and felt a little surge of pride that even the High Master's pet and Dworkin's top knights hadn't been trusted with this secret.

"Didn't you tell him about what we've seen at Barrier Ridge?" Nemclis laid his head on the ground again and released a sigh of steam.

Dworkin shrugged. "It didn't seem the time with so many people in the court. Besides, he gave me clear signs he didn't want to talk further about Darian so I took the hint not to mention more. Mattias isn't dumb. He suspects something but isn't sure what so can't act."

"I heard the same thing," Bartol growled, digging through the bag of food that Dworkin had tossed him. "People saying the High Master made a grand show of passing through the city but didn't stop to talk to anyone but the king."

"Which is very unlike Darian," Nemclis muttered sleepily. "Back when I could travel with him I used to get annoyed with how long it would take him to get anywhere because he had so many people to check in with."

"Exactly," Dworkin said with a small smirk, "that's what tells me it wasn't Darian that the King spoke to."

Bartol chose a meat pie then passed the bag on to Duntiel and Cantiem to dig through. "What do you mean? His Majesty would know who he was talking to."

"As well as Darian would know if he was talking to Master Frencis or not?" Dworkin raised an eyebrow, looking to Keslar.

Slowly, the gears started to click together in Keslar's mind. "This guy is a master of illusion. He pretended to be Darian to buy them some time, the same way he pretended to be Frencis to trick Darian. The real Darian was the injured friend."

"Exactly," Dworkin said, practically jumping into the saddle.

Cantiem still had a fruit tart hanging from his mouth as he tied the rest to his saddle then climbed up. "But where do we go? We still have no tracks."

"Here's a lesson for you," Dworkin waited as the rest of the crew saddled up, Bartol helping Keslar before climbing into his own, "every lie has a bit of truth to it. They told the king they were headed north towards the healers."

"I doubt this man is going to take Darian to the healers," Duntiel grunted then immediately flushed as Dworkin shot him a look.

"No, but he probably is headed North, so that is where we will go too."

Cantiem hesitated, pulling his horse up and messing with the pack horse's reigns until she tugged back a little. "What if the king is right though and we make a complete fool of ourselves?"

"You've never worried about making a fool of yourself before," Duntiel laughed, riding past to smack his friend on the back of the head. "You're just in a hurry to get home to that pretty new wife."

Duntiel blushed beet red as the others roared with laughter. After a moment, Dworkin motioned for them to quiet down even though he was still grinning broadly.

"I would much rather find my brother whole and have him laugh at me, than never find him." Dworkin raised an eyebrow and stared at the crew until they each nodded. "Let's ride out. The sooner we find Darian, the sooner we can all get home."

21

Darian growled as Litsen pushed him into the cell after another tedious dinner with Zarentle. Every night he was reminded that the luxurious room was still there and that the offer still stood. Every time he would refuse and quickly be sent back to his cell.

Litsen was just as bored and tired of this little game as Darian and growing more and more reckless. He would often leave the cell door open as he removed the bindings, but still, he was fast. Even though Darian had been doing any exercises he could think of in the cell to regain his strength, he didn't think he could make it past the Nelcant. He'd hate to give the creature an excuse to kill him without asking Zarentle first. That didn't mean he hadn't been formulating a plan.

For days now he had been picking at the underside of the table as

Zarentle talked. Finally, he had broken free a tiny sliver of the black wood and shoved it inside the lock of the shackles. It wasn't enough that they wouldn't unlock at all, but just enough to cause Litsen some trouble. When the lock didn't open right away, Litsen bent down to see what was happening, just like Darian had hoped. As soon as he heard the lock click free, he twisted his wrist and bashed the metal shackles into Litsen's flat nose. Litsen howled and gripped his face, falling back just enough for Darian to dart past.

Once he crossed the threshold, he felt his magic flood through him again and fill him with a new strength. He spoke a quick spell to knock Litsen out then shut the door with the big creature inside.

He turned back the way they had come, counting the turns and hallways just as he had every blasted day that he'd been here. On the second floor, voices and footfalls sounded down the hall so he slid into an alcove behind a dark statue. Two Nelcant strode past, not even looking his direction.

"Why Litsen boss best?" One of them growled. "Get human toy. We just guard."

The bigger one laughed. "Litsen no get play with toy. Just watch. We have fun soon and he stuck here."

Darian held his breath until the two were fully around the corner then set out again at a slower pace. He took a couple wrong turns and had to back track, and had to hide three more times before finally finding himself in the great central room.

To his right were the stairs that led up to the luxurious room, straight ahead of him the huge doors stood open like an invitation to freedom. He was tempted to just run straight for them but he could see shadows of guards milling about and a long stretch of open land beyond. He would be seen before he got anywhere and dragged back inside, at least.

Reluctantly, he turned away from the open door and continued to count turns down the hallway. He had to take out Zarentle. Or at least incapacitate him long enough to make a clean get away. It wasn't only his best hope at getting out of here, it was the best hope at saving Ramleaj. Even if his friends had noticed him missing by now, they would have no idea where to look for him or what they were up against. He was on his own. Again.

He skidded to a stop in front of the large door with the sea creature. It's one purple stone stared down at him, looking through him to pick out all of his doubts and fears. He had failed against Zarentle once, back when he was whole and healthy. What made him think that he would succeed this time? He didn't even have his staff and his magic felt weak and fluttering after being locked away for so long.

With a growl he turned away and searched the nearby halls for a Nelcant. He found a small one ripping apart some kind of meat and tossing the chunks into a pile. Darian shuddered as he wondered if that was the Neclant's dinner, or feed for some other kind of beast. He tried not to think too much where the meat might have come from as he quickly said a spell to extend his arm's reach and grab the Nelcant by the throat and lift it off the ground. A few more words recited and he laid a truth spell over the squirming creature then brought it closer to look into its eyes.

"Do you know the word that will open the door?"

The Nelcant smiled at him even as its claws raked at its throat trying to remove his magical hand. "Yes."

"Tell me what it is."

The Neclant was loyal to his master and tried to fight the spell. Darian pushed a little harder, hoping he wasn't wasting too much magic that he would need soon. The creature gnashed its teeth and rolled its eyes but he could feel it relenting.

"Reslark."

Darian twisted his hand, breaking the creature's neck and tossing it onto its own meat pile. His stomach rolled slightly but this was war and survival. It was him or them. At least, that was what he told himself as he walked back to the door.

"That can't be the word," he whispered to himself.

Maybe the spell had gone wrong somehow. The Nelcant could have given him any word if it was able to resist the spell, thinking that Darian would release him. No, he had felt the spell sink in, had felt the fight lost. Besides, how could a monster like that even know that name?

He placed a hand against the purple stone and spoke the name he hadn't uttered in years. There was an audible click and the door swung inward.

The room spread before him much as it did every night for dinner.

Zarentle rarely messed with the long walkway of dark carpet anymore. The need to impress and mystify long gone. Instead, he relaxed in a large chair at the table just ahead of Darian, the remnants of dinner having been cleared away. Back turned, he calmly sipped a glass of wine as he hummed a bouncy tune to himself.

Darian pulled the spell together in his mind, mouthing the words silently. It would take every bit of energy he had left but was strong enough to knock a dragon unconscious for a considerable amount of time. If only he had his staff, he could have concentrated and focused the power a bit more but you worked with what you had. Raising both arms, he whispered the final words and felt the magic rush out of him in a welcome warmth. A beam of purple light hurtled itself from the space between his hands towards Zarentle, gathering speed as he poured everything he had into it.

At the last moment, it spread into a thin mass and dispersed into the air as if having come in contact with an invisible wall.

"Well, well," Zarentle laughed, turning slightly in his chair, "once again you exceed my expectations. The things we could do together, my boy."

A test. It had all been another test and he had fallen for it completely. Thinking back, he should have realized how few guards there had been and how easily he had found the door in an ever shifting labyrinth. He hadn't been thinking. Had just rushed forward on emotion like he was always telling the young wizards not to do.

Any energy he had left drained out of him. He sank to his knees on the cold stone and folded in half, burying his face in his hands. He didn't even have it left in him to weep. His shoulders shook and his insides felt as if they were being ripped out of him, but no tears came.

A soft touch on his shoulder made him look up. Zarentle crouched over him, smiling gently, gray eyes almost kind.

"I'm never getting out of here, am I?"

Zarentle sighed and cocked his head as if speaking to a defiant child. "You can walk out that door any time you wish. Say you will join me. We can rule this world together, Darian."

"Just kill me." He tried to get to his feet but sat down hard as his head started to swim. "I'm not going to join you. Why won't you just kill me?"

"Because I still believe you will see it is where you belong. It is what you were born to do." Zarentle rose to his feet and started to walk away, stopping to lean against the high back of the chair. "Reslark did so well raising you, but you had to know you are much more than what she told you."

Darian growled and jumped to his feet, anger and disgust fighting with the exhaustion. "How dare you even say her name?"

"How much sense did her story make, really?" Zarentle grinned and moved closer. "A wounded knight that she had never met, they fall in love as she nurses him back to health, but he leaves before she even knows she is pregnant and is never seen again?"

He wavered on his feet. How many times had he begged her to tell the story, to explain why he didn't know who his father was? Even bastards knew who their father was, even if they couldn't be claimed. To not even have a name had left him feeling like half a person as a child. Still, there had been those who talked, who said that she had made it all up to protect the real father.

A chair appeared behind him just before he fell. He slumped in it, not wanting to follow the path his mind was trying to take.

"A knight who never once showed his face in court. So either he lied to her and was too low ranking to matter, or he never existed."

Darian closed his eyes for a long moment. So many years searching and wondering, and this was the answer he was always meant to find. As much as it hurt, it made a lot of sense.

"Why now?" He sighed and opened his eyes, motioning all around them. "I'm 33 years old. Why come try to play Daddy now?"

Zarentle returned to his own chair, turning it around to face Darian. "You were not the first. The spell on the barrier has been failing for a long time now. The others were horrible failures. I took them from their mothers at different ages and they never panned out. Besides, you were just a half breed, so I did not have very high hopes."

Darian could barely keep his eyes open but his brain jumped at those words. Something he had heard before, something important he couldn't quite remember.

"So I figured I would let her do all the work. I thought about taking you when she died but you were still so small." Zarentle shrugged and refilled his wine as if they were discussing the cleaning or tending the garden. "I must say, you turned out even better than expected. The Wizards did not do half bad teaching you to control your power, even if they could never understand it's true potential. I can help you unlock that potential."

He pushed hair from his face and grinned. "I thought you were all powerful. If you've been able to come across the ridge to make so many children, why wait so long for your revenge? Afraid they'll beat you just as easy as they did last time?"

"They did not defeat me, they trapped me." The wine glass slammed into the table hard enough to make some of the red liquid slosh over the side. Zarentle cleared his throat and wiped his hand before looking at Darian again, his face a calm mask. "Really, it is because you care so about Ramleaj you should help me. On my own, I will defeat them but it will be a long drawn out war and many will die. With our powers combined, we could take control before they even knew what was happening."

"It doesn't matter who you are or what you promise. I will never join you. I will find a way out of here and lead the charge against you."

Zarentle leaned forward with a patronizing smile. "I have been kind so far because you are my son, but should you continue to resist, things will grow far less pleasant."

"Aww, no more dinners with Daddy?" Darian growled, staring back at the man. "You really know how to break my heart."

Zarentle smiled slowly, gray eyes darkening. "You have no idea."

† †

He clenched his jaw and squeezed his eyes until tears leaked from the corners, trying to bite back the scream. The chains moved again, the mechanics clinking dully as another link slid into place. His arms pulled over his head, joints stretching and popping as they yanked away from where his feet were shackled to the floor. His shoulder wrenched out of the socket and stars flashed before his eyes. Another link and he couldn't hold it in any longer. The scream tore out of him, echoing through the small chamber.

"Litsen, what are you doing?" Zarentle sighed as he walked into the room. "I told you, you have to wait longer between pulls or it does not hurt as much."

"Sorry, master."

Zarentle had kept his promise. Darian had been dragged out of the fitful unconsciousness that passed for sleep at first light and hooked up to the chains. Zarentle had done the first couple of pulls himself, asking Darian if he had changed his mind each time, then left his minion to play at the controls. Darian had no idea how long ago or how many links he'd been stretched since then.

Zarentle turned to Darian with a bored shrug. "It is so hard to find good help."

"So they tell me." Darian grunted, fighting to stay conscious.

"Still joking, are we?" Zarentle motioned and Litsen pulled hard on the wench so that three links slipped through the ring, making Darian feel as if he was being torn in half. "You can stop this at any time, son. Just say the words."

He gasped for breath but forced himself to raise his head. "Don't call me that. You may have sired me but you'll never be my father."

Zarentle stared at him then slowly shook his head. He reached out and traced a finger down the long scar that ran from Darian's right shoulder and across to just above his left hip. There were plenty of others, trophies of adventures and delving into places people didn't want you to be.

With a swirl of his black robes, he turned to walk from the room again. "Let him down, Litsen. Pain will not work. We must rethink our strategy."

Litsen growled as he released the chains. Darian collapsed to the ground in a heap, unable to even raise his face out of the muck. Even breathing hurt. His throat burned for water but just the thought of swallowing was painful. For the first time in life, he wished for death.

"Everyone has a breaking point." Zarentle grabbed a handful of hair and yanked his head back. "I will find yours."

He coughed, bright red staining the dirt beneath him. "Go to hell."

"I have been there, and I have no intentions of going back."

Larsle tossed him unceremoniously back into his cell and slammed the door shut. He lay on the floor and just stared at the smooth black walls. He didn't have the energy to crawl up on the stone slab that passed for his bed, and it wasn't like it would be any more comfortable anyway. Breathing through the pain did nothing with his ribs protested every breath and there were no positive thoughts to think. He closed his eyes and prayed for death, or at least sleep.

The cold silence was broken by a low trill as something soft brushed his cheek. Instinctively, he reached up to bat it away, grunting as his arm and shoulder protested the movement. When he opened his eyes, there was a small white feather stuck to his finger. He looked up to see a night dove, hopping excitedly on the edge of the one window far above.

"You've traveled far, little one." He coughed, throat sore from lack of water and screaming.

The little black bird puffed up, showing off the small white patch on it's breast, then flew down to land in the dirt next to him. It hopped close and snuggled his head against Darian's grimy cheek. Darian smiled slightly then grimaced as he rolled over to pull the slip of paper from the tiny tube tied to the bird's leg.

"Yes, I missed you, too. It's been too long."

Night doves were a bird that lived only where Wylthem settled. They mated for life but also could be bonded with Wylthem or even humans. Miramel had given the bird to him when it had barely hatched, having him carry it around at all times so that it would bond with him and when given the command, would do anything to find him. She kept his mate's nest right outside her window so that he would then return back to her.

The tiny paper from the tube was barely larger than his thumbnail when unrolled. Written in silver ink was the symbol of a leafy vine twisting upon itself to create a circle around the symbol of a large oak tree. A single black line had been drawn through the symbol, Miramel's signal that she was concerned about something and wished to talk to him.

He crawled towards the doorway where Litsen was a little less thorough about sweeping the room and dug around in the dirt until he found a small rock. As carefully as he could, he used the dirt on the rock to scratch a line through hers. She should understand that this meant he had problems of his own and couldn't come to her right now. Hopefully, she would decide to go in search of him.

He rolled the paper back up and slid it in the waiting bird's tube then opened his hand for the little bird to hop into. One more quick snuggle then he held up his hand towards the window and gave a little toss to push the bird into the air.

"Fly back to your mate, little one. Give Miramel my message then lead her back to me."

He wavered on his knees for a moment, watching the bird as it disappeared out the window. It circled back once before disappearing from his view. Feeling the tiny stirrings of hope for the first time since he'd been taken, he curled in the dirt and tried to get some sleep, praying to every god he knew that Miramel would understand the message, and that he could survive until she came.

22

"This is hopeless," Keslar grumbled as he pulled Ebony to a halt next to Mist.

They had been traveling from sunrise to sunset for days and seen nothing but wide open land. Every village they passed had no reports of anyone resembling the High Master or the creatures that Keslar had seen. He wiped his face with the edge of his cloak and glared at the hot sun. Spring was already giving away to Summer and they were no closer to finding the High Master than they had been weeks before.

Dworkin took a long swig from his canteen and looked around. "We have to keep looking. It's the only lead we have."

"Did you find something?" Nemclis called as he crashed to the ground and lumbered over.

"Not yet." Dworkin shook his head. Every day he seemed a little quieter, a little less hopeful. "The men are searching to try and decide which direction to go next."

Kelsar gnawed on a strip of jerky, remembering longingly the bag of food from Marta that had ran out the day before. He loosened his grip on the reigns so Ebony could nibble on the grass but it was only moments before the stallion's head popped up again, his ears swiveling fast. Mist pawed at the ground, listening as well.

Bartol's horse thundered back towards them, both horse and rider out of breath and wide eyed. "Your Grace, there's evidence of a camp just north, a pretty big one. Remnants of a fire and other signs."

"Any sign of Darian?" Keslar asked, already shoving the tasteless jerky away and gathering the reigns.

Bartol shook his head. "Not that I saw but I only gave it a cursory investigation."

"Worth looking at," Dworkin said, holding Mist's reigns as she reacted to her rider's excitement. He put a hand to his mouth and let out two long bird calls, then waited a couple moments and made the same call.

Within moments, Duntiel and Cantiem came riding back from their respective directions. Dworkin quickly explained what had been found then they all set out following Bartol. He led them through the trees and down a small hill to a circle of scorched earth. Various rocks and logs had been rolled close to the fire, too uniform to be a natural.

Dworkin hopped from the saddle and slowly looked around the space. He placed his fingers into the pile of ash at the center of the circle then smelled them and rubbed the dust with his thumb.

"It's a campsite, for sure. Too old for me to tell just how long ago."

Nemclis curled at the edge of the site, letting his wings droop to the ground as he curled his front legs under his body. "Finally, a sign."

"Don't get too confident yet," Bartol grunted. "All we know is someone camped here, can't for sure link it to the High Master."

Dworkin motioned and the men spread out to scour the area. Keslar dismounted and tried to look around as well, even though he had no idea what he was looking for. As often was the case with these men, he felt horribly inept and a waste of space. He was just a tag along, getting in the way of these well trained soldiers and slowing them down.

After long moments, Dworkin raised his head and made eye contact with each man. Every one of them slowly shook their head. It was as if all of the air went out of Dworkin. His shoulders slumped and his face fell before he collapsed on the nearest log. The wood creaked and rocked back as he dug his heels in the dirt and buried his hands in his hair.

A sob caught in Keslar's throat as he walked over and sat next to the man. He had no idea what to say. To the rest of them, the High Master was someone to look up to and admire, someone who was important to Ramleaj. The Duke was his foster brother, they had grown up together and were well known to be close friends like was so rare to see in court.

His eyes dropped to the dirt between them. He had no fancy words or hope to give. Dworkin had been the one to keep them going so far, to stay focused and make the plan. All Keslar could do was sit and watch as a ladybug crawled in the dirt at their feet, disturbed by the movement of the log. Dworkin shifted so that his chin rested on his hands, his shadow moving. The returning light caught on something in the dirt, showing a small sparkle under the log.

Kelsar dug the thing from the dirt and brushed it off a bit before holding it up to the light. It was a man's ring, made of silver that had been intricately carved to hold a small purple stone at it's center. Something stirred in Keslar's mind that he couldn't quite place. He rubbed the ring against his sleeve then held it up to the light again.

"I've seen this before."

Dworkin turned his head with a grunt. The Duke's eyes went wide and his hand shook as he reached out to take the ring. He looked it all over before gripping it tightly as he started laughing and crying at the same time.

"It's his," he whispered then raised his voice as he looked up. "It's Darian's. I had it made for him when he became High Master. The stone comes from the same mine as the one on his staff. He never took it off."

Keslar's eyes drifted to the staff still attached to Ebony's saddle, the purple stone shining at it's top. He knew the High Master was advanced enough to not always need the staff to do his magic but that wasn't the point. It was something a wizard was never seen without. Beyond being symbolic of who you were as a wizard and what your status was, it was your weapon, your defense, your meditation aid. A wizard without it would be like a knight riding into battle without his sword. Now here was another item that High Master Darian would never leave behind willingly.

Even though he had watched the High Master be captured, a part of him had held onto the hope that the High Master had been able to fight back. Maybe even escape. But the more they found, and the more time went on, the less likely that seemed. His gut twisted and what little he'd eaten threatened to come back up. What kind of enemy could keep someone the power of the High Master captive for this long?

"We'll camp here as well," Dworkin said as he slid the ring into the pouch at his belt. "In the morning we'll fan out and figure out which way they went, but at least we know we're on the right track. If they were getting this careless they were probably pretty close to home."

Cantiem and Duntiel immediately set to work caring for the horses and getting a fire going. Bartol watched them with crossed arms before nodding with a grin and setting out to walk the perimeter like he always did when setting up a new camp.

"He's still alive, right?" Keslar whispered when it was just him and the duke. "I know we talked about how they could have killed him at the Isle but that was a long time ago and anything could have happened."

Dworkin shrugged and nodded. "You're right, it could have. But I have to believe he's alive. Until I see otherwise with my own eyes, I will assume that he is still out there causing hell for whoever started this."

23

Braslic

Braslic dismounted at the bottom of the hill and stared up for a moment. He really wasn't sure why they called it Healer's Mount. It wasn't anything near a mountain. Slightly larger than the hills surrounding it, with a nice flat top to build on, but really nothing all that special. Not that it really mattered. All that mattered was that he had finally arrived and could make his delivery then be on his way to the Wizard's Isle. He just hoped that things had not gotten too bad back home in his absence.

It was twilight as he led his llama up the hill towards the small white buildings. He hoped there was still someone awake that he could pass the gel off too. He didn't want to disturb the Healers or their patients but it was so much easier for him to travel when the sun wasn't as bright.

He reached a closed gate within the wall that circled the whole complex and stared up at the knocker hanging high over his head. With a growl, he jumped to grasp it, lifting it as high as he could before letting it drop against the wood. Repeating the process two more times, the dull thuds echoed into the quiet night. He was just trying to decide if he should try again, when the gate creaked open and a young human woman stepped out.

She looked about the hilltop for a moment before her eyes dropped to him and widened a bit. Her fingers played nervously with the amber stone that hung around her neck. "Yes, may I help you?"

"Just need to drop of some Marsim gel." He motioned to the pack strapped to the back of the llama. "Already paid for so I can just leave it with you."

She grinned and pushed the gate open wider. "The Great Mother mentioned some would be coming soon but she didn't tell us an actual Cregas would be delivering it. Come in, she will want to see you herself, I'm sure."

He gritted his teeth but followed her inside anyway. All he really wanted to do was get as far on his way to the Isle before it got too dark to travel and then get some sleep, but the Healers were their best clients and he couldn't risk angering them.

Just inside the gate was a pen with a handful of the massive beasts that humans rode milling about and looking asleep on their feet. The girl walked over to a large gate but hesitated before opening it.

"Do you think your animal would be okay in here with the horses? They're all pretty calm but I doubt they've seen anything like him before."

"She be a dam," he grunted, removing the saddle and pack from her back then gripping the reigns again, "and she be perfectly capable of taking care of herself if they give her any trouble."

The girl just shrugged as she opened the pen and waited for him to lead Lurp inside. He scratched her ears for a moment before unclipping the reigns from her halter and giving her a soft pat on the backside. Instead of running off to eat or play, she studied her new mates before giving him a side eyed look that said she wasn't impressed. He just laughed and stepped out of the pen, the gate closing with a soft clank behind him.

He untied his pack from the saddle and slid it over one shoulder before nodding for the girl to lead the way. They moved through the small building and connecting gardens silently. Everywhere they went, heads turned and people whispered to their companions. Some stared at him with open amazement while a few turned their heads away with curled lip or dark eyes. He couldn't help but wonder if any of the humans from the event on the far mountain had been brought here. While his people had lost three of their best, he was pretty certain they had at least injured some of their attackers.

He straightened his shoulders and tried not to think of that or the people staring at him. The Healers that came to market appreciated their supplies and everything it took to get them. The Great Mother was the kindest human he had ever met and had personally asked him to come. He stared at his young guide's back and tried to take comfort in the small and confining building. It was still too bright and warm to be his caves, but it was better than the great open expanse of outside.

Finally, they stopped and the girl knocked on a large wooden door. After a few moments, the door swung open and Great Mother Quinta stepped into the hallway. At first she looked confused but when her eyes fell on him, a bright smile filled her face and her hands clasped in front of her like a girl half her age.

"Sir Cregas, I am so glad you made it. We were starting to worry."

Braslic slid his pack off and untied the straps to pull out the bottles he had so carefully tucked inside. "I waited another day so that there could be more of the gel and even some of the Dulung powder. Plus, only being able to travel in the evening and early morning does slow me down some."

"I am so thankful to you for coming all this way. I have a patient desperately waiting for this." She passed most of the contents to the young girl with quiet instructions, but kept one bottle pressed to her chest. "Would you like to see how all your work helps my people?"

He swallowed a sigh. He really didn't care as long as his people received what they needed, but he hated to upset her. With lips pursed he gave a stiff nod and was rewarded by a bright smile and a small wave that he should follow her inside the room.

"I'll admit," he muttered, glancing around at the tables and shelves filled with all sorts of bottles and strange instruments, "I have wondered why you need medicines if you heal with magic."

She grinned at him before scooping out some of the gel into a dish and adding what seemed to be random other ingredients she grabbed from around her, mixing them over a low flame. "That is a common misconception even amongst other humans. Our magic doesn't actually heal. It goes deep inside to convince the body to heal itself faster than it normally would, but that still takes time and a lot of energy out of us. If there are things that can be healed by medicines that saves our energy for more dire cases, or like with this disease, it can help control some of the symptoms while the body does it's work. Come with me and I will show you."

They moved through a few more hallways before the Great Mother knocked on a door and then breezed in without waiting for an answer. Inside, a human man was curled on a bed with a book open in his lap that he didn't seem to be reading. One arm was wrapped in a thick white bandage, his other hand often drifting to stroke the top of the bandage then drifting away again.

"You haven't been scratching, have you?" Quinta sat on the edge of the man's bed with a smile and a wink.

"Trying not to but its so hard, Great Mother." The man's eyes fell on him and grew wide before narrowing. "Why would you bring that in here?"

Braslic's teeth gritted and his hand drifted to the dagger on his belt. If this was how all humans were going to react to him, maybe this whole trip was a waste of time.

Quinta clucked her tongue as she started to unwrap the bandage. "This is Braslic, the Cregas who traveled all this way to bring the medicine that you need. If you can't be respectful, then just be quiet and let me work."

The man gave a soft snort and turned his head away. Braslic found himself inching closer as the bandage fell away and the man's arm was revealed. The skin was raised and scaly, brown and yellow scabs surrounded by deep cracks of bright red that clear liquid seeped out of.

Great Mother Quinta closed her eyes and held her hand just over the skin as she whispered words in some other language. A soft light glowed around her hand and the wound until she stopped whispering and dropped her hand. The human gave a soft sigh and his whole body seemed to relax. Quinta poured a bit of the gel out and gently rubbed it over the wound before wrapping a new bandage around it.

"The medicine you have brought will keep the skin moist and stop the itching while the magic convinces the body to heal itself. Now if only we could figure out what is causing it or how it spreads." Quinta sighed as she tied off the bandage and stood up. She laid her hand on the man's shoulder, the soft light glowing again. "Rest now."

As the man settled down onto the bed and pulled a blanket over his shoulders, she motioned Braslic out the door and into the hallway. She shut the door behind her and leaned against it, looking so much more tired than just a few moments ago.

"You always seemed so worried about the Wasting, I figured it was a lot more than just a skin condition."

She rolled her shoulders and pushed off from the door. "It is. That is just the first stage. If we can't stop it before it gets into the bloodstream, it shuts down the body piece by piece until they just drift away beyond our grasp."

"I'm glad we can help in someway, but I really should be going Great Mother. I must get to the Wizards Isle and speak with Master Darian."

Quinta cocked her head. "Last I heard he had not returned since the attack."

"Attack?" Braslic froze, blinking at her. Could it be that it wasn't just them? He wasn't sure how he felt about that. It would be nice to know they weren't being targeted specifically but it would also be harder to get help if the humans had their own problems.

Quinta's eyes dropped to her hands as she lowered her voice. "The Wizards were attacked the night of that crazy storm. Hardly anyone survived."

A shudder passed through him. Something about that storm seemed to have spread a darkness over the land that reached much further than he realized.

"Do you have any idea where I can find the High Master then?"

"The last place he was seen was Darsile though that was quite some time ago. It was said he was coming our way, but I have not seen him."

He sighed and shrugged his pack higher on his shoulder. "Then that is where I will have to begin. Thank you, Great Mother."

"Just be careful, friend." She squeezed his shoulder and nodded her head towards the door. "There are way too many like him and worse out there."

24

Zarentle swirled the wine in his glass and stared at the covered dish in front of him, rage boiling in his chest and burning in his gut. What was it going to take to make this boy see sense? Every child who had come before him had gladly offered to join once shown what could be theirs. None of them had proved to be of any use and had been disposed of adequately but that only made Darian more frustrating. He was the perfect son, all the power combined with a deep understanding of just how broken the races are. Why could he not see that they would be saving the world from itself by ruling together?

    A portal of black and green light opened like an eye and a dark figure stepped out to stride towards him. She wore the black and sulphuric red of the world they had been trapped in for so long in tight leggings and a riding coat that seemed to shift colors as she strode towards him. Her skin was ashen gray from the hand that clenched the blade at her side through the delicately pointed ears poking out of silver white hair.

"You summoned me, my lord?" The Leranti's voice was lower than expected and held a hint of annoyance even though her face was a mask of calm.

Zarentle leaned back in his chair and eyed the female. "I summoned the leader of your people, Menir. What has happened to Minske?"

"I killed him," she stood a little straighter and raised her chin, "for suggesting that we not wait for your orders and just attack on our own."

Zarentle raised an eyebrow but just nodded. The Leranti weren't like the Nelcant or other simple creatures that filled his ranks. They had thoughts and emotions and magic of their own. They had been Wylthem once, before being turned cold and malicious by life across the border.

Menir grinned slightly but it was gone in an instant. "We do wonder how much longer you are going to toy with your plaything before you release us to fulfill your plans, my lord?"

"As long as I choose too. If I can convince my son to join me, there will not even be a war and all you will have to do is sweep up the scraps." Zarentle shrugged and waved a Nelcant forward to refill his wine glass. "If not, then I will kill him and we will move forward as planned. I would really rather not though, it took many tries to make such a fine magical specimen, I would hate to waste him."

He watched her back stiffen but her face betrayed none of the thoughts passing through her mind. "Is there a reason you have summoned us?"

"Yes, I do have a little errand you can do that might alleviate some of the restlessness you are dealing with. I have reports there is some kind of party drawing dangerously close to the tower. I would not be surprised if they are attempting to rescue our guest. Take a scouting party along with some of the beasts and take care of them for me."

"Yes, sir." She bowed stiffly before turning on her heel and heading back towards the portal she had stepped out of.

"Menir?" He waited until she turned to face him again. "There is a village between here and where the party was last spotted. You can let the pets play there as well, but bring me back one human. Alive."

She nodded and started to walk away but stopped to look at him again. "If you insist on waiting, we will follow your orders, my lord, but it is dangerous to lie to yourself."

"Really? And how am I lying to myself?"

She grinned and narrowed her eyes at him. "You do not work so hard to turn the boy because it would make the war easier. With him out of the way, my forces would take Ramleaj for you with little opposition."

Zarentle leaned forward. The Leranti was in dangerous waters and she knew it. Her conviction and sharpness might have helped her rise to the top of their ranks, but he was not sure he liked it being turned on him.

"Then why do I?"

Her pale eyes widened slightly and he wondered if she was laughing on the inside. "Because, as you say, you are loathe to kill him, but you also know, he is the only one alive who could kill you."

25

It seemed as if he had just closed his eyes when the door slammed open. Before he could even sit up, Litsen and another guard stormed into the room. Litsen quickly clamped the bindings around his wrists then the other guard kicked him in his already aching ribs.

"Gets up," Litsen commanded with a laugh. "Yous really done it this time. Boss gonna fry you and let Litsen chew you bones."

He didn't know what the creature was talking about, or really care anymore. He almost hoped that Zarentle really would kill him this time. He had lost all hope of finding a way out of here or anyone coming.

Hope. He remembered the tiny little bird winging it's way back to his friend. Maybe there was hope after all. A reason to stay alive at least a little bit longer.

With a grunt he pushed to his knees but when he tried to stand his legs wouldn't work. They were too weak to support him and every time he tried his head would swim and send him swaying. The Nelcant grew impatient and each of them grabbed his elbows and pulled him out of the cell. They moved through the hallways quickly and his head was still spinning by the time he was tossed onto the floor at Zarentle's feet.

With a wave of his hand, Zarentle sent the Nelcant away. The door thudded closed behind them, leaving just Darian and the Demon Lord alone in the room. For what felt like ages, Zarentle just stared at him. There was something different about the man. All of the fake sympathy had gone from his face, leaving his gray eyes dark and cold as he studied Darian who could barely keep himself in a sitting position.

"So, you still hold on to some vain hope." Zarentle growled. "Your will is stronger than I expected. Still, I did not think you would make such a stupid mistake."

"I don't know what you're talking about."

Zarentle reached across the table and pulled a silver tray with a large domed cover closer to him. He lifted the cover and carefully set it aside on the table, before lifting the tray and studying the contents. With a snarl, he flung the tray so that it skidded across the stone floor and came to a stop in front of Darian's feet.

All hope that he had tucked away in his heart, shriveled up and died. Spread out like an offering on the polished silver was the night dove, his message still tucked safely against the tiny leg. The neck was broken and lay at an odd angle, small drops of blood marring the white breast feathers and silver around it.

"Do not ever try anything like that again." Zarentle's voice boomed around Darian, not really penetrating his pounding head. "Next time, it will be the recipient of the message, not just the messenger."

A single tear slid through the muck and grime on Darian's cheek to splatter against the tray. He thought of the poor little female, waiting for her mate to return from his royal mission, of Miramel constantly checking the nest and wondering what had happened. She would probably never know. It was obvious no one was going to come for him now. He would die in this place, and the sooner the better.

"Please," he gasped, gently pushing the tray aside so he wouldn't have to look at it in his last moments, "just kill me. I'm not going to join you, and obviously I'm not going to get out of here. This game has dragged on for too long. Just end it. You win."

Zarentle pushed out of his chair and walked closer, squatting down in front of Darian. He reached out and grabbed Darian's chin with one strong hand, pushing his head back so that he had to look up at into that twisted face.

"Everyone has an opinion on what I should do with you." He turned Darian's face side to side then stared into his eyes again for a long time. "Mine is the only one that matters, and I am not done with you. There is still a spark in there, boy. When that spark is fully gone, then I will kill you. Until then, I will continue to find ways to show you the right choice."

26

Keslar

They set up camp with quiet efficiency. Everyone knew their job and how to do it without assistance or direction. By the time the horses had been cared for, a fire built, and Nemclis had caught them a wild pig for dinner, the sun had set. They sat around the fire as their half of the pig roasted on a spit, Nemclis curled nearby using a bone to pick his teeth after having consumed the other half.

Dworkin sat quietly with his elbows on his knees as he turned the ring so it glinted in the firelight. Keslar watched, wondering what thoughts might be going through the Duke's mind.

"Why now?" He said after a few moments of silence. "There hasn't been any sign the whole way. Why would they leave this camp and the ring?"

Dworkin shrugged and slid the ring onto his finger. "I doubt any of them noticed the ring. It always was just a little loose. If he were unconscious or," Dworkin hesitated, then took a shaky breath, "or incapacitated some how, it could have slipped off his finger without anyone knowing."

"As far as the camp," Bartol sighed as he slowly turned the spit so the pig cooked evenly, "my guess is they were getting near home. Had to be careful before, but no one has caught on to them this far so they picked up speed and got reckless."

"They don't expect anyone to make it this far looking for him," Nemclis muttered, stretching his neck and yawning.

"Or don't care," Keslar whispered, shivering as he remembered how easily the man had deflected the High Master's spell.

They sat in silence as the pig finished cooking and Bartol split it up between them. It wasn't long before Keslar could hear the dragon's soft snores behind him. He was growing more accustomed to having the beast around but that didn't mean he liked it. He still caught himself glancing over his shoulder, and watching the shadow as it passed over him. So far their goals seemed to align, but he wouldn't put it past the beast to turn at any moment. Still, he had to admit they had eaten a lot better since Nemclis had started to hunt for the group. He licked the last of the fat from his fingers and decided that was worth something at least.

A deep growl ran icy fingers up his spine. He jumped to his feet and searched the darkness. It had sounded so close, almost right in his ear, but he couldn't see anything moving beyond the fire's light.

"What was that?"

Duntiel leaned against his pack and stretched his legs out in front of him. "Just wolves, kid. Between the dragon and the fire, they won't come anywhere near us."

Keslar wasn't so sure. There had been strange noises in the night nearly every time they camped, but nothing like that. It had seemed just behind him and yet very distant all at the same time. There was something about it that had made him feel cold and exposed.

Dworkin and Bartol were staring at each other across the fire but after a moment, Bartol turned to him with a smile. "Try to get some rest, wizard boy. You're riding with some of the best. We can handle a few little beasties."

He still wasn't sure but Bartol's soft smile had a way of putting him at ease. When Dworkin nodded, he slid into his bedroll but kept his hand on his staff. He lay still, watching the fire die down and the men go about the usual nightly ritual. Cantiem wrapped a blanket around him and closed his eyes as Bartol and Duntiel stood up to start walking the perimeter. The ease and comfort of the men settled over him and he rolled over to watch the stars winking to life above him. He smiled softly, picturing the goddess that Bartol had told him about flying through the sky with her long cloak spreading behind her. The thought warmed him and he felt himself drifting off to sleep.

When he heard the growl again, from the other side of camp this time, he pulled the blanket higher and told himself Bartol had it handled. Shivering, he held his breath and caught himself listening for the crunch of leaves or brush of fur that would mark an animal's passage. A great snap like teeth gnashing near his ear sent him scrambling out of bed and closer to the fire. He nearly backed into the duke, the man's hand already on his sword.

"I heard it too."

His hands shook even though he gripped his staff so hard his knuckles hurt. His eyes scanned the darkness for movement as Dworkin carefully circled the dying fire to nudge Cantiem awake. The soldier took one look at his duke and was immediately on his feet with sword in his hand.

Duntiel jogged up from the other direction, out of breath and eyes wide. "There's something out there, sir. I could feel it following me."

Dworkin nodded and motioned both knights to his side. They all moved closer to Keslar, each facing a slightly different direction. Keslar backed up to join their formation as growls filled the night air again along with a strange hissing sound.

"Where's Bartol?" Cantiem whispered.

Dworkin started to speak but Keslar nudged him and pointed ahead of them. Something was moving just at the edge of the firelight. First, a large golden paw stepped into the light with claws flexing. Kelsar gulped, guessing it was bigger than his hand and imagining just how easily those claws could rip through flesh. The paw was quickly followed by the head and long body of the largest cat he had ever seen. Covered in golden fur it stood nearly as tall as him when on all fours, slit eyes taking in the surroundings. At the hind end, where a long tail should be, was the source of the hissing sound. Three long snakes writhed and snapped, biting at each other and the cat body they sprouted from.

"Kaldecs?" Dworkin gasped. "They're just a legend."

"Does the legend say anything about how to kill them?" Duntiel's voice shook a little but the grip on his sword was strong.

Dworkin sighed with a shrug. "Heart's in the normal place I figure. Never knew anything that cutting off the head wouldn't kill. Just watch out for those snakes, pretty certain they're venomous."

Another of the Kaldec's stepped up next to the first, something dangling from its mouth. Kelsar found himself leaning forward, trying to get a better look, when the creature dropped it and kicked it towards them like a game of ball. It rolled to a stop at their feet and they all risked a glance away from the attackers to look.

Keslar's chest burned as he forgot how to breathe through the bile rising in the back of his throat. He shivered as if ice water had just been dumped on him but his skin felt like it was going to burn off. He wanted to look away with every core of his being but just kept staring at the thing that stared back at him. Bulging brown eyes that had once been so kind looked blankly into his very soul, the scar across the cheek looking even more raised with all the color drained from the dark skin. They had decapitated him, bit clean through the neck, bone and all. Then brought his head to them to show just what they could do. Just what they planned to do to the rest.

"Oh Bartol," Dworkin whispered, voice thick with emotion even as he tightened his grip on his sword.

Cantiem and Duntiel exchanged a look before surging forward with angry battle cries. Dworkin pushed Keslar behind him and cast one more glance to the head of his guard, features permanently frozen in fear. The Duke took a breath and raised his sword as the first animal jumped towards them.

Keslar tried to follow the battle as Dworkin slashed and stabbed at the beasts, Cantiem and Duntiel working back to back nearby to take down just as many, but his eyes kept drifting to the head at his feet. Bartol had been so nice to him the whole trip, had always seemed so strong and capable. Would they all soon look just the same?

"I thought you said we were safe," he heard the whine in his voice but couldn't stop himself. "You said that as long as we had the fire and

Nemclis that nothing would come close."

Dworkin placed his foot into the quivering body of a Kaldec to pull out his muck covered sword and immediately swung it at a snake head too close to his face. "I was talking about regular beasties, not damn legendary monsters."

"Now Bartol is dead and the blasted dragon probably just took off and soon we'll all be dead too and there will be no one left to save the High Master and-" He only stopped himself by running out of breath. Gasping for air, his eyes burning, he tried to back further away from the awful eyes but felt the heat of the fire at his back.

"Nemclis wouldn't just abandon us," Dworkin snapped, gulping air as he fought off continuous attacks.

Duntiel kicked a Kaldec in the nose to get it to back off as he slashed at another. "I certainly don't see him helping."

Dworkin grunted and smashed the but of his sword into the skull of a Kaldec then slashed across the flank of another. "Keslar, stay tight against me and I'll make an opening for you. Find Nemclis and see what's going on."

His teeth practically sawed through his lip as he ran to the Duke's side, tip toeing carefully around fallen bodies and pools of blood. The Duke's sword was nearly a blur, swinging every direction to keep the cat's back. Keslar smacked his staff across the shoulder of one that tried to sneak up from behind and forced himself to keep moving. The warmth and light of the fire was fading as he ran into what felt like a massive, moving wall.

Running his hands over the wall, he could feel cool scales and the small lift and fall of breaths. Following the massive neck, he found Nemclis's head. The dragon's eyes were closed and soft tendrils of smoke wisped out between his lips with every breath.

"You have got to be joking," he screamed, bashing at the dragon's nose with his staff. "We're out here dying and you're asleep? What the hell kind of dragon are you?"

"Keslar?" Dworkin called, trying to fight his way closer. "What's going on? Did you find him?"

Keslar glared at the dragon and raised his staff to bash right between the stupid eyes but then he noticed it. A faint blue tinge glowed in the night around the dragons head. Magic? He highly doubted that the Kaldec's were advanced enough to have done this.

Squinting, he could just make out movement further in the darkness, the blue light dancing a path through the air to someone he couldn't quite see.

"He's under a sleeping spell. There's got to be someone else helping these monsters."

Dworkin growled and rolled his eyes as he pressed his back against Nemclis's neck. "Of course there is. Can you break it?"

"I can try." He hoped his voice sounded a lot more confidant that he felt.

He laid his hands next to the dragons eyes and spoke the words to show the spell. The blue flared bright enough to nearly blind him in the darkness then settled back into a soft glow. The spell was like nothing he'd ever seen before. Instead of words lined out in an orderly fashion, this was like a living and growing thing twisting itself around the dragon. What was he supposed to do with that? Words he could understand and find the opposite of or how to pull them apart, but this seemed to have no beginning and no end. All he knew for sure was that no wizard had cast this spell. Someone else was out there, someone with a magic foreign and elusive to him.

"Could you maybe try a little faster?" Duntiel yelled then grunted as he kicked a wounded Kaldec away.

Duntiel and Cantiem had fought their way back towards him and Dworkin. They stood back to back over Bartol's severed head, trying to protect what little they had left of their captain. With each swing, all three men's swords seemed to be moving slower, sweat soaking their shirts and hair despite the cool air. Even though the ground was littered with kaldec bodies, more just kept pouring out of the darkness.

He whimpered and turned back to the spell. His stomach tightened in knots, all the teasing and taunting from the other kids over the years ringing in his ears. He'd been taken in later in life than was customary and had had to fight to catch up. What came second hand to kids who had been there for years had been new and difficult for him. Maybe they had been right. Maybe he never would make it as a wizard. All those nights staying up to practice more, or to read every book he could get his hands on, had all been for nothing.

Wait. Maybe not. If he couldn't break the spell, maybe he could counter it. He closed his eyes and brought to mind the spell he had often used on those nights to force himself to stay awake, or to stay alert in class after having only gotten a couple of hours of sleep. Switching a few words around, he begged the Twins to give him enough power to make it strong enough to cover a whole dragon. Just this once let him do something amazing, then he could happily going back to being ordinary.

He yelled the words into the night and felt the power rush through his core and out his hands. The blue glow pushed back, trying to block his power, but it flowed out of him stronger than ever before. He growled and pushed every bit of his fear and desperation into the spell, begging Nemclis to wake up.

There was a low growling and the ground under his knees started to rumble and move like an earthquake. Only when Nemclis's eyes snapped open did he remember he wasn't on the ground, he was perched on the dragon's scaly nose. He slid off just as Nemclis, raised his head with a mighty roar that seemed to shake the trees.

Nemclis surveyed the scene with one swoop and fell into action. He slashed and bit at the swarming creatures, picking them up and throwing them aside like toys. As the few remaining cats slunk away from the dragon and the fire, Nemclis reared his head back as his sides heaved.

"Nemclis, no!" Dworkin yelled.

As Nemclis turned to the duke, Keslar could see sparks dancing around bared teeth. With a growl, Nemclis arched his neck towards the sky and shot a thick pillar of fire straight up.

In the odd, flickering light, Keslar realized the only kaldecs left were the ones that lay dead at their feet. Dworkin sheathed his sword then pressed his hand to a deep gouge in his left shoulder. Cantiem seemed mostly unharmed though he was covered in sweat and breathing heavily, but Duntiel had two scratches down his leg where sharp claws had found purchase.

Nemclis lowered his head, smoke still billowing from between his teeth. "Thank you for breaking the spell, wizard. I could feel it was an unnatural sleep but couldn't pull myself free. I could have been stuck there forever."

"And we would most likely be dead." Dworkin gave him a tired smile and nod. He looked to the rising sun and then the remains of the battle around him with a sigh. "We should get moving though."

"Shouldn't we look for Bartol's body? Give him a proper burial?"

Cantiem had tears in his eyes but no one felt the need to bring it up. Not even Duntiel who couldn't take his eyes off of the head at his feet.

Dworkin looked about to speak but all that came out was a painful guttural sound. After a moment, he shook his head and tried again. "I'm sure there won't be much to find. Besides, it won't take long for other creatures to smell the blood and be swarming this area, not to mention whatever was helping these things."

"We can't just leave him here," Duntiel whispered.

Cantiem nudged the other knight with a sharp look, but Dworkin nodded softly. He limped slightly as he walked over to his pack and dug through until he found an extra cloth bag. He seemed to be trying not to look too closely as he picked up the head and gently placed it in the bag then pulled the ties closed.

"We'll take him with us and bury what we have once we are somewhere safer, but right now I really need you guys to get moving. Round up the horses and any of our supplies that are salvageable. Honor him by doing as he taught you."

"I'll make sure there aren't any more attacks coming and see if I can't find a good place to take a rest for the day," Nemclis said before taking to the sky.

Keslar waited as the blast of wind from dragon wings blew his hair out of his face, then walked over to where Dworkin was quietly tying the bag to Bartol's horse. He hovered back for a moment. Dworkin's lips were moving but he couldn't hear what the man was saying, and doubted the words were for him.

"Let me guess," Dworkin coughed and straightened, swiping at his face, "you have a question."

Keslar's cheeks warmed as he moved a little closer, helping to gather the horse's tack from where it had been left. "I do, but it can wait."

"Go ahead." Dworkin glanced to him for a moment but just kept moving to calm Mist enough that he could saddle her. "There will be a time to grieve but this isn't it. We need to get somewhere safe first."

Keslar clenched his teeth at that thought but decided any questions attached to it were definitely better to be saved for a later time. "Why didn't you just let Nemclis use his fire on the Kaldecs? At that time we couldn't have been certain they were all dead."

"You and the dragon aren't as different as you think." Dworkin laughed with a wink. "Just like you're still learning how to be a wizard, he's learning how to be a dragon. He's still pretty young by their standards and at a disadvantage of having been raised by humans. He doesn't have much control over his fire yet and could have easily hit us or set the whole forest on fire."

Keslar yanked on Ebony's saddle a little harder than he meant to and caught a nip on the shoulder from the large horse in return. He didn't like to think of himself and the dragon as having anything in common, though he had to admit, it had been pretty nice having one along tonight. That still didn't make up for all the horrible things they'd done in the past.

27

Mist plodded along, Dworkin barely paying attention to where she was headed. They had camped out and tried to get some sleep but he was still exhausted. It was the type of tired that cut deeper than sleep could fix. His foster brother was missing, they had been traveling for only the Twins knew how long now, and his decisions had led to the death of one of the best men he'd ever known. Bartol had been a dedicated soldier and a good friend who gave his life in search of a man he barely knew.

"Looks like there's a town up ahead," Keslar called from the front of their sad little line. "Maybe they'll have seen something."

Cantiem barely looked up while Duntiel stayed on high alert, constantly scanning the surroundings. Each man had taken the loss in his own way. Cantiem had withdrawn and barely spoken a word since, while Duntiel seemed to be trying to be certain they were never caught off guard again. Keslar was trying hard to keep everyone's spirits up but his eyes held a darkness that shouldn't be in one so young.

Dworkin took a couple deep breaths and forced himself to move Mist forward to catch up with Keslar. "If nothing else, maybe we can spend a night in an actual bed."

They passed small farms surrounding the outskirts of the city. Dread started to settle into Dworkin's stomach the closer they got to the city. He didn't see anyone out working the farms, no animals grazing about, and no sounds coming from the town proper. It was still early in the evening. People should be out shopping and socializing, children should be playing. There didn't seem to be a soul about. As they drew closer, the wind shifted and they were accosted by the all too familiar scent of rotting flesh.

Dworkin pulled Mist to a stop just outside the twin churches flanking the main road. Small, simple buildings but with lovely stained glass windows that someone had spent ages of time and care on. He forced his eyes from the churches to slide down the street and the desecration that had swept through.

The town was littered with bodies. Whole families lay together as if merely resting from an evening out, if it weren't for the chunks of flesh ripped off or the gaping wounds. Every face that was turned towards them was frozen in the same look of terror that Bartol had worn.

"Kaldecs." Keslar pulled his cloak over his face against the stench. "Think it was the same pack that attacked us?"

Dworkin nodded as he dismounted and studied the ground. "Probably, but they weren't alone. Look at these tracks."

Overlapping and crisscrossing the giant paw prints, were large four toed prints with long strides and often traced in blood. Moving along the edge of the road, in more regimented lines were some kind of a cloven hoof like a goat or deer but as large as a horse, footprints of someone wearing small, fine boots following close by.

"What are they?" Duntiel asked, moving closer.

"I'm not sure. I've never seen anything like this." He pushed to his feet and tried to study the town, something off in the distance catching his eye. "Cantiem, stay with the horses. Duntiel, take Keslar and check out that store. See if there's anything we can use."

Keslar raised his eyebrows. "Wouldn't that be stealing?"

"None of it's going to be much use to these folks and our supplies are getting a bit low." Cantiem grimaced with a shrug. "That's battle, kid. You going to travel with us, you may as well get used to it."

Dworkin shot the young knight a look before digging in his pouch, his heart twinging as his fingers brushed past the necklace from Leslien and the medal from Darian. He pulled out a few coins and placed them in Keslar's palm.

"Leave these on the counter if it makes you feel better. We'll rejoin Nemclis on that hill and make a plan of what to do next."

Cantiem pulled the other horses a little bit closer to take Mist's reins as the other two walked off. "Where are you going?"

"To check something out." He kept his voice as calm and level as he could. The young knight would never have questioned him as long as Bartol was around to smack some sense back into him. "Stand guard and keep the horses ready. There's no guarantee all the attackers are gone."

Cantiem nodded and straightened a little, but there was still an odd look on his face. "Of course, sir. Just, be careful."

"I will. Keep an eye out for the others." He smiled and patted the young man on the shoulder before jogging off in the other direction.

He strode down the street, trying not to look at the townspeople in the horror that they had been left in. Each body that he passed made him both more angry and more concerned. This hadn't been a battle, or even really an animal feeding. This was killing just for the sake of killing and then moving on once done. Pure evil. If these creatures came from whoever was holding Darian, what were they doing to him?

If he was even still alive.

He reached the corner where he thought he'd seen movement but couldn't find anything. He searched up and down the alley but didn't find so much as a mouse moving around, much less something large enough to be the flash of white he'd sworn he'd seen. At the mouth of the alley, he bent down and picked up the ragged remnants of a what looked to be homemade doll. Fighting back tears, he reached forward and laid it in the outstretched hand of the little girl who couldn't be more than a year older than his own daughter, her throat ripped so violently her head was barely still connected.

"Such a horrible tragedy," a smooth voice sighed from behind him.

Dworkin spun around with his hand on his sword. Leaning against a doorway, calmly munching on a piece of fruit, was a man dressed in white from head to toe. Even his boots were white and somehow had avoided becoming stained with blood or dirt. He didn't seem to be carrying any weapons but that didn't mean he wasn't a threat. Dworkin relaxed his hand away from his sword, but every muscle stayed tense and ready to spring.

"Yes, it is. Are you from here?"

"Oh no, just a traveler much like yourself, your grace." He bowed low and grandly, a dark smile spreading across his face as he looked around. "Such a gruesome thing to come across, but I'm sure a warrior such as yourself is quite used to such sights."

Dworkin tried to swallow the lump in his throat but it refused to move. "I don't think you ever get used to it."

"You'd be surprised what can become ordinary with enough time."

"I'd really rather it not." His eyes darted back to the little girl before shaking his head and trying to force his mind to function. "My men are checking the store for provisions. We'd be happy to share if there is anything that you need."

He looked back to the doorway but found himself staring empty air. The man had completely vanished, leaving no trace behind. Searching the area, Dworkin almost wondered if he had been talking to himself the whole time.

28

Litsen was unusually talkative as he cleaned out the small cell. He babbled on and on in his broken Common about how unfair it was that the others had gotten to go play while he was stuck here guarding the Master's son. He relayed the stories the others had told about all the fun they had had in sickening detail.

Darian sat on the stone cot with the tatters that remained of his cloak wrapped around him. He tried to feel bad for the small town Listen described but just couldn't find it in him. His world had shrunk to this tower and the constant pain and misery that it encompassed. His life before felt like a distant dream, or an imaginary story a child would come up with to comfort themselves. It was hard to care about a world that you weren't even sure really existed.

Litsen winced as the door slammed open but Darian barely raised his head. Zarentle stood framed by the doorway, arms crossed and face dark. That was different at least. The boss rarely came to the cell himself, usually sending guards to drag Darian to him. All Darian could do was wonder what new horror this development would bring with a detached curiosity.

"I don't think you took me seriously," Zarentle snapped. "Come. There is something I want to show you."

Litsen sighed and leaned the broom against the wall then pulled out the shackles. Darian just held out his wrists with a tired sigh.

"No," Zarentle gave a soft laugh, "we won't be needing those."

Darian raised an eyebrow but didn't say anything. He tried to stand but his legs wouldn't support him anymore. Litsen growled and hefted him easily with one arm, throwing him over a shoulder before nodding to Zarentle.

He counted the turns as they moved down the hallways. If his calculations were right, they were headed for the torture room. He was surprised to feel relief bubbling in his heart. Maybe this time would be the one that finally released him from all of this. He sincerely doubted that his body could take another round in the chains. Then he could finally rest.

Litsen deposited him in a heap on the floor before stepping over him to move to the controls. He lay there for a moment, waiting to be hooked to the chains but it never came. Instead, a familiar scream cut through his fog as the chains clinked through the loops.

He forced himself to sit up, her name catching in his throat. Her red hair had been cut to her chin and her clothes hung in tatters. Every inch of exposed skin was covered in welts and cuts, blood running in tiny rivulets to pool on the floor. The chains already stretched her body to it's full, lean height and further. His joints stung just thinking of the way they would yank and pop with each link that slid through the hook. Her cat eyes went wide as Litsen yanked the controls again, pulling a scream from her throat.

"Darian," she gasped, tears filling her eyes, "help me. They're going to kill me if you don't do something."

Miramel. His beautiful and strong Wylthem princess. How had they even gotten to her? Rage burned in his throat and pulled on reserves he didn't know he had left. He pushed to his feet, feeling his magic stir.

"Let her go, Zarentle. She has nothing to do with this."

Zarentle smiled at Darian before walking calmly around Miramel, studying her. He cupped her chin in his hand and turned her to face him, before rearing back to slap her.

"She has everything to do with this. I told you, everyone will suffer. The longer you refuse to join me, the worse it will be for the ones you love the most."

"Please, Darian," Miramel gasped, tears streaming down her face to join the blood from her mouth, "just do as he wants. Please, just make it stop."

He closed his eyes and sank to his knees. Had he done this? He could hold out as long as he was the one suffering but Miramel? Then Dworkin would be next surely, probably his lovely wife and children too. Could he bear to listen to them beg him to make it stop, to ask the one thing that he couldn't do?

His eyes snapped open as his mind cleared. Miramel was strong, probably stronger than him. She was a warrior and a princess who always put her people ahead of herself. She would never, ever ask him to join Zarentle. No matter how much pain she was in. This had to be another of Zarentle's illusions meant to trick him into agreeing.

He grinned as the power built inside him. It was weak and pale but it felt good to dip into the well again. He grasped at the first spell he could think of, saying the words quickly and raising his arms to send it crashing through the illusion, already imagining how it would splatter against the wall behind.

But it didn't. The spell crashed into the woman before him, making her body shudder and twist in agony as an endless scream echoed through the tower. The illusion fell away as Zarentle laughed. It wasn't his Miramel, but it wasn't the empty chains he expected either. A human woman hung from the chains, her blue eyes wide and pained as she stared at him for a second before slumping in the chains and breathing out for the last time.

Zarentle wandered up and inspected the woman's limp body before turning to grin at him. "See, my boy? That was easy wasn't it? You can't tell me you didn't get a little enjoyment out that. I saw it on your face."

His stomach rolled and he heaved into the dirt at his feet but

nothing would come. He had nothing left to give.
"By the Twins, what have I done?"

29

Dworkin

Dworkin gasped as they crested the small hill next to the dragon. By the time they had rejoined him outside the city, he had nearly twisted himself into knots. He insisted he had something amazing to show them and it couldn't wait. Dworkin had hoped to take some time and process what they had seen, and try to figure out who that strange man he had talked to might be. But he had to admit, this had been pretty big.

He'd passed through this area many times on patrol and the most unusual thing he'd ever noticed was the looming feeling of the Barrier Ridge towering over you. Other than that the land had been wide open fields, only unsettled do to the agreement to stay away from the barrier. The landscape that spread out below him was nothing like anything he'd seen before.

The land was completely desolate, stripped of any life in a wide circle. A single tower rose from the center, like an accusing finger reaching out of the dry and cracked land to point at the heavens. The high walls were so black they seemed to absorb all light, reflecting nothing back on it's surroundings. There were no windows that could be seen and only one large set of doors at its front. Over the whole mess hung heavy low clouds that blocked the sun and made it almost as dark as night in the land below.

"Do you think that's where Darian is being held?" Keslar whispered.

Nemclis raised his head from the lower ground next to the hill, still easily on level with them. "All signs point to it, young wizard."

Cantiem grunted and shook his head. "How are we supposed to get in there? The place is swarming with Kaldecs and other creatures."

Dworkin nodded as he studied the tower. Kaldecs roamed the barren land, snapping and growling at each other. Overseeing them, and guarding the massive doors, were hulking beasts with green skin and long arms that looked like they could twist a man's head off without breaking a sweat. Patrolling through the whole mess were two almost human looking figures riding a beast similar to a black horse but more delicate and with a single black horn protruding from their forelock.

"The green ones are Nelcant. I don't know about the others." Dworkin growled and kicked at the grass. "Damn it. These demons aren't even supposed to exist outside of the stories told to scare children. What the hell are they doing in Ramleaj?"

Duntiel gave a soft snort. "No offense, your grace, but I think we can worry about the how or why later. Right now, the question is what. As in, what are we going to do?"

Cantiem tossed a grin over his shoulder to them. "I suppose just walking in the front door is out of the question."

Duntiel snapped at Cantiem who rose to the bait and snapped back. As the two continued to argue, with Keslar ordering them to stop with no luck, Dworkin turned and walked back down the hill. He paced the small area as his head swam with thoughts. This was a situation like he'd never faced before. He tried to think of what Darian would do but all of those options included magic and he doubted

Keslar was strong enough to do any of the type of spells they would need. After a while he grew tired of pacing and bent down to doodle in the sand with a stick.

Nemclis's massive head blocked the light as it drifted down to him, the others slowly striding down the hill. They must have stopped arguing long enough notice he was gone. Keslar squatted down just outside the dirt filled with doodles, wrapping his brown cloak around himself like a blanket.

"Do you have a plan, your grace?"

Dworkin glanced to his frightened eyes, then the frustrated faces of his knights. "Maybe, but we're all going to have to work together and get the timing just right. So no more fighting. Remember, all the things Bartol threatened, I can do as well. And worse."

Dworkin and his men snuck through the scraggly trees that remained just outside of the desolate circle. It didn't get them near as close as he would like but it was the best cover they had. Nemclis flew above in ever tightening circles, the tower at the center of his focus.

The creatures had already noticed him. A call to arms was raised and the lazy wandering turned to scrambling for weapons and some sort of organization. A few Nelcant pulled out massive looking crossbows and started setting bolts as large as a tree branch into them. Dworkin grimaced and sent a prayer up to the Twins. He hadn't counted archers into the plan. Hopefully Nemclis wouldn't have to be in the air for long and could remain safe.

Once close enough, Nemclis released his fire into a smooth circle around the tower, spiraling closer and closer. Each pass he left just enough of an opening for them to run through towards those large front doors. About half of the creatures turned and started fighting the fires, while the others kept their focus on the dragon above. It wasn't as good of numbers as Dworkin had hoped for but it would have to do.

He gave the signal and they ran from the cover out into the open field. Kelsar shouted a spell next to him and two large spell lights flared to life on either side of the tower, adding to the confusion and hopefully blinding at least some of the enemy. He nodded to the two knights who ran alongside him and pulled his sword, slashing at any creature who got too close.

Right next to his ear, the twang of a crossbow drew his attention. He spun and buried his sword in the back of the Nelcant who had fired it but it was too late. The bolt was already flying directly towards Nemclis. Banking sharply, the dragon avoided the shot but his head turned and fire engulfed the tower, spewing from the top and what must have been a wooden roof. Sheepishly, Nemclis grinned down with a shrug of his front legs then flew off to wait for his next step.

Duntiel called out as his sword flew dangerously close to Dworkin's face, and sliced into the paw of a Kaldec who had been lunging for him. He nodded his thanks to the young knight, angry at himself for getting so distracted, then motioned them forward to the doors. Just like he'd hoped, the creatures had delved into chaos and were streaming out of the tower to fight the fire or attempt to flee from it. In their haste the doors had been left wide open. He motioned his men through then pulled them tightly closed behind him.

"What happened to that figure on the black unicorn?" Keslar whispered, eyes darting around the large space.

Dworkin took in the massive room with a sweep. It felt too big to fit into the tower that they had seen from the outside, and too pristine for all the creatures that had moved about. The black marble floor stretched for ages before joining a staircase that moved upward and a hallway that split in two directions at the back.

"I don't know but keep an eye out for them, I'm pretty sure they're the ones in charge." He nodded towards the hallways at the back of the room. "Let's sweep this level before going up. Cantiem and Kelsar take the left, Duntiel and I will head right."

"May the Twins protect you, Your Grace," Kelsar called, already jogging off down the hall.

Robin Rhoden

"You too, sir wizard. Stay alert, Cantiem."

30

Menir stepped from the portal and into the grand throne room, her steed's hooves echoing on the marble floor. She had been riding patrol around the tower when the dragon had started spewing his fire. Once it became obvious the Nelcant and Kaldecs were not going to listen to her, she had decided it wasn't worth risking her neck for.

Zarentle looked up from pouring himself another glass of wine with an eyebrow raised. "I did not summon you."

"My lord," she clenched her teeth for a second, fighting to keep her voice even, "the tower is under attack. I can only assume they are trying to rescue your prisoner."

He grinned and took a long sip of the wine. "Yes, I know. They are just humans, Menir. The beasts will take care of them in due time."

Menir just stared at him, silently begging the dark god to strike her down where she stood. If she had to spend one more day in the service of this idiot, she just might lose her mind. Maybe she should just let the humans have their way with him. It would mean a change of plans but nothing that could not be handled.

"Humans are like ants. They may be small and inferior but they are strong, especially when working in teams. Once set upon a goal they keep going no matter what is thrown at them. We have already taken out one of their crew and they just kept coming."

Zarentle set down his wine and rose to his feet, power gathering in swirls around him. "Let them come. You think I can not handle a few humans? I will squash them like the bugs they are."

"The tower is compromised and the creatures are so crazed they are turning on each other. I will not hang around for this." She sighed and rolled her eyes, surprised she was even thinking what she was about to say. "Come with me, Zarentle. We can regroup and come back even stronger to make Ramleaj in his image."

She winced as the wine glass clattered across the floor. Zarentle towered above her, his dark eyes swirling with anger. She swallowed hard and took a cautious step back. He might not be the best planner or the most stable, but he was extremely powerful and could take her out with just one spell. Contempt had made her lazy and overconfident and she would have to think fast to be sure it did not cost her life.

"I do not know what plan you and he think you have going but you can go back right now and tell him that Ramleaj is mine. I will not leave without my son, and I will not leave until I have laid to waste every corner of this blasted land."

She bowed low, carefully backing towards the portal without ever turning her back on Zarentle. "No plan at all, my lord. Merely trying to help you realize your goals but you do not need me."

31

Keslar had to slow as they found the steps leading downward. They were covered in moss and lichen that squished under his boots and threatened to send him sliding. As they descended, the light dimmed until he was barely able to see more than the next step right in front of him. Whispering the words, he concentrated on his staff until the amber at the top started to glow softly.

"Should you be wasting your power like that?" Cantiem whispered, the pale light glinting off the sword in his hand and throwing his features into sharp contrast.

Keslar shrugged and continued to the bottom of the stairs. "This is child's play. How to control every aspect of your staff is one of the first things you learn when you join the guild."

The base of the stairs widened into a single room piled high with various weapons, all in different states of repair. Hooks lined the wall, some empty and some with rings of keys hanging from them. Keslar studied them for a moment before grabbing the biggest ring and shoving it in his pocket.

"How do you know that's the right one?" Cantiem glanced down the single hallway that led out of the room then back to him.

"I don't. I'm just hoping it's the master set because it has the most on it."

Cantiem seemed to consider the thought for a moment before nodding. He checked the hallway one more time before motioning them on again. Keslar couldn't help but grin. For all their bickering and joking, it was obvious that both these young knights had been trained by Dworkin and Bartol and had taken their lessons seriously. He had to admit, he felt a lot safer having the armed knight exploring the dark dungeons with him.

They wound their way through the maze of hallways with dirt walls and dirt floors, praying they weren't walking in circles as everything looked the same. More than once they had to press their backs to the wet and dirty wall as creatures raced past in an adjoining hallway. Each time Keslar would hold his breath and listen to the pounding of his heart wondering how the whole world didn't hear it, but the creatures were intent on their tasks and paid no attention to the young wizard or knight.

Slowly, the dirt walls started to give way to iron bars and simple locks. Keslar's stomach swirled and fear of a different kind crept into his mind as he studied each one they passed.

"These cells would be no problem for a simple Master, much less the High Master. How did he not escape?"

Cantiem grunted but kept his eyes forward, constantly looking for threats. "Maybe he was knocked out or something?"

Keslar's step faltered for a second. That was entirely possible but he didn't really want to consider it. If the High Master had been unconscious for this long, there was a high chance he was dead. He took a breath and tried not to think about that. They couldn't have come all this way to already be too late.

After a couple more turns, Cantiem motioned for them to stop then motioned to his ear. Keslar squinted and looked around, then he heard it too. A soft muttering somewhere up ahead. Two voices for sure but he couldn't make them out well enough to tell what they were saying or who they belonged to. He nodded and Cantiem motioned them forward again, following the sound.

After a few wrong turns and back tracking they found the hallway where the sound was the loudest. The iron bars gave way to a thick stone wall with a single door set in it and standing slightly ajar. Just being near the wall gave Keslar an odd squeezing feeling at his core and the light in his staff dimmed.

"Yous gots to eats," the first voice was saying from the other side of the door. "Litsen no care. Boss care. Say keeps yous alive."

"Go away, Litsen," the second voice muttered.

Keslar's heart jumped and he couldn't help but smile. He had definitely heard that voice before. Everyone knew the way it would boom down the hallways to greet another Master or fill the lecture halls when giving special presentations on whatever obscure topic had become his latest obsession.

"But yous-" The clatter of metal against stone interrupted the first voice, which growled in response. "This stupid. Litsen should be fighting. Litsen not babysitter. Litsen should strangle yous and be done."

As they crept slowly to the door, Keslar mouthed the words to the only attack spell he knew. He wasn't even supposed to know it but had found it in a dusty book at the back of the library and practiced it on inanimate objects until he got it right. It wasn't enough to kill but it would certainly knock someone back. He'd always figured it didn't hurt to have something ready if the bullies got too out of control without a Master around.

He poked his head in the door, holding his breath on the last word of the spell so it wouldn't release until he was ready. The pitiful figure huddled against the far wall nearly knocked the breath from him. Curled up in a ball, the man was nothing like he remembered. Thin and pale, his hair hung in dirty clumps around his face. Holding a tattered and stained purple cloak tight around his frail form, he seemed to be trying to retreat from the rest of the world. There was little life left in the gray eyes that widened as they noticed Keslar slip into the room.

Keslar pressed a finger to his lips then turned his attention to the creature. It was a Nelcant, a bit smaller than the ones they had seen outside, with one ear a shredded and tattered mess. It was leaning over with it's back to him, muttering as it scooped food from the floor and back onto a metal plate. Keslar let the last word slip out on his held breath and pointed his staff at the creature, waiting for the exhilarating rush of power.

Nothing happened. The power never came even as Keslar repeated the word and reached deep into the well the Masters had taught them to imagine as the source of their power. Suddenly, his well hadn't just gone dry, it had been sealed and locked up tight then tossed out of his reach. He gasped and nearly doubled over, the sudden loss leaving him hollowed out and cold.

He barely noticed as Cantiem pushed him out of the way to step between him and the Nelcant who was lunging directly at them. The Nelcant's eyes shifted to the sword pointed at him but couldn't stop quick enough. There was a soft slicing sound as the metal slid into the creature's stomach and up towards it's chest. Cantiem grunted and pushed a little deeper and gave a swift twist before pulling the blade free and tossing the lifeless body to the floor.

"What are you doing here?" Darian's voice was rough as he turned slightly to look at them.

Keslar shook himself out of his stupor and ran over to lift the man's all to thin hand. "Come on. We've got to get you out of here."

To his surprise, Darian just yanked his hand away and curled back towards the wall. "Go while you still can, Apprentice. Forget me. Zarentle will never let me leave."

"Zarentle? Is that his name?" Cantiem laughed then grimaced as he wiped the blood away. "Duke Marslic is dealing with him."

Darian's head jerked around and his eyes snapped to attention. "Dworkin is here? And going to face Zarentle?"

Keslar smiled broadly and shrugged as Cantiem nodded.

"That idiot will get himself killed, damn it!" He held out an arm to Kelsar and motioned him over again. "Help me up, kid. We've got to get out of this room so you can loan me some power."

Keslar slid himself under the High Master's arm and helped him to stand. He could feel every bone in the man's body, nearly afraid that if he touched him too much or moved too fast, something would break. He swallowed and glanced up at the High Master even as they made their slow way to the door.

"I don't know if I can. There's something wrong with my magic. I can't feel it anymore and I couldn't call on it just now."

The High Master grunted and leaned against the wall to catch his breath for a second before nodding for them to continue on. "That'll clear up once we get out of this blasted room. Do you know the spell for Power Transference? No, of course you wouldn't, that's a spell for an Accolade."

The High Master kept muttering to himself as they moved out into the hall and around the corner. Just as the man had said, Keslar felt a rush of his power coming back to him. It gave a warm tingling inside and he once again felt whole.

"Okay, kid, I need you to repeat exactly what I say and imagine some of your power feeding into mine. Not too much though, you don't want to knock yourself out. Just enough to wake mine up."

Keslar nodded even though his mouth had gone dry and there was an empty feeling in the pit of his stomach. Was he really going to attempt a spell two levels above his station? Even with the High Master as his temporary tutor, that was just insane.

The High Master was still just staring with those intense gray eyes so he shook himself and nodded again. He repeated the words carefully, imagining a thread of his power passing out of him and through their joined hands to fill up the gaping hole inside of the High Master. After a few moments, Keslar was starting to feel lightheaded and sleepy when the High Master yanked his hand away.

"Careful, kid. Not too much, but thanks."

The High Master was standing straighter and there was a bit of life back in his eyes. He pushed hair from his face and looked around before pointing down a hallway and moving forward. He was still way too thin and stopped once in a while to catch his breath, cursing quietly each time, but could move without having to lean on Keslar.

Cantiem cleared his throat as they moved through the brighter, and cleaner, halls of the main level. "If you take the next right, we'll be back outside and-"

"Run outside if you want, little knight," High Master Darian snapped without even looking back at them, "I have to stop my brother before he gets his blasted self killed, and, if we're lucky, end all of this before it goes any further."

32

Dworkin

Dworkin and Duntiel slipped through the silent hallways as quietly as they could. Everything looked just the same and they were starting to worry they would be walking in circles forever. The place was an absolute maze of black and white marble that never seemed to change.

"What's that?" Duntiel tapped him on the shoulder and motioned down a hallway to the left.

Dworkin nodded and moved that direction. Set into the wall was the largest set of metal doors that he'd ever seen. Carved in painstaking detail was some form of tentacled beast, grasping at gemstones. A single amethyst glinted at the very center. Dworkin patted the pouch at his belt, thinking of the ring tucked safely inside, and figured they must be in the right place.

There were no handles to be seen so he tried pushing on the doors but they wouldn't budge. With a nod to Duntiel, they both slid their swords away and backed up a few steps. He silently counted to three and they both rammed their shoulders into the metal on either side of the opening. They didn't open but he could hear a cracking inside so they stepped back to repeat the process. Just as their shoulders met the door, the doors flung open and they hurtled to the marble floor beyond.

Black boots marched up into his field of vision, black robes swirling just above them. "Well, I am impressed. I figured my pets would have already taken care of you."

Dworkin pushed to his knees, wincing as his shoulder protested, and looked up into a pair of gray eyes that were strangely familiar and yet so cold his heart skipped a beat. Before he could even react, power slammed into him and knocked him flat on the floor again. The man raised his arms and it was as if two giant hands gripped Dworkin by the neck and lifted him off the ground.

As Dworkin struggled against air and fought for breath, movement over the man's shoulder caught his eye. Duntiel was struggling to his feet, sword drawn. He rushed the man with sword high, aiming for the killing blow.

Dworkin dropped from the air like a stone into a pond, if the pond were made of hard granite and the stone could feel pain.

The man had turned his attention to Duntiel. With a swipe of his hand, the young knight flew through the air to crash against one of the stone pillars. Bile rose in Dworkin's throat as he could hear the crack of Duntiel's head colliding with unforgiving stone. His limp body was lifted again and smashed into the floor until a wide pool of bright red spread across the endless black of the floor.

"Now I'm going to have to get someone to clean that up," the man said, clucking his tongue casually. "You are turning out to be quite the thorn, aren't you?"

Dworkin forced himself to his feet, still gasping for air, and drew his sword. "You'll pay for that, you monster, and I'm going to enjoy every second of it."

"Not really a man of words, are you?" The man laughed, green light forming around his hands. "I'd hoped this would at least be entertaining but you continue to disappoint, so I think your time is up here."

33

Darian cursed as he had to stop and catch his breath again. He could feel his magic growing and stirring but his body just couldn't keep up. At this rate they would never reach Dworkin in time. He couldn't let his brother die on his account. Especially after the man had tried to warn him and he'd just laughed it off. If only he had taken Leslien's premonition a little more seriously, maybe they wouldn't all be in this situation.

The young wizard just stared at him until he was ready to move again. Darian couldn't remember his name but vaguely remembered seeing him around the island and noticing he was a good study. Touching his magic had been a surprise however. There was a much deeper well hidden in there than one could possibly expect, especially with so much of it still untapped.

He nodded and they continued on, the young knight wearing Marslic colors guarding their backs. It seemed to take a lifetime but finally they were at the doors to the throne room. His heart dropped to see them already standing open. Did that mean that Dworkin had already found this place, or was it just one of the creatures being careless? He'd never seen them forget to shut the door before, but then the tower had never been filling with smoke before either.

He pushed his way in and took in the scene with a single sweep. Another young knight lay on the floor surrounded by a painfully large pool of blood. Directly in front of him, Zarentle towered with a sneer on his face and a ball of energy forming between his fingers as he stared down at Dworkin.

From somewhere deep inside, Darian found one last surge of energy. He threw himself forward, pushing all of what little weight he had left into Dworkin just as Zarentle released the spell. Dworkin fell to the side, sword clattering away, as Darian turned to face the ball of energy. It was too late, there was no way to avoid it. He threw up his hands and sent his mind diving down into his magic, trying to say the words of a shield spell fast enough.

He didn't have time. The energy enveloped him, surging through is body violently. His mind stood apart as his body was thrown backward to collide with the wall and fall to the floor in a heap. He could hear bones crunch and muscles rip, but it was like it was happening to someone else. He opened his eyes for one brief moment to see Dworkin sliding up to him on his knees, before everything went black.

34

Dworkin didn't breathe as he yanked his gloves off and fumbled around for a pulse. It was faint and uneven but it was there. He growled and turned Darian's face to him. It was so thin and gaunt, he barely recognized his brother through the blood and dirt.

"Come on, Darian, open those eyes." He begged, emotions choking his throat. "Wake up, you fool. I didn't come all this way just to lose you now."

The monster hovered over them, face contorted in anger and something almost kin to regret. Dworkin reached for his sword but realized it was still well out of reach, forgotten where it had fallen in his haste to get to Darian.

"Now look what you made me do. You humans and your false

sense of loyalty. Too much like your mother, boy." The man growled then suddenly turned away. "Take him to your little healers or whoever you have to. When he wakes again, be sure and tell him, we have unfinished business to attend to."

Dworkin remained rooted in place, hovering protectively over Darian. His brain struggled to process it all but just couldn't seem to grasp hold of anything.

Cantiem raised his sword as Keslar started to chant a spell. The man just glanced their way and snapped his fingers with a sigh. Both young men froze in place, their eyes wide as they struggled to move without any success.

"I am tired and bored. No more games today."

The man just shook his head and kept walking towards the raised platform where a dark rift was opening in the air. Power crackled around the edges, a scene as black as the night sky shimmering just beyond. With one last glance back at Darian, the man stepped through the rift and disappeared. After a second, the edges sealed back together and dissipated as if they had never been there.

As soon as he was gone, the two young men were released and stumbled forward. They stared at each other for a moment before rushing off in different directions. Cantiem ran to Duntiel's side, his agonizing wail ripping Dworkin's already bruised heart in two.

"Is he okay?" Keslar whispered as he knelt beside Darian.

Dworkin ripped his eyes from Cantiem to turn his attention back to Darian. "He's alive but he won't wake up."

Keslar swallowed hard, his eyes wide and filling with tears. "What do we do now?"

"We do exactly what that creature said." Dworkin grunted as he slid his arms under Darian's limp body, way too little effort needed to lift him close and stand. "We get Darian to the healers. Everything else can be figured out after that."

He turned and nodded to where Cantiem had regained his composure but wouldn't leave Duntiel's side. They hadn't been able to bury Bartol and that seemed to have weighed heavily on the young knights. He couldn't ask Cantiem to leave another friend behind, but he was barely going to be able to make it out with Darian's weight.

"Can you help?" He whispered to Keslar, nodding towards the two men.

Keslar nodded and walked over, laying a hand on Cantiem's shoulder before starting to chant the words to a spell. Pale light glimmered around his hands before spreading to surround Duntiel's broken body. As the light grew, Duntiel lifted off the ground and floated whatever direction the kid moved his hands. Cantiem leaned over and whispered something to the kid before jogging over to grab Dworkin's sword and lead the way out the door.

Moving as quickly as they could with Dworkin carrying still unconscious Darian and Keslar guiding Duntiel, they jogged towards the door. Dworkin skidded to a stop in the entryway as the whole tower seemed to shudder and there was a great crash above them.

"Was that the roof?" Cantiem yelled.

Dworkin hefted Darian a little higher and started again as the tower rumbled for a second time. "Most likely. We need to get out before this whole place comes down around our ears."

They set out at a run out of the building and across the grounds. The creatures milled about and watched them go, no longer attacking just like their master. They didn't stop running until they reached the green grass of the hill that Nemclis waited on. Dworkin laid Darian next to the dragon as Keslar carefully lowered Duntiel to the grass then fell over himself. The kid was sweating profusely and rubbed at his temples with a soft moan.

They all turned as the tower continued to shudder and smoke, tilting dangerously to the side. But just as it seemed the black stone would tumble to the ground, the fires went out and the tower righted itself. By the time the final plume of smoke cleared, it was as if nothing had ever happened.

"What in the Twins name is happening here?" Nemclis growled.

Dworkin settled onto the grass next to his still sleeping friend. "We can only hope Darian has the answers, and that he wakes up in time that they'll be useful to us."

35

Miramel winced as the staff collided with her shoulder. She gritted her teeth and chided herself for getting distracted. She should have easily seen through that feint and blocked his clumsy swing. She was supposed to be the teacher here but the bruises she was collecting today told another story.

"My apologies, Princess." The young soldier remained in a defensive stance as he had been taught but his eyes filled with concern and possibly fear.

She forced a smile for the boy then glanced over her small class. "I deserved it. Let that be a lesson. No matter how much more experienced you are, if you let your guard down your opponent will get the best of you. Had that be a Human's sword or a Cregas ax, I would have lost my arm and probably my life."

"If a Cregas could reach that high," someone whispered and a quiet laughter rippled through the class.

"Underestimating someone for their size is just as dangerous." She looked them each in the eye until they quieted down and returned their attention to her. "I think that is enough instruction for today. Pair off and show me what you've learned."

She paced the yards, feeling restless and unsettled. Periodically she would correct a soldier's form or chide them for missing a parry but her mind was only half in it. Her heart raced as if she were running at full speed and the pounding at the back of her skull had returned. A deep and urgent fear consumed her but she could not say why.

"How goes the training today, Princess?"

She glanced up to smile at the Wylthem hopping the fence to enter the yards. "Idilm Larsle, perhaps these young fools will listen to their future commander if he tells them to keep their guard up, even in practice."

"If they will not listen to their future queen then I am not sure what help I will be."

She laughed as he winked at her. The first genuine laugh she had felt since the dark rains. Between watching Reilin slowly fade away, and all the others being added to the infirmary with smaller but just as dire wounds, and the chaos going on in her mind, there had not been much to smile about recently. She reached out to squeeze his arm, thankful he never held a grudge when they squabbled like siblings.

She gasped as light flashed in her eyes, blinding her. She gripped Larsle's arm hard and threw her other arm up in front of her face though it did no good. The pain was hot and searing as it coursed through her body and stole her breath away. A scream that wasn't her own echoed through her mind and then everything went black.

The first thing she noticed when she started to come back to herself was that the headache was gone. But that wasn't the only thing. There was a gaping hole in her consciousness where a warm, and familiar presence had taken residence for so many years. Even as she opened her eyes, she searched and reached for him.

"Miramel," her father's soft voice called, the warmth of his magic rushing through her, "my Inonym, come back to us."

She blinked and realized that she was laying on the ground in the middle of the practice yard. Father and Larsle hovered over her, with her young trainees just a little further back. Father smiled and helped her sit up, pressing a glass of cold water into her hands as he lightly rubbed her back.

She dutifully took a couple sips of the water before setting it aside to hug her knees to her chest and bury her face in them.

She could hear Father quietly shooing everyone away, saying that she needed space and air. Most of the footsteps receded until she could no longer hear but noticed that Larsle's only moved a small bit away. Father sighed but didn't argue with him further.

"Inonym, please, look at me."

She forced herself to raise her head and meet his concerned brown eyes. He pushed her hair back from her face and kissed her forehead.

"You terrified us all." His voice was thick and breathless, hands trembling where he clutched her shoulders. "Can you tell me what happened?"

She closed her eyes for a moment, trying and failing to choke back a sob before looking at him again. "He is gone. I do not know what happened but he is gone."

"Who is gone?" Larsle moved closer, ignoring her father's dark glares.

"Darian," she whispered, knowing neither of them would like the answer but not caring. "It is like he has been ripped out of me."

Larsle growled and rolled his eyes but Father's face went pale as he just stared at her. She stared back, almost daring him to rebuke her for speaking a human's name in his court again.

"You feel him when he is not with you? His joy, his pain, you feel those as if they were an echo of your own?"

She narrowed her eyes but shrugged. "He has been a presence in my mind for many years now, though the connection is small. He is a dear friend. Though recently he has been on my mind much more."

Father rocked back on his heals and studied the ground with a deep sigh. "The tiredness, the cold, headaches. That can not be a good sign. You said he is gone, Inonym, how does that feel? Is he dead?"

"I do not think so." She closed her eyes and searched her heart.

"His life force is still in the world, but I can not touch his mind. Something is very wrong, Father."

He reached out a hand and helped her to her feet but didn't release her hand once she was standing. He studied their joined hands for a moment before sighing deeply and looking into her eyes again.

"More than you know, my Mira," he whispered before straightening and transitioning from her father back to High King of the Wylthem. "Go and pack your things, Princess. Go to Arnis, it is the nearest hub of information. See what you can learn and if it is possible to get a message to the High Master."

She studied him, almost not daring to hope. "You mean it, Father?"

"I will go with the Princess," Larsle stepped forward and snapped to attention, "to keep her safe, your majesty."

"Thank you, Idilm Larsle, but no. It will be safer for her to travel alone so that she might slip through unseen as is her greatest skill." He bowed his head slightly as Larsle saluted and walked off stiffly, then turned back to her with a wink. "Yes, I am serious. Go, before I change my mind, but please be careful and come home as quickly as you can."

She tried to bow to him as would be proper but could not resist hugging his neck as tight as she could, refusing to let go until he squeezed her back. "Thank you, Father. I will be back, I promise."

36

She straightened her jacket and took a couple of deep breaths as the portal started to form. "Do you know why he has summoned me?"

Melteze shrugged, fiddling with the lace on his suit instead of looking at her. "No one ever knows with him. He's half crazy after being locked up with only his pets to talk to for so long."

"Why do we even bother with him? My forces, with your power behind us, could easily take care of things without all of his drama."

Melteze raised his head with a smile that made her shiver. "There are more pieces at play than you know, Menir. You'll have your chance to ride into battle soon enough. For now, his antics buy me time to be certain other matters are handled."

She swallowed and gave a sharp nod. Though her face remained blank and passive, her mind bounced around like a youngling given too many sweets. Would she ever learn to just hold her tongue and do as she was ordered? Sometimes it amazed her she had remained alive long enough to rise in the ranks to this level.

She took one more breath and started to walk toward the portal but Melteze placed a hand on her shoulder. This close, she could feel the power practically crackling off of him, but laughter shone in his dark eyes.

"Find out what his plans are now that he's lost the wizard. Just try not to anger him too much. I really don't have time to train your replacement."

"Yes, sir."

Her skin tingled and the usual wave of vertigo slid through her as she passed through the portal. She stood still for a moment to gather herself and orientate to her surroundings. He had not called her to the throne room as she had expected, but to the warm and cozy room that he had prepared for his son. He sat on the thick bed, staring into the crackling fire, not even looking up to her.

"You summoned me, my lord?"

"They have taken my son from me, Menir."

She pursed her lips and swallowed the first words that came to mind. Better not to mention that the wizard had not wanted to be there in the first place and that it was not as if they had the usual father son relationship.

"Yes, my lord. I know."

He rose from the bed and turned to her. "They have taken him to their human healers. They will not be able to fix everything that is wrong with him. I need you to follow them and be sure that they take him to Melcader. Good old Jarelt will know what to do."

"Just to clarify, my lord." She cocked her head and raised an eyebrow. "You have taken him out of the equation, but you wish me to make sure that he is healed."

He grinned at her before walking over to the window and staring out at Ramleaj. "I need him whole to complete my plans."

She bit the edge of her tongue, only her years of personal training keeping the smile off her face. These men and their plans constantly delaying things. Both of them had more than enough power to just take this land and bleed it dry, yet they kept delaying for reasons they didn't want to share. Maybe they didn't fully understand them themselves.

"I can practically read your thoughts, Leranti." He turned from the window to stare at her coldly. "No, I do not need my son to take Ramleaj, but I am not the idiot that you and your boss think I am. I know he thinks as soon as I have Ramleaj in my grasp, all he has to do is destroy me and he will have it without putting in the effort, and he probably could. But with my son and I's powers combined, he will at least have a fight on his hands."

"I do not-"

He waved away her protests as he turned back to the window. "Do not bother trying to deny it. Just get out there and do as you are told. Fail me, and you will not live long enough to run back to Tez for protection."

37

For probably the thousandth time that day, Dworkin caught himself glancing over to the prone body stretched across Nemclis' back. They had been traveling for nearly a week, moving as fast as the horses could handle, and Darian had not stirred or moved the whole time. If it weren't for a steady heartbeat and quiet, easy breathing, Dworkin would have sworn they had lost him.

"Are you sure it is wise to let him go, Dworkin?" Nemclis lowered his head and nodded to the speck within a small cloud of dust that was all they could see of Cantiem as he took the fork in the road that would lead to Darsile.

"The king needs to be notified of what we've seen and that I'll be along as quickly as I can." Dworkin sighed and shook his head.

"Besides, I don't think he'd be much more use to us. He's a good soldier but this trip has nearly broken him."

Keslar grunted and tried to stretch his legs, sore from so much time in the saddle. "I'm a little surprised you did not also include a message back home."

"My wife will not be happy until she gets word of Darian. I'll send her a message from the Mount when hopefully I have better news to share."

He pulled her necklace from his pouch and rubbed his hand across it as thoughts of home tugged at his heart. Keslar leaned in closer trying to get a closer look.

"I've seen you pull that out off and on through the whole trip but never noticed it glowing before."

Dworkin glanced at the kid then back to the green gem wrapped in silver that lay in his palm. As usual, the kid was right. In the dimness of the trees, the gem seemed to have a faint glow to it that he had never seen before. For a brief second the thought crossed his mind that he should tell Darian, that the man would be fascinated by it and probably figure out the answer. Then he glanced to Nemclis's back and remembered that he couldn't tell his brother anything at the moment.

Dworkin sighed and climbed back in the saddle, giving Mist's neck a friendly pat. "Come along. If we can keep this pace, we'll be at the Mount tomorrow evening."

They rode in silence for a while before Keslar leaned a little closer, gaining a snort from Ebony. "I still don't understand. Zarentle almost seemed sad that he had injured the High Master, and then he just let us go. Why?"

Dworkin looked up at the gray sky as a cold raindrop landed on his neck and slid along his collar. With a sigh, he pulled up his hood and looked to Nemclis. The dragon was already lifting one wing so that it curled like a canopy over his precious cargo.

"I have no idea. It's obvious he wants Darian alive but as the why or any sense in the things he's done, I just can't make it out."

"Do you think the Healers will be able to help?"

"We have to keep up hope," Nemclis said softly. "When we get to the Mount, they'll know what to do."

They rode on in silence, allowing their doubts and fears to go unspoken. The rain slowed the horses down, making it two more nights before they would finally dismount at the base of the hill. Dworkin rested an arm across Mist's neck for a moment before starting to climb the hill with her reigns loosely in his hand. Kelsar did the same and Ebony took a moment to stretch and shake before following politely. The poor things had been pushed to their limits and deserved a rest. They couldn't be left at the base of the Mount, but they didn't have to carry a rider up either.

Three Healer women came running out of the compound and down the hill towards them, their white dresses flowing around their ankles. A sigh of relief spilled from him as he recognized the woman in the middle. Her short hair had gone more gray and thinned out since he'd last seen her, curling just under her chin. The long red belt at her waist marked her as a Mother Healer, equal to a Master Wizard, and the golden emblem clasping the ties that hung down the front marking her as the Great Mother, leader of their guild.

"Duke Marslic," she called out from still a few yards away, pushing hair from her face, "what brings you to me with a Wizard and a Dragon, looking like you could barely walk another step."

Dworkin passed Mists reigns to Keslar and motioned the Great Mother to follow him over to Nemclis's back. The dragon lay down and folded his wings tightly so as to reveal the passenger he had so carefully carried all this way.

"It's our mutual friend, Great Mother Quinta." Dworkin's throat constricted seeing that there was still no change. "High Master Darian has been gravely injured and needs your touch."

Quinta reached out a hand to brush back a lock of Darian's black hair. She snatched her hand back with a gasp, her eyes widening with shock. "This child has been touched by dark magic like none I have seen before."

"I can't tell you much beyond what I saw." Dworkin shrugged and scrubbed at his face. Now that they were here the exhaustion he'd been holding at bay was settling on him hard. "I don't understand it myself."

The Great Mother nodded and motioned for the other two women to carry Darian away. "We will do what we can for him, Your Grace."

"That is all I can ask."

He started to walk back to where Keslar stood, meaning to take his horse and care for her as she desperately needed. Suddenly, the world tilted under his feet and he felt himself sway. He would have fallen if Nemclis hadn't stretched out a wing for him to grasp onto while he tried to catch his breath and wait for his vision to stop spinning.

Great Mother Quinta laid a hand on his shoulder and a soft warmth flowed through him. The pounding in his head dulled to a quiet roar and he found he could stand straight again. He blinked and found her staring up at him with an eyebrow raised and mouth turned in a deep frown.

"And when was the last you have slept, your grace? How did you expect to care for your brother if you passed out along the way here?" She shook her head and motioned Keslar over to them. "You look half dead as well, Apprentice. Leave the horses here with the dragon and my girls will come for them. You need caring for yourselves."

"Please, just focus on Darian, Great Mother. We'll be-" Another wave of dizziness and nausea cut off whatever he had been about to say.

Great Mother Quinta snorted and practically pushed them both up the hill. "Nonsense, child. There is more than enough care here to go around. Do not make me put you to sleep and have you carried up this hill, Duke Marslic."

He glanced to Keslar who was trying to hide a smile then bowed his head to the woman. "Yes, Great Mother. Thank you."

38

Keslar leaned back and just enjoyed the sun on his face and the soft smell of plants around him. After the touch of a healer and a nice long nap, he was starting to feel like himself. The sores from so much time in the saddle, the scrapes from the Kaldec attack, and even the deep exhaustion from overusing his magic, were gone. If only the worry and pain of his heart could be healed so easily.

Having wandered the grounds, he was amazed at how similar and yet how completely different they were from those on Wizard's Isle. Where back home there were soaring towers and high balconies, things here were much quieter and more conservative. The complex was made up of one story buildings connected by cobblestone paths. Made of white stucco with overhanging red tiled roofs, they looked almost like giant mushrooms clinging to the hilltop. Tucked into every unused corner were tiny gardens like the one Keslar rested in. They were meant to be calming and healing to the patients but even here no space was wasted. Every plant had been carefully chosen and cultivated for its healing properties. There was basil to draw out poisons, honey suckle for sore throats, thyme for coughs, and many many more. Most of them Keslar didn't even recognize.

Shortly after the Wizard's Guild was formed, it had been realized that magic power took a different form in women. They couldn't use their powers to attack or cast spells. Only to heal. The one power that had escaped men. The Healer's Guild had formed as a mirror image to the Wizard's. Both shared the same five levels and colors to identify them, the wizards in their cloaks and the stones of their staff, the healers in their belts and necklace. Both had a high council all others answered to.

Or did, Keslar thought with a sigh. It was still hard to believe their great guild had been reduced to just him, the King's Wizard Clesum, and the High Master. Assuming High Master Darian could be healed.

"We heard that you were on the island for the tragedy. That must have been horrible. We all wish there was something we could have done."

The tragedy. Was that what it had been reduced to already? An event with a name that any time someone mentioned it everyone would shake their heads and click their tongues saying how horrible it was? He thought about all the events he learned about in history class and realized that people had actually been there and had to deal with the fall out and the misery that went along. Suddenly he wished he had paid a bit more attention to their stories.

His heart twinged thinking of the two men that history probably wouldn't remember. By now everyone knew of all the wizards lost and while they deserved to be mourned and remembered, how many would know of Bartol and Duntiem's sacrifice. Both of their deaths flashed before his eyes and stabbed at his heart just as much as watching the Wizard's Council fall while he was hidden away. Swallowing a sob, he promised himself to tell their stories to anyone who would listen.

He opened his eyes and found a tall dark haired Healer hovering nearby. She was a young, thin girl with wide inquisitive eyes and a gentle smile. A deep green belt circled her slender waist. A disciple, one step below a Mother.

"Thank you. There was nothing that could be done."

"Two of our best Mothers are helping the wizards restoring the Isle." She smiled as she sat down next to him. "We would have sent more but could not spare them with all of the mysterious animal attacks and of course the Wasting."

Keslar started to ask her about the animal attacks, wondering if maybe they were from Kaldec or Nelcant, but stopped and cocked his head. "What Wizards? They're all dead. Dworkin and I buried them ourselves."

"Not all were at the Isle, Apprentice." She laughed lightly, touching his shoulder. "Many were away on missions, others have assignments elsewhere like the King's Wizard, Master Clesum. Some Masters choose to live at home instead of on the Isle. Your numbers have dwindled greatly, but there is still hope."

He shook his head with a snort. "I knew all that. Why couldn't I think of it?"

"Sometimes when grieving for the dead, it is easy to forget the living."

He nodded slowly. "There have been too many dead. Sometimes I almost forget myself."

"Grief is a thing to be felt, Apprentice. Do not push it away."

Dworkin stepped into the garden, looking as rested and refreshed as Keslar felt. He had bathed and changed, the wound on his arm cared for. That glazed look was gone from his eyes so Keslar figured he had gotten at least some sleep, probably healer induced to keep him from worrying about the High Master too much to rest. Still, there was a tightness about his jaw that didn't raise Keslar's hopes very high.

"Keslar, can you come with me?"

He scooted to the edge of his seat, excitement and fear warring for place in his heart. "Is it the High Master? Is he going to be okay?"

"The Healers are finished with him. He... I..." Dworkin pursed his lips and pushed a hand through his hair. "Would you please just come?"

"Of course." He rose from the bench and turned back to the girl, clasping his hands in the traditional deference to an elder guild member. "Thank you for listening, Lady Disciple."

She smiled and adjusted her skirts. "Injuries of the body aren't a Healer's only focus, though sadly the heart and the mind do take much longer to heal. Go and be well, Sir Apprentice."

Dworkin didn't say another word as he led Keslar through white corridors and quiet gardens until they reached the central, main building all others seemed to branch off of. He was brooding, with shoulders nearly to his ears and a stiffness to his gait. Keslar's heart tumbled from his throat to his gut with every step, imagining the worst and still wishing for the best. He let his hand run along the rough stucco of the walls and tried to come up with something to say to the High Master once they were face to face. Back in the dungeon things had been insane, but this was the moment he'd been waiting for ever since the Master had brought a scared little orphan in front of the council.

Dworkin stopped before a plain wooden door. He grasped the small knob but turned to Keslar instead of opening it. "I should warn you, Darian... well, isn't quite himself."

"What do you mean?"

Dworkin shook his head. He seemed to search for the words but couldn't find any so just opened the door instead. Keslar could see that something was gravely wrong, but couldn't fathom what. They had gotten the High Master to the healers, to the Great Mother herself. Everything was supposed to be all right.

"Darian." Dworkin's voice took on a gentler, almost parent like tone as they stepped into the small room. "This is Kelsar. He's an Apprentice Wizard. He's the one who helped save you."

High Master Darian sat with his back to them, staring out the window. His hair had been washed and once again hung in thick black waves to his shoulders, his tattered scraps of clothes had been replaced with a set of high quality travel clothes that by the size Keslar assumed had come from Dworkin's own pack. He didn't react to Dworkin's voice or them entering the room.

Keslar moved around the chair, bowing slightly with his hands clasped, hoping that no one could see the way they shook. "It is an honor to finally meet you again, High Master."

The High Master continued to stare out the window without moving a muscle. There was an emptiness to his dark gray eyes, almost as if this wasn't even the real man but some kind of living statue made of him.

Keslar's eyes burned and his throat wanted to close up. "What's wrong with him? We came all this way, just about killed ourselves getting him here. They were supposed to fix him."

Dworkin started to speak but Great Mother Quinta walked into the room and touched the Duke's arm before turning to Keslar. She stepped closer, resting her hands softly on the High Master's shoulders. "We healed his extensive physical wounds, wounds you do not want to know the tally of. Our friend went through a lot during his time in captivity. Probably more than we know. However, what still ails him is out of our expertise."

"What's wrong with him?" Keslar flinched as he heard his own voice crack.

Dworkin sat down on the edge of the bed and buried his face in large, calloused hands for a moment before folding them and pressing them to his lips almost like a prayer. "We think that he's locked inside his own mind, or possibly in his own magic. His body can do everything he needs to stay alive. He can walk, eat, sleep, whatever he's told or led to do. But he can't speak, can't even react. He's just a shell."

"Not an empty shell," Quinta whispered with a soft smile, "more of a vault. A safe and secure place to protect the most important parts of him until they can be unlocked and put back in place."

"Can he hear us?"

Mother Quinta shrugged. "We can't be sure, but it's good to think positive. Treat him as if he can and then it's of no harm either way."

Keslar nodded. That, at least, was logical and he liked logic. The order of it and the reliability. Like the cadence of a spell.

"Is there nothing we can do for him?" He whispered, tearing his vision away from those empty gray eyes.

His heart wrenched when he saw the desperate way Dworkin looked at the Great Mother. He was so used to seeing the Duke as powerful and in control. Even after the deaths of Bartol and Duntiel, he had been the one to hold them all together even though he was hurting himself. To see him look so broken and helpless scared Keslar more than anything.

"Let's get you both something to eat and we'll discuss it. The High Master should rest."

39

Darian wanted to scream more than he ever had before in his life. He could sense all of them standing around looking at him as if he were dead, could feel the Great Mother's warm hands on his shoulders, and could do nothing. He wanted to jump up and tell them all that he was here and perfectly fine, to tell young Keslar that he remembered him and was so proud of how far he'd come from that scared little orphan. Mostly he wanted to hug his brother and take away those stress lines forming around his eyes.

The walls that he had thrown up around himself and his magic to block the blast wouldn't release the way they were supposed to. He'd tried every spell he could think of, tried pounding against them, even pleading. Nothing would work. If their magic was a well inside them, he'd fallen to the bottom and someone had slid the cover over the top. Nothing he did seemed to make any difference.

Footsteps started filing out of the room. Soon he would be alone again. He wasn't sure what was worse, being stuck in the silence with no ability to do anything about it or being surrounded by friends and being unable to interact with them. Two sets of feet left the room, but the heaviest set paused and came back to him.

Dworkin squatted down in front of him, eyes shining with unshed tears. For the longest time he just remained there as if waiting for a response he knew wouldn't come.

"Why couldn't you have just listened to me?" Dworkin growled, hands balling into fists on Darian's knees. "I told you what Leslien saw, I told you that you were in danger, but you just couldn't listen. Why do you always have to be so blasted stubborn?"

He didn't have an answer even if he could have spoken it. He'd been in such a rush that night and distracted by the storm and his annoyance at being called to a meeting so late. Even his own senses had been on high alert and telling him something was wrong but he had pushed them away and barreled through. He would never be able to repay Dworkin for all the pain and suffering that mistake had caused, but if he could just find a way out of his own mind, he'd spend the rest of his life trying.

Dworkin sighed and pushed to his feet. "It's my fault too. I should have rode out looking for you instead of using the storm as an excuse to trust you and wait. I should have killed that bastard before he had a chance to harm you or Duntiel."

You never would have been able to, Darian thought with a sad little laugh, *even I couldn't do that.*

"I know you're in there, brother, and I know you can hear me." His hand landed heavy on Darian's shoulder, shaking slightly as it squeezed. "We're going to figure this out. No matter what it takes, we'll figure it out just like we always do. I can't lose you, too."

Dworkin made a choked sound in his throat before quickly leaving the room and pulling the door closed behind him.

His brother's tears stoked the angry fires already boiling inside Darian. He kicked and smashed his fists against the wall. He tried to climb it but there were no hand holds. He tried to dig underneath it but only found black darkness that resisted his touch and burned his thoughts. Frustrated, he retreated back and sat cross legged on the ground, cloak wrapped around him. He wasn't giving up, just like he knew Dworkin wouldn't, but he needed time to think and plan.

Dworkin was right, somehow they would solve this puzzle just like they always had in the past. Then Zarentle would pay. Darian wasn't sure how but he would have his revenge. For being kidnapped, for this spell, for the pain Dworkin and young Keslar had been put through, for all the wizards and two fine knights that had been sacrificed in his name, even for the deception and abandonment of his mother. More than anything else, for all the lonely nights he'd spent longing for the father he never knew, and wished that he still didn't.

40

He nodded his thanks as the girl set a plate of food in front of him but he wasn't hungry. Keslar scarfed it down as if he had never seen food before and in some ways Dworkin envied him that. To be so confident in the adults around you that you could still be starving when everything seemed to be falling apart. It was no fun being the adult that everyone looked to to hold everything together. He picked at the food but his stomach was already too full of emotion to eat much.

Instead, he studied the faces around him. A handful of healers floated around the room, serving food or checking in on those eating, but most of the people around him were patients. Most were bandaged in one way or another, a few even missing limbs. Dworkin had seen a lot of injuries and a lot of suffering in his time, but to have so much of it in one place was unsettling. Even though the healers did everything they could to keep the patients comfortable and calm, there was still a horror in every set of eyes that met his that he couldn't shake. Still, it had to be better than the cold, blank look that Darian wore right now.

"Gentlemen," Mother Quinta called, leading a young girl to their table, "this is Disciple Carly. She has seen things that just might be able to help."

Keslar's eyes went wide and he nearly choked on a bite of meat. When he was able to breath again, his cheeks flamed bright red. Dworkin couldn't help but smile. Carley was a lovely young girl and he recognized her as the one who had been speaking to Keslar in the garden.

"By all means," Dworkin pushed away his still full plate and motioned to a seat at the table.

Carly and Mother Quinta settled onto the benches, Mother Quinta gently pushing the plate back towards Dworkin. Carly clasped her hands in her lap nervously and barely looked up from where she picked at a fingernail, while Mother Quinta leaned her elbows against the table and smiled encouragingly.

"Before I came to the mount, I lived in a little village between Arnis and the Great Forest. There was an old man who lived on the edge of town who had pretty strong magic but had never been trained."

Keslar winced with a hiss and Dworkin turned to him with an eyebrow raised. The boy shrugged. "If someone with magic is never trained, it can make them go crazy. The stronger the magic, the crazier they can become."

Dworkin blinked, remembering how his father had hesitated sending young Darian to the Isle for training. He hadn't been certain it would be best for a young boy who had already been uprooted so many times. Considering the level of Darian's skill, what could have possibly happened had they not sent him?

"Yes, and this man was no exception," Carly continued with a nod. "The children of the village always seemed to annoy him but my older brother more than most. One day Micah, my brother, was caught stealing apples from the man's tree again. The man chased him down the street, yelling some words none of the village understood and waving his hands at Micah. My brother just laughed it off and went to bed, but the next day he woke up covered in boils and sores. He could hardly move without one popping open and causing him great pain."

Dworkin cleared his throat. "I'm very sorry, Disciple, but what does this have to do with Darian?"

"Patience, your grace," Mother Quinta said quietly.

He was practically crawling out of his skin but he forced himself to give a nod. Carly glanced at them all before taking a breath to continue.

"My parents tried everything. All the home remedies they could find, the town wise woman, and even saving up money to travel here to the Mound. Nothing would work. The Healer's told them that it was a magical wound and nothing could be done so they brought him home and tried to make him as comfortable as possible. Then, one day, a tall man passed through the village. He had long red hair with pointed ears poking through and his eyes were slit like a cat's."

Keslar gasped and leaned forward. "You've seen a Wylthem? Up close and in person?"

"I didn't realize it at the time but yes." Carly nodded, her eyes glazing over as if she relived the moment. "He saw my brother laying in the sun on the cot Mom had made for him since the heat seemed to help dry up the sores for a little while. He walked up and talked to my brother for a few moments, then ran his hand over my brother's whole body and gave my mother some herbs from his pack. He told her to have Micah drink a tea from the herbs that very night. The next morning, the sores were completely gone as if they'd never been there. Micah never would say what the Wythelm said to him but he was a changed boy after that."

Keslar practically jumped out of his chair, a wide grin spreading across his face. "So all we have to do is find the Wythelm and they can heal Darian."

"And how do you expect to do that?" Dworkin growled, pushing a hand through his hair. "No one knows how to get into Melcader, except the man who can't talk to us. People have searched the whole of the Great Forest without having found it, or they're dragged out looking like pincushions from archers no one ever saw."

Keslar stared at him open mouthed for a moment before

collapsing back into the seat. He hated to take away the boy's hope but it just wasn't realistic.

"That is true, your grace," Mother Quinta said quietly, patting his arm, "but you of all people should know there are those with Wythelm blood amongst us. I know of a man in Arnis who runs a shop just outside the castle walls. He came to me when the wounds on his ears became infected."

Keslar cocked his head. "Wounds on his ears?"

"From humans cornering him and cutting off the tips of his ears." Quinta's eyes dropped to her hands for a moment before looking back up at the young wizard. "Not everyone is as excited to see a Wylthem as you are, child, even those that are only half breeds."

Keslar's eyes widened and he shrank into himself. "Yeah, I know how that feels."

Mother Quinta tapped Keslar's dark hand with a nod. Dworkin pressed his lips together with a grunt. He'd seen the way some had treated Bartol when the man first came to Marslic, heard whispers at court. It broke his heart that such a fine young man had had to deal with the same, or that someone could be so evil to the half breed that Mother Quinta spoke of. He thought of his wife and was thankful that her ethereal beauty did not come with such obvious signs of her heritage.

"Or anything different for that matter," Mother Quinta continued, her eyes ablaze. "Why just last week there was a Cregas here delivering some medicine. At least one patient nearly denied treatment knowing it was from them. Come to think of it, he was in search of the High Master."

"What for?" Keslar asked even though his eyes drifted to Dworkin.

Quinta shrugged. "I'm really not sure."

Dworkin gritted his teeth to stop himself from saying he didn't care what a Cregas wanted with Darian. Probably to ask forgiveness for slaughtering more humans or something. He would let his friend deal with it once they had him healed. He cleared his throat and tried to bring the subject back to the matter at hand.

"And this half breed, he has the healing power of a Wylthem?"

Mother Quinta nodded. "Probably not as strong as a pure blood but yes, he seemed to have some. He helped a few of our more serious patients while he was here. You'll find him along the East wall of the city, selling teas and other herbs. Though please, his name is Jalden, not half breed."

"I really should go to Darsile to consult with the king over this new threat." Dworkin scrubbed a hand over his beard, his gut twisting in knots. "I have to get Darian the help he needs, but I'm honor bound to put kingdom above all else. I can't be in two places at once."

Quinta rose from the table and straightened her skirts. "It's late. Stay the night and maybe an answer will present itself in the morning once you are fully rested."

41

Keslar

He lay in the borrowed bed, staring at the too low ceiling, as Dworkin tossed and turned on the other side of the room. He listened to the older man grunt and growl for long moments before rolling over to face him.

"What does it mean to be honor bound?"

Dworkin sighed and flopped on his back. "It means that I made an oath to king and kingdom. I vowed to put the safety of Ramleaj and her people above anything or anyone, including my own family."

"A lot of the Masters like to complain that the High Master doesn't take his oaths serious enough."

Dworkin sat up and stared at him, face twisted by shadows in the dim light. "For what? I've never known a man more dedicated to service, and diplomacy, and all the other stuff you wizards are supposed to stand for."

"I know that," Keslar whispered, fiddling with the edge of the blanket he had been given. He really shouldn't have said anything but there was no turning back now. "You know how a wizard isn't allowed to marry or have children? A lot of the older Masters pretty much took that as meaning that we shouldn't have any ties outside the guild. No family at all, and Darian refused to give you and your family up. They told him that it was a conflict of interest being so close to a Duke and that it would make the other dukes and lords think he was showing favoritism. He told them that the moment they could prove he had done such a thing, he would consider renouncing his station, but he would never renounce his family."

Dworkin was quiet for such a long moment, Keslar almost wondered if the man had finally fallen asleep. When he spoke again, his voice was thick with emotion. "How do you know all this, Apprentice?"

"I listen. Not eavesdropping mind you, I just kind of blend in to the background so people forget that I'm there and can hear them."

"Well," Dworkin gave a small laugh and fell back on the bed, "that certainly does sound like something that Darian would say, but being High Master he has a little more leeway than I do. If the king feels that I have broken my oath, he very well could take Marslic from me and it has been in my family for many many generations, ever since Yerlin and the Sword of Light. Then where would my children live? Who would care for the people that have come to depend on me?"

Keslar perked up, resting his head on his fist. "Sword of light?"

"Yerlin was my ancestor and the first Duke of Marslic." Dworkin yawned as his voice slipped into the cadence of a story told many times. "According to legend, Rosewood forest was a lot bigger back then and a wild, dangerous place after the Wylthem left. Yerlin used the Sword of Light to clear it out and make it safe. The sword was a magical thing that could light your way through the darkest night or glow to let you know trouble was near, it could cut down the most evil creature in one swipe where all others would fail. They say if you held it to a man's heart it would tell you if he was lying by the color it glowed."

Keslar snuggled down into his blanket, images of Dworkin

wielding a glowing sword filling his mind. "What happened to the sword?"

"It was lost to antiquity generations ago, if it ever even existed." The bed creaked as Dworkin rolled towards the wall and pulled the blanket over his shoulder. "Get some sleep, kid. We'll figure out what to do tomorrow."

He yawned and stretched then sighed. "There's nothing to figure out. You'll go to the king like you have to, and I'll take Darian to Arnis."

"Of all the cursed places in the world, why did it have to be Arnis?" Dworkin mumbled, sounding half asleep.

"What's wrong with Arnis?" Keslar sighed with a small laugh. "It's a city much like any other. All I really learned about it in history class was that it's mostly a fishing port."

Dworkin growled and shifted position again. Keslar grinned thinking of the man who could pass out without a problem on the hard ground or leaning up against a tree.

"It's the Dukedom of my uncle, a greedy and nasty man who was always jealous that my father inherited the better dukedom and he had to marry to obtain one. He always seems to be trying to come up with one trick or another to take Marslic from me."

"All the more reason for you not to go there then."

Keslar grinned as Dworkin growled again. He had seen the way the man looked at Darian the whole trip to the mount. These men weren't just friends, they were brothers in every sense except blood and it made sense why Darian refused to give that up. The fact that Dworkin had larger responsibilities that kept him from being the brother he felt he should be must be eating the man alive inside, but if this continued, neither of them were going to sleep that night.

He hummed softly to himself, weaving the words in his mind long before saying any of them out loud and even then as quietly as he could. The spell lilted like a lullaby and a soft sparkle formed close to the ceiling and started drift down over them.

"I know what you're trying to do and it's not going to-"

Dworkin's protest was cut off by a sharp yawn and not picked up again. The last thing Keslar heard was deep snores before he whispered the last line of the spell and fell into a dreamless sleep himself.

42

The Golden Gryphon was crowded and loud. A small band played music in the far corner while people talked and laughed at the various tables or around the long bar that dominated one wall. The whole place reeked of too many food smells mixing together, of ale both fresh and stale, and all the mixtures of smells that humans seemed to constantly carry around themselves.

No one noticed the lone figure that slipped in the door draped in a robe the same browns and blacks of the woods and shadows, the hood far over her face. Her eyes scanned the room as she slid along the wall to take a seat at a back table, as far from the rest of the patrons as she could get.

Letting the hood drop from her head, Miramel checked to see if anyone was looking her way. Even though no one seemed to be and her powerful hearing didn't pick up any changes in the conversation or laughter, she kept her hand close to the sword on her hip. Arnis might be a bit more of a melting pot than the rest of the human world but that didn't mean it was safe. She had left her bow with Arilla in the small stable but her silver sword and the daggers hidden within her clothes were plenty to protect herself.

"Didn't think I'd be seeing you again after the last time, deary."

She smiled up at the bent old woman who hobbled over to her table. Selte and her brother Raslen had been running this establishment for nearly as long as Miramel had been visiting. They did their best to be certain anyone was welcome and free from harassment under their roof. If only there were more humans like them.

"Those men got what they deserved treating a poor healer that way just because his ears were a different shape," she growled, cupping the warm mug Selte set in front of her, "but, not everyone sees it that way so it was best I lay low for a while."

The old woman slid into the seat across from her with a smile and a wink. "No arguments here. What's brought you back out of your forest though?"

Her eyes swept the room again before she leaned forward. "I fear something is wrong with a friend and need to find him."

"And you thought to start here since this be were ye two met," Selte laughed. "Or because the last ye saw of each other was when you had that bit of fun here?"

Miramel frowned and leaned back. "I never said it was fun. Doubt he would either."

"I know, I know. Sorry to say I haven't seen him since I have you, I assumed he was dealing with the aftermath of the attack."

"Attack?" Miramel's heart practically pounded out of her chest as her throat went dry. What had they missed staying isolated deep in their forest?

Selte's eyes widened and her lips pursed over toothless gums. "You haven't heard? The Wizards Guild was attacked, nearly wiped out in one night. No one knows who could have done it."

"And the High Master?"

"Lord Ranklus claimed to have seen him in the King's court but between you and me, some of his men say the High Master didn't seem himself and that Duke Marslic came searching for him not long after." Selte reached out to pat her hand then pushed out of the chair. "I'm sure you two will find each other soon enough. Ye always do. Now, let me get you something to eat."

Miramel just nodded as the woman ambled away. She sipped at the warm mug and tried to work through everything she knew. Something in her gut told her the attack had been the night of that cursed storm, when she had seen the vision of Darian facing a dark stranger. He had been at the attack, she was certain of that, just as certain he had survived. But that still didn't explain what she had felt just the other day, or why the foster brother he spoke so highly of would be searching for him. She shivered despite the warm liquid sliding down her throat. Nothing she saw could explain what kind of force could not only get on to the Island but take out the whole Wizards guild. Or what that meant for the rest of them.

43

Standing at the crossroads and watching the two horses amble away nearly killed him. He breathed deep through his nose and let it out slowly through his mouth but it did nothing for the swirling feeling in his gut. He shaded his eyes with his hand and watched them until they were barely more than specks.

The Healers had found an old brown mare called Mercy that they could spare for Keslar so Darian was once again astride Ebony, though his tattered purple cloak had been replaced with one of solid black. From this distance you would never know something was wrong. He rode with his back straight and head forward, if asked he would dismount and walk, if food was set before him he would eat. But it wasn't him. His eyes didn't crinkle with laughter when Dworkin told a horrible joke, or roll if someone had a different plan than he did. He should be casting spells just to show off for young Keslar, or lecturing Dworkin about such a crazy rescue attempt. They had his body, but they still didn't really have Darian.

"I will be with them the whole way." Nemclis lay his massive head on the ground at Dworkin's side. "We'll get this fixed and join you in Darsile soon."

Dworkin absently scratched the dragon's scales and sighed. "You can't go into the city with them."

"No harm will come to either of them. I promise it on my life."

The force of the wind as Nemclis took to the air nearly knocked Dworkin off his feet. Seeing the massive shadow catch up to the two riders calmed his nerves slightly, even if Keslar did glance up then shake his head in that annoying teenager way.

He continued to watch until he could no longer see them, just as he had watched the dove flit into the sky early that morning, taking his message back to Marslic. He'd thought about lying to his wife but knew that she'd see right through that, so had painted everything in the best light he could without outright lying. Hopefully, by the time he had to face her wrath everything would be set right and she'd be too happy to stay mad at him. Now both dove and companions were gone and he was left alone on the road, his heart split in three directions.

"Come on, old girl." He patted Mist's neck then swung into the saddle and turned her head towards the other fork. "We have our own duty to fulfill. Standing on this road isn't going to help anyone."

44

She grinned from the shadows of the forest as she watched the small parties go their separate ways. She considered taking out the human warrior as he stood there alone. It would be so easy to be upon him before he even knew she was coming. But something had caught her attention. A feeling radiated from him, or something he carried that had made her curious. She wouldn't be done with him until she figured out what it was.

With a hand on the neck of her steed, she turned and opened a portal, stepping through to Zarentle's throne room.

He was still moping on his throne as she approached, a Kaldec sleeping at his feet like a fine hunting hound. She moved to the center of the floor and stood at attention, waiting for him to acknowledge her.

"Are the humans caring for my son?"

She wet her lips as the Kaldec raised it's head, snake tails springing to life to snap and wave in the air. She placed a hand on her steed's black neck to calm him and cleared her throat.

"They have taken him to the human healers and cared for his physical wounds. Now they have parted ways. My guess is that the human warrior rides to consult with his king as your son and the young wizard are headed in the direction of Arnis, just outside of the Great Forest."

She didn't mention how intrigued she was by the shiny bauble the human warrior carried. Every time he pulled it out, it was as if the thing was singing to her. She would love to follow him and try to learn more about it, but she had a feeling that was not the path Zarentle would put her on.

Zarentle nodded and held up his hand, a glass of blood red wine appearing out of no where. "They are on the right path at least. Stay with them and keep him safe. I do not trust that scrawny child to watch over him alone."

"Of course, sir." She took a step forward, trying not to react as the Kaldec started to growl. "If the human king is to be notified, he will probably raise his forces and make plans to attack. Should we prepare for battle, my lord?"

He sipped at the wine and grinned. "And what do you think they will be able to do against me? I have already taken out their wizards and they fight amongst themselves nearly as much as they do the other races. Let them come, it will keep the pets busy until Darian returns and we can take this land for real."

Her teeth clenched. She hated to admit that he was probably right. Of all the dimensions she had helped Melteze take, there was a reason he had left this one to Zarentle to move on first. It was not seeming like she would get to taste the excitement of battle or the joy of victory this time. She would be relegated to baby sitter for a spoiled little prince who didn't even want the title while the inhabitants basically destroyed themselves.

45

Braslic

Braslic sat in the pub and stared at the gates. Getting into Darsile hadn't been a problem. The massive tiered city had so much traffic flowing in and out that hardly anyone had noticed a tiny Cregas and his crabby llama entering. He'd found halfway decent lodging in the bottom tier and every day walked his way through the second tier and up to the final gates that blocked off the regular people from the royal lands on the very top of the hill.

For days now he had tried to gain an audience with the king and been turned away every time. He'd even tried invoking Darian's name just to be told the High Master wasn't in residence and to go away. Many times he'd thought about just turning around and going back home but then this whole time would have been a waste. They would be right back where they were before he left. Or maybe worse. Who knew what had happened while he was gone.

"Hey, Tarik," a voice called out nearby, "you letting children drink at the bar now? Maybe we should get a cushion so he can reach the table properly."

Braslic bristled but tried to keep his head down. Drawing attention to himself or causing a ruckus wasn't going to help his cause any.

"Leave it be, Fanir." The old man from behind the bar called back.

Fanir didn't listen. He and his friend rose from their table and moved over to circle around him. One kicked his feet under Braslic's and they all had a good laugh over how Braslic's didn't touch the floor. Braslic just set his mug on the table so that his hands could rest in his lap, much closer to dagger or ax but not touching them just yet.

"I have no business with you, humans."

"Well, maybe we have business with you," Fanir snarled, leaning in until the smell of ale on his breath was overpowering. "You Cregas think you're untouchable up there in your mountains, making the prices of metal so high blacksmiths struggle to stay in business. Then you turn around and set up shop in a town, selling goods at half the price because they don't have to pay your ridiculous mark up."

Braslic swallowed. He knew a few Cregas had chosen to leave the caves and live out in the human world but had heard none of this. The price of ore was supposed to be the price of ore. Buyer did not matter.

"I have no idea what you're talking about and just want to finish my ale."

One of Fanir's friends laughed and smacked Braslic hard on the back. "Then I guess you know nothing of the ones who took over the caves out by the shore and demand tribute from any fishing boats or they destroy the ships?"

No, he didn't. He realized he really didn't know much beyond the caves and the small news he got from Darian. Why hadn't Darian ever mentioned any of this?

Before he could say anything, one of the men slapped the large hat off his head. The bright sun immediately blinded him and his skin felt like it was being held to the fire.

"I told you to leave it be," the old man snapped much closer.

Braslic's hat was shoved into his hands so that he could shove it back on. As his eyes adjusted again, he realized his attackers were no longer paying attention to him or the old barkeep with a broom hovering over him. Everyone was staring at the gray horse thundering through the city towards the castle gates. The rider was a tall man, dressed in light travel armor with his blond hair laying over a red cape, a rearing stallion emblazoned across it.

Braslic leaned for a closer look. He had seen that symbol somewhere before. As the gates swung open and the man rode inside without even slowing, he thought of a mountaintop battle and three soldiers slaughtered.

"Wasn't that Duke Marslic?" One of the men gasped.

Fanir nodded, his jaw slack. "In a real hurry too. Maybe the rumors be true. Something be happening. Something big."

Braslic fell back in his chair with a sigh. Duke Marslic, good friend of Darian and the man who's men had attacked them in that mountain pass was the same man? Guess there were a few things the High Master had chosen not to share.

46

He paced the small meeting room feeling like a bird in a gilded cage. As soon as he'd strode into the great hall, Matthias had insisted that they speak in private. Of course, a king couldn't just disappear without raising suspicion so he had been waiting for at least a half hour for Matthias to find a proper time to excuse himself.

Finally, the king rushed into the room and shut the door firmly behind him. "You look absolutely exhausted, my friend. Sit and have a drink."

"This isn't just a friendly chat, your majesty," Dworkin snapped but collapsed in the nearest chair with a sigh anyway, "but a bit of brandy wouldn't be turned down."

Matthias smiled as he poured two glasses and passed one to

Dworkin before sitting down across from him. The smile disappeared quickly though as he stared into the glass before taking a long swig.

"Your man passed through nearly a week ago with your message. I was growing fearful about not hearing from you again for so long."

"As I stated in the message," Dworkin glanced towards the door and tapped his ear before sipping the drink, "I had to see to a friend before I could come."

Matthias waved a hand to the door and leaned back in his seat. "You can speak freely in here, Dworkin. I've had Clesum double check all the wards on the door that keep people from listening. What is said in this room will not leave it."

"I still don't understand what you see in that man. You could have any master you wanted in your court and you stick with the worst of the bunch."

Matthias winked over his glass. "Well, Marslic had already stolen the best, not that Darian would ever allowed himself to be tied down the way a King's Wizard must be. Clesum does as he's told and stays out of my way for the most part. Anything beyond that I call for Darian."

Dworkin's eyes dropped to the drink he suddenly didn't want anymore. Matthias gave a soft snort and slowly shook his head.

"I was almost starting to believe Darian invincible, he's come through so much with nary a scratch. Problem is, I think he was starting to believe it too." Matthias poured a little more brandy for each of them and leaned forward to lower his voice, despite his talk of the wards on the room. "How is our friend? Your message really wasn't clear."

Dworkin shrugged and tossed back the drink, sliding the glass on the table and shaking his head when Matthias offered another refill. "I didn't want to say too much since I didn't know who would read that message. He's not well, Matthias, and the Healers can't help him. Another wizard is currently taking him to Arnis to see if a special healer there knows anything more."

"And it's killing you being here instead of going with him."

Dworkin raised his eyes to the king but only saw his old friend. There was no annoyance or reproach in those eyes that studied him so intently. Not trusting himself to speak, he just grimaced and nodded slowly.

Matthias grinned with a small chuckle. "I was so jealous of you two. The first time your father brought the two of you to court together, you were what, about six? I was fourteen and had just met the woman I was betrothed to marry. My father's health was waning and I feared I would have to take the crown soon. Watching you two run about together as thick as thieves and giving the castle staff hell, I couldn't help but think that that was what childhood was supposed to be and regretting that I had missed out on all that."

Dworkin didn't know what to say. He remembered that trip, too, and the way two little boys had looked to the young prince in awe. How so many of their games had revolved around being knights in his service and conducting grand deeds, saving maidens from castles, and slaying dragons. They had all grown up to fulfill their dreams in their own way, but it certainly wasn't how they had imagined it.

Matthias cleared his throat and swiped at his face, a touch of wetness left on his cheek matching the burning in Dworkin's throat. "He will be fine and back to driving us crazy in short order. In the meantime, it is up to us to be sure there is a kingdom for him to come back to. Tell me more about this threat that we face."

"I really don't know what I can tell you. This man, or whatever, has magic like I've never seen before. Magic that even Darian couldn't handle. He took out the whole Wizard's Council and held the High Master captive. What are we supposed to do against a man like that? Especially without Darian."

"We have to do something," Matthias roared, jumping to his feet to toss the glass back on the tray. "People are already wondering why I have not acted on the attack of Wizard's Isle and if they find out that the High Master is injured, or that there is some menace just north of here that I haven't handled? They'll have my head on a platter, Dworkin, and maybe yours right next to it."

Dworkin scratched at the beard that had grown too long being on the road and wished he had an answer. "Darian is the only one who truly knows what we are up against. We can not make much of a plan until we are able to speak to him."

"And when will that be? Can you promise me that this healer in Twins forsaken Arnis will be able to bring him back?"

"No." Dworkin choked on the sob that filled his throat. No matter how positive he tried to stay, every moment of his life was consumed by the thought that he would never get his brother back. "But we have to buy some time. Going in to battle without all the information is foolish and will get many of our men killed. We at least have to give Keslar a chance to try."

Matthias sighed and leaned his hip against the table, nodding slowly. "They should reach Arnis by the end of the week, we can't expect to move out that quickly anyway. You will remain here and start preparing our troops, call it training or whatever you have to. This threat to the north and Darian's condition stays between us until we receive word from your wizard friend, or hopefully, Darian himself."

47

Clesum

The King's Wizard grinned as he leaned back in his thick arm chair and released the listening spell. He wasn't certain if Matthias was a trusting fool or just doubted his abilities to do anything of the like, but either way, he would realize just how wrong he was soon enough.

Clesum picked up the scrying glass next to him and said the activation spell. The light pulsed around the glass until finally Master Fenim's face filled the glass. Clesum fought not to roll his eyes. The fool had answered his call right in the middle of Arnis's grand hall judging by the sights and sounds behind him.

"This had better be important, Clesum. I'm knee deep in festival preparations and don't have time for any more false leads."

Clesum snorted. "Important? This is massive. Blast it, Fenim, isn't there somewhere you can speak privately?"

Fenim growled a little but the image turned to red tinted black as he shoved the glass in his pocket. After a lot of shuffling and shifting, Fenim appeared again, red faced and out of breath but seemingly alone.

"I really don't have time for this, Clesum."

"Oh, so you and your duke no longer hope to get rid of Duke Marslic, or maybe Matthias himself?" Clesum raised his hand as if about to wave away the connection. "Sorry to have bothered you then."

"Wait." Fenim sighed and glanced around. "What do you have?"

"Secrets, my friend. The king and Marslic do not want anyone to know that the High Master was gravely injured in the attack of the Isle. They fear the people will lose confidence if it is known he was wounded and they have done nothing."

Clesum watched the information sink into Fenim's tiny brain. He'd decided last minute to keep the information about the supposed dark power to the north to himself. At least until he could look into it more.

Fenim sneered. "The people do love that little upstart, but as soon as he's been to the Healers he'll speak out in their favor."

"They have tried that already but there is still something wrong. They are trusting a mouthy apprentice to sneak him into your city to see some kind of special healer."

"I bet I know just the one." Fenim started to pace the room, tapping his chin as he thought. "An annoying thorn in his own right but not hard to deal with, and an apprentice? What were they thinking?"

Clesum grinned. "They were thinking no one would know, and if they want to keep it that way they will pay dearly."

Fenrim started to smile then stopped suddenly. "But who's to say once they get the High Master back they won't just fix everything, or toss us all in the dungeon?"

"Who said we were going to give him back?" Clesum laughed. "Once they've made the proclamation there will be no way to change it without revealing themselves. Then we quietly dispose of the bastard and his little apprentice. No witnesses and we get everything we've ever wanted."

"Finally," Fenrim said with a wide grin. "I will inform the duke right away and set things in motion."

"Proceed carefully and remember not to mention my name. We can not risk being tied together just yet. We'll talk soon."

48

Finally, the city of Arnis came into view. Keslar pulled the horses to a stop and took a deep breath of the salty sea air. The city spread out below them, a walled fortress except for the side open to the sea. The coast line curved to make a small bay that sheltered all the docked fishing ships, the rocky coast dotted with dark caves culminating with a lighthouse built of the same sandy colored rock that surrounded the city.

"We're almost there, High Master," he said, pulling Ebony closer. "You'll be back to normal soon."

It had been a long journey with such a silent companion. Day after day of being so close to his idol but having the man stuck in this diminished form had drained him in ways he had never imagined. He had taken Great Mother Quinta's advice to heart and talked the whole trip, to the point where if the High Master could hear him, he was probably sick of the sound of his voice.

"You're going to have to stop that." Nemclis dropped his large head close, the rest of his body still halfway down the hill. "No one can know who you travel with until he is healed, especially in this city."

He sighed and cut his eyes at the dragon before looking back to the city. "I know. It's bigger than I expected though, and a lot more crowded."

"Arnis used to be a jewel in the crown of Ramleaj, now its a den of thieves and corruption. Nemclis raised his head and studied the city before blinking. "As for the overcrowding, I think that's partly because of the festival. People come from all the surrounding small towns to join the festivities."

Keslar rose in his saddle and shaded his eyes to see better. "The festival, already? How long have we been traveling?"

"Too long," the dragon snorted, plumes of smoke escaping between his teeth.

Keslar dropped back in his saddle, his chest constricting as his heart shrank into itself. "I was supposed to be a Student by now. Students and higher get to go to Darsile for the High Master's show. Now neither of us will be there."

They sat in silence for a long moment, just watching the people stream in and out. People were dancing and laughing, bright music played from somewhere in the city as colorful flags flapped in the wind. All absolutely oblivious to the dark clouds that hung over them. His eyes drifted north, as if he could look hard enough to see the tower with it's circle of scorched earth.

"This is as far as I can go," Nemclis whispered. "From here on, it's all up to you."

He swallowed hard. Mercy sensed his unease and danced a little in place. He found himself reluctant to part ways with the dragon. The creature had been gentle and caring with the High Master, as well as keeping them safe and taking watch every night the whole trip. Or maybe it was just fears about going it alone from here on out and having everything be up to him.

He nodded and tightened his grip on Ebony's reigns before lightly tapping Mercy's sides with his heels. Together, they made their way down the slope and were quickly swallowed up by the river of people traveling into the city. They were jostled and bumped but moved a little easier being on horse back while most people moved about on foot. He kept Ebony's head as close to Mercy as he dared and held his breath as they approached the gates.

The guards stood to either side of the gates, letting people travel in and out without trouble for the most part. Keslar pulled his hood a little bit higher, worrying he might be questioned, but all around him folks of his coloring and even darker moved about freely without being stopped. Did they not fear the people from the Southern Isles here as they did further North?

Even so, he tensed as he drew closer to the guards but they didn't look his way. As he passed under the great wall, they seemed distracted talking to two individuals that were the size of human children but wore broad hats and covered by layers of loose clothing. Keslar was so busy craning his neck and trying to see if these were the legendary Cregas he had so much about, he almost ran into the Master Wizard standing in the middle of the road. He heard a spell being spoken and turned his head just to see the man wave his hand and put up a small wall that caused Mercy to stop and Ebony nearly run into the back of her.

"My apologies, Master," he called, hoping his voice didn't shake as bad as his legs were. "I got distracted and didn't see you there."

The master moved closer to grip Mercy's halter and pet her long neck. He was a short squat man, with a head full of silver hair and dark eyes that seemed to look straight through Keslar.

"There is quite a lot for a young apprentice to see. What brings you to our fine city?"

"The festival, of course." He kept his voice as bright and light as he could. "With things still not back to normal on the Isle, I took the opportunity to come and see for myself."

The Master nodded slowly. "Yes, yes, such a tragedy. How are things going with the rebuild?"

"I wouldn't know." He swallowed. At least that wasn't a lie. "I haven't been to the Isle in quite some time. I was visiting family when the attack happened and haven't had the courage to return."

Keslar's heart was pounding in his ears and his throat went dry.

It was such an easy lie to call him out on. There was no way the masters would have allowed him to go home to visit family right in the middle of testing season. But the master just smiled and nodded towards Darian. Of course, that just made Keslar even more nervous.

"What about your friend here? Why doesn't he show his face?"

He'd spent much of the trip practicing an answer for just such a question but could still barely find the breath to say it. "This is my uncle, sir. He was injured as a child and it left him deaf and mute. His face is really scarred so he doesn't like to show it much, but I thought he might get some enjoyment from the sights."

"I see." The master shook his head and clicked his tongue. "Poor chap. While you are here we have many powerful healers in residence, even some of less conventional means. Perhaps one might be able to help. Tell them Master Fenim sent you."

"I will keep that in mind, sir. Now, I do apologize but we should get going. We've been in the saddle a long time and would appreciate a rest."

"Yes, of course." The master released Mercy and stepped back. "Welcome to Arnis, apprentice. May it hold all you can imagine."

He nodded to the master with the best smile he could muster then urged Mercy on. He didn't breathe easy until they were dismounting in the stable yard of the inn Nemclis had mentioned, saying he and Darian had frequented it when he was small enough to travel with the High Master.

"The Golden Gryphon, we made it," he muttered, helping the High Master from the saddle. "You recognize this place? I could really use a real sleep. That was too close for comfort, but I guess he believed me so we'll just keep moving."

49

"Your majesty."

Matthias just kept walking. He was deep in conversation with Duke Righteous himself and completely oblivious to any others around him. Their heads bent together over some scribbled report, they rushed down the hallway in their own little bubble like they had been doing for the whole week that Duke Marslic had been in residence. Clesum assumed it had something do with the threat to the North that they had mentioned but still wasn't sure what that was, or a safe way to find out.

He growled under his breath and ducked down a side hallway, jogging to reach the end of the hall before they did and step out in front of them.

"Your majesty," he repeated.

Finally, both men looked up. Duke Marslic had the same annoyed look as usual when they were in the same room. It was no surprise. He was best friends with that cocky little child that Master Frencis had practically handed the world to. King Matthias' expression was more blank, tired and overwhelmed.

"Did you need something, Master Clesum?"

Clesum cleared his throat and straightened his cloak. "The people are concerned, Your Majesty. Tomorrow is supposed to be the big show but there has been no sign of High Master Darian."

Duke Marslic's face went white as he glanced to Matthias. Clesum had to fight not to laugh. They thought they were being so sly and that no one would realize something was wrong.

Mattias cleared his throat and glanced to Duke Marslic before looking back to Clesum. "The High Master has been held up by important business and will not be able to join us for the festival this year. Do you think that you could fill in for him?"

"Of course, Your Majesty," he said, bowing low. "I'm sure I can throw something together."

Matthias nodded and motioned to Duke Marslic that they should continue on. "Thank you, Clesum."

He smiled as they started to walk away. This was his chance to use all the ideas that he had had over the years and prove that he deserved to be the King's Wizard. After this year, even if Darian came back, the king would know that he didn't need to depend on the High Master. He already had a wizard who could do anything that was needed.

His excitement only grew as his pocket started to glow. This had better be good news. As much as he knew his powers were enough to impress at the festival, it would be even better if their plan all came together. Being the King's Wizard was an honor, but there was a position that he wanted even more, and by chance, there was suddenly an opening.

He rushed to his quarters, shutting and locking the door before pulling the scrying glass from his pocket. "What?"

Master Fenim glared at him through the glass. "It took you long enough to answer."

"I was in a meeting with the King. Now what is it?"

Fenim snorted but after glancing over his shoulder settled into a grin. "They arrived just as you said. I spoke to the young wizard as he entered the city. He honestly believes I fell for his story but it was obvious who they were."

"Excellent." Clesum laughed. Everything was finally going his way. "Proceed with things as planned."

Fenim's face fell and he started fiddling with the edge of his cloak nervously. "There is one other thing. The guards said they saw the boy talking to a dragon outside the city."

His teeth clenched and he fought not to roll his eyes. Why did that brat have to have so many powerful friends? What was it about him that people were willing to look beyond the cocky demeanor and hand him everything.

"That must be the dragon pup that he raised. You'll remember the hell that beast caused on the Isle." Clesum cleared his throat and fought to feign confidence. "This can work in our favor. Instead of depending on a courier, we can use the dragon to deliver our message. Less chance of anyone else finding out and we don't have to wait as long for our payoff."

"Are you insane? The beast will swallow me whole as soon as I get close!"

That wouldn't be much of a loss. The only reason Clesum even bothered with Fenim or his Duke was as a means to an end, a way to get what he wanted. Still, he wasn't quite finished with them yet.

"You're a wizard, I'm sure you can figure out a way to protect yourself until you get him to listen to you. Then you make it very clear that if he harms you, Darian is done for. Now just get it done."

Fenim rolled his shoulders and lifted his chin a little. "I have my own duties to complete, King's Wizard, and it is getting late. I will send the dragon your direction first thing in the morning."

Clesum snorted and rolled his eyes. The master had to choose now to grow a spine and insist on having a say? Once this was all over and Clesum was head of the council, he would make sure Fenim paid for this insolence. For now, he would have to let it slide.

"If this all falls apart just because you need a night's sleep to find the courage, I promise you I will be sure that you spend the rest of your life with crotch itch and arms too short to reach. Do not fail me,

Fenim."

50

Dworkin

Dworkin slipped into the first empty room he saw as soon as they were out of sight of the wizard. His only thought had been to be alone for a moment but Matthias followed him silently in and closed the door tightly.

He paced the small sitting room, hands buried in his hair as he tried to remember how to breath. His chest burned and it felt like the small lunch he'd forced himself to eat was going to find it's way back up. He'd spent the whole week bottling up this feeling every minute of the day. It was nearly impossible to keep up the demeanor of running young soldiers through drills and smile at courtiers at dinners he couldn't bring himself to eat, when it felt like his whole world was falling apart. He wanted to scream and shout, to curl up and cry, to pummel something just to get the anger and anxiety out, but if he did any number of those things then someone might know something was wrong. Someone might question him why Darian wasn't at the festival, and just his friend's name would send him spiraling again.

Matthias waited patiently by the door, not saying anything or making any movements. Just waiting for Dworkin bring himself back under control. Somehow, this only annoyed him all the more.

"He's going to be all right," Matthias whispered after a few moments. "They should be at Arnis by now. The young wizard will find the healer and before you know it, Darian will be swooping in with one of his grand entrances and annoying us all."

"I wish I had your confidence. You didn't see him, the shell that he's become. Or the way even the Great Mother recoiled from the magic inside him." He leaned against the back of a settee, his nails digging into the soft fabric. "But it isn't just him, Matthias. I told my wife when I left that I would be home for the festival and I'm not and I have no idea when I will be. We've become complacent and our men are vastly under trained. There is no way I can get them ready to face the type of enemy I saw up there. I lost two men just trying to get Darian out, possibly lost Darian himself. I can't look at these young men and tell them we're just running drills when I'm mostly likely sending them to their death."

Matthias crossed his arms and leaned against the wall, his eyes dropping to the floor. "I know."

His eyes jerked up, meeting his old friend's and for the first time seeing just how the march of time had settled on the king just like the heavy crown he wore. Not even ten years older than Dworkin, he looked much older, more tired than Dworkin had noticed before. There were worry lines around his eyes and streaks of gray starting to show in his hair.

"How many times have the Southern Isles threatened to invade, or a delegation from another country not gone well, or a city cause problems, and you, Darian, and I have quietly fixed it before anyone else could know? How many times have we made sure that our people feel safe and secure by making sure that they don't know about all the political crap that is constantly going on?" Matthias stared at him until he shrugged. He really couldn't count the number of times since it had become so common place. Matthias sighed and shook his head.

"Now imagine how many more things I handle every day without your help. How much else must be going on that you don't even know about. But I still attend balls, and dinners, and endless meetings about trivial things people could fix themselves if they would just try. We may not have asked for this power or all heartache that comes with it, but it's what our fathers and the Twins entrusted us with. All we can do is our absolute best not to make them regret that trust."

Dworkin nodded, forcing himself to straighten and take a couple of breaths. He was still shaky and his stomach in knots, but it was as if he remembered who he was. He wasn't just a man missing his family, or terrified of losing his brother. He was a Duke and a knight of the king, and he needed to start acting like it.

Matthias seemed to read his mind because he pushed off the wall and walked over to lay a heavy hand on Dworkin's shoulder. "That doesn't mean we aren't human, that we don't feel things or get afraid. Fall apart around me any time you need to, friend."

Dworkin nodded and breathed deep, trying to gather the final pieces of himself back together. A sharp knock at the door had them both glancing at each other and then towards the sound. Matthias looked Dworkin up and down and must have decided he wasn't quite ready because he gave a small shake of his head before pitching his voice towards the hall.

"Whatever it is can wait."

There was a sound of shuffling outside the door and then another, not as loud knock at the door.

"Apologies, your majesty," came a soft feminine voice, "but everyone seems to believe you would know where my husband is."

Dworkin's breath caught and he nearly fell over and Matthias just grinned and stepped out of the way. Dworkin pushed past, practically leaping over the furniture to rip open the door.

Leslien stood in the hall, still with her travel cloak on and braided hair looking wind whipped. Their son slept peacefully on her shoulder with thumb in his mouth, as their daughter clung to her skirts, face lighting up as soon as she saw him.

"By the Twins, what are you doing here?" He gasped, catching his little girl as she jumped at him then sweeping the whole family into the room.

Leslien's eyes flicked to Matthias and then the children, her expression dark. Matthias gave her a soft nod before putting on a large smile for the children and holding out his arms for the sleeping little boy. Darius fussed slightly but fell right back asleep in the safe arms of another father as Matthias turned to the blond haired angel clinging to Dworkin.

"Well, hello miss Lera," Matthias cooed, dropping to be on eye level with her, "how about we go get Prince Bran and see the new puppies?"

"Want Daddy," she pouted, hugging his neck even tighter.

Dworkin sighed and kissed the top of her head. "Daddy isn't going anywhere. I just need to talk to Mommy for a minute."

"If there's a puppy you like, we might even be able to talk Daddy into letting you take it home with you," Matthias said with a wink, holding his hand out.

With a slow glance between all the adults, Lera finally nodded and allowed Dworkin to set her on the floor. She took the king's hand and allowed herself to be led out of the room with only a few glances back. Dworkin's heart twisted a little more thinking his daughter was so used to him leaving even the promise of a puppy wasn't enough for her to trust that he would still be there when she returned.

As the door shut, he let out a long sigh then turned to his wife. "Leslien, what were you thinking? It is way too dangerous for you and the children to be traveling right now."

"And I am supposed to know that from the cryptic messages you send? It almost feels as if I would know more if you hadn't sent any at all." She winced as she heard her own voice raise then stepped closer to him, her hand brushing down his arm. "You have been gone way too long and have told me way too little. Dworkin, what is going on? Where is Darian, and our men?"

The carefully curated control that the king had helped him find again crumbled under her gaze. He folded on himself, eyes burning and stomach clenching as it all rushed back on him. Her eyes went wide but she pulled him close, both of them collapsing onto the settee and clinging to the other. It seemed forever before he was able to gather himself to tell her the whole story and by the end they were both crying again.

"Poor Reva," she gasped, thinking of Duntiel's young wife, "she'll be devastated. And Bartol."

Dworkin leaned his head back against the padded seat, his wife snuggled in his arms. He felt like a heel having never really given his men the proper mourning they deserved. It had been just one thing constantly added on top of the other with no time to stop and deal with any of it.

His hand rubbed up and down her back slowly. "I'll tell her personally when I'm able to come home, and of course we'll take full care of her."

"What about you?" She whispered, lifting her head to look him in the eye. "Who has been taking care of you this whole time? I'm certain you aren't doing a very good job yourself."

He snorted and shook his head. "I'll rest when I know my brother is well and my family is safe from that monster."

"Darian would punch you if he heard you say that, you know as well as I do. I've never seen you so exhausted, love."

He kissed her hair and laid his cheek against her forehead, sighing deeply. "I've never been this frightened before."

51

Darian stretched his mental form and yawned even though his physical body did nothing. Not being able to do much of anything, he found himself sleeping most of the time. The rest of the time was spent trying to find ways to bring the walls down even though he knew nothing he'd tried so far had worked. He liked young Keslar well enough but day after day of listening to the kid babble without being able to do so much as respond, was enough to make anyone feel ready to lose it.

But the kid had mentioned the Golden Gryphon. Of course he remembered the place. He might not be able to look around but he could smell the rosemary that Selte added to the rushes to try and combat the smell of stale beer and too many people squeezed into one place. He could hear the horrible band that Raslen had never had the heart to fire so they continued to play in the corner over the chatter of multiple voices. This place had always been a haven in an unfriendly city, and the safest place he could imagine for the young wizard.

"How can I help you, boy?" Raslen called as Keslar led him up to the bar and pushed him into a seat.

Darian quit listening as the boy asked about a room and meal. Something was tickling his awareness. He growled and wished he could turn his head. Something was there, something important, and he couldn't even look to see what or alert Keslar.

His body was moving again. Kelsar must have gotten a room from Raslen and was leading him towards the stairs. They wound through the tables to the back of the room, the general chatter ebbing and flowing around them. Then there it was, a pocket of silence within the noise. Something that brought the thought of the wind blowing through the trees, a brook dancing over the rocks, and animals burrowing through soft earth. Layered on top of the usual scents he caught the soft smell of flowers and moss, of warm dirt and green things growing.

"Miramel," he whispered, pushing again on the walls of his mind. "You're here. Can you feel me? Can you hear me? Miramel, I need you like never before."

Keslar kept walking and the feeling faded but it was still there. Darian kicked against the walls and screamed but nothing changed. Salvation sat a table not ten yards from them, and he couldn't do anything about it.

52

Her eyes never left the stairs as she waited for Raslan to come back down. She would have been curious about the pair he had led up to the rooms anyway. An apprentice wizard and a man with a thick black hood over his face were not exactly an everyday sight, no matter where you were, but it was the feeling she got as they moved past that had really caught her attention. She could not quite place it, and it was nearly too quiet to notice, but it had almost felt as if someone was calling her name. She'd been half out of her seat before deciding to have more caution.

Finally, Raslan walked back down the stairs and towards the bar. She slipped out of her seat and moved to the corner of the bar, waiting for him to look her way.

"What be your need, Missy?" He laughed, glancing her way as he wiped down the bar.

She leaned forward, fighting not to wrinkle her nose at the stench of the cleaner he was using. "That pair that you took upstairs, what is their story?"

"The wizard and his companion?" Raslan snorted with a grin. "Kid says they're here for the festival but he seemed awful jumpy. His friend was an interesting sort as well, wasn't he? They asked about your friend too."

She raised an eyebrow. "What friend?"

"Jalden, the healer you and the High Master helped a while back. Wonder what they be wanting him for."

Selte bustled out of the back with a tray balanced on her hip. "I would assume they be looking for some healing, wouldn't you? Girly, if you're so curious why don't you help me out a bit and take this up to them? Sure looked in need of a good meal if you asked me."

Miramel grinned and took the tray. Selte just winked and bustled back to the kitchen while Raslan added a ticket saying which room number they were in. It just happened to be the room right next to hers. She looked at him for a moment and shook her head before turning. Sometimes she suspected these two of knowing a lot more than they ever let on.

Balancing the tray with one hand, and holding her long robe out of the way with the other, she carefully climbed the stairs and found the proper door. She rapped her free hand against the wood and waited, listening to the quiet whispers and bustling inside.

"Wait right here, okay?" The younger one was saying to his companion. "That's probably just the food I ordered. This will all be over soon, High... uncle."

Her head cocked as the door creaked open. That was an interesting hesitation.

The boy's smile disappeared as he noticed her. He glanced over his shoulder and pulled the door a little further closed before glaring up at her. She found herself liking the kid on sight. She didn't get a single bad vibe off of him besides nerves and secrecy and he obviously cared about whoever it was that he was sheltering.

"You don't exactly look like a serving wench," he said even as his eyes fell on the tray she held and his stomach growled loudly.

She took a deep breath and decided to take a chance, praying that her curiosity was not over riding her common sense. With the flip of her head, the hood fell away and her hair tumbled out around her shoulders. She smiled as gently and warmly as she could, registering how the boy's eyes widened and the hand he held the door with started to shake.

"I am a friend of the owners and offered to help them out since things are so busy." She motioned to the tray and then to the door. "So, can I set this down for you?"

"I'll take it. Thank you." He grabbed the tray from her hand and backed into the room, letting the door start to close.

She rolled her eyes and shoved her foot in the doorway. "Raslan also mentioned you were looking for Healer Jalden. I could take you to him but, after an unfortunate incident, he does not take just anyone. I will need to know what you need him for."

The boy hesitated, looking deeper into the room and back to her. She could feel the fear and confusion radiating off of him, plus a deep tiredness underneath. He had seen a lot in his short years and been holding onto secrets bigger than himself for a very long time. She pursed her lips and sighed, pressing a shoulder into the door gap.

"I understand, youngling. Who ever you have in there, I can see that you care about them very deeply and it is hard to know who to trust. I swear to you that I mean you no harm. Healer Jalden trusts me and if you will do the same, I promise I will take you to him, but you will not find him on your own. He has had to take too many precautions."

The boy thought it through for a moment longer, the swirling feelings inside him nearly making her sick to her stomach. Finally, he pushed the door open and nodded her inside. She smiled gently for him, trying to shove feelings of calm and trust his way as she patted his shoulder before moving past.

The stranger sat on the edge of the bed, not moving, the hood still pulled firmly over his head and face. The odd feeling grew stronger, like someone calling her name from a long distance or through a thick doorway. She moved to stand in front of him but he did not turn to look at her or respond in any way. She raised her eyes to the young man who set the food on the table but did not touch it even though he was obviously starving.

"What ails him that you would be looking for Jalden? There are plenty of very talented Healers in the city."

"We have already been to Great Mother Quinta herself," he whispered, not able to look her in the eye. "His injury is of a magical nature. She suggested that a Wylthem healer might be able to help him and told us about Jalden."

She laughed as his eyes drifted to her ears then dropped to the floor again. "Yes, child, I am Wylthem. My name is Miramel, but the healing abilities seemed to have skipped me. I can handle minor wounds but that is about it. I can, however, tell you whether his injuries are of a type Jalden would be able to help with if you will let me examine him."

She remained as still and silent as possible as the child struggled with the decision. What had life dealt out that this poor child was dealing with such big issues all on his own?

"I guess we don't have much of a choice." He sighed with a shrug before collapsing into a chair. When she did not move and continued to stare at him, he gave a sad little nod.

She smiled softly for him then turned to the stranger. She was not sure why she was so nervous as she reached to flip back the black hood. As the fabric settled around his shoulders, her heart jumped into her throat and her eyes started to burn. Black hair fell across his face as gray eyes stared blankly forward. She was not sure whether to feel horror or relief as she dropped to her knees in front of him and gripped his hands tightly.

"Carame," she gasped, pushing the hair from his face despite the skin crawling feeling that touching him gave her. "Oh, Darian, I have been so worried. What has happened to you?"

The boy jumped to his feet and moved closer. "You know him?"

"We are old friends, youngling. The darkness radiates off of him. How did he become like this?"

"Have you heard about the attack on Wizard's Isle?" Emotion choked the young man's voice as memories filled his eyes. She touched his arm and nodded. "That whole thing was so that the man, or whatever he was, could take the High Master into custody. When we tried to rescue him, he was hit by a massive spell and has been like this ever since. The Healers fixed him physically but couldn't fix his mind."

She laid her hands on either side of his head, choking back a sob as his hair fell over her fingers. "Let me in, Carame."

She closed her eyes and pushed her awareness into his mind, forcing herself past the shuddering darkness. The child was correct, he was physically intact and well, but everything that made him unique and human seemed to be missing. She delved a little deeper and suddenly was assaulted by memories. She held on and forced herself not to run as the images flashed through her mind. She bit the edge of her tongue until she tasted blood to keep from crying out as she relived flashes of everything he had gone through. She fought against the remaining terror and a hefty amount of guilt she did not understand, searching for that which made Darian, well, Darian.

Finally, she saw him even though he could not see her. He stood behind a shimmering purple wall, screaming and pounding against the wall with no effect. She reached out to try and touch the wall but it burned her and knocked her right out of his mind. When she pulled back and dropped her hands, her face was wet with tears.

"The problem is not with his mind," she whispered, wiping at her cheeks. "It is with his magic. He has become locked in his own power without a way out. I do not know if Jalden can help, but he is our best hope within the city. We will go see him first thing in the morning."

She was shaking as she rose to her feet and replaced her own silver hood. With one last long look to Darian, she turned and headed for the doorway. She needed to get to her own rooms before she collapsed, his emotions still rolling through her and his memories filling her mind.

"Miramel?"

She turned and forced a smile for the young wizard.

He blushed a little then made himself busy pulling the hood back over Darian's head. "If you don't mind my asking, what did that word mean? The one you called him? You were whispering it as you did, whatever that was."

"Carame? It is a term of endearment for someone who means a lot to you and you have a close bond with." She smiled, wishing that she could offer the young man some comfort but was afraid that if she touched him, some of the craziness rolling inside of her would rub off. "You are doing a good job with things way beyond what you should have to deal with, Keslar. I will be right next door should you need anything, but try to get some rest and we will head out in the morning."

He walked with her to the door but did not shut it right away as she stepped into the hall. "How do you know my name?"

"He told me." She smiled and nodded to where Darian sat, still as a statue. "He thinks you are doing a good job too. Rest, Keslar. We are all going to need it."

53

Keslar

He was already dressed and ready to go when there came a light rap at the door. To be honest, he had barely slept all. It was all too much in too short of a time. His mind was too full of thoughts, and questions, and fears to relax enough to get some sleep. He doubted he would truly get any rest until the High Master was back to normal and could take on all these responsibilities. As it was, he was really starting to wonder why he had ever been in such a rush to grow up and reach master.

"Come," Miramel whispered as soon as he opened the door, "let us try to get to Jalden while most are still sleeping off last night's revelry."

He nodded and helped Darian to his feet, leading him by the cloak to the door. Miramel smiled sadly and reached out to take Darian's hand, a slight shudder passing through her.

"Darian, I know you can hear me. Just be patient a little longer and all will be fixed." She sighed and moved her hand to his temple, frowning as she seemed to concentrate for a moment. "Follow me. Stay close and do not get lost. Same goes for you, Keslar."

He just nodded and grabbed his staff from where he had leaned it next to the door. He said a quick prayer to the Twins that Darian's was still safe and sound with Ebony's gear.

The city was quiet as they wound their way through the roadways. The only people about were those few opening their shops and stalls for another day. None of them so much as gave the odd little bunch a second glance once it was clear they weren't looking to spend coin.

Miramel stopped in front of a small building in the shadow of the walls at the edge of the city and knocked on the bright blue door. When there was no answer, she growled and knocked louder.

A figure leaned out a window above them, rubbing at his eyes. "What do you want?"

"Are you Healer Jalden?" Keslar called back up. "I was told you might be able to help my uncle."

Miramel grinned but didn't say anything. The man pulled a face then yawned dramatically.

"I am not really taking clients right now."

Keslar's heart sank and his eyes dropped to the ground. He was about to turn around when Miramel took a couple steps back to be seen from the window. She tossed her hood off and crossed her arms, staring up at the man.

"Just open the blasted door, Jalden."

The man sighed and waved his hand, a soft clicking sound coming from the door.

"Come in. I'll be down in a second."

Miramel pushed the door open and ushered them inside. It was like stepping into a different world. The air was cooler and the salt smell of the ocean stronger. Multiple fountains bubbled throughout the crowded room, plants and herbs growing in pots on every available surface. Keslar stopped to look in one bowl and saw a small starfish calmly waving back at him.

"This is incredible."

Miramel smiled and ran her hand over a small fern, the plant seeming to bend and twist until it was fully wrapped around her hand and wrist. "Jalden is water born so it does not surprise me."

"Water born?" Keslar glanced to her then went back to looking around the room.

"There are actually four different types of Wylthem. I am forest born, my affinity is for plants and animals that live in the deep woods. My mother is rock born, she was born in the Ykor Mountains and is tied to the rocks and gems. Water born love any water from streams to lakes but especially the ocean herself. Meadow born are the softest and quietest, liking wide open spaces and plants like crops or wildflowers. Every type used to have their own city spread across Ramleaj but all have been lost except for Melcader."

"I never knew that." He gave a small snort even as his eyes ran over the spines of the books lining a high shelf. "So even just being half Wylthem, he still has an affinity like that?"

Miramel crossed her arms and raised a fine eyebrow. "Well, yes, it is hereditary but why would you think he is half?"

"That's what Great Mother Quinta said."

"Because that is what I told her." The man who had leaned out the window breezed down the stairs, now dressed in a white flowing shirt and tan pants, his feet bare on the wooden floor. "It is slightly easier to fit in when you can claim some ties to the group you are surrounded by. Has not always worked though."

He sighed as he tucked his hair behind one ear. Keslar tried not to stare but couldn't help but see the jagged and scarred skin where the top of his ear ended in a straight line instead of the delicate points like Miramel's.

Miramel crossed her arms and shook her head. "I stuck up for you to father when you wanted to leave the community, to be closer to the ocean, but if he knew about this-"

"I don't care what the great King Jarelt does or does not know. I am not one of his subjects anymore."

Keslar's eyes went wide as he stared back and forth between them. Was he suggesting that King Jarelt was her father? Had Keslar been in the presence of a princess this whole time and not even realized it?

"What about your mother?" Miramel dropped her eyes for a moment before looking back to Jalden. "You should visit. She is not doing well."

Jalden nodded. "I do not figure she is. I tried to convince her to come out here closer to the water with me."

"It is not just..." Miramel stopped as she and Jalden seemed to be listening to a sound Keslar couldn't hear. They all turned as there was a small crash in the back of the shop.

A young human woman slunk forward, hair covering most of her very red face. She was dressed only in a thin shift with a bundle of clothes bunched in her arms. She glanced to the rest of them before giving Jalden a small grin and a wink then rushing out the front door.

Miramel's eyes tracked the girl before turning back to Jalden with a disapproving eyebrow raised. Jalden shrugged with a smile, leaning against a nearby table.

"What can I say? I'm exotic."

"Can we just get to the point here?" Miramel growled. "I would like to be out of this blasted city before another day is done."

Jalden's face grew serious as he pushed up the sleeves of his shirt and motioned to Darian. "There is some massive dark energy flowing off of that one. Healing him is going to cost you. Who is paying?"

Keslar swallowed hard. He had been so focused on getting here, he hadn't really thought about payment. Really, he hadn't even thought of it at the Healers Mount but surely Dworkin took care of it. He still had a bit left of the coins Dworkin had given him for room and board in the city but doubted it was nearly enough.

"You already owe him," Miramel snapped.

Jalden just stared at her coldly. "I do not remember having any debts."

With a sharp growl she paced over and yanked the hood off of the High Master's head. "Who do you think took out the fools who cut off your ears when Duke Arnis would not do anything? Did you think it just accident that you have been able to walk the streets without fear since then?"

Jalden's face drained of color as he pushed off the table and slunk forward. For a long moment he stood eye to eye with the High Master, every now and then glancing to Miramel and then back.

"That was you guys?" he whispered.

Miramel rolled her eyes and nodded.

"I just assumed that it was someone else they had made angry. I never thought a princess and the High Master…We're not even really friends."

Miramel's eyes drifted to the High Master with a tiny smile. "You think that matters to him? There was a wrong in the world, someone was in danger by no fault of their own. He can not just let that slide."

Keslar's heart twinged as foggy memories flashed through his mind. Sitting alone in the smoking ruins of his town, next to the lifeless bodies of his mother and sister, too little to know what to do next. Until the High Master had come in a swirl of purple and scooped him up, given him a hot meal and a good nights sleep before testing him for magical ability. He owed everything about his life to the High Master, and was starting to understand that he wasn't the only one.

Jalden's throat worked like he was preparing to say something but no words came out. Finally, he just nodded and motioned to a chair at the corner of the shop. Miramel smiled as she leaned in to whisper something in the High Master's ear before leading him to the chair and gently pressing him into it. Jalden bustled about for a moment, lighting incense and holding his hands in a fountain of what smelled like salt water for a moment before coming to stand in front of Darian.

Keslar moved closer, curious how any of this might work, when movement towards the back of the shop caught his attention again. This time it was a handsome young man who strode out in just breeches, a shirt and cloak tossed over his bare shoulder. Without even looking at the rest of them, the man strode over and kissed Jalden on the cheek then sauntered out the front door.

This time it was Jalden's face that turned red as he glanced to Miramel. "Like I said, exotic."

54

Nemclis dozed fitfully on the hilltop. He didn't like sleeping so out in the open and couldn't stop thinking about all of his friends. He didn't like having them spread so far apart, and especially didn't like having only the young wizard to watch over Darian. Not that he didn't like the little man, despite their rough start, he just wasn't prepared. If only Nemclis was still small enough to ride in a pouch on Ebony's saddle and spit fire balls at anyone who got too close.

"Wake up, dragon."

He shook himself and blinked his eyes open. A small master wizard stood in front of him, a magic bubble surrounding him as if he expected Nemclis to attack on sight. That wasn't a good sign off the bat.

"What do you want, wizard?"

"You are going to deliver a message for me, Dragon."

He raised his head and laughed, baring his teeth. The little master could only hold that bubble for so long and what happened after that, strongly depended on what he had to say next. "And why would I want to do that?"

"Because you care about High Master Darian and want to keep his secret." The little Master laughed as shock registered in Nemclis. "That's right, we know he's here and we know he's injured. If you don't want his injuries to become more, permanent, you'll listen to what I have to say."

Nemclis lay his head on the ground and allowed small tendrils of smoke sneak out from his clenched teeth. He would comply for the safety of Darian but they wouldn't forget who he was or what he was capable of, and first chance he got he would make them very aware.

"Watch yourself, dragon." The wizard pulled a slip of paper from his robe and held it out. "Take this to Duke Marslic in Darsile, be certain that he knows the importance of it."

Nemclis plucked the paper between two claws and held it up to his eye but couldn't make out the tiny writing. Fire bubbled in his stomach but he just growled and stretched his wings. He took a small satisfaction in watching the wizard be knocked to the ground as he took off, before turning and angeling himself towards Darsile.

55

Darian perked up as another presence entered his mind. He recognized the over dramatic and frivolous feel of Jalden immediately but pushed away the annoyance. No matter what else he was, Jalden was a good healer. Maybe he would be able to do what Mother Quinta hadn't. What Darian hadn't been able to do despite any attempts since.

He stood up and moved closer to the wall as Jalden walked up to him. He couldn't help but grin at the Wylthem's projected self image. He was dressed in flowing robes in all shades of blue and green with embroidery around the edges that flowed in an unfelt breeze. Power glowed around him, shooting out in snake like tendrils to seek out the source of the issue, zipping back to him quickly any time they touched the glowing purple wall.

"Nice to see your little mishap hasn't diminished your self image at all," Darian laughed, pointing to his own ears.

Jalden's face scrunched and he shook his head. Darian sighed. No one outside the wall could hear him, much like out in the real world. That certainly complicated things.

Jalden motioned for him to wait and started to inspect the wall. It circled all the way around Darian, much like the well that he had always described his magic as. After a walk around, Jalden thought for a moment before squatting down and placing his hands against the ground. Darian could feel the gathering of power as Jalden's light grew brighter.

The walls started to shudder and Darian felt the first inkling of hope. Closing his eyes, he reached out and tried to meet Jalden where he worked, sending what he could grasp of his own power. If they could just get the walls to open enough, he could banish the dark energy from his own mind and break this prison. Blue mixed with purple and cracks started to form on the walls.

Suddenly, Jalden stopped and pulled back. Darian felt a whimper rise in his throat and rushed to the walls, begging him wordlessly not to give up. They were so close, why would Jalden pull away?

Then Darian saw what the Wylthem had. Every where that cracks had started to form, a blackness was growing and pressing inward. It was the same dark matter that he had found while trying to dig under the wall, the burning flow that seemed to block his every move.

There was a loud sound outside, pulling at Jalden's attention even as he tried to stay. His image wavered and shimmered before darkening again. Darian raised his head and could faintly hear Miramel shouting and other voices answering. Jalden said something and pointed to the black but Darian couldn't hear what was said any more than Jalden could hear him.

"Stay with me, Jalden," he muttered, sending as much power as he could into the process.

Jalden's image wavered and faded again. Darian could feel a surge of energy as he tried to hold on, but then the healer and all of his power were yanked away. The sudden ripping of Jalden from his mind and body sent a burning pain that made him scream as he was tossed backwards.

56

Braslic

Braslic pulled his llama closer and fought against the crowd. Way too many humans all crammed into one place and only caring about themselves. The caves might be crowded but there was order and organization, not just everyone bumping into each other and pushing past.

That was where he was going. Home. It was obvious he was never going to talk to anyone important without the High Master and no one seemed to know where he was. It had become the talk of the town that he wouldn't be around for some big show. Braslic couldn't care less about the show, he just hated that he had wasted so much time here with nothing to show for it.

He broke free of the crowd and out of the city gates, taking what felt like his first deep breath in ages. He'd never thought he would miss the big wide open spaces of the countryside but anything was better than being caught in that throng of people and animals. He sighed happily as a large cloud passed over the sun and he was enveloped in cool shade for a moment.

He stopped as the shade moved on much quicker than any cloud he'd known. He watched it move further down the path from him then turn sharply to the left and circle around. He definitely had never seen a cloud move like that.

A gust of wind nearly blew his hat off, then the ground shook as a massive green form seemed to fall from the sky onto the hill just ahead of him. As legs, head, and tail seemed to reform themselves into proper form, he realized it was a dragon. He wasn't certain but he was pretty sure that it was the dragon that had allowed him to pass on the mountain path.

"Nemclis, was it?" He called, inching cautiously closer. "Are you all right?"

The large head swung around to face him and rows of teeth showed in what he hoped was a dragon smile. "Little one, I didn't imagine I would ever see you again. You might be just what I need though."

"I'm in your debt after you saved me from that other dragon, but what could I possibly do for you?"

Nemclis held out one foot, a folded piece of paper clutched tightly between two claws nearly as long as Braslic's arm. "I need to get this message to Dworkin, Duke of Marslic, urgently but he's somewhere inside there and I can't get in. Do you think you could find him for me?"

"I've been trying to get in for over a week and the guards won't even look my way. Besides, I have no love for this Duke Marslic. I would help you if I could, dragon, but not if it's to aid him."

Nemclis growled and snorted smoke. "Blast it, little one. This isn't about your issues with the humans or theirs with you. This is about Darian, and possibly so much more."

Braslic's ears perked up and his eyes went wide. He snatched the paper out of Nemclis's claws and unfolded it but it was written in human and he could only pick out a word here and there. Nemclis leaned his head closer but didn't seem to fair much better.

"I don't know exactly what it says," the dragon growled, "but I know that if Dworkin doesn't get it and do as it says, they've threatened to make Darian's injuries permanent, if you get my meaning."

Braslic's attention jerked up to the dragon. "The High Master is injured? Is that why he isn't here?"

"Keep your voice down." Nemclis glanced around before nodding. "Yes, the High Master is gravely injured and seeing a healer as we speak. But if those buffoons get to him before he can protect himself, they'll use him as leverage to get whatever they want from Dworkin and the king. Then probably kill them all and take over the kingdom."

Braslic chewed on the inside of his cheek for a moment. He really didn't care about human politics. One king was about the same as any other in many ways, and Duke Marslic was far from high on his list of people to assist, but they were at least an evil he knew. If someone else took over, there was no telling how it would affect trade or prices, or those humans constantly trying to take what they didn't want to pay for. Besides, the life of the one human who had always been kind and helpful to them was on the line.

"Watch Lurp," he sighed and tied the llama to a nearby tree, "I'll figure something out."

He took another deep breath and headed back into the fray. It was a little bit easier moving with the flow of the humans. He ducked under arms and circled around extra congested areas, until the castle walls were in sight. The gates were open but the guards were checking passes before letting anyone in. From what Braslic had gathered over the past few days, only a few lucky people got to watch the show from inside the castle walls, anyone else had to line the streets and watch for anything that was high enough in the sky to see.

"Pass," one of the guards said in a monotone voice as he drew close.

Braslic swallowed and waved the bit of paper. "I don't have one but I do have this very important message that needs to get to Duke Marslic right away."

"What kind of message?"

He shook his head, shoving the paper in his pocket. "Can't say but it is very urgent. You have to let me through."

"We ain't got to do anything, you mini-man. Now get out of here."

Braslic clenched his teeth as the guard swung the butt end of his pike at Braslic's legs. Tired of talking and tired of constantly being told no, Braslic jumped onto the end of the pike and spring boarded off of it to catch the stone wall above the guard's head. Even as the guard screamed and yelled at him, the stone showed him where her hand holds and foot rests were located and he scrambled up to the top.

He took a second to survey the crowded landscape below him, as guards ran towards him from both directions. How was he supposed to find Duke Marslic in that mass of people before the guards caught up to him? With a grunt and a sigh, he tossed away his large hat and prayed this was one time that being small in a world of large people would actually work to his benefit.

With the guards closing in, he jumped from the top of the wall to land on a vendor's outstretched canopy and slide from that down to the ground. People barely noticed as he squeezed his way into the crowd. He wove his way through, ducking under arms, crawling through or around legs, and all other sorts of demeaning things he'd seem human children do in the large crowds of the city. He figured someone of high standing like the Duke would be near the front with the king, and just prayed that he was still headed that direction since he couldn't really see.

The crowds grew thinner as he neared a large barrier with it's own set of guards. These ones either hadn't been alerted to his presence yet or assumed he would never make it that far. Just beyond the fence holding back the massive crowd, a group of benches had been set up in front of a stage where the Wizard had just started his show. Everyone ooh'd and aah'd over the glittering creatures he created in the air but Braslic searched the crowd.

There, seated just behind the king, leaning in to speak to a dark haired woman, was the man he had seen riding in on horse back. He was dressed in court finery, the bright red cape with a white stallion once again draped over one shoulder. Braslic said a prayer to Mother Mountain that those jerks had been right and took a deep breath. He thought he heard someone behind him yelling to stop but knew that wasn't possible. With clenched teeth, he took a running start and dove through the space between the boards of the fence, straight past a guard who immediately reached for him and just barely missed.

"So sorry, boys," he called over his shoulder, sprinting out in the open now, "important message, can't hang around to chat."

57

Lera squirmed in her father's lap, making lots of little girl sighs and whines. "This boring."

Dworkin's cheeks flushed and he tried to figure out how to admonish her without disagreeing but the women around him just laughed. Leslien patted her daughter's head while Queen Narlise leaned down between her and Prince Bran with a wink and a smile.

"It's definitely not the same as when Darian does it."

Dworkin sighed. The whole crowd seemed to agree. There was a lot of movement and muttering amongst the crowd as Clesum put on his show. No one seemed to think it the dazzling or inspiring show that the King's Wizard had promised.

"Where is Uncle Darian?" Lera whined.

Dworkin swallowed as his throat went dry and his chest tightened. "He's busy, dear. You'll see him soon."

Narlise leaned back again to whisper to Dworkin, "Any word on how things are going?"

"Nothing yet." He sighed and tried to count the days since he had said good bye to Keslar. They should be in Arnis by now. Had they found the Healer? He couldn't shake the nagging feeling that he should never have left them to go alone, no matter what his oath was.

A ruckus behind them caught the crowds attention and had everyone turning away from Clesum's show. Not that people had exactly been in awe anyway. As the sounds from the stage got louder to try and regain the crowd, Dworkin slid his daughter onto the bench between him and the queen then turned with hand on his sword. In front of him, Matthias turned as well, dagger sliding into his hand from the pocket under his sleeve.

At first all he saw was guards rushing about, looking like fools trying to catch a cat or something. Then, from behind the benches, a small figure jumped out and angled directly for them. He had a brief second of wondering why the guards would be chasing a child then he took a closer look. The figure may be tiny but it was a full grown man, with hair so pale it almost disappeared in the light and an ax swinging at his hip, something gripped tightly in one hand.

Dworkin climbed over the bench to stand in the walkway, blocking the royal family and his own loved ones, then pulled his sword and held it out in front of him. "Not a step closer, Cregas."

He took notice of the gasps of the crowd and the aggravated sigh from Clesum, but kept his eyes fully on the Cregas. It skidded to a halt mere inches from the tip of his blade and glared at him, pale eyes rolling within a red face as he heaved for air.

"Of course this is what I get for trying to help humans. Damn you and damn that dragon."

He tossed whatever he had been holding towards them and tried to dart off into the crowd again but the guards had had time to catch up to him. One scooped him up under the arms while another rushed forward to disarm him.

"Take him to the dungeons until we figure this out," Matthias bellowed.

As the Cregas was carried away, Dworkin looked down to the dirt to see what it had thrown. There was a balled up scrap of paper at his feet with some kind of writing on it. He sheathed his sword then bent down to pick it up, carefully unrolling it.

His stomach dropped and the world tilted, his worst fears bubbling to the surface. Duke Arnis knew of Darian and his injuries, possibly had him in custody already. He was willing to hold Darian, and young Keslar, hostage and even threaten to kill them unless Dworkin came to speak to him personally. He wasn't to tell the king, and had to come alone. Dworkin already knew what those talks would entail but it didn't matter. He had to go.

"Dworkin, what is it?" Narlise placed a soft hand on his shoulder, trying to lean around to read the note.

He crumpled the note and shoved it in his belt. "I have to go."

"Daddy?" Lera called, climbing up on the bench, "are you going to get Uncle Darian?"

He sighed and kissed her blond curls then shook his head to Leslien as her eyes questioned him. "There's just something I have to take care of. I'll see you soon."

"Go where? What is happened?" Matthias called but he was already striding down the aisle and didn't pause to look back. "Duke Marslic! I order you to stop."

He closed his eyes and winced. He had never disobeyed a direct order from the king, had never had a reason to. Hopefully, everything would turn out fine and he could explain to his friend later. Right now, the whole kingdom could be burning to the ground and he would still keep walking. It was time to do what he should have done in the first place and be there for his brother.

"Duke Marslic!" Matthias's voice roared again behind him as people all around started to talk and whisper.

He knew if he turned around he would fall apart. He would feel the need to explain to his king, his wife, his children, but that would only put them and Darian in more danger. So he gritted his teeth, and started to run.

Mist thundered out of the city at a full gallop. She seemed to sense her riders mood and kept tossing her head and snorting as she ran. Dworkin gripped the reigns tight and leaned over her neck, trying to keep her under control while also pushing her as hard as he dared. He was already doing the math in his head, trying to figure how many hours a day she could handle and how quickly he could get to Arnis. Not near quick enough by his calculations.

"Dworkin," a loud voice called out, startling Mist and causing her to sidestep, "he made it to you! I had my doubts but the little guy must have done it."

Dworkin pulled Mist to a halt as Nemclis' big head lowered down towards him from a hill next to the road. The dragon's words filtered down into his anxious mind. Had Nemclis sent the Cregas? He had mentioned something about a dragon and about trying to help. And they had thrown him in the dungeon for it. He would have to get word to the king to release the Cregas without saying why. As soon as he could figure out how.

"I can't stop to talk, Nemclis. I have to get to Arnis."

Nemclis cocked his head. "I know, I'm the one the stupid little wizard had deliver the message. You'll never make it there in time on horseback."

"Don't see what choice I have," he yelled back, trying to hold Mist still as she pranced along the path.

Nemclis grinned and walked down the hill a few steps, laying his long neck along the ground. "If you can get Mist somewhere safe, I can take you. Darian and I have tried it out just for fun, figured it would probably come in handy someday."

He took a deep breath as he slowly dismounted. He wasn't sure he liked the idea of flying through the air on a dragon, but he also wasn't sure he had much of a choice. He removed Mist's bridle and folded it neatly inside her saddlebag, pulling out the red slip that he kept there for just such an instance. He tied the red flag to her saddle then, with a hand on her neck, turned her back towards the castle.

"Stable, Mist," he commanded, giving a light slap on her haunches. He watched her run back down the road for a moment, before turning to the dragon. "How does this work?"

Nemclis rolled the muscles of his shoulders just above where his wings attached. "Just climb on and hold on tight."

Dworkin hopped on, searching for a hand hold. He shrugged and grabbed the spines that ran down the dragon's neck, finding that his hands were shaking a bit. His stomach lurched as the massive wings started to beat and they lift a little ways into the air.

"Been hitting the festival banquets a bit hard?" Nemclis grunted, wings beating a bit harder.

As the ground moved further and further away, he leaned forward and gripped the dragons neck tighter and closed his eyes. "I was guarding the king and queen, I'm wearing armor."

"If you say so," Nemclis grunted.

"This was your offer. Just get us there and quit complaining."

58

Keslar

For all the build up, it didn't look like much was going on. Jalden's hands pressed against the High Master's temples, a soft blue glow surrounding them. Other than that, they just stood there not moving or reacting. Keslar leaned against a table, half dozing, waiting to see if it would work.

"We've been here pretty much all day." He yawned, digging through his pouch for something to eat.

Miramel glanced at him with a shrug. "You never know how long healing will take."

Her head jerked up and her eyes went wide, her hand flying to her hip. Keslar straightened and tried to figure out what she might have heard. A moment later, there was a loud rap at the door. Miramel glanced to Jalden and the High Master then back to Keslar, her hand to a smaller dagger she pulled out of her boot.

"I will send whoever it is away," she whispered, nodding her hand to the healing process, "be sure they are not interrupted."

He hefted his staff and moved between them and her. "By who? And how?"

"I don't know yet," she hissed, her hand already on the door, "and you are a wizard, figure it out."

"Just an apprentice," he whispered. He thought he'd said it quiet enough that she wouldn't hear but she raised a disapproving eyebrow at him. He sighed and shrugged. It was the truth after all.

She opened the door a crack and was immediately pushed backwards to crash into a table holding a fountain and many bottles of herbs and liquids. Five men burst into the small shop. Four of them wore the blue and yellow of the Arnis guards, two of them hovering over Miramel with weapons drawn while the other two pushed their way deeper into the shop. The final intruder was wrapped in red. Keslar squinted for a moment then realized it was the master that he had met in the market the day before.

"What are you doing?"

Master Yarlin grinned and motioned to the back of the shop. "Uncle, is it? Just because you're the color of dirt, doesn't make you the crown prince." He turned to the two guards with a vicious grin. "Seize him."

Keslar moved between them, trying to think fast. His eyes fell on yet another bubbling fountain and pointed his staff at it. Calling out the words as fast as he could, he commanded the water to obey him, causing it to jump from the fountain and spill across the floor. The guards slipped in the sudden puddle, nearly dropping to the floor.

Yarlin laughed then rattled off a spell of his own. Within seconds the water dried up and the guards could walk freely again. They marched to the back of the shop, yanking Jalden's hands away from the High Master and tossing him to the side.

Jalden screams filled the shop. His hands flew to his head as he writhed in pain on the floor. The High Master's face was still perfectly blank, his eyes empty.

Keslar tried to move towards the High Master but found he couldn't. A red light colored his vision as the Master moved closer, grinning and continuing to whisper the words that locked him in place, as his staff tapped a slow rhythm on the floor. Meanwhile, Miramel was still trying to get past the two guards blocking her path as the others hefted the High Master by each arm and started to drag him out of the shop.

"What are you doing?" Keslar growled, pushing against the spell. "He needs help. Guild members are supposed to work together."

Yarlin grinned and clucked his tongue. "Aww, that's so sweet. You still buy into all that 'we're your family now' bull. Of course, what should we expect when they let your kind in."

"A lot better than anything from you apparently," Keslar snapped back with his teeth gritted.

"The guild is about power, child, and getting this one out of the way is just my ticket to gaining some."

Out of the corner of his eye, Keslar noticed Miramel cast him a glance and a wink. While the two guards blocking her fell back to join the ones holding Darian, she slid her hood onto her head and practically disappeared. If he hadn't been looking directly at her, he wouldn't have been able to pick out her outline as she slipped out the door.

Gathering his strength, he pushed all his power against the spell and threw the Master off of him. He stumbled for a second, then gained control of his limbs again and raced after her but skidded to a stop just outside the door.

Master Yarlin had brought a lot more than just the four guards that had entered the shop. There was practically a full regiment waiting outside at attention. Miramel threw off her hood as she dove into the fray, her first kick landing to the back of the head the man carrying the High Master's arm. He fell aside, the other man pulling his sword while trying to hold on to Darian's other arm. Miramel grinned just before she spun, kicking the man's sword away and landing with her own in her hand. It shown silver in the dropping sun, long and wafer thin, the air humming every time she moved it.

A flash of red drew Keslar's attention away from the swirling dance that Miramel was caught in as the men beset her. Yarlin had recovered and was rushing out of the shop, already reciting a spell that had fire gathering around the ruby at the top of his staff. Keslar spoke the first spell that came to mind and a tiny raincloud formed over the man's fire, dousing it before it could fully form. Yarlin turned and swung his staff in a low arc and yelled a couple words, sending Kelsar flying backwards. His head collided with the wall of a neighboring shop, the darkness closing in rapidly.

He blinked, coming to enough to see a dark figure leap from the roof of the shop and bury a long black sword in Yarlin's back. Blood spilled to follow the cracks in the tiled ground as the figure pulled her sword from the limp body.

Keslar squinted, wondering when Miramel had changed into all black. No, this figure was shaped like her but was different. He tried to focus as the new one grinned at him, but could only stare back for a moment before losing consciousness completely.

59

Miramel

She hovered over Darian's body as the men stood in shock, staring at her. Certainly they had thought that this would be an easy mission. Follow their wizard to take an incapacitated wizard from a healer and a little boy. They had not counted on her being there, or what she was willing to do to keep her friend safe. Still, they had their orders and returning to the duke without his prize would probably bring about a punishment worse than facing her blade.

The men seemed to glance at each other and remember that it was all of them versus just one of her. One man feinted in and the whole scene devolved into chaos. Men came at her from every direction, some with weapons drawn, and some with their bare hands. A very long lifetime of training kicked in and her body moved almost without thought. Her blade moved through the air like a blur, knocking the thicker and heavier steel blades away, jabbing and slicing through skin when needed. She tried to make space for herself by using her feet and elbows to drive men back as her eyes scanned the area.

Normally, she would move to the high ground to have an advantage, but there was no way that she could leave Darian and she couldn't pick him up without exposing herself. She searched for the little wizard but couldn't see him over the men pressing to reach her.

A grunt and the sound of another blade caught her attention. She stabbed her sword into the gut of a man on her right, then pulled it out to slash across another man before she could look up. Half the men had drawn their attention away from her and were facing some new attacker. The figure was dressed all in black and danced with two short black swords.

Miramel was so transfixed by the grace and speed of this newcomer, she lost track of her surroundings and a man yanked her head back by the hair. Her elbow drove into his belly but he didn't release her hair. When he slipped on the blood soaked ground, they both nearly went down. She turned best she could to swing her sword at his arm, but the black figure was already on top of him, driving a blade into his throat. The grip on Miramel's hair loosened and she was able to stand straight again.

For a moment, she and the fighter just stared at each other while the remaining men scattered, screaming and yelling about something. Pale eyes with the same vertical slit as her own stared back at her from an ashen face. Silver hair was tied back in layers of tight braids to keep it out of her face and away from small pointed ears. Miramel shuddered as she stood, gripping her sword at the ready, the other mimicking her movements.

"I know what you are, though I thought you a myth," she whispered. "Why would you help me?"

A sly smile crossed the other's bloodless lips. "So did I until I was set free. Go ahead, say it. Say what I am, princess."

"You are darkness, and evil, and torture. You are Laranti. Why help me?"

"Zarentle wants his toy alive and put back together. Once you finish that task, you and I will meet under different terms."

The Laranti glanced up over Miramel's head then bounded away.

She jumped to the top of a nearby cart and onto a rooftop then was quickly out of sight. A part of Miramel wanted to chase after her, to track her down and understand. Maybe to learn who this Laranti had been before her darkening. But she had Darian and Keslar to think of, and the need to get away before anyone saw the chaos they had created.

60

Wind buffeted his face and the ground raced by beneath them. He estimated they were traveling at least three times as fast as a horse could and would be at Arnis before the sun set. As they moved, he loosened his grip on Nemclis's neck and leaned back a little, feeling the press of the speed and the air against him.

"Almost there," Nemclis called back, his voice rumbling under Dworkin's legs.

Dworkin leaned forward a little and looked down at the walled city fast approaching. There was some kind of commotion going on just inside the walls. He saw a flash of red and a mob of people crammed into the small street.

"What's that?"

Nemclis banked a little towards the area of the city. "Let's find out."

Banking his wings, Nemclis slowed and dropped toward the city at a dizzying pace. Dworkin leaned forward as the dragon tipped his head up, dropping massive hind legs onto the large stone wall surrounding the city and finding buildings to rest his smaller front feet on. His left foot broke through some thatch and he nearly lost his balance, Dworkin pitching sharply to the right.

Growling, Dworkin righted himself as the dragon adjusted his footing. The street below them was chaos. Men dressed in the uniforms of Arnis guards battled with two spinning figures, one in flowing silver and one in tight black clothes. Dworkin was mesmerized by the speed and fluidity of the two fighters, seemingly oblivious to each other as they mowed down larger and stronger men. The one in black jumped and flipped through the crowd but the one in silver seemed to be protecting something at her feet.

"Is that Darian?" Nemclis growled, lowering his head.

Dworkin didn't waste time responding. He climbed down the dragon's neck until he was close enough to jump to the ground. At the sight of the dragon, most of the Arnis men had turned and ran off but Dworkin drew his sword to be safe. He strode towards the figures, the one in black disappearing into the city as the one in silver watched.

"Are you the one I have to thank for my brother's safety?"

She spun towards him, impossibly thin silver sword high and ready to strike. Cat like green eyes studied him for a moment, bouncing from his sword to the cape fluttering over his shoulder and up to his face nearly faster than he could process. Her stance relaxed a little but her sword didn't lower.

"You are Dworkin, Duke of Marslic and friend of Darian?" Her voice had a softness that belayed the calloused hands and the haughty tilt of her chin.

"I am." He sheathed his sword and held up his hands, walking slowly towards her. "I mean you no harm, Wylthem. I just want to be sure my brother is okay. There was also a young wizard with him?"

Her head jerked up and she looked around the courtyard. "Keslar?"

"Over here," a voice groaned nearby. The boy stumbled towards them, wincing as he rubbed at the back of his head. "Dworkin? How did you get here? And when did you change back, Miramel?"

"What are you talking about?" Miramel snapped.

"By dragon." Dworkin laughed, pointing up to where Nemclis's head hovered over them. "You okay, kid?"

Keslar shook his head, his eyes looking a little cloudy. "Hit my head pretty hard but looks like we survived that mess, whatever it was."

"That was Duke Arnis trying to get to me through you guys." Dworkin glanced to the crowd starting to gather and realized how they must look. People might know that their Duke wasn't the best but they would never imagine figures standing amongst a pile of dead guards and one dead wizard would be the good guys. "I'll explain later. We need to get out of here."

Miramel took a step back as he leaned down to Darian. He sighed and shook his head, seeing no change in his friend other than his expression frozen in a look of horror. With a grunt, and a little help from the Wylthem, he hefted Darian over his shoulder and nodded towards the nearest city exit.

"We need to get the horses," Keslar said, jogging along next to them, picking up his staff as they passed it. "They're at an inn called the Golden Gryphon."

Dworkin nodded with a sigh. "I know the place but it's pretty far out of the way."

"I'll get them when I get my steed and meet you outside the walls. I just have to check on Jalden first." Miramel motioned them on then glanced at the dragon looming above them. "Keep an eye on them Nemclis and get them as far from the city as possible. I'll find you."

Dworkin wanted to argue. He didn't like the thought of their new friend fighting out of the city on her own. Then again he had seen her fight. She was probably more prepared to make it out than any of them.

"Go," she whispered, brushing a hand over Darian's shoulder. "All that matters is getting him out. I'll be fine."

They ran until Dworkin couldn't carry Darian any further. He motioned Keslar into a small stand of trees on the far side of a hill and carefully leaned his still friend up against one of the trees. For a long moment, they just huddled together, catching their breath and waiting for whatever the next threat might be.

"It doesn't look like we were followed," Nemclis called from just outside the trees.

Dworkin rose and strode back out into the setting sun, looking over his shoulder at Keslar and Darian. "You should be safe here and I'm sure the Wylthem will find you soon. Nemclis and I have one more thing to do."

"We do?" Nemclis laughed and cocked his head. "And what might that be?"

"To make sure my dear uncle knows to never try messing with my family again." Dworkin grunted as he climbed onto Nemclis's shoulders again.

Nemclis nodded and took to the air, circling the castle at the center of the city. Dworkin leaned over the dragon's neck and tried not to scream. For a city so dirty and overcrowded, the castle was filled with lush gardens and delicate walkways that were all perfectly immaculate, and a perfect waste of space. They found the duke in one such garden, surrounded by giggling ladies fanning themselves as he munched on fruit and sweetmeats.

"How close can you get me, Nemclis?"

The dragon searched the area then nodded his head towards the castle. "That low tower be close enough? I think I'll fit on the roof."

Dworkin pulled his sword and adjusted his grip on the dragon. "It'll do."

Nemclis circled, his massive shadow catching the attention of everyone in the garden. The women shrieked and ran to the imaginary safety of the pergola while the guards stationed around drew their swords. For a brief moment, Dworkin's throat tightened. He ached for the men who had lost their lives today in the service of a Duke who would never mourn them the way he still did Bartol and Duntiel and many others lost before. As Nemclis perched on the edge of the tower, wings spread for balance and dramatic affect, Dworkin rose to his feet on his shoulders.

"Duke Arnis. Dear Uncle Hebrent."

Shock fell from Hebrent's face to be replace by contempt. He had grown even fatter than the last time Dworkin had seen him, brown hair hanging around his pockmarked face, clothes stained from food and wine. Dworkin couldn't help but wonder how they were even related.

"What are you doing here, nephew?" The word fell from his lips like a curse. He glanced over as his female companions crept out from the pergola, their eyes on Dworkin as they whispered and giggled to each other. "I suggest you remove yourself and that monster from my castle before I have you arrested."

Dworkin laughed. "Your guards couldn't even retrieve you an incapacitated man and an apprentice wizard today. I'm really not concerned."

"I should have the king insist you pay me damages for the forces that I lost, and my court wizard."

"Then you might have to explain to him just why they were attempting to arrest those men in the first place," Dworkin grinned. "Besides, I didn't kill a single one of them. The fight was over by the time I arrived."

Hebrant's face was growing red as he waved his flabby arms in the air. "Then why are you here?"

"Can we hurry this up?" Nemclis whispered. "This isn't exactly a comfortable position."

"Have you been working on your accuracy? Give me just a moment more." Dworkin adjusted his footing as a small laugh rippled through the dragon then turned back to his uncle. "I'm here to deliver my own message. Next time you think to threaten myself or the people I care about, try to remember that I have very powerful friends, with powerful talents."

Dworkin could feel the heat emanating from Nemclis's belly and start to travel up his throat. With a motion that felt very much like a deep cough, the dragon turned his neck and tossed a small fire to the roofing of the pergola. Ladies screeched and ran while Hebrent stood staring in shock. The wood caught quickly and the structure was a complete loss in only moments. Guards and servants rushed about retrieving water in every container they could find, trying to save the surrounding garden.

"Next time you try a stunt like you did today," Dworkin laughed, sliding back onto Nemclis's neck and motioning for the dragon to take off, "it'll be your whole castle. Don't test me, Hebrent."

61

The crowd was starting close in on her as she watched the men dart off towards the wall. She ducked back inside the little shop and threw the bar across the door, sliding a large chest in front of it for good measure.

Jalden was still on the floor but had stopped screaming. His eyes were glazed over and he just blinked at the wall as if not seeing. She sighed and placed a hand on his shoulder, glancing back towards the door before closing her eyes.

The inside of his mindscape was like being able to breath under water. She found herself swimming like a fish, searching for him and calling his name. His screams still echoed inside his mind, harsh and painful but at least they gave her a direction. Following the sound she found an area that ended with a jagged edge as if the whole world had been ripped wide open. Water spilled out like a massive waterfall into nothingness with Jalden at the bottom, tossed and turned on the churning rocks.

"Take my hand," she yelled, leaning as far over as she could.

At first he looked at her lost and confused, then his hand gripped hers. She pulled back with all of her might, dragging him into the calmer parts of the water. As he gasped and clung to a rock, she turned to the gaping hole. She had no expertise with water but even here there were plants. Placing her hand in the sandy bottom, she pushed out her power and called to the seaweed that swayed like grass in the wind. It resisted her strange touch at first then began to move slowly, picking up pace as it grew until it had formed into a mesh net that crisscrossed over the hole and stopped the pouring water. Pulling back every trace of her power into herself, she carefully exited the way she had come until she was fully back in her own mind.

She opened her eyes to Jalden blinking at her as humans pounded on the door. "That should hold until you are able to repair yourself. You will be all right?"

"In time," he answered horsely then pushed her away. "That door won't hold long and my story that I had no part in this won't work if you're still here. There's a secret exit through a wardrobe at the back of the shop. Hurry."

She nodded and rose to her feet, glancing to the door then back to Jalden. "Darian?"

"I nearly had it, but that is some strong magic, Mira. Take him to your father, but tell the king to be careful of the darkness. Every time I made a crack it would fill with this black goo." He rolled his eyes to the door that was starting to splinter then back to her, dropping his voice. "Get out of here! And, tell my mother I will try to visit as soon as it is safe to."

She smiled at him before slipping through the doorway to the back room. She had to move a few boxes to get to the wardrobe he mentioned, but the mechanism was easy enough to figure out and she was soon stepping out into the twilight. She could hear voices yelling from the other side of the building and considered her options. With a sigh, she gritted her teeth and ran out to where they would see her.

Yells erupted through the crowd and a handful of men darted her direction. She ran in a zigzagging pattern through the city, keeping them just far enough that she would not lose them until she was ready but they would not catch her either. She could have done like the Leranti had and moved to the rooftops to get away from them quicker, but the longer they followed her the less likely they were to turn their attention to the others. Once she felt a sufficient amount of time had elapsed, she darted into an alleyway then used a few crates and a window ledge to propel herself up to the rooftop and across it to the next alley over. She squatted on the eaves, and caught her breath while listening to the frustrations of the men below when they couldn't find her.

Standing up, she assessed where she was and where she needed to be. A dark shadow moved two roofs over and for a second she thought it might be the Leranti back to make good on her promise, but it was just a cat out for it's nightly prowl. The thought of the Leranti sent her heart racing again even as the high of battle wore off. She had heard of them, of course, every youngling had. They were the creature that stalked the night, the monster that would grab you should you venture too far into the forest alone or worse, dare to leave the protection of the community all together. Even in her worst nightmares, she had never imagined actually meeting one. Especially one who knew who she was.

She shook herself and puffed out a quick breath. Now was not the time to think about that. She had to get back to Arilla and the horses and then get out of the city. In one piece if she was going to be of any use to the men. Jalden would be fine eventually but his healing powers would be compromised for quite some time. Father was Darian's only hope now, and there was no way they would make it through the forest without her.

She dropped back to the street, willing her cloak to match the dark grays and blacks of the city at night. As she pulled the large hood over her head, she practically disappeared into her surroundings, slipping through the streets unnoticed until she stood outside the Golden Gryphon.

"Why did I have a feeling you were at the center of all that ruckus I'm hearing about?" Raslen laughed as she entered the stables.

She blinked and cocked her head at him. Ebony and the boy's

brown mare were already saddled and haltered, while Arilla stood calmly nearby, her bow and quiver hanging from the steed's long white neck. Could word really have traveled that fast back to the other side of town? Still, she knew better than to ask questions of Raslen. You would never get a straight answer out of the man.

She laughed and tossed him the full pouch from her belt. "This should cover both rooms and any other trouble. You are the best as always."

"You take care of those boys." He grinned with a wink as she jumped onto Arilla's back and took the reigns of the other two.

"I am trying, Raslen. I am sure we will see you again soon." She leaned forward and patted Arilla's neck. "Time to go, old friend."

Arilla tossed her head with a neigh that sounded distinctively like a laugh. "Outworn our welcome already? Such a shame."

62

Keslar was nearly asleep in the saddle by the time Miramel felt they were far enough from the city to camp for the night. She bypassed any of the small towns and inns that littered the road and led them down a path that was barely more than a game trail until they reached a piece of the great forest that jutted out into the land like a peninsula reaches into the sea. As soon as they were under the thick canopy, she seemed to take a deep breath and her shoulders relaxed away from her ears.

Nemclis lay his head down just outside the trees and let out a long sigh that washed them all with warm air. "Where you go next, I can't follow."

"You've been a great help, Nemclis." Dworkin smiled as he

dismounted then moved to help Darian off of Ebony. "There were many times we would have been lost without you."

Nemclis closed his eyes and tipped his head a little. "I will return to the mountains and tell my people everything we've learned. Maybe I'll fly over the tower and see if there are any changes. Once you get Darian healed, he'll know how to contact me if you need."

"Travel safe, dragon friend," Miramel said quietly, laying a hand over her heart.

Keslar kicked at the ground with his foot and stared off into the trees. He was surprised to find he didn't want the dragon to leave. He still despised the red beast that had taken his family, and wasn't sure he would trust any other dragon, but Nemclis had proven himself time and time again. Whether it be because he had been raised by humans, or it were true that not all dragons were the same, was still up for debate in Keslar's mind.

"It has been nice traveling with you," he finally whispered, unsure what else to say. "Don't get yourself killed before we can meet again."

Nemclis raised his head and gave a toothy grin. "From you, young wizard, I will take that as high honors."

They all watched as the dragon lumbered away until he was clear enough of the trees to take flight. He quickly rose into the night sky, looping in and out of the lazy clouds that drifted by until he couldn't be seen anymore. Quiet and sullen, the group moved deeper into the trees and started to set up camp. Miramel disappeared into the woods and returned in short order with two small rabbits to roast over the fire that Keslar had built.

"Somehow, I assumed the Wylthem wouldn't eat meat. I mean, we hear about how connected you are to the land and all that."

She smiled and slowly turned the spit so that the rabbit would cook evenly. "A bear, or bobcat, or wolf are all connected with the land and eat meat. We all have our place in the circle that is nature, and as long as we take respectably and never more than we need, she continues to bless us."

"It seems quite the coincidence that you were in Arnis just as Keslar and Darian needed you, my lady." Dworkin grunted as he finished brushing down Mercy and tried to move on to skittish Ebony.

"Dworkin!" Keslar hissed, tossing an apologetic look to Miramel before glancing back at Dworkin.

"It is fine," Miramel said with a smile. "It was not a coincidence, sir duke. I was specifically looking for Darian."

They all grew quiet as eyes drifted to where Darian lay under a tree, not asleep but not really awake either. They had had such high hopes for the healer in Arnis and really it hadn't gotten them anywhere. All that trouble and all those guard's lives lost and they had nothing to show for it.

"Ever since the storm I felt there was something wrong with my dear friend, and when he did not answer my message requesting his help it only compounded my worry." She took a shaky breath then busied herself with removing the rabbit from the fire and carefully cutting it up with one of her many knives. "Then one day it was as if his very essence was being stripped from my mind. I knew then that I had to figure out what was going on. It was my father who suggested beginning at Arnis though."

Keslar nodded and gave as brief a run down as he could of everything they knew had happened to the High Master. He still shuddered at the thought of that cell and how it had blocked his magic. Not being able to access his power for that brief moment had been one of the scariest things he had ever felt. He couldn't imagine having to deal with that for as long as the High Master had.

Dworkin still didn't seem convinced as he gave up on grooming Ebony who only wanted to pay attention to Miramel's slender white mare. He settled next to the fire and took the bowl of food Miramel offered with a stiff nod.

"I will admit that Darian has mentioned your name before but never how you met."

Keslar tossed Dworkin another glare but the man wasn't paying attention to him. Why was he questioning their Wylthem guide so much? She'd already saved his life once and seemed to really care about Darian.

Miramel on the other hand just smiled and tipped her head to Dworkin. "I can see that everything Darian has said about his foster brother is true. You are just as wise and cautious as he described. It is no wonder he trusts your judgment."

Dworkin's eyes grew wide and sad as he glanced to Darian's still form then looked down to his food. Keslar's chest constricted watching him. Had the duke really not known how Darian felt about him? How much the High Master would use him as an example when speaking of strategy or leadership?

"Anyway," Miramel continued as she worked quietly pulling some nesting cups from her pack and a small sack of herbs that she sprinkled into each cup, "I first met Darian in Arnis when he was still a young child traveling with his mother. He had wandered away from her, as I take was his want, and gotten himself lost in a not so safe section of the city. From the moment I returned him to his mother, he seemed to continue to pop up in my life at the oddest times and a deep friendship formed as he grew."

She pulled a pot of boiling water from the fire and poured it into each cup, tasting one herself before passing the rest to them and walking the final cup to Darian. She leaned in to whisper in his ear before pressing the cup into his hands and watching him slowly drink.

Keslar sniffed at mixture, a few scents seeming familiar from the gardens at the Healers Mount but others foreign and mystical. Dworkin raised an eyebrow at him then shrugged.

"Do not worry, it is merely a tea to help you rest and to ease some of the aches that come with so much travel and heartache." She rose to her feet and picked up her silver robe from where it lay on top of her pack. As she clasped the fabric at her neck then pulled the hood over her head, the silver shifted and shimmered until it was a mottled green and brown that nearly disappeared into the landscape around her. "I will take first watch while you get some rest."

Keslar blinked and shook his head, seeing similar shock on Dworkin's face. "How did you do that?"

"Wylthem cloth," she laughed, holding up her sleeve to show how it shifted back and forth from silver to camouflaged, "part magic, part skilled weaving. Now, please, get some rest. Tomorrow we shall enter my father's land and I will need you awake and aware if we are to make it all the way to the city without you getting yourselves killed."

63

Braslic

Braslic curled into the corner of the cell and tried to sleep. He had come all this way just to end up behind bars and of no help to his people. He should have listened to Gerent Selick. He should have known better than to think humans would care.

"Not so smug now, are you?"

Braslic growled and turned his back. "Go ahead and gloat, Lord Ranklus, we both know who is the real criminal here."

"Big talk from such a little man," Ranklus laughed, "especially one behind bars."

Braslic shrugged and curled tighter into himself. He didn't have any energy left to fight with the human. Maybe this was what he deserved, what Mother Mountain had planned for him when she pushed him from home. He had done no crime but would pay penance for the Cregas who had brought dishonor to their people. For all he knew, he would lose his head tomorrow but he wasn't sure he cared. He had failed his mission and their people. There was no reason to go home anyway.

"Hey, I'm talking to you," Ranklus yelled and shook the bars. When Braslic didn't react he gave a hard snort. "Wonder how your people are doing without you? Probably wouldn't be too hard to just go take what should be ours anyway."

Braslic was on his feet and at the bars before he could think. His hand reached for his ax then fell as he remembered the guard had taken all his weapons. Ranklus stepped just out of his reach and grinned like a fool.

"Lord Ranklus," a soft female voice called from the darkness, "why are you down here bothering our guest?"

Ranklus paled before bowing deeply to the two women who rounded the corner. One was so fair she practically glowed like she had brought a piece of the sun with her. Blond hair hung to her waist and sharp green eyes narrowed at the lord. The other was darkness wrapped in velvet. Deep brown eyes were tired but quick, skin the warm brown of a dravite gem, raven hair bound at the back of her neck and around the gold band that encircled her head. In her hands was a steaming bowl that smelled heavenly and set Braslic's stomach growling.

"Your majesty, Lady Marslic," Ranklus stammered, "no offense, but this Cregas is a prisoner, not a guest."

The blond woman raised her chin with a sniff. "I would think a disagreement in terms between the king and queen would be a bit above the second son of a second son."

"Yes, of course. My apologies."

Braslic grinned watching the young lord practically fall over himself. There was still a darkness to his eyes that said he didn't really respect these ladies but his actions said he knew enough to not show it. When he didn't move or say anything else, the queen inclined her head towards the stairs with a small smile.

"You are excused, Lord Ranklus."

The women waited until the young lord had disappeared around the corner and his footsteps could be heard on the stairs before approaching the bars. The queen held out the strong smelling bowl as the blond pulled a crusty end of bread from a pocket in her skirts. Braslic's stomach growled loudly but he hesitated.

"It's okay," the queen whispered, pushing the bowl closer. "They're leftovers from our own meal and there is plenty to go around. If my husband wanted you dead, poison would not be his first choice."

Braslic nodded and took the bowl, using the bread to scoop up a heavenly bite. The rabbit stew with thick and tender vegetables was the heartiest meal he'd had since leaving home.

"Why are you being so kind to me?" he muttered between bites.

The queen smiled and glanced to her friend. "We have both known how it is to be thought of as different and have people not fully accept us because of it. Only powerful friends have allowed us to be where we are."

"Also," the blond took a step closer, leaning against the bars, "you brought that message to my husband, the one that made him leave without a word to anyone. Please, do you know where he has gone and why?"

Braslic struggled to believe these two lovely and kind women could possibly be married to the two men who wanted him locked up and possibly dead. He finished off the soup and passed the bowl back with a shrug.

"All I know was that it had something to do with High Master Darian and some people who wanted to use him against Duke Marslic and the King. I'll admit, I have no love for either of your husbands, but the High Master has always been a friend."

"To us as well," the queen muttered, backing away as she retreated into her thoughts.

The Lady Marslic gripped the bars and gritted her teeth. "It has to be that snake, Duke Arnis. Isn't there something we can do about him?"

"Not without proof." The queen shook her head before looking to Braslic again. "Thank you for your help, Cregas. I will work on convincing my husband that you meant no harm and should not be in here."

He watched them start to walk away, already convinced he would never see them again. Yet somehow, he found himself caring.

He didn't know if it was the sadness in their eyes or the kindness they had shown, but he didn't want them to leave.

"Braslic," he called. When both women turned back to him with questioning looks, he shrugged and buried his hands in his pockets. "Name's Braslic, not Cregas."

The queen smiled and gave a small nod before lifting her skirts to climb the stairs. "Of course, Braslic. Thank you for trying to help. I am sorry for the misunderstanding that ended with you here."

64

Dworkin

They picked their way through the forest for three more days before Miramel stopped in front of two trees that looked just like any other of the thousands they had seen since entering the forest. She laid a hand on her steed's shoulder and almost seemed to talk to it for a moment before turning to them. Dworkin pulled Ebony closer to him, an odd feeling tracing over his skin. He glanced up to Darian, strapped to his stallion's saddle with black cloak still pulled over his head, and then over to Kelsar who led Mercy, before looking back to their guide.

"You have been on Wylthem land since you entered the trees. We have been followed by at least two scouting teams that you did not even notice." She sighed and glanced over her shoulder once more before continuing. "I do not tell you this to frighten you but to help you understand. Once you pass between those trees, you will be in the city of Melcader and you will be watched constantly."

Keslar stepped a little closer to study the two trees but didn't seem to come up with anything more special about them than Dworkin had. "If the city is just beyond those trees, then why can't I see anything."

"Because it is hidden by a magical portal. If you had somehow made it this far without me and without the scouts filling you with arrows, the portal would shift you to another set of trees just like this in a different part of the forest. This is why humans who wander too deep into our forest feel like they are walking in circles."

Dworkin licked his lips and cleared his throat. With Darian as a best friend, he'd had to grow used to things he couldn't explain but this was different. A wizard studied and learned, there were certain things to say and do to make specific spells happen. Just like he could teach his body different sword fighting techniques or military strategies, Darian could teach his power different spells and ways of using his magic. The things Miramel and her people did seemed to be as natural and a part of them as breathing or walking.

"We understand, Princess," he finally said with a soft bow. "Please, lead on."

She nodded then turned towards the trees, her hand on Arilla's snow white neck. "Stay close and keep moving."

She moved towards the trees, steed silent by her side. Just as it looked like they would pass under, the air shimmered and they disappeared completely. Dworkin shook his head in disbelief then motioned Keslar forward. The boy took a deep breath before leading Mercy and the pack horse forward to disappear as well.

A slight rustling sound caught Dworkin's attention and had him glancing behind him. He searched the trees and foliage but couldn't see anything moving. Maybe it was just an animal, or maybe one of the scouts that Miramel had mentioned. Either way, nothing was getting done with him just standing out here. He pulled Leslien's necklace from his pouch, holding it in his hand as he had come to do for comfort over the trip, then turned back to the two trees.

"Come on, Darian," he whispered, giving Ebony's reigns a soft tug, "this is our last hope. If this doesn't work, I don't know what to do."

With a lump in his throat, he stepped through the trees. The air had a warm feel, like a summer breeze brushing across your skin. From one blink to the next, he moved from an empty forest, to the edge of a great city. He shook his head again with a small laugh before moving towards the massive stone structure.

A figure dropped from the trees in front of him. The Wylthem stared at him with muddy brown eyes and a dark smirk. Silently, more Wylthem dropped from the trees to completely surround him and Ebony, bows drawn and pointed directly at them. His hand flew to the hilt of his sword out of instinct, necklace sliding to the ground as a low growl filled his chest.

"Not a wise idea, human." The first Wylthem laughed, drawing his own thin silver sword as the archers pulled their bows taught. "You would drop far before it even cleared the scabbard."

Dworkin lowered his hand from the sword but continued to glare at the Wylthem. "We are here by invite of Princess Miramel."

"Oh I know, I've had one of my scouting teams following you for days." The Wylthem stepped a little closer, smile spreading wider. "Still, the safety of this city and the royal family are my responsibility. It is bad enough that wizard always brings trouble with him, now there is a whole group of you."

"Idilm Larsle, stand down," Miramel snapped, rushing back to them.

Keslar slid through the crowd to Dworkin's side, leaning in close to whisper. "Idilm is one of the highest rankings in the royal guard. What have we stepped into?"

Dworkin just shrugged. He honestly didn't care as long as they survived long enough to get Darian the help he needed.

Larlse grinned and slid his sword away as he backed up. At his nod the archers lowered their bows but kept arrows at the ready. "Just welcoming your guests, my princess."

Miramel spoke quickly in words that Dworkin couldn't understand. The language sounded lilting and rhythmic like a birdsong on the breeze but her tone gave him the distinct impression that there might have been some curse words mixed in. Larsle shot back just as harshly, gaining himself a dark look.

"I have this handled, Idilm Larsle. Return to patrol." Miramel snapped, eyes sharp as the two Wylthem stared each other down.

Larsle's eyes drifted to Dworkin and Darain one more time before giving a stiff bow to Miramel. With barely even a hint of movement, he disappeared back into the trees, his team following quickly behind. Miramel watched them go with a dark glare before turning to Dworkin.

"I thought I told you to stay close."

Dworkin rolled his eyes and crossed his arms. "I thought I heard something in the woods. And I have a feeling your friend was planning that little show of force no matter what I did."

She sighed and started to say something but instead bent down to pick up the necklace from at his feet. In her hands, the glow was even brighter, enough to cast a pale green light across her hands and face.

"Where did this come from?"

Dworkin grunted and held out his hand. "It belongs to my wife. She gave it to me before I left, for luck."

"How would your wife be in possession of something with Wylthem origins?" Miramel snapped, still holding the necklace.

He hesitated but figured there was no use in lying. "It is said that she has Wylthem blood, and that necklace came from her however many greats grandmother. Though it's only started glowing since we rescued Darian from the tower."

"Meadow born," Miramel whispered as if to herself, studying it for a moment before handing it back to him. "Certainly an heirloom to be kept safe then."

"Um, excuse me, but, is that a," Keslar stammered as he moved closer to them, his eyes on Miramel's steed.

Arilla tossed her head and made a sound somewhere between a neigh and a laugh. All argument fled from Dworkin's mind as he realized her coat practically sparkled in the soft sunlight and there was now a single white horn jutting from her forelock. She leaned her head towards Keslar and seemed to give an almost human wink.

"Unicorn is the term in your language, wizard." Her lips didn't move the way a human's would but it was obvious the voice was hers.

Keslar just blinked and stared as Miramel's face softened to a small smile. She glanced his way with an apologetic look before turning to rub Arilla's neck and smile at Keslar.

"She can choose to hide her true form if she does not feel safe, and

Arnis is definitely not safe. Now that we are home, there is no reason to hide." Miramel took a deep breath and moved to help Darian off of Ebony. "Come. Let us get on to our purpose of being here."

65

She smirked, and glanced over the forest again as the portal opened. The human knight had almost spotted her. Would he have even known what he was looking at if he had? Or would he have thought her just another version of Wylthem that he didn't know of? Either way, she had gotten cocky and careless. She would not make the same mistake again.

The princess had sensed her presence, that much was clear, but there had also been the Wylthem scouting party following the little group. That seemed to cloud the princess's mind enough that she did not pay much attention to a loan figure and mount following their every step. A mistake she did not expect the daughter of Jarelt to make but was thankful for.

She stepped through the portal and bowed stiffly to Zarentle. At least he was not moping on his throne anymore. He had summoned a large table, filled with maps and plans and other paraphernalia she wasn't sure of. Her eyes widened to find Melteze leaning casually against the table, his white suit as pristine as ever and a sly smile on his lips.

"My lords," she swallowed, trying to catch her breath and her surprise, "Darian and his friends have entered Melcader with the intent of speaking with King Jarelt. Do you wish me to follow them into the city?"

Melteze's grin grew a little wider. "Would you like that, Menir? To go home?"

"Melcader was never my home, my lord." She sniffed and straightened her uniform. "I lived there, yes, but I was meadow born. My home was stolen by the humans when I was a youngling."

Zarentle leaned against the table and closed his eyes as if fighting memories of his own. When he looked up again, his eyes bore into Melteze's back as to burn a hole straight through him. "Yes, they and the others have much to pay for. No, I do not need you to enter the city. I am certain that Jarelt will heal my son and send them on their way shortly."

Menir nodded and bowed again, turning on her heal to leave the room. If there was no longer a need to follow the wizard and his princess, she could finally get back to her troops. She wondered if they had kept up with their training in her stead or if she would have to beat some sense back into them.

"You have not been dismissed," Zarentle roared after her.

She turned back, eyes darting between Melteze's teasing grin and Zarentle's clear anger. It was always uncomfortable to be in the same room with both of them. They both despised each other for reasons she wasn't privy to, yet seemed to think they needed each other for some reason. She knew they each wondered where her and her people's allegiance would fall should it come down to it but that wasn't something she had an answer to just yet.

"My apologies, my lord. There was something else you needed?"

"Yes, I need to show my son just how hard it will be on these people he cares so much about if he continues to deny me." Zarentle straightened and rolled up one of the maps to hand to her. "Gather your troops, Leranti. It's playtime."

66

Keslar couldn't hide his awe as they reached the city of Melcader. If you could really call it a city. It was one large palace, a rambling building winding it's way in and out of the trees, big enough to house the entire city of Darsile and maybe part of Arnis as well. Varying roof lines and high towers suggested private living quarters as well as large communal areas. Delicate carvings filled the pale stone over every archway and under each roof line topped with warm brown and green tiles. Doors and windows were just open areas in the stone, allowing nature to grow right up to and sometimes inside the building. He watched as a small lizard crawled out of a doorway and into the green grass while two birds chased each other in and out of windows. The whole place exuded a timelessness, as if it had grown up with the ancient forest. As if it always had been and always would be.

All about them, Wylthem stopped what they were doing to bow as Miramel passed by. Many waved and called out to her in their native tongue. She would smile and wave back, sometimes commenting with a few words of her own, obviously well loved by her people and loving them deeply in return. Faces would change as they fell on the humans trailing behind her. Shock, fear, distrust, and even anger flashing at the sight of them.

Keslar gripped his staff and tried to stay close to Miramel. These people may be tall and elegant with the colorings of the very plants that surrounded them, but he had already seen more than once just how dangerous and deadly they could also be. She led them to what seemed to be the main entrance. Large stone columns carved into a spiral rather similar to Arilla's horn framed an arched opening.

"Arilla will take the horses to be cared for. Do not worry about your packs, I will show you where they are later."

Keslar's hand brushed over Darian's staff where it had stayed in Ebony's saddle ever since they had found it on the Wizard's Isle. It sparkled and shone in the dappled light, making his with just the two stones and muddy brown bit of amber at the top look like a child's toy.

He caught Dworkin smiling at him and felt his cheeks flush. "He'll need it soon, right?"

"My father is the best healer in the land," Miramel whispered, motioning them closer as Arilla led the horses around the building and out of sight. "If anyone can fix this, it will be him."

Dworkin grunted and cleared his throat, a thousand emotions crossing his face. "Leave it for now. He'll know where to find it when he's ready."

It wasn't quite the answer he had hoped for but it was more hope than they had had thus far. He nodded and stepped back, gripping his own staff as Dworkin draped an arm across Darian's shoulders.

Miramel hesitated for a moment, studying them but seeming to be thinking about something else. He wanted to ask what was causing her to pause, but the look on her face passed as quickly as it had come. She smiled and motioned they should follow her, passing into the cool dimness of the archway.

They moved through what seemed like a maze of hallways and rooms before exiting again into an open air central courtyard. The space was dominated by a massive tree carved out of stone with so much delicate detail you would almost swear it was real. Water trickled over the leaves and branches to gather in the large pool at it's base.

Miramel gasped and dashed to the edge of the fountain, bending down to pick up a stone from the ground. Drifting closer, Keslar realized it wasn't just a stone, but a small leaf just like the ones that remained on the branches of the stone tree. The ground around their feet was littered with the carved leaves, a few also at the bottom of the pool of water.

Miramel straightened but her face was pale as her eyes searched the surroundings. "Stay here while I find my father."

"No need to search, Inonym." A soft voice said from the other side of the courtyard. "Did you think that you could return home with such an entourage without word reaching me?"

Miramel ran to hug her father as he and Dworkin shifted awkwardly where they stood. When she pulled back, she held one of the stone leaves out in both hands like an offering.

"What is happening to the tree, enomym?"

The king looked over her head to them then folded her hands over the leaf. "First we will discuss your guests. I see you found what you were looking for."

Keslar bristled a bit and frowned. He didn't like Darian being referred to as a 'what.' By the way Dworkin's jaw clenched and he moved protectively closer, he felt the same.

Miramel cast them both a look before leading her father to Darian, flipping back the black hood to reveal his blank expression. They spoke quickly in their own language. By the few words Keslar was able to pick up on, she was giving the king a quick explanation of everything that had led them to this point.

The king asked a couple more questions then nodded, turning to Darian. "You are lucky my daughter cares for you so, Wizard. I do not usually concern myself with the problems of humans."

Keslar couldn't stop the snort and just barely held in the eye roll. The king turned to him with one dark eyebrow raised.

"Is there a problem, child?"

"My apologies, your majesty." Keslar bowed deeply, ignoring the looks both Dworkin and Miramel were giving him. "It just seems a waste. I can feel the power of this place, and your daughter says you are the most powerful healer in Ramleaj. To hide all that away for only your people feels a bit selfish. I've been to the Healer's Mount and they do amazing things, but there are many that they can't help the way your power could."

Miramel started to speak but the king stopped her with a look. "There was a time we helped the humans, tried to live side by side with them. We paid a hefty price that we could not afford to pay again."

"Your majesty."

"I have lived more summers than you can hold in your mind. I will not be scolded by a child of what, ten?"

"Sixteen," Keslar said with a growl.

The king just nodded and turned to his daughter. "The infirmary is full. Bring him to my office. I will retrieve your mother and meet you there."

"Full?" Miramel gasped, gripping the stone leaf to her heart. After a second she seemed to gather herself and nodded. "Yes, enonym. Thank you."

No one moved as the king practically glided from the courtyard. Once he was gone it was like a collective breath was released. Dworkin reached around Darian and lightly smacked Keslar on the back of the head.

"Really, kid?"

Keslar rubbed the back of his head and glared at the Duke. "What was that for?"

"You don't insult a king, especially one you just met. And especially when you're asking for his help."

His cheeks flared but he refused to look away. "Was I wrong?"

No one answered him. Dworkin rolled his eyes skyward and seemed to be fighting a grin as Miramel made a study of her feet.

"Stay here." Miramel took Darian by the arm and grinned at them. "I'll either come back for you or send someone."

Keslar nodded and stepped back out of the way. Miramel stopped next to him and looked him up and down before winking.

"And try not to insult any more of my family members while I'm gone."

Keslar grinned back and raised his eyebrows. "You still haven't said I was wrong."

67

He couldn't sit still, pacing the small area between the walls like a caged animal ready to strike at the first thing he saw. He had known the minute they crossed the barrier that they were in Melcader. The power in the land and the people had always sung to him and even now it energized him and stirred his resolve. He just had to pray Jarelt wouldn't hold their past arguments against him and would actually want to help. This was probably his last hope.

The presence entered like a breeze playing through the trees. The soft smells of pine needles and woodsmoke drifted to him long before Jarelt walked up to the wall. He turned to face the Wylthem, smiling sheepishly with a small shrug.

King Jarelt walked up to the wall with an exasperated look on his face. Darian knew he was only doing this as a favor to Miramel and that he would have to find a way to show his appreciation. He was trying to figure out how to get a message across when Jarelt seem distracted by something. The king turned from the wall and looked over the expanse that was Darian's mind space. The whole of Ramleaj was echoed here. Trees of the Great Forest towered just to the south as the Ykor Mountains shimmered in the distance to the North. Jarelt bent and dipped his fingers in the flowing water of a small river, closing his eyes and cocking his head as if listening to something. After a moment, his eyes snapped open and the color leached from his face. He rose slowly, staring at Darian as if seeing him for the first time.

"What?" Darian screamed even though he knew the Wylthem couldn't hear him. "What did you find?"

Jarelt just shook his head and turned to inspecting the wall. The blackness had grown since they had left the Jalden. Cracks left by him being yanked out of Darian's mind had given it space to flow and grow amongst the shimmering purple. What would happen when the walls fell? So far they seemed to be the only thing holding that bit of Zarentle away from the core of him, but they were also what blocked him from fighting back against the monster. Was this a no win situation he'd found his way into?

Jarelt circled the wall then came back to stand in front of him. Reddish brown hair swished about his shoulders as he slowly shook his head. The last reserves of energy dropped out of Darian as he slid to his knees, face in his hands. If Jarelt couldn't fix this, then no one could. Someone may as well run him through with a sword and put him out of his misery.

"Wizard," Jarelt's voice drifted to him, soft and hard to latch onto like from a great distance but it was there. It was the first voice that he didn't hear with just his ears, but that spoke deep within him, "I can not fix this."

He sighed and settled onto the ground, his back against the buzzing wall. "I appreciate you trying, your majesty. Please, thank all my friends as well. They went through a lot to get me here."

"Maybe you are not the wizard that everyone thinks you are if you are willing to give up that easily." There was a touch of laughter to Jarelt's voice, but a tired annoyance as well. "I can not fix this, because only you can."

Darian jumped to his feet and turned to face the king again, pounding his fist against the blasted wall. "You think I haven't tried? Every spell, every incantation, I've tried it all. Nothing works."

Jarelt moved a little closer to the wall, surprising him by sitting down. "Nothing has worked because you will not let it. You put up these walls to protect yourself from more than just a spell. Whether it is this darkness or something else that I can not see, that is for you to figure out. The walls will not come down until you are ready to face whatever it is. I can give you added energy to assist, but the work is yours."

Darian fell back a step as if he had been punched. He wanted to say it was the darkness. Hadn't he just been worrying about what would happen once the walls fell? But he knew in his gut that wasn't it. Images flashed through his mind as bile rose in the back of his throat making him gag. The woman hanging from chains in the torture room, the woman he had killed. The black cloak and warm room and just how close he had come to giving in. The way Zarentle had smiled as he revealed that he was indeed Darian's father. How was he supposed to come back from all of that and just go back to his friends and life as if nothing had happened? It wasn't like he could tell them any of that. They would never look at him the same way. He wasn't even able to look at himself the same way.

"Darian," Jarelt called to him again, quiet and calm amidst the storm that was his thoughts, "whatever it is, staying trapped inside there will not change it. I have never seen you shy away from a fight before, do not let your own mind be the one that you will not face."

He closed his eyes for a moment and forced a few breaths through his raw throat. When he thought he was ready as he ever would be, he opened his eyes and copied Jarelt's posture. Kneeling on the ground, he buried his hands in the grass around him and pressed his awareness deep, searching for the root of the walls. Again, the darkness flowed against his every movement, blocking him and pushing him back into his self imposed prison.

"I can't break through," he said, trying not to sob.

"I can hold some of this back, but do not take too long. Even being here is draining me quickly." Even as Jarelt spoke, some of the darkness receded, drawing back like snakes sliding into their den.

He gave a nod and turned back to his own work. He didn't think about spells or proper words to use. He let his mind dive into the well that was him, was his power. The one thing that made him special and set him apart from the rest. The one thing that he could use to fight back against Zarentle and save this land and it's people.

It seemed he would dive forever before he finally found it. A pulsing ball of black and purple wound together like a lady's ball of yarn after a kitten had gotten into it. He knew the strands well even before he touched them. Purple for his knowledge and power, for his friends and the love they had shown him through this, for everything that he still had to offer to the world. Black for the temptations, for the harm he'd done, for the lineage he couldn't control, for the pride that had gotten him into this mess in the first place. Each strand was like a column, holding up the massive walls

"Darian, hurry."

He shook his head, unsure if Jarelt could even see him. The last thing he needed right now was a distraction. Just because he had found the problem, didn't mean that he had any idea what to do about it. These black strands weren't just going to go away. They were a part of him now and something he was going to have to find a way to live with. Still, they were blocking him from the most important thing he needed to do right now. Killing Zarentle. Once that was handled, he could deal with the rest of this.

His teeth clenched and hands shaking, he reached out and grabbed the whole glowing mess. Once in his hands, it shrank from something he couldn't even wrap his arms around to a ball he could hold between his hands. The thought kept circling in his head that these were all a part of him, the good and the bad, those he needed and those he wished he could forget. Swallowing hard, he took one more deep breath then collapsed around the ball, clutching it tight to his chest.

His screams picked up right where they had been cut off back in Zarentle's throne room. Something inside him was being ripped apart and pieced back together as a great thundering echoed in his ears. A bright flash of light blinded him before everything faded to black.

68

Miramel tried to focus on the tour that she was giving Keslar and Dworkin but they were all distracted. Father had all but pushed her out of the room, saying that her energy was too chaotic for him to work. She couldn't help it that her heart felt like it was going to pound through her chest and every nerve was on edge.

Keslar's fascination and thirst for knowledge seemed to override his nerves. He asked a thousand questions and was fascinated by what he saw. Dworkin was polite and interested but she could feel the fear radiating from him. She remembered Darian calling the reserved duke his foster brother but had never realized just how tight of a family they had become, tighter than some blood families she knew. His fear swirled against hers, each compounding each other and making it hard to think or focus.

She was showing Keslar a pair of twin baby unicorns that had been born recently when the scream hit her. Though the sound knocked her back and punched her in the gut, Keslar and Dworkin showed no reaction. She was hearing it with her head and heart, not her ears.

Her hands shook as she rose from the straw and brushed her pants off. She was trying to think of something to say when Dworkin looked at her with eyes widening.

"What do you know? Is it Darian?"

She smirked, having not realized how her emotions had shown on her face. "I am not certain of anything yet. Follow the pathway there and you will find yourself in the courtyards just outside my rooms. I will go see what I can find out and meet you there as soon as possible."

She did not wait for the response but set out at a jog the other direction. Wylthem jumped out of her way with only slight grumbles, used to their princess often dashing about on whatever mission had excited her this time. It seemed to take forever to reach Father's office with the scream still echoing in her mind.

She raised her hand to knock on the door, one of the few in the whole compound that was ever actually closed, when it swung open and Father stepped into the hall. His eyes were tired, the power that always radiated off him coming in small and weak waves. His hair had escaped it's ties to fall around his face, age showing more than she remembered.

"Did it work?"

"It is up to him now. I created the path for him, we will have to wait and see if he still has the strength to walk it." Father pulled the door open a little wider and motioned her in. "I must rest. You may sit with him to see if he comes around but do not push him too hard."

She hugged her father's neck tightly, the back of her eyes and throat burning. "Thank you, enonym."

"I would do anything for you, my Mira, but this was for Ramleaj. We need to know what this evil is that we are facing and he seems to be the only one with those answers."

She nodded, studying him before stepping back and releasing him. There was something different in his eyes, a knowledge he wasn't yet ready to share with her. The urge to ask questions was strong, but even stronger was her concern about Darian. She kissed her father's cheek and gave a small push towards his rooms. He nodded as Mother stepped out of the room as well, taking his arm and leading him down the hall.

Miramel took a breath before dashing into the room to take Darian's hand. The scream had faded from her mind but his eyes were still closed and his breathing slow.

"Darian," she whispered, squeezing his hand and pressing it to her cheek. The tears she had been holding back ever since he'd been ripped from her slipped out to run down her face. "Darian, you can do this. Come back to us."

A warmth started to grow in her, making her breath catch in her throat. It started as a trickle, a whisper in her mind of a familiar voice. She held her breath, waiting and praying, until his presence flooded her mind again. There was more pain and sadness attached to it, some pieces blocked off from her touch but it was him and he was whole.

She opened her eyes to find him staring back at her. He grinned and winked at her.

"Hi there."

With a laugh she lunged to hug him, never happier to feel his arms tighten around her. "Do not ever scare me like that again."

"It's not like I planned on it." He laughed, leaning back to stare at her with those mesmerizing gray eyes. For a moment they just stayed there, heart's thudding in unison as they clung to each other. He softly brushed hair from her face, sighing deeply. "Thank you, Carame. I knew you would find me."

"Every time. Now come on. I know some other friends who are pretty anxious to see you." She laughed and stood up, tugging his hand.

He started to rise but his eyes glazed over and he collapsed back into the chair with his head in his hands. She pursed her lips and cursed herself. He had been through a lot, of course he would need to rest. She moved to squat down next to him, gripping his knee where the black cloak had bunched.

"It is okay. Take your time. Gather your strength."

His hand moved to grip hers but started to shake and tugged the cloak out instead. He gasped and jerked away from her, tugging and yanking at the cloak. He finally ripped the clasp open and tossed it away from him, scuttling to the very corner of the chair as if he couldn't get far enough away from it.

"Hey, what is wrong?" She whispered, picking up the fabric to glance it over.

He closed his eyes and took a deep breath before trying to grin at her. "Nothing, nothing. I'm fine."

"Darian," she dropped the fabric and walked back to him, her movements slow and voice soft as if not to startle a wild animal, "when I found you in Arnis, I touched your mind. I saw some of the darkness there, what you were put through, what he did to you. I'm sure there was much more than the flashes that I passed trying to find you. Do not lie to me and say you are fine."

He pressed his lips together and closed his eyes for a brief moment. After a few deep breaths, he looked at her again with tears filling his eyes. "Please do not ask me about those things, Carame. Not yet. Maybe not ever."

"Okay."

His hand reached out to brush the edges of her cloak, trying to force a watery smile. "You wouldn't happen to have some spare fabric laying around?"

"Of course." She grinned, surprised she did not think of it herself. "I will have some dyed our finest purple for you as you rest."

His breathing slowed and his body relaxed as he grinned up at her through his hair. "I know it's asking a lot, but a blue one as well, and might your mom have a sapphire she'd be willing to spare?"

"What are you planning this time, Darian?" She laughed and shook her head, grabbing a blanket from a pile in the corner. "No, don't even bother telling me yet. You just rest and I will take care of everything."

69

Braslic

Braslic pushed away the bowl of mush, convinced he couldn't touch another bite of it. He'd lost count how many days he'd been locked inside the human's dungeon. It really wasn't too bad. The stone walls and cool air reminded him of home, other than the whole locked doors and guards posted everywhere and mush for nearly every meal. The queen and Lady Marslic came back when they could but not too often, probably at the behest of the king.

"And what are you in for, Small one?"

Braslic moved to the bars and looked out. He had thought himself alone in this area since they had released the thief next to him a couple days after he'd arrived. In the cell across from him, a tall human sat on the stone bench, lightly twirling a very large and very white hat. The whole rest of his outfit was just as white and just as impractical for sitting in a dirty jail cell. Not that anyone got dressed in the morning thinking they would be arrested that day. Dark eyes grinned at Braslic, making him shiver even though he wasn't sure why.

Braslic scoffed and rolled his eyes. "For trying to help a human. You can be certain I won't be doing that again."

"Oh, I wouldn't be so sure of that." The man laughed as he placed his hat on top of dark hair, adjusting it until it was tilted just right. "We can surprise even ourselves if the situation is right."

Braslic grunted but decided that he wasn't up for an argument. "What about you? What did a dandy like you do to get tossed in here?"

"Me?" The man grinned and rose to his feet. "Oh no, I'm just visiting."

Great. He was penned up next to a raving lunatic. Next thing you knew the guy would be claiming he was the king himself and could get them both out of there. Shaking his head, Braslic turned back towards the bench and his own thoughts.

"King? No, that would be step down really. And I think you'll do just fine getting yourself out of here soon."

That wasn't possible. Braslic was certain he hadn't said those things out loud.

His head jerked up as the whole earth seemed to rumble and shift. Screams filled the castle and men started to yell. Guards rushed past the cells, weapons drawn as they yelled at each other.

"Hey, you?" Braslic yelled as one rushed past. "What's happening?"

The guard turned to glare at him. "Is this your people's doing? Trying to rescue you?"

"What are you talking about?"

But the guard was already running up the stairs and out of sight. Braslic sighed and looked towards the cell across from him. Maybe the dandy knew something of what was going on. But there was no sign of the man in white or any evidence that he had ever been there.

"Great, Braslic. You're losing your mind too."

He could hear boots dashing back and forth upstairs as men yelled at each other, one voice rising above the rest. He knew those sounds.

There was some sort of battle going on, and he was stuck here like a rat in a hole just waiting for someone to come and kill him. He growled and rattled the bars but they wouldn't budge. He searched the surrounding area, trying to find anything that he could maybe break the lock or find some other way out. He couldn't just sit there and wait to die.

Another blast shook the castle, the sound of things falling and people yelling filling the night. A louder crash sounded just above him, dust and pebbles showering down on him. He dropped and covered his head until the air seemed to clear. When he looked up again, moonlight was streaming into the cell.

He moved towards the outside wall to inspect the damage. It looked like a large stone from somewhere higher on the castle had been blasted off and rolled into his wall, knocking a hole in the side. There wasn't much space, but it might just be enough. Climbing up the damaged stone, he squeezed and shimmied his way through until he was out in the open air.

The whole castle was in chaos. Soldiers were rushing to the walls to form some kind of defense as civilians ran towards the castle for protection. At the center of the chaos was the human king, armor thrown over his sleeping clothes and sword in his hand as he shouted orders and encouragement to his men. No one noticed Braslic as he slipped to the wall and climbed a ladder to try and find out what was happening.

Poking his head over the wall, his heart dropped into his stomach and his throat went dry. The land outside the castle was filled with dark, moving shapes. In the flickering firelight, he could see green beasts with yellow eyes holding growling Kaldecs at the end of long chains. It was the creatures at the back of the line that sent shivers through him. Pale skinned and riding pure black mounts with glowing eyes, they paced the area yelling orders to the beasts and periodically tossing large balls of magic to collide with castle walls. So far the deep ditches and moat that surrounded the city was keeping them back but that would only last for so long.

One ball smashed into the wall next to him, blasting dirt and smoke into the air. Men screamed, scattering in multiple directions to reassemble elsewhere. One man didn't rise and move on with his compatriots. Braslic slunk closer, keeping his head lower than the wall until he reached the fallen man. He hesitated for a second, swallowing a feeling he didn't like. In death, the human boy didn't look all that different from all the fallen Cregas he had given back to Mother Mountain.

"Sorry, sir, but these won't be much use to you now and I don't know what they did with mine." He muttered, feeling along the soldier's uniform for weapons. The longbow and broadsword were of no use to him, but he found two daggers that seemed sharp enough and well balanced. They would do. "Now, to figure my way out of here without dying."

Going over the other side of the wall would never do. He'd be wide out in the open for both the humans and attackers to see. Crawling back to the ladder he climbed down and hung to the shadows, trying to decide what to do.

"Your Majesty," a breathless soldier yelled, rushing through the front gates, "they've breached the third wall."

The king cursed and looked around. "We need to get those people out of there. Half of you fight your way in and get as many of our people out as you can, the other half man the second wall and cover them."

Braslic dropped his own curses and slid further back into the shadows. If the walls were being breached, there was no way he would be able to slip out. He'd just have to keep himself alive and try to slip out when the battle was over, no matter who the winner might be.

70

Dworkin leaned back in the chair and watched the forest around him. It was so similar to Rosewood Forest and yet so different at the same time. For the most part it was the same trees and animals, the same sounds and smells, but the feel was different. Here, the animals were braver and bolder. He watched as two foxes chased each other and pounced their way through the underbrush not six feet from him. A little while earlier a chipmunk had bounced down from a tree right on to the table to steal some of the food that had been spread out for him. He should be experiencing everything he could and cataloging it all away to describe to Leslien when he finally made it home, but all he could think about was Darian and that they should have heard something by now.

They had been in Melcader for nearly a full day and still there was no update. Any Wylthem that he tried to ask would just say the King or Princess would most likely be with him soon. Still, they had been kind and welcoming hosts. All except for Larsle who seemed to go out of his way to make sure Dworkin knew they were being watched. After Miramel's tour, they had been given rooms where they could clean up and change, or sleep as Keslar was still doing.

When Dworkin couldn't rest for thoughts of his brother, they had brought him to yet another courtyard and laid out a veritable feast for him. Fruits and berries floated in a rich cream, there was duck roasted in savory herbs and vegetables, as well as some dishes he didn't even recognize. He'd picked at the food a little to try to seem polite but even sipping the sweet berry wine was hard when your mind was so distracted.

"You should try the duck," a voice laughed behind him, "it's amazing."

He almost didn't dare believe even though he knew that voice nearly as well as his own. A slow smile spread across his face as he gripped the arms of the chair, forcing himself to stay still even though he wanted to leap out of his seat.

"See, I thought you'd go for the berries and cream, because you're fruity if you think I'll ever forgive you for scaring the life out of me."

When Darian didn't respond, Dworkin feared he'd imagined the whole thing. He turned slightly in the chair and just stared at the man standing there. The Wylthem had replaced his trademark purple cloak, though it still hung a little loose with all the weight he'd lost as did the fine clothes he'd obviously dug out of his bags left with Ebony. He leaned a little heavy against his staff but he was standing, and breathing, and speaking.

Dworkin scarcely dared to breathe as he rose to his feet. They'd gotten their hopes up and been disappointed so many times now that he still found himself waiting for the let down.

Then Darian grinned at him. That mischievous light sparkled in gray eyes that once again crinkled with laughter as he held his arms open. Dworkin crossed the space between them in two long strides to hug his brother as tight as he could. Darian squeezed back as they laughed and cried like they'd lost their minds.

"It's really you." Dworkin gave one more squeeze before leaning back to look at him again. "Really and wholly you."

Darian's smile softened as he squeezed Dworkin's shoulder. "Because of you, brother."

"Well, everyone-"

Darian cut him off with a wave of his hand and shake of his head. "I will forever be grateful to Miramel, and the kid, of course."

"Kelsar," Dworkin laughed. "His name is Keslar and he practically idolizes you."

"I know. I listened to him talk nonstop the whole way to Arnis. He's a good kid." Darian paused to take a deep breath. "But you're the one who tried to warn me, the one who came searching and wouldn't give up until you found me. I know what you went through and what you lost on my behalf. I can't possibly express how very sorry, and how deeply thankful I will always be for that."

Dworkin's throat tightened and his vision misted over again. "It's what family does."

A dark look passed over Darian's face and he seemed to retreat into himself for a moment. Dworkin wanted to ask what was on his mind but knew Darian would speak when he was ready. Who knew what kind of horrors he had gone through during those weeks in captivity. That couldn't be an easy thing to carry, or talk about.

Darian forced a smile that didn't reach his eyes. "Well, I'm lucky to have the best. Which is why I know you'll be happy to help me with a little surprise I have planned."

"Not even awake a full day and already scheming."

"As you said, it's me." Darian laughed and threw an arm around his shoulders to start guiding him back down the path. "But, if you want to talk about out of character, did you really deny a direct order from Matthias?"

Dworkin groaned and rolled his eyes. "Yeah, I guess I did."

71

Keslar

Keslar didn't know where he was for a moment, just that someone was desperately shaking him awake. He jerked up and grabbed for his staff, heart pounding in his chest as he wondered what danger was coming this time. More Kaldecs? Those green creatures they'd seen in the dungeon? Or something new and even more horrible?

"Calm down, boy."

He took a breath and looked around. He was in one of the rooms the Wylthem had given them, with a soft summer breeze blowing on his face and the smell of something mouthwatering nearby. Dworkin hovered above him grinning like a fool as he tossed Keslar's pack onto the foot of the bed.

"What is it? Is it the High Master?"

Dworkin scrubbed at his beard for a moment before motioning to the pack. "Wash up then dress in the finest clothes you have. We're being summoned before the king himself."

Keslar swung his legs off the bed and pulled his pack close but never took his eyes off Dworkin. Why hadn't he answered the question? Keslar's heart sank into his stomach. Were they being called before the king to be told that there was nothing to be done?

"Dworkin?"

The Duke just turned and walked towards the door, but stopped to motion to a platter sitting on the side table. It was piled with food, a thick looking red wine, and cool clear water. That's where the amazing smells were drifting from.

"The Wylthem brought you food so eat up but don't dawdle." The ghost of a smile crossed the duke's face as he glanced back. "I'm told the duck is really good."

Keslar stared as the Duke walked out the door, almost swearing he heard the man chuckle once he was out in the hallway. Once alone, he let out an exasperated sigh. Seriously, what was with adults and not answering questions and being so cryptic and weird all the time?

As quickly as he could, he scarfed some of the food then washed his face and combed his hair before getting dressed. He really didn't have anything nice enough for an audience with the king, but his tan breeches and maroon shirt would just have to do. It would be mostly covered by the tattered and road worn brown cloak anyway. He grabbed his staff from the bed, once again thinking of the way the High Master's had sparkled and wondered if they had come all this way for nothing. What would happen to Ramleaj if the High Master couldn't give them the answers they needed to fight whoever, or whatever, that had been?

He shook himself and decided he was as ready as he would ever be. When he stepped out into the hall, the guard Miramel had called Larsle stood at attention waiting for him. His heart clawed it's way into his throat as the Wylthem studied him with quiet disdain. That couldn't be a good sign. Maybe his words had offended the king more than he had thought.

"My princess has asked me to escort you to the throne room." Larsle turned and started down the hall without even looking back over his shoulder. "Please keep up."

He swallowed hard then jogged to catch up with the Wylthem's long strides. They moved in and out of the building, through small gardens and courtyards until they reached the statue of the great tree again. Keslar glanced to his feet, wondering if Miramel had ever gotten an answer about the leaves, but Larsle cleared his throat in front of a large archway. With an embarrassed grin, he sped up again and followed Larsle through the archway.

The throne room was the largest interior room he had seen yet, and surprisingly empty. The two thrones at the far end of the hall were empty, as was the rest of the room. The tan tile under his feet and stone of the walls were painted by the setting sun as it drifted in through tall windows and the open ceiling showed stars just starting to fill the darkness through the tree branches. Only two people stood in the large hall, both dressed in their finest and grinning at him like fools.

Miramel had changed into a dress of the softest green that floated around her, gauzy sleeves slit to show her lithe arms and sandaled feet barely visible under the long skirts. Her red hair hung loose down to the small of her back other than the tiny braids woven around the silver crown that rested on her brow. Dworkin stood next to her, dressed in his court finery, short red cape with the rearing stallion of Marslic draped over one shoulder. He had left off the formal sword belt and hilt out of respect for being a guest in a foreign court but Keslar had no doubt that there was at least one weapon hidden somewhere on his person, of course the princess probably had at least a couple herself.

Larsle stopped in front of the two and bowed stiffly, giving Dworkin a hard look before smiling for Miramel. "The apprentice wizard, Keslar, as requested."

"Thank you, Idilm Larsle," Miramel said quietly as she motioned him aside then looked to Keslar. "Come forward, young wizard."

Somehow, having just these two made him even more nervous than if the full court were in session. If they wanted to tell him bad news, this was probably how they would do it. They would try to give him a moment of privacy to process it without a whole audience to see. His footsteps and the click of his staff on the stone floor were the only sounds as he moved closer, wishing they would just get it over with.

"What is going on here?"

Dworkin glanced to Miramel then smiled. "We're not the ones to ask. We're only witnesses."

He cocked his head but didn't have a chance to ask any more questions. Three loud taps echoed through the room, bouncing off the walls until he couldn't tell what direction it was coming from. His breath caught and his eyes went wide. He knew that sound. That was the sound of a staff tapping on stone with purpose, the sound of a wizard calling the room to attention because he had something important to say.

As he held his breath, something swirled in the darkness behind the two thrones. He glanced to Miramel and Dworkin to find them both grinning from ear to ear. Just when he thought he might burst from anticipation, the shadows coalesced into the form of a man and the High Master stepped forward. A new purple cloak swirled around his ankles and the confident tilt to his head that Keslar had always noticed around the Isle was back.

High Master Darian was back.

He leaned a little heavily on his staff as he walked towards them, but it was definitely the High Master and he was fully in control of himself. Coming to stand between Miramel and Dworkin, he turned and carefully handed them each a package. Dworkin took the larger and tucked it under his arm, while Miramel could hold hers in the palm of her hand. The three of them shared a look before the High Master turned to stare down at him, face becoming devoid of any emotion at all.

"Apprentice Keslar of the Wizard's Guild, your staff and cloak please."

He started to sweat even though the breeze drifting through the windows was cool, his stomach doing somersaults as he passed his staff to the High Master and unclasped his cloak to lay it across the man's outstretched arm. He couldn't help but notice how drab and dirty it looked next to the High Master's bright purple.

Darian passed the brown cloak to Dworkin, then traded his own multicolored staff to Miramel for the small package that she held.

"As High Master of the Wizard's Guild, I speak in the absence of a council member. Being the highest ranking, and surviving," he paused for a moment and licked his lips, blinking rapidly before continuing, "member of the guild, this decision is still binding. Kelsar, I hereby strip you of the title of Apprentice."

He forced himself to stay standing, to not fall back a step even if he felt like he had been kicked right in the gut by Ebony. As his eyes dropped to the floor, he could see the High Master's boots move a little closer then just remain there. After a moment there was a soft snort of annoyance and Dworkin whispered something quietly.

"Look up, boy. I strip you of the title of Apprentice," the High Master's voice was softer, almost laughing. Kelsar didn't know why he felt the need to repeat it but raised his head as he was told, and found the High Master holding Keslar's staff out in one hand and a flawless sapphire about the size of a man's eye in the other, "to offer you that of Student."

He gasped and swayed a little where he stood. A sharp pang ran through him, remembering just how similar Head Master Frencis had looked just before the attack. Had he really come all this way, and through everything he had seen, to end up full circle? Only this time it was the High Master himself attending. Still, it didn't quite feel right.

"I never took my tests, never passed the trials."

The High Master's face softened as he lowered the staff and gem, leaning into Keslar a little. "Those silly things? They're nothing compared to what you've done. I could hear everything you said and Dworkin has filled in the holes for me. You survived the attack on the Isle and relayed the information to someone who could help, you save my friend Nemclis from a sleeping spell, dared enter an unknown dungeon to look for me, and so very much more. No mere apprentice could have ever handled himself or his magic the way you have. Now please, take your final test and prove what I already know."

The words washed over him like water and made him feel all warm and squirmy inside. He knew his cheeks must be bright red but he took his staff from Darian's outstretched hand and touched his fingers to the lump of amber at the top. With a few words, he released the amber from the wood then reattached it to the notch just above the small piece of ebony that he had received after his first year at the Isle.

Darian nodded and passed the small sapphire to him. He took a deep breath an slid it into the slot at the top of his staff. He whispered the words and focused all of his concentration on where wood and stone met, willing them to become one. Some stones were harder to control than others and had been set to progressively respond to a Wizard's level of expertise. High Master Darian had been the only one to ever be able to force the rare and precious amethyst to his will.

Saying the last of the spell, he pulled his hand back from the stone. For a breathless moment he just stood and watched, expecting the stone to slide off to the floor at any moment but it held firm. Carefully, he wet his lips and took a step backwards. His movements started off slow and clumsy, the staff spinning awkwardly through fighting stances in his shaking hands, but quickly muscle memory took over and it was sliding through the air. Neither stone moved. With a smile, he tapped the butt of the staff on the stone then walked forward again to present his staff to the High Master.

The High Master looked over the staff briefly before giving a stiff nod and holding out his hand to Dworkin. When the Duke pulled the package from under his arm, the High Master shook it out to reveal a long cloak of the most beautiful blue that Keslar had ever seen. With a quick snap of his wrists, the High Master tossed the cloak over Keslar's shoulders and clasped it at his neck.

"You have proven worthy, Student Keslar." The High Master's hands rested heavy on his shoulders as that smile beamed down on him. "May I be the first to congratulate you."

High Master Darian stepped back to retrieve his own staff from Miramel, tapping it three more times against the stone to end the official announcement.

Keslar didn't know what to say. He stood in shock simply staring at the beautiful gem that was now a part of his staff and the cloak that rested heavy over his shoulders and across his arms. Dworkin practically pounced on him, wrapping an arm around his shoulders and pulling him in tight.

"Sorry for the misdirection, kid, but the look on your face was definitely worth it. I knew you could do it."

"Comairdas, Student Keslar," Miramel said, stepping closer to softly pat his arm and then hold up the edge of the new blue cloak. "This is Wylthem fabric, and we do not give it to just anyone. It will not change color like mine, but it will keep you warm and dry in even the worst weather."

"Thank you, your highness." He wasn't sure whether to laugh, or fall over, or let all the thoughts in his head just tumble out. He smiled for Dworkin then looked back up at the High Master. "Thank you, High Master. It is an honor to have you preside over my trials."

The High Master cleared his throat and blinked a couple of times. "It should have been Frencis, but I am honored to stand in his place. And Keslar? You can call me Darian."

"I'll try, High Master Darian."

72

Darian tried to stifle a yawn as they waited at the large round table. The whole day had been extremely exhausting and now the stars sparkled in the dark sky, the night animals stretching and coming out from dens and burrows. All he wanted to do was sleep for about a week and eat everything in sight.

Dworkin turned from his right and raised a concerned eyebrow. "Are you sure you shouldn't be resting, brother?"

"I'm sure the king would understand," Keslar whispered from his left, still softly stroking his new blue cape. "I mean this guy hasn't done a single thing since we broke you out. What's one more night going to hurt?"

He gave them each a soft smile, wondering how he had ever gotten such good friends, but shook his head. "I'm not really going to be able to rest until that bastard is destroyed once and for all this time. Every day he's breathing is another day that he has a chance to destroy something that I love."

They both nodded and shrugged, thankfully not fighting him. He leaned back in the chair and wrapped his cloak tighter around himself to fight off a shiver. He couldn't tell them the rest of his worries. How as long as Zarentle was around someone might learn the real reason the monster had held him captive. Would his friends look at him the same if they knew who is real sire was? Even more frightening, was the thought of the darkness the spell had left in his mind. The falling of the walls had been so blinding, he hadn't been able to take notice of what happened to it and had been too frightened to look inside of himself since.

Larsle stepped up to the other side of the table, not even attempting to hide the sneer on his face as he looked over the three humans. Darian just smiled back and forced himself to sit straighter and run a quick hand through his hair, nudging young Keslar to do the same. Of course, Dworkin was the picture perfect duke, ready for any court function at the drop of a hat, just like always.

"Presenting Lord of the Forest and protector of all, King Jarelt ep Terieum, Lady of the stones and speaker of the Mountains, Queen Piala ep Marimelsem, and their daughter, Idilm and Princess Miramel ep Jarelt."

Kelsar glanced to him with a side eye and raised brow. He grinned and just nodded. The fact that Miramel was a princess and could also be a high ranking general of the royal guard probably seemed a bit odd to humans, but he had grown used to the Wylthem ways a long time ago. Besides, Miramel wasn't exactly someone who could be told she couldn't do something.

His breath caught as she walked to the table and waited by her seat, smiling at him. He still couldn't put a finger on exactly when their friendship had turned to so much more in his heart. As a child he had seen her as this mystical creature that floated in and out of his life, as he grew she was unchanging and beautiful as ever and their bond had deepened. The first time she had called him carame, he'd known that he would never feel for another the way that he did for her. Not that she felt the same, or that there was any hope for them. Wizards didn't marry so that you could always put Ramleaj first, and Wylthem Princesses certainly didn't marry humans, even if she had wanted to.

Queen Piala was just as lovely as always in her dress the red of garnets with emerald accents at her neck and dangling from her pointed ears. She smiled at each of them, giving Darian a small nod. Jarelt, on the other hand, looked just as tired as Darian felt. The normally ageless Wylthem had bags under his eyes and deep lines creased into his forehead and around his mouth. Sharp eyes studied Darian without revealing anything of what he saw. Jarelt was the only person who had seen the darkness in his mind. Did he know what had happened to it as the spell broke? Darian was afraid to ask.

The three Wylthem royals took their seats as a servant passed more berry wine around the table and set a platter of fruits and cheeses at the center. Keslar started to reach for the fruit but Darian shot him a quick look and shake of the head. You never ate before the king offered. The kid blushed and pulled his hands under his cloak but couldn't take his eyes off the platter. In response, Darian's stomach growled loudly and Miramel had to hide her smirk behind her glass.

"Please, guests, enjoy the wealth of our forest while we talk of such dark matters," Jarelt said, pushing the tray a little closer to them before his eyes locked on to Darian. "I sense you have much to tell us, High Master."

He gave a small nod and smile to Keslar before turning to the king. Suddenly, he'd lost his own appetite. "I will tell everything I can, your majesty, though it is not much."

"My daughter has already filled me in on your captivity and the journey that brought you here." Jarelt nodded as his wife placed a few pieces in front of him, even as Dworkin shoved a heaping plate in front of Darian. "What no one seems to know, is the name of your attacker."

Darian rolled a blueberry between his fingers, keeping his eyes and voice low. "He told me his name was Zarentle, the Demon Lord."

Dworkin nearly choked on his wine while Miramel's eyes went wide. Out of the corner of his eye, Darian noticed the king and queen share a quick look even as Keslar laughed with berry juice on his chin.

"That's impossible," the boy said, wiping his face when Darian motioned then continuing with a grin. "Yeah, until recently I thought the stories were just stories but even they say that the Demon Lord was destroyed by the Wizards at the end of the war."

"Not destroyed," Jarelt whispered, his face pale and hand gripping the wine glass just a little too tight.

Darian nodded and fell back in his chair. "The Wizards tried but could not destroy him, so they created the Barrier Ridge in the Ykor Mountains and, with the help of the other races, locked him behind it. It was supposed to be his prison for all eternity, but by his reports, he has been sneaking into the world off and on for some time now."

"That would explain why he attacked the wizards first," Dworkin leaned forward, his eyes darting around the table for validation of his idea, "to get revenge on those that struck the final blow."

"And stop them from doing it again," Keslar added with a proud snort.

Darian dropped his eyes to the edging on his cloak before looking directly at King Jarelt. "Yes and no. I'm sure that was an added bonus, but his main objective in being on the Isle was to take me. It was a trap and I walked right into it."

Jarelt stared at him as if he could see straight through to his soul still, but it was Miramel who spoke.

"That is what I do not understand. Why was he so determined to get to you, but had no plans to kill you? And has not tried to take you back since you were rescued?"

Darian swallowed. "He wants me to join him. Did everything he could to break me, offered me everything you could imagine."

Chatter broke out around the table but he barely heard them. Keslar and Dworkin nearly laughed at the thought that anything could make him give in, while Miramel spoke of just how horrible that must have been and how proud she was he had stayed true to his heart. He would never have the heart to tell them just how close he had come to breaking. To giving Zarentle whatever he wanted just to make it all stop.

"It is as we feared," Piala whispered, grabbing her husband's hand.

"Yes, carame." He squeezed her hand and straightened in the chair a bit before raising his voice to silence the rest of the table. "The wizards were not the only ones that he attacked that night. The storm he brought was more than a distraction, it was a direct assault upon the Wylthem, upon his people."

Darian's throat closed up as his heart dropped into his stomach. His people? Was Jarelt possibly saying what he was thinking?

Miramel pulled something from her pocket and laid it on the table. It was a stone leaf that looked to have come from the great tree at the heart of Melcader. Her hand brushed it lovingly before pushing it towards her father.

"You mean like Reilen, and the others. The tree losing it's leaves and the infirmary being full. You think that is all connected back to the storm, and in turn, to Zarentle? But why?"

"Each leaf that falls from the tree, is a Wylthem that now sleeps in the infirmary." Jarelt swallowed hard, his hand covering the leaf as if he couldn't look at it. "What we thought to be just a skin condition, a rapid aging, takes hold of them and worsens quickly. The more skin that was touched, the more they are affected."

"That sounds just like the disease Mother Quinta was talking about, the one they use the Cregas medicine for," Keslar whispered as he leaned around Darian to look at Dworkin.

Dworkin nodded but waved him off as Darian's eyes stayed riveted on Miramel. Her face had gone pale and her hand shook slightly as it covered a spot on her arm. She caught him looking and forced a small smile before turning back to her father.

"But why would you think this a deliberate attack from Zarentle?"

It was Piala who sighed and rubbed at her temples. "Because we saw him control the weather similarly when he was still Harshim, though it didn't have the same poisonous properties then. He always did love to show off by making it rain."

Dworkin looked to Darian but he just shook his head. He was as much in the dark here as the rest of them.

"I'm sorry, your majesties, Harshim?"

"Long before he was Zarentle, he was Harshim and my best friend. We were nearly brothers, much like you two." Jarelt leaned his elbows on the table, dropping his eyes to creased hands as if the past could be found there. "He was prince of Femias, the city of the water born outside what you now call Rosewood Forest."

Darian remembered climbing through the ruins they had found on the beach that one summer, the depth of magic that he had felt there and the way it had called out to him. By the way Dworkin's eyes hazed for a moment he was facing the same memories.

"His father, along with mine, were the last to give in to being pushed from our cities by Human and Cregas alike. Our fathers strongly disagreed on how this should be handled though. My father insisted that there should always be a Wylthem presence in Ramleaj, no matter how small, while his was tired and just wanted to find somewhere they could live in harmony with the water and without anyone else trying to take it from them. They agreed to split what was left of the Wylthem people in half. Whoever wanted would stay here in Melcader, and those that did not would travel away with them. Those who did not get a choice were my younger sister, Dialia, and Harshim. It was decided for them that Dialia would go with those looking for a new home, and Harshim would stay here with us."

"I can see why you are so protective of Melcader," Keslar whispered.

Miramel nodded with a sad smile. "It is all we have left."

Jarelt leaned back in his seat with a sigh, his eyes falling once again on Darian. "Harshim and I stood side by side on the hill Marslic is now built upon as his people sailed out towards the portal, storm clouds rolling over his head in his anger that he wasn't allowed to go with them." He took a deep breath, eyes shimmering with dredged up pain. "Then just as the portal opened, the clouds broke and Melteze appeared. He had not been seen in centuries, but somehow heard about their journey and destroyed all the ships before they could reach the portal. Harshim screamed helplessly in my arms as his father's ship burned and sank to the bottom of the sea. There were no survivors."

Darian's mind spun but he didn't want to grasp on to those thoughts just yet. He had to be understanding Jarelt wrong.

"Who is Melteze?" Dworkin growled, obviously struggling to keep up with all of this.

"He is the Dark God," Miramel explained with a shudder, "the lord of everything dark and evil in the universe and murderer of the Bright God, lover of our Lady of the Forest."

"Why would he want to destroy the ships?" Keslar leaned forward, wrapped up in the story.

"He most likely thought they carried at least some of the Carseels with them." Jarelt held up a hand before any more questions could be asked and proceeded. "The Carseels are four great weapons that the Wylthem have guarded as long as our history can remember. Used by the right people they are the only thing that can destroy him. What he did not know was that they were still hidden away somewhere in Ramleaj. Even I am not certain where."

Miramel shook her head. "So you are telling me Zarentle was once a Wylthem, your friend, who's family was killed by Melteze? I always thought Zarentle was a servant of the Dark God."

Darian swallowed a chunk of fruit and tried not to look as interested as he was. Miramel had put the words of his heart into the air. If Zarentle was his father, and Zarentle had been Harshim. He stopped and shook his head. It was all too confusing.

Piala patted her husband's hand and nodded to her daughter. "Grief can do crazy things to a heart. As we all grew, he became more and more obsessed with revenge. He blamed Melteze yes, but even more he blamed the Humans and the Cregas for pushing us off our land, and the rest of the Wylthem for not stopping it. Melteze took notice of his anger and hatred and offered him the power needed to take the revenge that he so craved."

"He disappeared from Melcader, somewhere beyond our reach no matter how hard we searched," Jarelt glanced around the table before sighing, "before returning years later as Zarentle, the Demon Lord, bent to destroy Ramleaj."

"Which led to the War of the Races," Keslar whispered. "All three races, joining together to stop him."

Darian's chair scraped the stone as he pushed quickly to his feet. "Then that is what needs to happen again. If we leave right away, we can be to Darsile in just over a week. I can send a message to Nemclis as soon as we are out of the trees and he can bring Gerent Selick from the Ykor Mountains to meet us there."

"The Cregas?" Dworkin growled, leaning forward to stare at him.

He sighed. He didn't have time for his brother's prejudices right now. While he understood their origins, and knew that members of each race were going to feel similarly about each other, it would do them no favors right now.

"Yes, the Cregas," he snapped, glaring at his brother and daring him to say anything more. "Along with Matthias to speak for the humans, I will speak for the Wizards. King Jarelt, your majesty, will you come with us and speak for your people? Will you help me convince them that we all must work together again if we have any hope of surviving this?"

Jarelt rose from his seat but slowly shook his head. "While I agree with you for once, High Master, I can not leave my people right now. Too many of them are already ill and more succumb every day."

"But—"

He smiled and rested a heavy hand on his daughter's shoulder. "Miramel shall go in my stead. She is heir to the throne, Idilm in our guard, and wise beyond her years. She shall speak for our people, High Master."

As Miramel's cheeks flushed, Darian forced himself to nod then grabbed his staff from where it leaned against the table. "It is settled then. Everyone grab your things and be ready to ride out within the hour."

"Tonight?" Keslar groaned. "Wouldn't it make more sense to get a little rest and wait until morning?"

Darian felt every cell in his body sing in agreement. All he wanted was a nice long rest in a soft bed, and a full meal in his stomach, but his heart was pounding as he thought of the small atrocities that he had already seen Zarentle do. He knew exactly what Zarentle was waiting for before attacking the rest of Ramleaj, what he didn't know was just how long the monster was willing to wait. Locking eyes with King Jarelt, just confirmed that the Wylthem King felt the same.

"I'm sorry." He glanced to Keslar and Dworkin, hating the memories he had to dredge up for them. "You saw what he did to Wizard's Isle, to that small town up North, to Bartol and Cantiem. Can we really take chances on how long it will be before he gives up waiting for me and turns that kind of wrath on the rest of Ramleaj? On Darsile, and Marslic, and Melcader?"

"Come on, kid," Dworkin said, already on his feet and waving Keslar over, "as usual Darian has the right of it. I'll help you pack." He strode a little ways and stopped to grip Darian's shoulder. "Good to have you back, brother. You always were the brains between us. I know you'll figure out how to make this all work."

"Couldn't do it without your strength and the people's loyalty to you." He patted Dworkin's hand, eyes serious as he hoped his message would get through. "Matthias and many others will take your word over nearly anyone else's. I will need you to back me up on this."

Dworkin's eyes darkened but he gave a sharp nod. "I'll do my best."

"That's all any of us can do," Darian whispered, leaning heavily against the chair as the others all brushed past him to prepare.

Once everyone else had left, Jarelt leaned against the table next to him. They remained that way in silent companionship for a long moment before Jarelt finally spoke.

"You are wondering what I saw in your mind, and what I will tell my daughter of it."

Darian didn't look up, he still wasn't certain he wanted to know. "The darkness. It's still in there isn't it?"

"We all have our dark spots. The things about us or the thoughts that we have that we do not share with others. What we do with them is what matters. That is not what I meant." Jarelt moved a little closer and lowered his voice. "You have Wylthem blood, that combined with the human magic on your mother's side is what makes you so strong. And what made Zarentle want you."

His hands gripped the chair until they hurt. "I didn't know, your majesty. Until he told me, I had no idea."

"And the others do not have to until you decide to tell them," Jarelt whispered, tapping his arm until he looked up to meet the Wylthem's dark eyes. "Just remember. Harshim's father was just as kind and caring a man as my own and yet he turned out to be pure darkness. The reverse can be true as well."

73

Braslic

The night was wearing on and the battle was being lost. He was surprised to find himself caring that the human city was being over ran. Whether they would feel the same way about his people or not, no one should lose their home. He slunk along the wall of the innermost castle, muttering to himself for going soft. The second wall had been breached and it was only a matter of time before they crossed the third. He needed to find somewhere safe before he got caught in the middle of a battle that was already lost.

"Daddy?" A voice cut through the night somewhere off to his right. "I want my daddy."

"Shouldn't be here," another little voice muttered as someone sniffled and tried not to cry.

Braslic slid around a large bolder and peered out into the night. Just at the door of the castle stood three small figures, unnoticed by those fighting to protect the walls. One dark haired boy with a little blond haired boy clinging to a slightly older girl who was the tiny copy of Lady Marslic. What in the depths of the mountain where tiny children doing out when there was a battle raging on?

A flash of red filled the night as a wizard rushed past, seemingly oblivious to the fighting around them. The children's faces lit up as they noticed him, reaching tiny hands out for his cloak. Braslic let out the breath he'd been holding and started to back away, thankful the children would be safe without him having to step in.

"Leave me alone, you little brats," the wizard snapped. Braslic turned back just in time to see him pulling his robe away from questing little fingers. "I have important things to be doing. Where are your nurses or mothers?"

The dark haired boy started to cry, silent tears running down his face. "We don't know. Please, Master Clesum. We're scared."

"I don't see how that is my problem."

Braslic couldn't believe what he was seeing as the Wizard turned and rushed away from the children. He ran directly for the wall, sidestepping the main gates that soldiers were adding supports to and slipping out a side door hidden within the rock.

In the brief moments the door was open, a massive Kaldec slipped in snarling and leaping for anyone within reach. It sliced down the two guards next to it, viscous snake tails biting at least one more, before raising its head to sniff the air. When it turned and started to stalk forward, Braslic's gut clenched. It had taken notice of the three children and was stalking them as a house cat might a mouse in its sights.

Even as more magical projectiles erupted overhead and the ground shook, Braslic pulled out the borrowed blades and rushed forward. No child should be left in harms way, but these one's mothers had been kind to him. There was no way he could just stand by and let the most important things in the world be taken from them.

The children screamed as he rushed towards them with blades drawn but he skidded to a stop in front of them and turned to the animal as it drew ever closer. "Stay behind me, little ones, and slowly make your way to the castle. Whatever you do, do not run."

They whimpered and clung to each other but did as they were told. The animal drew ever closer, snarling and snakes snapping. It swiped out a long paw but Braslic jumped over the claws and stabbed down hard with the knife. As they reached the steps up into the castle, it lunged again, catching Braslic across the leg. He screamed and nearly dropped but knew if he went down the animal would be on the children before he could get back up. Pushing underneath another hard swipe he punched the giant cat in the nose with the hilt of one knife then buried the other as deeply as he could into the creature's eye.

The cat reared back with a sharp roar, paws flailing in the air as the tried to shake the blade free. Braslic moved under the beast, trying to avoid the paws and snakes while trying to find an opening for a killing blow. He was down to just one knife and would have to make it count.

Before he could lunge at where he guessed the Kaldec's heart to be, the animals head dropped to one side of him and the body to the other. Even as the body was still twitching, a massive sword covered in its blood lowered to point at Braslic.

"What are you doing with my son and the Marslic children?" The king roared, many heads turning towards them.

Braslic rolled his eyes and dropped the blade he still held. Was there really any use trying to explain? It wasn't as if the humans were going to listen any better than they had last time.

"Oh, thank the twins," the queen gasped as she and Lady Marslic ran out to scoop the children up, "we've been looking for you everywhere."

"They were with this prisoner." The king snarled, pointing the blade even closer to Braslic's face. "How did they even get out of the nursery?"

The queen stepped up next to Braslic, hugging her child close. "Their nurse was injured in one of the blasts. They must have gotten frightened and ran out."

"Bran wanted his Daddy. I wanted to stay with Bran." The little girl sobbed from where Lady Marslic held on to her and her little brother.

The prince lifted his head from his mother's hair to pick up the story. "Big kitty tried to eat us, but small man and Daddy saves us."

Braslic straightened a bit as the sword lowered from his face. The king stepped forward and kissed his son's head before kneeling down in front of Braslic, swiping a hand over his dirty and sweaty face.

"I guess I owe you my apologies and gratitude, Cregas."

"Braslic, your majesty." He grunted, trying to hold back a self assured smile. "My name is Braslic, and I've been trying to speak with you for some time now."

The king nodded with a sigh. "Well, if we survive this fight, we'll have to sit down and have that talk."

Braslic jerked and listened around him. He'd been so caught up in thinking he was about to die, he hadn't noticed the lack of explosions or yelling around him. He looked around and men at the wall were just standing around and watching the other side, as those holding the gates collapsed against them with exhaustion.

"I think the fighting is over," he whispered, looking up to the rising sun, "for now at least."

74

Clesum

Clesum growled and shook his robe back into place after stepping out of the door. Damn kids and their grubby little hands. What were they doing outside the castle anyway? No one had time for the little pests right now.

The protection spell he had planned died on his lips as he realized the monsters were all moving away from the castle. They streamed past him, leaping and snarling, seeming to race each other to get away. What was happening? There was no way that Matthias' men had dealt any kind of final blow to get them to run away. The castle had been nearly taken just moments ago.

The rising sun glinted in his eyes and warmed the air as he raced down the hill after the animals. Every now and then one would swipe or growl at him but they all seemed to be too focused on where they were going to really care about him.

He stopped in awe just outside the last gates. Just ahead a massive portal shimmered in the air, blues and blacks and purples swirling together as the creatures poured into it. He could feel the very power radiating off of the figures standing on either side, holding it open, as black unicorns pawed the ground next to them. A hunger surged in him and pushed his feet forward despite the fear souring his stomach. If he could have even half that power he would never have to bow to anyone again, not the council, not the king, and especially not that brat they called High Master.

"Halt, human," one of the figures manning the portal called. She looked him over with pale cat eyes, hand drifting to the blade at her belt.

One more bow couldn't hurt. He cowered and made himself small, sidling up to her with empty hands out where she could see.

"I take it you are in charge here, madam. I hear your master is a great power, someone strong enough to take on the full Wizards guild and hold the High Master captive. I wish to offer my services to such a man."

A small smile curved her lips as she glanced over the dwindling forces as they slipped through the portal. "And what could you hope to offer, human?"

"Knowledge." He stood a little straighter and offered a smile of his own. "I work closely with the king and his most high ranking subjects, including the High Master. I know the castle layout by heart and any other tidbits he might could use."

She raised a single eyebrow looking much less impressed than he'd expected. "And what do you ask in return?"

"Simple. Only power, and a shot to knock the High Master down a few pegs."

Her laugh caught him off guard. It was much too high and light for such a dark creature and suddenly he had the mental image of wildflowers dancing in a summer breeze.

"Come," she said, still laughing and shaking her head as she motioned to the shrinking portal, "this will be entertaining if nothing else."

75

Keslar

Keslar blinked and shaded his eyes from the morning sun as they stepped out from under the trees. Had a full day and night really passed since they had entered Melcader? How long had it been since the attack on the island? His whole sense of time had been skewed by so much travel and so many events. He'd seen more of Ramleaj in the past weeks than his whole sixteen years before.

"Okay," Darian called, hopping into Ebony's saddle, "what's the plan? Should we go straight to Darsile or swing by the Isle and see if any of them would be free to help first?"

Keslar's head popped up as he scrambled into Mercy's saddle with a lot less grace. "I'd love to see how the Isle is doing but wouldn't that take a long time? We'd have to ride all the way around the forest."

"Did you not pay attention?" Miramel laughed as Arilla slid up next to Mercy, her horn sparkling in the light. "We exited from a different portal when we left Melcader and are all the way on the other side of the forest. Your Island home is only about two days ride to the northwest, and Darsile about five or so days that way. Wait, what is that?"

As soon as her eyes had swung more to the East, her whole body had tensed. She sat a little straighter and shaded her squinted eyes with one hand. Darian struggled with Ebony's reigns as he turned to glance at her then looked wide eyed to Keslar.

"Kid, you know Eagle Eye, don't you?"

Keslar shrank down in the saddle. He knew the spell but had never been very good at it. Why didn't Darian just do it himself. "Yeah, but—"

"No time to argue, just tell me what you see."

Maybe this was his first test as a Student, or maybe the High Master was still too tired. Either way, this was his chance to show what he could really do. He said the words clearly and carefully, pronouncing each one in a soft cadence before tossing his awareness up into the sky. His stomach dropped and he was dizzy for a second before his vision cleared and he was floating high above the world. He saw their little group huddled at the edge of the woods below, the glittering lake that held the Wizard's Isle just a little off like Miramel had said. The thought of flying down and taking a look crossed his mind but he could already feel his power slipping and his hold on the spell weakening. He turned his attention the way Miramel had been pointing and gasped.

"What is it, kid?" Darian's voice was harsh and impatient, the distraction causing the spell to waiver for a moment.

"Smoke," he called back.

With a few blinks and all the focus he could muster, the image shifted and the area of the smoke grew. He cried out as the three tiered city came into view, damages ravaging the perfect layout he had been so impressed with before. The shock knocked him out of the spell and back into the middle of their group with everyone staring at him.

"It's Darsile. Smoke coming from Darsile, there's damage to the lower two walls and smoke coming from everywhere. I couldn't get any closer."

"We're too late," the High Master whispered, slowly shaking his head. "It's already begun."

Arilla pranced in place and tossed her head, Miramel just as fidgety and anxious in the saddle. "Then we should get going. It's at least a four day ride, if the horses survive going that fast."

"That's too long." Dworkin's face went white as he gripped the High Master's leg. "Darian, my family is in Darsile. Leslien and the kids."

The High Master cursed and stared in the distance for a moment before nodding and climbing out of the saddle. With a sigh, he gripped Dworkin's shoulder then passed over Ebony's reigns and motioned that Miramel and Keslar should dismount as well.

"Everyone get in tight, I've never done this with so many before."

"Done what?" Keslar asked, moving Mercy as close as she would come to the other steeds.

The High Master didn't answer him, just closed his eyes and started chanting a spell. Keslar caught a word here and there but not enough to figure out what the spell was. As Darian chanted, a purple light formed in a bubble around them all, stretching and shrinking then stretching again as his face scrunched and his words grew harsher. When he said the final word and snapped his fingers, the light flashed so bright Keslar had to close his eyes for a moment, then blink away spots of purple before he could see again.

Once he could see clearly, he almost didn't believe it. They stood at the center of Darsile's inner courtyard. Where just a moment ago there had been trees and grass was now stone and dirt. He could tell by the way people were looking that it was as much a surprise to them as it was to him.

"I've never even heard of anything like that." Keslar laughed, looking around.

"I wrote it, though I usually only use it for myself," Darian waved him off and started to look around them, but Keslar could see how his hand shook a little and his voice seemed strained. "What happened here?"

"We were attacked. Thank the gods to see you whole and well." King Matthias rushed into the group and pulled Darian into a tight hug, giving three sharp pats to the High Master's back then holding him at arms length. "We're going to need you. I have a feeling the bastards will be back."

"Yeah, probably." Darian nodded, wavering a bit as Matthias turned to clasp hands with Dworkin.

Dworkin nodded to the king but rose on his tiptoes, head searching the grounds. "Sorry I wasn't here, Matthias."

"That was my—" Darian started to mutter but let the statement trail off. His face turned pale and his eyes rolled back before closing, as he dropped to the ground.

76

Dworkin and Matthias both lunged for Darian but weren't able to catch him before he fell. Exhaustion and fear mixed in Dworkin's heart as he knelt next to his brother, gently patting his face and checking for a pulse.

"Don't do this to me, Darian." He growled, tempted to shake the man. "I just got you back."

Gray eyes blinked unfocused then a weak hand pushed his away. "Calm down. Just used a bit too much magic too soon. I'll be fine."

Dworkin sighed and rocked back on his heels. Deep inside him, something started to crack and boil. He really wasn't sure how much more he could take of this constant fear and desperation.

Miramel squatted down next to him, hand brushing his shoulder before reaching down to grip Darian's hand. As she stared into his eyes, a bit of color came back to his face as his gray eyes cleared. After a moment, he nodded and let them pull him to his feet.

"King Matthias, may I have the honor of presenting the Princess Miramel of Melcader." Darian smiled and pushed Miramel forward slightly.

Dworkin quit paying attention as the two royals exchanged pleasantries. He turned in a slow circle, taking in what damage he could see. The walls were charred in some places, bracings still on the main gates where someone must have tried to push their way through. Pieces of the castle had broken off and littered the grounds. Some rooms of the castle must be uninhabitable, but the structure seemed sound enough that there were no concerns of the whole thing collapsing.

All about, people rushed to and fro on different tasks. Castle servants were setting up makeshift tents and residences, helping to organize the people from the city and town beyond that wouldn't fit within the castle itself. Healers moved about in their white gowns, tending to wounded soldiers and citizens alike. Every now and then one would stand and shake her head then a pair of soldiers would carry the still body away.

"They struck at sundown," Matthias said quietly, moving up next to him with the others. "Monsters out of nightmares just like you mentioned. The riders on dark horses threw some kind of magical projectile at the walls and castle, while the creatures swarmed the gates and broke through the lower walls. We were certain they were going to get through the final wall when they suddenly just stopped and retreated."

"Those were not horses. They were Delani," Miramel sighed, and rubbed a hand down Arilla's neck, "unicorns that have been twisted until they are as dark and evil as their riders, the Leranti."

One of the soldiers working to move bodies turned to look at them. Dworkin almost didn't recognize the man as he strode towards him. He still wore the blue of Arnis but his fine clothes were dirty and ripped, some stains looking suspiciously like blood. Brown hair spread in dirty and sweaty wisps across his face as blue eyes narrowed.

"Now you get here. Where were you when we actually needed

you? You were supposed to be leading our men, not running off to whatever game you and the High Master were up to this time."

Dworkin stepped forward, hands gripping into fists at his sides. "Why don't you ask your father where I was, Ranklus?"

He winced and sighed as the king's head spun around to him. He had said too much without thinking. The king was never supposed to know. His issues with Duke Arnis were his own and none of Matthias' concern.

Ranklus fell back a step and stared at him wide eyed. "I have no idea what you're talking about."

"Neither do I, Marslic," Matthias growled.

Studying Ranklus for a moment, he was surprised to find he actually believed the kid. He ran a hand through his hair and tried to calm himself down. "It doesn't matter. I'm here now and there are more important things to worry about."

"I'll decide what should and shouldn't be of concern."

Dworkin looked to Matthias, pleading him to just let it go. The whole thing had been taken care of and they had much bigger concerns. Besides, to tell the whole story he would have to reveal details he wasn't sure Darian wanted everyone knowing.

"Oh for the twins sake, Dworkin," Darian scoffed, pushing his way to the king's side, "quit trying to handle everything by yourself. I was a bit, indisposed, and Student Keslar took me to Arnis to see a healer. Duke Arnis and his court wizard somehow knew we were going to be there and tried to take us captive to use as blackmail to get Dworkin to give up Marslic. To be honest, your majesty, if it had worked they probably would have come after you next. I'm assuming Dworkin told you what was going on with me, so you would have been complicit to keeping it quiet."

"Something it certainly isn't now," Dworkin growled.

Darian just shot him that infuriating grin. "It's over now. Nothing anyone can do with the information."

"Other than make Arnis and his wizard pay for their crimes as soon as we're not in the middle of a battle." Mathias crossed his arms and shot Dworkin a hard look.

Miramel walked up to them with a small laugh. "You won't have to worry about the wizard. He was killed in a little skirmish when they tried to take Darian away. I just never could figure out how they knew these two were going to be there before they even arrived."

Matthias nodded, turning his attention back to Ranklus. The boy actually looked scared as he backed away shaking his head. Dworkin sighed, as much as he couldn't stand Ranklus, there was no way he could have known, much less passed word on to his father.

Dworkin stepped between the king and Ranklus with a hand on his chest. "Your majesty, can we please worry about that later? We need to figure out what is going on here and prepare. You said yourself that they would probably be back."

"So are you going to run off again without even saying hello to your children?"

He couldn't decide whether to smile or roll his eyes. Leslien strode towards him like a vision, her hair coiled around her head and first aid supplies in her hands. He jumped around the rest of the small crowd that had gathered and swept her into his arms, spinning her around before pulling her tight. For a moment, they were the only two people in the whole world and everything was right with their hearts beating in unison. As he set her back on her feet, he pulled the necklace from his pouch and clasped it back around her neck.

"Back where it belongs. As promised."

"Daddy!" The kids yelled, running up behind her to jump and pull at him.

He bent down to snuggle and kiss each, taking in their unique little kid smell and reveling in how their little arms squeezed his neck. Setting them back down on their feet he grinned at each one then pointed over their shoulders.

"I bet someone else would love great big hugs like that, too."

Darian grinned and shook his head at Dworkin but was all smiles and open arms as the kids turned. "You can't be my little niece and nephew. You're way too big."

"We growed, Uncle Darian. You gone long time," Darias said with all the seriousness a two year old could muster.

Lera seemed quieter, pulling at a string in her dress as she looked between him and Darian. "You should come last night. Was so scary. We get lost and end up out here. Wizard guy wouldn't help but the little man hurt the cat and then Bran daddy chop it up."

Cold dread poured over Dworkin. His children had been in danger and he hadn't been here to protect them. He had already sworn his life to king and kingdom but would do so again a thousand times over before he could make up for what Matthias had done. He started to turn to the king but something else his daughter had said stuck in his mind.

"Little man?"

Leslien raised her chin in that way that meant she knew he wasn't going to like what she said, but she was going to say it anyway. "The Cregas that you two had shipped to the dungeon just for trying to deliver a message to you. He put himself in harms way to save your childrens' lives."

His jaw hung open. He really didn't know what to say or think. Leslien stared at him as if daring him to disagree.

"Lera," Darian was saying quietly, his hands on little shoulders, "you said the wizard wouldn't help. Which wizard?"

Her little mouth skewed and she shrugged. "The one who did the show. Why weren't you here? Your shows are better."

"I'm sorry I wasn't here to give you a good show. I promise I'll make it up to you." Darian kissed her head and rose to his feet, letting her cling to his arm even as he turned to raise an eyebrow to Matthias. "Where is your King's Wizard, your majesty?"

Mathias paused and looked around, his eyes growing dark as he scowled. "Come to think of it, I haven't seen him at all since before the battle."

"I wouldn't be surprised if we've learned how Arnis knew I was coming," Darian sighed and took in the devastation around them, "and possibly so much more."

77

Braslic

Braslic's stomach swirled and knotted as he was led through the castle. Most had been kind enough to him since the attack, allowing him to bathe and change and eat, then giving him a place to rest, but there were still the stares and outright avoidance that he had seen everywhere else. Even protecting their prince didn't seem enough for them to look at him as anything other than different. Now he was being called in front of the king. He just hoped he hadn't somehow offended someone and fallen out of what small grace the king had offered him.

Instead of the grand hall that he had noticed earlier in the day, he was taken down a maze of corridors deep into an area that didn't seem to be used much. A part of him relaxed, the close walls and low ceilings reminding him of the tight tunnels of the caves, even the winding stairs that seemed to lead up forever were close and damp. The page leading him stopped silently at the top of the stairs and pushed open the door, motioning him inside.

All the way up the stairs and as long as the door was closed, he had been enveloped in the quiet of stone. All he could hear was the slight drip of moisture within the walls and small creatures scurrying about. As soon as the door opened, he was assaulted by raised voices all talking over each other and loudly enough he was surprised the whole kingdom couldn't hear.

"Your majesty," the page raised his voice and cleared his throat to catch the rooms attention.

The room went silent and all heads turned towards him. The page nodded and quickly turned, shutting the door behind him and dashing down the stairs, his footsteps quickly growing further and further away. Around ten pairs of eyes focused on him, a thousand different emotions seeming directed at him. The King and Queen both smiled from the head of the table and motioned towards the one empty chair. Lord Ranklus snarled from his seat as the other lords looked confused and glanced to their king for confirmation.

Bright green cat eyes stared at him and his heart skipped a beat. A Wylthem? He'd only heard stories about them, hadn't even been certain they still existed.

The remaining figures were the picture of opposite. Duke Marslic studied him with hooded eyes, a mix of emotions across his face. Had he heard about what happened with the children? Was that enough to excuse what happened on the mountain top so many months ago? Probably not, it certainly wasn't for Braslic. A young man in a blue cloak leaned over to whisper something to the Duke but he didn't seem to even hear.

The final figure rose with a broad smile and a sparkle in his gray eyes. He spread his arms, throwing back his purple robe to wave towards the table. "Braslic, how did I know it would be you?"

"High Master," he gasped, moving towards the chair and simultaneously wondering how he would ever climb up into it, "you have no idea what I've been through trying to find you."

Darian uttered a few words and the chair shimmered before lowering itself nearly to the ground. Braslic hesitated but slowly climbed on, gulping slightly as it rose again until he could comfortably reach the table and was on eye level with everyone else.

"My apologies." Darian sighed and settled back in his own chair. "I've been on a bit of an adventure myself."

"Which can be discussed later," the king said, rising from his seat to address the group. "I hereby call this war tribunal to order. Along with myself and her majesty, Queen Narlise, every dukedom is represented, High Master Darian and Student Keslar will speak for the Wizards. We are graced with the presence of Princess and Idilm Miramel of the Wylthem, and Aegis Braslic of the Cregas."

For a moment everyone just looked at each other. Braslic felt most of what he thought he saw on their faces. His people may have been fighting the creatures for some time now, and the odd skirmish with humans, but no one had seen actual war for decades. And never had a war tribunal like this been called since the original war of the races.

Matthias sighed and returned to his seat. "Lord Ranklus, you were the first to notice the attack last night, please describe what you saw."

Ranklus stood and straitened his fine clothes. Braslic swallowed a growl but couldn't keep the sneer off his face wondering if the man's arm had healed. He saw Darian swat Dworkin's arm as he made a similar face. It felt odd having a common enemy with the Duke.

"I was patrolling the walls at sundown, since we're so short on commanders," Ranklus glanced Dworkin's way with a sniff, "when it looked as if a dark hole opened just outside the gates and those creatures started pouring out of it and attacking. It was obvious the Wylthem on the black steeds were the leaders."

"They are not Wylthem, not anymore," Miramel snapped. She bowed her head slightly as all eyes turned to her. "My apologies for the interruption but they are Leranti. They were Wylthem once but have been held in the dark realms of Melteze until they are twisted and evil shadows of their former selves."

Ranklus rolled his eyes. "Semantics."

"It is not semantics, it is fact. You can not blame my people for something they did not do."

"If we're going to talk about things people have actually done," Braslic heard himself saying before he even realized it was coming out of his mouth, "I'm not sure why we are trusting the words of a thief."

Ranklus fist slammed down on the table as he leaned towards

Braslic. "Are you trying to suggest something? Actually sitting as high as the rest of us so feeling big now?"

"I'll say it outright if you want me to. Do all your friends here know how you spend your trips to the mountain markets?"

"Oh, like your people are much better." Miramel rolled her eyes with a laugh. "Stripping the mountain with little care for what is good for her or the creatures who call her home. As long as you make a profit that is all that matters, right?"

Again everyone was speaking over each other and yelling until Braslic wasn't even certain who he was arguing with or about what anymore. He just knew he couldn't sit there and have his people, or himself dishonored that way, and shouted louder to try and be heard.

A sudden silence fell over the room, pressure pushing on Braslic's head as if the air had somehow grown thicker. People around the table's lips were still moving but as no sound would come out, their eyes grew wide and panicked. Braslic tried but couldn't even hear his own voice either.

A bright purple glow filled the room, drawing all eyes to a very angry Darian. He glared around the table at each of them in turn before sighing and shaking his head.

"My apologies, your majesties and esteemed guests." His voice practically thundered in the silent room as he pushed his chair back, leaning against his staff with the purple gem on the top still glowing. "I understand there are years of bad blood here that can't be dealt with in one day. Ranklus, everyone knows you try to steal from the Cregas but rarely succeed. You're a fine fighter and you have a brain. Don't follow in your father's pathetic footsteps."

Ranklus' eyes dropped to the floor as he fell back into his chair. Darian just continued to sweep his eyes around the table.

"Miramel, I know your mother and her kind could teach the Cregas even better ways of mining the mountain that would benefit all, you and your father could teach our healers a lot too. But you can't complain about someone not knowing if you aren't willing to come out of your forest and share your knowledge. Dworkin, brother, I mourned beside you for your men but that battle was not all the Cregas fault, nor was it yours. There is no reason the Cregas can not expand to other mountains and you still feel safe within the borders of Marslic. You just need to talk to each other, not attack first."

Braslic and Dworkin's eyes locked for a brief moment before they both looked away. He had to admit, he'd just been thinking about how perfect the mountain would be for a small satellite community. Not how close it was to a human settlement or how it might look them snooping around. He'd always just considered the mountains their territory.

"Here's what you all need to understand. We aren't talking about some warlord from the Southern Isles, no offense to Keslar or her majesty," Darian paused to nod to each of them before sighing and continuing, "or a disgruntled knight thinking he's going to lead a rebellion. This is Zarentle, the Demon Lord that all our kind worked together and could not defeat last time but merely locked away. If we do not work together and figure out some kind of plan, he will send his pets back and we will be destroyed, along with the rest of Ramleaj and your families. Now, I'm going to release the spell but I only want to hear from someone who actually has something useful to say."

The pressure released from Braslic's head as the light drained from Darian's staff. Darian lowered himself slowly into his chair, his face pale and dark circles under his eyes. Whatever the adventure he had mentioned might have been, it seemed to have left him weakened and exhausted.

King Mathias cleared his throat, casting dark glances Darian's way. He seemed ready to say something when the Queen laid a hand on his arm and leaned forward instead.

"I would think," she said quietly, everyone leaning in to listen, "the place to start would be figuring out why they left this morning when they nearly had us beat. That might also tell us when to expect them back."

The younger wizard sat up a little straighter, his head cocking each way as he seemed to think. "Lord Ranklus said they showed up around sundown last night. Judging by the time we arrived and how much had been done, I would guess they left about sunrise?"

"About that, yes." Matthias sighed, patting his wife's hand.

"When we were at Zarentle's tower," Keslar hesitated and glanced at Darian before clearing his throat to continue, "There were low clouds that hung over the land and kept everything dark, the inside of the tower was pretty dark too."

"You were inside his tower? Why didn't you just kill him then?"

One of the lords interrupted with a scoff.

Dworkin threw his hands in the air. "You think we didn't try? This bastard killed two of my best men and injured—"

Grumbles circled the table as the duke let the statement trail off. Just as things were about to boil over again, Darian let his staff tap the stone floor once with a sigh.

"And injured me. The only reason that Dworkin and his men were in the tower in the first place was because I was being held captive there. Two fine soldiers were killed and I was nearly trapped inside my own magic forever. Now please, can we just focus on how to stop him."

"That's what I was getting at," Keslar said quietly. Darian smiled and motioned that the boy should continue. "I don't know about the Leranti, but it seems like the Kaldecs and Nelcant don't like the light. Maybe that's why they left at sunrise."

One of the other human lords in attendance curled his lip as he looked the young wizard up and down. "Why are you even here, Island Boy? You'll just surrender to him like last time. Probably take the rest of us down with you."

Braslic leaned back as if struck as the boy's eyes dropped to the table. So the humans were just as nasty to each other as they were to his people. That was impressively disgusting.

"That is enough," King Matthias snapped as he rubbed at furrowed eyebrows.

Darian half rose from his chair and leaned across the table towards the lord, teeth clenched and bared. "This young man has already faced down more trials and evils than you've seen in a lifetime sitting in your fancy hall. Sit down and shut up unless you have something actually constructive to add."

The whole table went silent for a second, everyone staring at each other. The young wizard cast shocked looks to the High Master out of the corner of his eye while the High Master winced and turned to his king.

"Apologies, Matthias."

"Save them for when you've actually done something to apologize for, Darian." The king grinned and winked at the High Master.

When no one else spoke for a long moment, Duke Marslic rose from his chair to stand behind the young wizard, big hands on the boy's thin shoulders. "Keslar speaks the truth about the tower, though I hadn't even thought of it until he did. The creatures stayed in the dark and didn't follow us out of it. If that's true, they'll be back tonight as soon as it's dark."

"That doesn't give us a lot of time to plan, but at least it's something," Mathias grunted, rising from his chair. "And maybe a little time for rest. We are all asleep on our feet."

As if on cue, Darian tried and failed to stifle a yawn. All three of his friends surrounding him shared worried looks and leaned towards him even though he pretended not to notice. Braslic shook his head and sighed. He couldn't even imagine someone being able to hurt the High Master to the point people were treating him like an invalid. And this was who they might be facing later that same evening?

"Yes, rest is a definite must for everyone," Darian said, stretching his way out of the chair, "but if the rest of you could possibly work on military tactics, Keslar and I may have just the spell to help you out. Can we maybe gather in the great hall around dinner and compare notes?"

Mathias rapped his knuckles on the table then rose from his seat. "I think that's the best idea we have. Everyone get some rest and then prepare your men, if you have them, and maybe try to get a message back home if that's possible?" The king's eyes brushed over Miramel and Braslic. She immediately nodded but he hesitated until Darian motioned for him to nod. "Then we will gather tonight and do our best to be ready. Ladies and gentlemen, say a prayer to whatever god or goddess you believe in and try to find some joy and love in this day. There is no telling how our world will look by the next dawn."

78

Keslar

Keslar just stayed at the edge of the group as everyone else stood around to talk to each other or ran off in different directions. He had followed everyone down the stairs as they filed out of the room, but didn't know what to do with himself from there. Part of him was still in shock. He had not only sat in on a war tribunal with many of the most important people in the whole of Ramleaj, he had actually been useful. But mostly, he didn't know where to go or what to do now.

Everyone else seemed to have a purpose. The lords and dukes gathered together in groups to chatter, a few of them catching a very tired looking King Matthias in their conversation. Dworkin had dashed off as soon as the king had released them, undoubtedly to see his wife and children then start to prepare the men he cared nearly just as much about. Keslar wasn't sure where the Cregas had gone, and Miramel was speaking with the Queen. All he wanted to do was curl into a bed and sleep as long as he could, but he wasn't even sure where that should be.

"Are you coming, kid?" Darian called from the doorway, turning back to smile at him. "We've got work to do before we can sleep, and I'm really looking forward to getting some sleep."

He couldn't hide his grin as he pushed off the wall and jogged to catch up with the older man. The High Master's arm landed heavy around his shoulders, steering him down the hallway and out into the bright daylight.

Darian's step slowed as they moved through the central courtyard. The rubble from the night before lay strewn about, testament to the devastation these creatures could cause. Nearly every usable space was taken up by tents for displaced families to live in, or tables for food and blankets to be handed out and the healers to continue their work. It seemed everyone who moved about sported some kind of bandage or visible injury. From every face, hopeful eyes watched them pass, looking to them to fix this and make life go back to the way it had been.

"I want you to remember this," Darian whispered, stopping in the middle of the chaos. "Tonight when things get tough and scary, or years from now when you've completed your studies and take the red cloak. Look back on this moment, these peoples' faces and remember that this is why there are Wizards in the world. This is why we were given the gifts we have. It isn't for the kings, or the glamor, or the status, it's for folks like these."

"And for orphans crying in their burnt out villages with no where to go," he whispered, eyes focused on a little boy in his mother's lap with shocked and empty eyes.

Darian's cheeks flushed a little as he grinned and ruffled Keslar's hair. "Yeah, them too. Now come on, let's go find that spell."

They climbed the winding stairs to the very top room of Darian's tower. Keslar settled cross legged on the bed as the High Master started digging through the multitude of books that lined the shelves and sat in piles around the room. He would flip through a few pages, then toss it over his shoulder until the whole room was littered with strewn books.

"What about Nemclis?" Keslar gasped as he glanced over the dragon on the latest book Darian had thrown his way. "He said to just contact him and he could help if needed."

Darian grunted as he pulled another book. "I sent word to him as soon as we got here but it'll take all day to arrive. I don't think they'll make it in time."

"If you told me what you were looking for, I might be able to help."

Darian muttered to himself as he flipped through another book, then slammed it down on the desk with a sigh. "No, I'll find it soon. Oh, that's Atreal by the way."

For a second, Keslar had no idea what he was talking about and then there was a shift in the bed like weight being added. He glanced behind him to find a large orange cat stretching and yawning his way over. Atreal head butted Keslar with a soft purr before curling up in his lap and going back to sleep.

"I didn't know you had a cat."

Darian glanced up from another book to laugh. "Oh, he's not mine. He comes and goes as he pleases and does what he wants. Seems to like you though. Where is that blasted spell?"

"You sure I can't help?" Keslar sighed, petting the warm orange fur and trying not to fall asleep. "I spent a lot of time reading and know about a lot more spells than most Apprentices, even if I can't do very many of them yet."

Darian grinned as he slammed the book closed. "Student, and probably not. It's a spell I've never used but I remember seeing it somewhere in one of these. Luciembe de something."

"Le Luciambre de Numbria," a voice rumbled in Keslar's head. "The small blue book. Top shelf, third from the left."

Kelsar glanced around, trying to figure where the voice had come from but saw no one but him, the High Master, and the cat quietly washing his paws. Shaking his head, he chalked it up to being extremely tired.

"Have you tried that one on the top shelf? The blue one?"

Darian raised an eyebrow to him but reached up and pulled the book down. He flipped through a few pages before collapsing on the bed with the book open between them. "Le Luciambre de Numbria, in darkness find the light. How did you know it would be there?"

"Lucky guess?" Keslar said with a small shrug. "Maybe I've seen the same book in the library. So, what are you going to do with this?"

Darian studied him for a moment but just shook his head with a smile. "We, actually. To do this on the magnitude we're going to need, I think it's going to take both of our powers. Especially since I'm still feeling kind of weak."

As the High Master's eyes dropped to the blankets, Keslar quietly looked over the spell trying to work through his own emotions while letting the High Master face his. He couldn't imagine how hard it must be for someone so powerful to feel weak and his heart broke for the High Master, but it also surged with pride that the man would trust him with both his vulnerability and such an important mission.

"I'm barely a student, and never been at the top of my class," Keslar whispered, looking over the old and complicated spell. "Are you sure you don't want to try to get a master from the Isle to help you?"

Darian reached out to scratch Atreal's ears before grinning up at him. "Don't forget, I've felt the magic inside you back at the tower. You have so much more potential than you think, kid. Will you trust me?"

Heat flooded his cheeks but he forced himself to meet those intense gray eyes. "Of course, High Master."

"It's Darian, Keslar." Darian laughed, pushing up off the bed and stretching. "But first, I want to show you something."

He followed Darian back down the stairs, the cat right at his feet, until they stopped at a door about halfway down. Darian pushed it open and motioned Keslar inside. It was a small room much like the one they had just left except empty save for a few random baubles that looked to be overflow of Darian's extensive collection. Keslar walked inside and looked around before sitting on the bed.

"Do whatever you want with the place, I never use it for more than storage."

Keslar blinked and narrowed his eyes at the Master. "I'll leave it just how I found it, I promise. It will be nice having somewhere private to nap though."

"No, kid," Darian laughed, shaking his head as he backed out of the room, "this place is yours for as long as you want it. I know how it is not having a place to go besides the Isle."

Keslar gasped, looking around with new eyes. "Thank you, High Master. I could never repay you."

"Yeah, you can, just by being the wizard I know you can be. Live up to that potential I saw." Darian yawned and stretched, pulling the door to behind him. "And by getting some sleep. I'll need you at your best later."

"Thank you," he whispered again then thought of something just before the High Master was about to close the door. "Could I ask just one more thing?"

"I have a feeling it's never just one more question with you, but go ahead."

He chewed on his lip for a second, the mention of the men they'd lost having stirred his mind. He'd promised Bartol he'd do something and so far had not had a chance to live up to that promise.

"Are all those books you have about magic? I was hoping that you might have some on the history and lore of the Southern Isles. I'd like to learn more about my father's people."

The High Master's eyes seem to narrow and darken for a quick second and his whole body went rigid. Keslar backed up a small step, afraid that he might have offended the High Master somehow but couldn't imagine how. Darian glanced over his shoulder for a second and seem to let out a long breath before looking back with a smile.

"I think I've got a couple and I'm sure the royal library will have some more. We survive this night and I'll be sure to find you everything you could possibly want to know. Okay?"

"Okay. Thank you again, High Master."

"Darian." The High Master's voice and laughter echoed even as he closed the door and started to climb back up the tower steps.

79

Miramel's throat was tight and eyes moist as she watched Darian walk away. Was his arm over Keslar's shoulders out of companionship or for support? She had never seen him this weak and that frightened her more than she cared to admit.

"Your highness," a soft voice spoke next to her.

It wasn't hard to force a smile as she turn to incline her head to the soft spoken queen. "Please, call me Miramel, your majesty."

"Only if you will call me Narlise," the queen smiled and inclined her head in return then motioned down a nearby hallway. "I know we are all tired but I was hoping I might could speak to you about something."

"Certainly."

Narlise led her down the hall and up a side flight of stairs. She pulled a small key from her pocket and unlocked the door before leading Miramel inside and locking it again. The queen's frail shoulders shivered and she rubbed at her arms under her long sleeved gown.

Miramel moved to the large fireplace along one wall and set flame to the logs already piled there. Before long the crackling fire was chasing the chill from the room.

Narlise settled onto the cushioned settee and poured them each a cup of tea from the service that had been set out. "I asked the maids to prepare the room, hoping that you would agree."

Miramel glanced around the small sitting room with its comfortable seating, rich fabrics, and various sewing accouterments. Add a few rocks and gemstones and it would have looked much like her mothers rooms back in Melcader. She guessed it was fair to say that no matter what race, women of power needed a cozy space of their own to escape to.

Miramel settled on a nearby chair and accepted the cup, sniffing to determine what herbs it had been brewed with. Taking a sip she tried to remember if she had brought hers with her so she could suggest a different blend for the queen.

"Please excuse my bluntness, but why all the secrecy just to ask if I can do anything for your illness?"

Narlise sighed and set her cup down. "Our favorite wizard has been talking."

"No, though he should have. I can see it written all over you, and saw the way you looked at me when Darian mentioned my people are healers. Why would it have been a problem if he had though?"

"That was quite the show he put on. He didn't say anything that wasn't true though." Narlise laughed then her face fell before looking up at Miramel through her lashes. "You are a princess, I'm sure you at least partly understand. I am an extension of my husband, I represent the goddess of the twins on earth. I can't have the people thinking I am weak or it could reflect poorly on him and the kingdom as a whole."

Miramel set down her cup and leaned forward with her elbows on her knees. She had not really taken the time to unpack everything he had said, was not sure she wanted to. But she did understand what Narlise was saying. Being royalty was so much more than wearing a crown or making decisions.

"If you are asking me, I will assume that your own healers have not been able to help?"

"The great mother herself wasn't able to figure it out."

Miramel pursed her lips before moving to sit on the couch next to the queen. Anxiety swirled in her stomach and every beat of her heart said to run away, but the pain and desperation in the woman's eyes wouldn't let her say no without at least trying.

"I should warn you that I am no where near the skill of my father and have not done this for quite some time."

Narlise just smiled and gave a small shrug. "For seven years I have felt as if I were a foreigner in my own body. No matter how much I sleep, I'm tired. No matter what I eat, or don't eat, I feel ill. It's as if something is eating me alive from the inside out and if nothing changes, I will just fade away. If Darian has faith in you, then so do I. What do you need me to do?"

She took the queen's hand in hers, feeling every tiny bone beneath the skin. "Just lay back and relax, sleep if you can. Try not to think about what I am doing or you might accidentally lock me out."

Narlise nodded and laid her head against the back of the couch and closed her eyes. Miramel wet her lips and adjusted to a more comfortable position, before turning her attention inward. She had seen her father, and even Jalden, do this a few times and knew they walked right in as easy as opening a door and it frustrated her that she had to slowly think through each step. With Darian it was different because of their connection, someone she did not know so well made it infinitely harder. If anything went wrong, it could damage her or the queen in ways that she did not even want to consider.

Carefully, she dove into herself and grasped onto her own center. She visualized her spirit as a thin thread that she could run through her fingers and wind into a tight ball that fit into her pocket. The loose end she tossed out and tied around her physical body, double checking the knot then circling back to check once more. Finally satisfied, she set out to slide into Narlise.

There was a small resistance but she was able to push through and open her ethereal eyes within Narlise's mindscape. The queen's spirit took on the form of a warm valley sheltered by high mountains.

A lovely place filled with light and life. Miramel guessed it was probably a beloved place from childhood by the sheer perceived size. Somewhere, a young lady had felt safe and happy. But even here something marred the perfect landscape. Many of the trees and flowers were withering, a few even dead already.

The sky grew darker and the dead more frequent as Miramel walked deeper into the valley. Heavy clouds rolled above her, the scuttling of bugs along her skin and an acrid smell burned her nostrils as she stepped past the mountain and onto a circle of desolate land. Floating ahead of her was what looked like a pulsating blob of ink with long tendrils stretched out in every direction.

Miramel swallowed her fears and concerns to try and focus on finding a source. Her finger brushed one of the tendrils and it hissed against her skin. Nausea turned her stomach as words of hate and malice echoed in her mind. This was no natural illness, that was for certain, there was nothing natural about it. The magic reeked of human even though there wasn't the lacing of color like she had noticed followed Darian and Kelsar's skill.

If only Darian had the ability to mind walk so he could look at this. She spoke the few words he had taught her to force the spell to show itself and tried to memorize what she saw, but it was all so strange. Everything was done in duplicate with odd symbols laced through. It was by far like nothing she had every seen before. She would write out as much as she could and show it to him once all this talk of battle was done. Maybe there was a key word or something that would disable the whole thing. Not that such matters were so easily handled in her experience, but she could only hope.

At the edge of the devastation, she squatted down to press her hand into the dirt. She pushed as much of her own energy as she dared into the land, trees and flowers sprouting and growing to maturity in minutes all around her. Concentrating on the circle, she willed the trees and bushes to grow together, to criss cross and join until a thick wall surrounded the blob. She could not remove it completely, but hopefully she had slowed it long enough to find a better solution.

Slowly and carefully, she followed her string out of Narlise. As she passed, flowers and trees perked up, spreading their leaves to the sun that was the queen's warmth and love of family and kingdom.

Miramel pulled her string, tightly rewinding it to be sure nothing of her was left behind except the work she had done.

Within a few moments, they both opened their eyes. While Miramel was worn and ready to curl up and sleep forever, Narlise looked refreshed and rejuvenated.

"I have not felt so alive in years. Does that mean you fixed it?"

Miramel pulled her arms in tight against her body and leaned against the back of the couch, shaking her head. "No, I'm sorry. This type of magic is beyond me and I'm afraid of touching the wrong thing. I did what I could to stop it from spreading, though. That is probably why you feel so much better."

"Spell?" Narlise closed her eyes for a moment and let out a shaky breath. "So it is as I feared. It's not just a rare disease, someone has purposely done this to me."

Miramel rose, stretching and yawning. "I'm afraid so, your majesty. I promise to try and figure out who but first—"

"Yes, of course, dear. We all must rest for the battle. Thank you for taking the time to speak with me."

She smiled and gave a soft nod, pausing to glance over the relief and fear mixed in Narlise's eyes. If she had never agreed to try, Narlise would have gone on thinking she just had some rare disease the healers couldn't figure out, likely until it totally destroyed her, and the perpetrator would remain unknown.

If they could do this to the queen, could there be others out there suffering just the same? She thought of the way her own people were suffering and the whispered comment Keslar had mentioned about Cregas medicine. Maybe Darian spoke a bit more truth than she cared to admit.

80

Keslar

Fire raged around him, as far as he could see. The city, and the whole world it seemed, had been fully consumed. He stood high on the walls of Darsile, the fire licking at his feet and pulling at the edges of his cloak. The heat blew into his face, ashes floating through the air.

"High Master?" He called, clutching his staff to his chest. "Dworkin? Miramel? Someone, help me."

"There's no one left to save you little wizard."

He spun around, searching for the voice then wished he hadn't. Zarentle floated in the air above him, black robes blowing in the wind and a viscous grin on his face. He raised his arms and called down more fire, falling like meteors from the sky to crash around Keslar.

"You failed them all, and now they're gone."

"No," Keslar gasped, backing up until his feet were on the very edge of the wall and the fire licked up his back. "I didn't do anything. I didn't cause this."

Zarentle floated closer, eyes narrowed. "Are you sure? Death certainly seems to follow you wherever you go."

"That," he gasped, heart dropping as he nearly lost his foot, "those weren't my fault."

"Maybe not, but you are the common link, aren't you?" Zarentle raised his arms and the fire took on a life of it's own, rising in front of Keslar and twisting itself into shapes until he watched the worst parts of his life pass like shadows. "First your family and the whole town, then the Wizard's Council. Poor Bartol and Cantiem."

Tears streamed down his eyes and he shook his head. He didn't want to watch but couldn't tear his eyes away as Master Frencis was sliced open by the Nelcant, as Bartol's severed head rolled to his feet, at Cantiem's lifeless body sprawled on the marble floor."

"Yet, somehow, you still made friends. People still trusted you. Now, even they're gone."

The flames twisted and jumped again flashing the faces of the people who had come to mean the most to him. Miramel's shock and horror as a Leranti ran her through with a blade, King Matthias backed into a corner of his own castle with Nelcant creeping up on him. Bile rose in his throat as he watched Dworkin collapse on his children, trying a last ditch effort to keep Kaldec claws from them. And Darian, eyes again glazed over and lost as he was carried away into the night. Back to Zarentle's tower.

"No," he screamed again and again until his throat was raw and his voice cracked. "It's not my fault. It's not my fault."

"Keslar! Kid, wake up!"

Something was shaking him, he tried to fight it off but they wouldn't stop.

His eyes opened and he took a gasping breath. The strong hands quit shaking him but didn't let go. The sun shone in bright reds and oranges through the window of the tower, painting Darian's face in stark relief as he stared at Keslar.

"Hey, kid, there you are," Darian whispered, gray eyes soft and full of concern. "It's okay. You're safe."

He tried to talk but his throat was raw and his stomach clenched. Tears pricked his eyes and wouldn't go away no matter how many times he blinked. Darian sighed and released his shoulders, scooting just a little closer on the bed. Even though he hated himself for it, the tears overtook him and he collapsed into the High Master's shoulder, strong arms tightening around him.

Darian calmly rubbed his back until the tears dissolved into a hiccuping mess but didn't let go right away. "How?"

"How what?" Keslar muttered, sitting up to swipe at his face and bury himself in the jumbled mess of blankets.

Darian smiled gently, staring at the wall instead directly at him. "How has a boy of only sixteen, gotten this far and seen all the things you've seen, without falling apart long before now?"

Keslar opened his mouth but no sound came out. He tried again to the same affect, so gave up and snuggled lower in the blankets with a shrug and a grunt. Warm fur brushed against him as Atreal shoved his way up through the blankets and into Keslar's lap, purring loudly. The heavy presence and soft vibrations of the warm cat helped bring his breathing back to an even keel and banish the lingering fear. In its place quickly rushed shame and embarrassment that the High Master would see him this way just when he seemed to be gaining the man's respect.

"Do you want to know my guess?" Darian scratched under Atreal's chin and waited for an answer so Keslar just shrugged again. "I think, up until now you've had something to focus on, a task that needed to be done. First you had to figure out how to get free of the council room, then you had to find me, then you had to care for me. Now, you don't have a task so all that stuff you've been shoving aside is catching up with you."

"The spell," he muttered without lifting his face from Atreal's fur.

Darian shrugged. "A battle that may or may not happen tonight, and you are currently safe and sleeping in an actual bed with all of your friends safe and around you. I'm just sorry I didn't think of it before and saved you a little bit of trouble. Though they are feelings you'll need to work through. Keep them buried too long and they'll haunt you when you're awake as well. Understand?"

"Yes, Master."

"Now, get yourself together and come down when you're ready.

Matthias thinks it a good idea if we have an extra church service before the sun sets and there's still some things to prepare for the spell." Darian patted his leg before rising and walking to the door. "And kid?"

Keslar sniffled and poked his head out of the blankets just a little more. "Yes, Master?"

"Don't be ashamed to let Dworkin or I help you work through those feelings. He and I have cried to each other many times over many things, there's no shame in you doing the same."

Keslar nodded but just sat staring at the door long after it was closed. He raised his knees to closer snuggle the warm cat and let the words roll around in his head. It was hard to imagine the Duke or the High Master breaking down the way he had. Yes, Dworkin had been on the edge a couple of times while they feared for Darian, but he'd always kept himself in control and the group moving forward.

"Focused on a task," Keslar whispered, to the cat or himself. "Like High Master said."

81

Dworkin closed his eyes at let the peace of the service wash over him. As the priests went through the motions of lighting the incense and saying the traditional prayers, his heart called out with a prayer of his own. His thoughts cried out to the god and goddess to hear their plea and be with them. Every one he loved and cared about were within the city walls, just waiting for demon spawn to descend upon them.

In front of him, Matthias sat in full royal armor, back rigid and crown glittering in the soft candle light. Next to him was the brother he had only just gotten back and still seemed so weak and the young man next to him trying to hide tears on his face. The rest of the church was filled with lords and knights and common soldiers, all just as scared and anxious, whether they chose to admit it or not. Across the street, the church of the goddess, where his wife and the Queen sat, would be full of wives, daughters, and healers making the same plea.

"They searched the whole castle, can't find any sign of Clesum. Not that I'm surprised."

"Darian," Dworkin hissed and kicked his brother's leg.

Darian straightened from whispering to Keslar and grinned sheepishly. "Sorry."

Dworkin just sighed. After what Keslar had told him the last time they were in Darsile, he understood but it still annoyed him. Darian may not carry the same level of devotion to the church, but the least he could do was be respectful.

Darian seemed to read his thoughts and nodded more seriously. Dworkin nodded back with a small smile and turned his attention back to the service. The priests in their bright yellow robes lowered the large golden sun disc, symbol of their god and his power. Brother Odin bowed his head, everyone in the congregation quickly following suit.

"Oh great god, brother to our goddess, protector and creator of all," Brother Odin's strong voice echoed through the hall, "we call on you to bring your light and your protection. Turn your shining face to our great city and hold us within your hand. Let not those within our walls who's hearts are not pure turn your love from us."

Dworkin opened his eyes just slightly to glance around. Darian and Keslar were sharing a glance as a few others shifted nervously in their seats. This wasn't quite like the prayers he was used to growing up or in Marslic.

"Your children cry out to you, oh lord and god, to guide us through this night. Let your children survive as a sign of your might and your grace so that we might turn back to you and bask in your light. You are the one true god, the only one meant to control the heavens and the earth, life and death. Show us your mercy so that we might be reminded."

Matthias gave a small snort as everyone raised their heads and got to their feet. Dworkin looked around for a moment before leaning forward.

"What was that?"

Matthias shook his head. "I'm not really sure what's going on with

Brother Odin. He's becoming more and more radical and outspoken by the year. I just pray the god and goddess are with us either way."

"I'm not sure if he would recognize the god if he were right here in the church with us," Keslar grumbled, following them out into the aisle.

"And you would, young wizard?" Brother Odin called from behind them. "Or do you look to the man teaching you to play at being a god instead."

Darian stepped forward, his eyes flashing, but Dworkin pulled him back. There would be enough enemies to fight tonight. They didn't need to waste the energy on their own people.

Shocked gasps filtered through the crowd as a lone figure strode up the aisle. People fell aside, opening a wide path for the Cregas to march towards them. He had cleaned up and looked a little more refreshed, ax and dagger strapped to his hips again. Dworkin felt his teeth clench but tried to tap down the feeling. Once this was all done, he fully intended to ask Darian what he had meant back at the war council, but old hurts were still hard to ignore.

"Your kind is not welcome here, Cregas," Brother Odin snapped, pointing a shaking finger at Braslic. "This is the house of the god and only his children should enter."

Braslic shrugged with a laugh. "Trust me, I didn't want to but that Wylthem friend of yours thought it best she not come into the boy's side of things and someone had to tell you the sun is just about to set."

"Thank you, Braslic." Darian sighed, glancing through the stained glass windows at the angle of the sun then laying a strong hand on the Cregas' shoulder. "Did you have time to sing to the ancestors?"

"Aye, though it doesn't sound quite the same outside of the cave, I'm sure they heard and will have our backs."

"As will the Lady of the Forest and the Lord of the Land," Miramel called from the door, Leslien and Queen Narlise at her side. "But we can have all the gods helping we want and it won't make a difference if we don't prepare."

Brother Odin's face went red and a guttural growl spilled from his clenched teeth as he threw his arms in the air. "Neither of you should even be here, do not defile this place by calling on your heathen gods as well."

Miramel and Braslic seemed unperturbed but Darian was offended enough for all of them. Rising to his full height, he spun Braslic around then gave a tug on Keslar's arm. "Come on. We are finished here and there is much to do, my friends. Coming Dworkin?"

"In just a minute." He stared back as Darian's gray eyes bored into him.

Matthias nodded and motioned to the door, his voice much lower and more controlled than Dworkin felt. "Go ahead, High Master. We'll be along in just a moment."

Dworkin and Matthias stood between the seething Brother Odin and the rest of the congregation filing out of the church, many casting curious glances back over their shoulder. Once the door clanged shut, Matthias sighed and crossed his arms.

"You can not do or say anything to me, Matthias," Brother Odin sniffed, looking the king up and down.

Matthias just grinned and rubbed at his beard. "You personally? No, I can't. I could however, stop coming to services all together and only worship the god and goddess in the old ways around the castle. How many lords and ladies do you think would still attend if their king was not?"

"A kingdom can only survive when built on a solid foundation," Odin hissed, stepping closer to the king than anyone would dare if not within the protected walls of the church. "If you turn away from the god, your reign will crumble and fall around you, taking us all down as well. Maybe it already is given all the recent events."

Dworkin sighed and decided to try a different tactic. "Brother Odin, I've known you nearly my whole life. You were always one of the most devote and caring men I had ever met. You recommended Brother Piet for Marslic and he has been a perfect fit for years now. What has changed, my friend?"

"The world has changed, Duke Marslic. You prepare for battle as we speak. You can not tell me that there is not a growing darkness in our world that only the god of the sun could cure."

Dworkin and Matthias shared a look, unsure what to say. They really did not have time for this tonight and needed to prepare their troops for when the real darkness descended. Matthias nodded his head towards the door and Dworkin followed, quickly losing the bit of peace and hope that he had found from the service.

"You should not anger them so," a frail voice spoke up from one of the pews as they passed, Brother Odin hot on their heels. "You risk turning strong souls away from the faith when they are needed the most."

Dworkin glanced back to see a small bent man still seated on one of the benches. Watery eyes looked up as Brother Odin stopped to stare at him, head cocking and eyebrows furrowed.

"I'm sorry, sir. Do I know you?"

The old man shook his head sadly and sighed. "You did once, but I'm not so sure anymore."

"Sir, can the Duke and I help you get somewhere before the fighting begins?" Matthias called back from the doorway. "Most are taking shelter within the castle. I can take you there myself."

The old man turned and smiled a toothless grin at them then shooed towards the door with a twisted hand. "Thank you, your majesty, but I am right where I should be and you have much to do."

82

Night crept upon the land slowly. The castle of Darsile and her surrounding city were shrouded in complete darkness. Not a single torch had been lit or spell light called, making it seem as if all the inhabitants had taken to hiding beneath their beds. Even as they marched towards the castle, Menir doubted that was the case. The humans had fought strongly and passionately the night before, and now both Darian and the princess, Miramel, had joined them. Still, she had her marching orders and would do as she was told. Even if it was a fools mission.

Four of her fellow Leranti rode on either side of her. She had wanted to bring a whole platoon and end this quickly but Melteze said it wasn't time yet. She wasn't sure where Zarentle stood on that opinion, but figured as long as nothing was said, it best not to anger anyone. Ahead of them, the Nelcant lumbered. They laughed and muttered to each other, anxious for another night of fun, herding the Kaldec ahead of them. She wished they would be quiet for once. Miramel would hear them coming from at least a mile away. Not that it would make much difference.

She started to doubt as they climbed the hill to the castle, passing through the gates and over the walls without opposition. As they neared the third and final gate, she rose in the saddle to look around.

A bird call sounded, drawing her attention to a rooftop just above her. A second later, a bright searing light flashed. She was blinded for a second as her eyes adjusted but the Nelcant and Kaldec screamed. They would be blinded by the light and practically useless.

"Hold the lines," she screamed.

She gasped as her eyes adjusted. The humans had actually outwitted them. In the bright light, her animals hissed and swung blindly. The gates of the castle flung open, a force thundering out towards them. Even as she considered retreating, another force spilled from the houses and storefronts behind them. They were trapped in a vice that was tightening quickly.

The fast twang of a bow snapped above her and the Leranti to her left fell. She caught a glimpse of Miramel pulling another arrow to her bow. Menir dropped from her steed and slid under the awning of the building. Two more Leranti fell in quick succession, leaving only her and one other. She pulled her swords with a hiss. That princess may be her father's daughter, but she had some of her mother in her for sure. More than expected.

The animals were already being over ran. She did not have much time. She glanced across the battle and realized the humans had left the gate wide open. Just above it was the source of the light. She couldn't look for long but got a clear enough view to see two figures in long cloaks standing together. That would be her prey, she was certain of it. Slashing at anything that moved too close, she slid through the shadows, stalking her true mission as the battle was lost around her.

83

Dworkin was already growing tired and sweating under his armor. The stench of blood and death was all around him. His men moved in a perfect formation, wedging the creatures back towards the king's ranks at the gate. The plan had worked perfectly but there was still danger in these close quarters.

He glanced up to the wizards above as the light wavered for a second then surged back to life. He prayed they could hold on just a little longer. His sword buried deep into a Neclant's chest with a dark squish as a kaldec fell to his right. He felt a presence press up against his side and nearly swung out with his elbow but noticed Ranklus's blood stained face.

"Do you think they can hold out?" Ranklus yelled over the

screams and roars. "If we lose that light, this is going to be a very different battle."

Dworkin shook his head. There were still so many creatures. Ranklus was right. If they lost the light and the creatures were able to attack better, all could still be lost.

"Darian will hold it as long as he can," Dworkin grunted, ducking under the club of a Nelcant, "even if it kills him."

A small ax buried into the brain of the Nelcant he'd been fighting. Braslic jumped from seemingly nowhere to the creature's shoulders to retrieve his weapon with a smile. "Then we should kill these damned demons so that it doesn't go that far."

Dworkin nodded. Braslic jumped from the beast as it fell to the ground. He turned to choose his next opponent, nearly slipping on the blood soaked ground. Ranklus didn't fair as well, his feet going out from under him. He reached for Dworkin but was on the ground too quickly.

Dworkin and Braslic jumped into the fray as animals tried to swarm Ranklus. Dworkin grunted, watching out of the corner of his eye as Braslic used his size to his advantage. The Cregas ducked under swings, scrambled up Nelcant backs, and slipped out of reach of Kaldec claws.

"Neither of you should care," Ranklus gasped as Dworkin pulled him back to his feet.

Braslic landed next to them again with a grunt. "For now, we're on the same side. Besides, I already knew you weren't that great with a sword."

Dworkin's laugh died quickly as Braslic screamed. Ranklus reached out and sliced off the tail of the Kaldec but it was already too late. One of the snake heads was still clamped on to the Cregas's shoulder. With a grunt, Ranklus shoved his sword back in its scabbard.

"What are you doing?" Dworkin yelled, trying his best to cover them both.

Ranklus hefted the unconscious Cregas over his shoulder. "You two saved me. I can't let him die because of it."

84

Miramel moved from roof top to roof top. She tried to keep one eye on the battle below, sending out a well placed arrow when needed. The creatures were well under control and would be taken out soon, as long as the light held. That was not what she was worried about. She was certain there had been five Leranti to begin with and only four had fallen to her bow. The other one still had to be around somewhere, and she had a sinking suspicion she knew where.

Two buildings from the castle walls, she picked up her pace to gain momentum. At the last moment she pushed off the slippery tile and flew through the air, rolling to a landing on the top of the wall. She dropped her bow and pulled her sword as she crept towards Keslar and Dworkin.

As cheers erupted from below, the two wizards released their spell. People were quickly lighting lanterns and torches inside so they were not plunged into complete darkness. Miramel watched Darian turn to pat Keslar on the back when she noticed a dark shadow behind him. Another figure crept forward, dark blade in each hand and deadly focus on Darian. She crouched and cursed herself for dropping her bow, doubting she could reach Darian before the Leranti did.

"Carame," she screamed, hoping he could hear her over the celebration starting below, "behind you."

Darian spun with purple power already forming in his hands but he never released it. The light glowed in the Leranti's face as she rose to grin at him. Miramel pushed to her feet and started to run. Still, she doubted that she could make it on time.

"Darian. She's Leranti. Stop her."

He glanced her way then back to the Leranti. Miramel wondered for a second why she wasn't striking then realized, she was calling on power of her own. Miramel's skin prickled and crawled as the power of the night gathered around the Leranti. She wasn't sure what the Leranti had in mind but did not want to find out. She reached out with her own power but there just were not enough living things close by for her to call from.

Darian still hesitated, holding the purple magic as if waiting for some sign. Keslar looked to her then back at Darian before growling and pushing his master out of the way. With sharp staccato words, blue magic tossed from his hands and smashed into the Leranti's chest. It wasn't enough to kill, or even seriously injure, her but she stumbled back and the crackle of her power dissipated in the air.

Miramel pushed past the wizards with a glance to Darian. His face was frozen in shock and horror as the power faded from his hand. She shook her head. Whatever he was going through would have to be dealt with later.

The Leranti was getting back to her feet. Miramel adjusted the grip on her sword and prepared herself.

"I told you, princess, I have other things to handle before you and I get to play."

Miramel grinned. "You are not getting anywhere close to my friends unless you make it through me."

"As you wish."

They both dove at the same time, meeting in a clang of metal. Again and again their swords clashed at a dizzying pace, neither gaining the upper hand. Miramel backed up a few steps and tried to rethink her approach. The Leranti did not follow, instead testing the waters with her shorter swords. She tapped the end of Miramel's sword, expecting a reaction. When she tried again, Miramel took the opening and dived forward with her blade pointed directly at the Leranti's heart.

Instead of parrying, the Leranti jumped backwards, somersaulting off the wall and down into the courtyard below. Miramel growled and followed, landing low to the ground to protect her knees.

Just ahead of her, the Leranti stood with swords slack at her side and jaw open. Miramel paused a second then looked around.

Only a few feet away, Leslien stood next to the queen as they prepared to treat the wounded. The Lady Marslic and the Leranti stared at each other in shocked silence as the gem around Leslien's throat glowed brightly.

"Idonlynta" the Leranti gasped.

Miramel nearly dropped her sword in shock until the Leranti took a single step towards Leslien. She raised her sword and dashed to the lady's side, even as three guards rushed from behind them. The Leranti growled and slid back into the darkness, leaping over the wall and back into the night.

"That was the Leranti you were talking about? The ones who used to be Wylthem?" Leslien whispered at her side, lightly fingering the necklace as its glow faded. "What did she say?"

Miramel swallowed and shook her head, barely believing it herself. "Literally child of my child. Closest translation would be granddaughter."

85

Darian stumbled back against the parapet as Miramel pushed past him to deal with the Leranti. He closed off his magic with a sharp snap like slamming a door. Even as the colored glow faded from his hands, his heart continued to pound and he couldn't catch his breath. Keslar was at his arm saying something but he couldn't hear over the storm in his mind.

By the Twins, what if Keslar had been hurt by his hesitation? What if Miramel hadn't shown up when she did?

The spell had come to mind so easily, his magic answering just the way it should. He wasn't sure it would kill someone like a Leranti, but it would have knocked her back at least. The release word was on the tip of his tongue when it struck him that it was the same spell he'd used back at the tower.

He'd frozen, thinking of that poor woman hanging from the chains. Her screams as his magic fried her every nerve still echoed in his ears over the cheers of the crowd around him. Using his magic for transport or light hadn't bothered him, but the moment he used an attack spell she had come to mind. He didn't even know her name.

"Master?" Keslar still stared at him, wide eyed.

He made a show of straightening and adjusting his cloak but his mind was still racing. What if the darkness wasn't from being blasted by Zarentle's spell like he thought? What if it came from being his son and had been spurred to life by that kill? Could he ever trust himself to use his magic as an attack again?

"Master? Are you okay?"

The boy's voice sounded miles away but Darian's nod and weak smile seemed enough to calm him.

"Tired. I guess my magic isn't fully recovered yet." He patted the boy's arm and started for the stairs. "I couldn't have done it without you. Come on, sounds like the celebration has started without us."

Keslar followed a little too closely as if afraid Darian would fall over at any moment. As soon as they reached the ground level, they were swarmed by people cheering and clapping them on the back. Keslar's face burned a bright red as people thanked and congratulated him, shoving a drink and food into his hands. Darian just smiled and nodded for him to go enjoy himself.

Dworkin stepped up and clapped him hard on the back. "Nice work, brother. The plan worked perfectly."

"The war is not won yet," he sighed and shook his head, then forced a smile as his friend's face started to fall, "but we have survived the night and for now that is enough. How bad were the losses?"

Dworkin crossed his arms and kicked at the dirt. "We lost a few, a lot of injuries. The healers are working their magic now."

"Miramel? Braslic? The king?"

"Matthias suffered a slash to the leg but nothing major. He is being stitched up by a healer as we speak."

Ranklus strode towards them, his uniform stained with dark blood and stress showing in his eyes. "The Cregas is with the healers also. He lost a lot of blood but they think they'll be able to stop the poison in time to save the arm."

Darian raised an eyebrow to Dworkin. The Duke grinned and shrugged, giving him a look that said they would talk later.

"I am here," Miramel called, storming up to them, "and I need to speak with you."

"Mira, about that—"

She glared at him then glanced to the crowd. "Not that, well, at least not yet. There is something else I need to discuss with the two of you."

"Darian." Zarentle's voice boomed over the castle, loud as thunder.

Everyone still in the courtyard stopped and turned to the wall where he and Keslar had just stood. Dworkin was already pulling his sword, his other hand on Darian's shoulder.

Darian prayed his brother couldn't feel the way he was shaking, couldn't see the effect Zarentle still had on him. His eyes narrowed at the figure cloaked in red at the top of the wall.

"Clesum?"

Clesum spread his hands and the master's cloak flapped around him like bloody wings. His eyes shone with a dark light and his pudgy face was twisted into an all too familiar expression.

"Darian," Zarentle's voice spoke through Clesum again, "this is your last chance. Join me so that we might put your pets out of their misery quickly."

Darian shrugged Dworkin's hand off and moved forward a few steps. "That's never going to happen. You've tried your worst and I'll still never join you."

Clesum started to rise into the air as Zarentle's laugh pummeled Darian. "You have not come even close to seeing my worst."

"Try me, the outcome will be the same," he yelled back before turning, not at all surprised to find his friends right behind him. "Get everyone inside. Now!"

Dworkin raised his sword. "We're not leaving you alone with that."

Keslar nodded as Miramel motioned for a nearby soldier to hand her his bow. Darian gritted his teeth. He loved them for their bravery and devotion but they had to get these people to safety. Everyone was just standing there staring as light began to gather around Clesum's body.

"I know," he forced himself to say. "I'll hold him off while you get everyone inside and bar the doors. Circle around from the back and he won't see you coming."

Dworkin growled but turned and started to herd people inside the damaged building. Keslar rolled his eyes and Miramel stared at him for a moment longer before starting to help. Darian was already magically sealing the back doors and preparing a spell for the front as he jogged back up the stairs to the wall.

Clesum had started to scream. The light twisted and swirled as his body grew, morphing and changing in the air. The sound of breaking bones and Clesum's agony filled the night. There was a bright flash that forced Darian to shade his eyes for a second. When he blinked away the dots from his vision, Clesum was gone, replaced by a hideous and grotesque creature.

Tatters of the red cloak floated around leathery wings that blocked out the fading stars, a spread ribcage that sprouted four massive arms ending in long fingers that spread like claws. The skull like head tilted and cracked, jaw dislodging to let out a guttural scream that Darian felt in his bones.

Finally, the doors closed with everyone inside. He slammed the lock spell against them and double checked the ones at the back doors. He let out a breath and gripped his staff. At least they would be safe while he tried to figure this out.

The creature turned and dove for him. Wood spun in his hands in well practiced movements. It connected with jaw bone, sending the creature careening as he spun through to keep from jarring his arms. Before he could even set his feet again, the creature had recovered and was baring down on him again. Over and over they repeated the dance with no easy end in sight.

Darian grunted as another impact sent him stumbling backwards. He was getting winded already and his staff felt like it weighed three times as much as usual. He was still weaker than he wanted to admit and tiring fast.

The creature circled around him again, catching him from behind. Claws ripped through his arm, sending searing pain through him and knocking his staff from his hand. He dove but the wood slipped through his fingers and off the wall to clatter on the courtyard far below.

"What's wrong, boy?" Zarentle's voice taunted. "No magic left? Or are you scared to use it? Afraid you'll like the feel?"

He dove towards the stairs, rolling across stone as the creature attacked again. Hot wind fluttered his hair and cloak as the claws passed just over him then rose back in the air. He gagged against the hot smell of death that followed and clutched at his arm, hiding within the staircase for a second to catch his breath.

"I swear, if I survive this," he growled, forcing himself down the stairs, to hell with the rules. Dworkin's teaching me to use a damn sword."

"Why are you dragging this out, my boy? You're just making it harder on yourself and your friends. Join me now and maybe I'll even let you spare one."

He waited until the sound of flapping was the farthest away before rushing out to grab his staff. His arm was dripping blood and burned with every movement but he planted his feet and gritted his teeth.

"You will never have me and as long as I am breathing, you'll never take Ramleaj."

The creature spun and grinned at him. "Then I guess its time you stop breathing. A shame. I had such high hopes for you, my son."

86

Keslar and Miramel grunted as they pushed the last board in place across the doors then gave Dworkin a nod. The Duke nodded back then climbed on a bench and clapped his hands for everyone's attention.

"Good people of Darsile," his voice rang over the crowd, "everything is under control. Please just remain calm and this will all be over soon."

Keslar looked over the crowd in amazement. Of course they were still exhausted and frightened but there were no hysterics or panic. The Duke's words settled over them like a balm, soothing nerves like a healer might soothe pain.

He paused and cocked his head as Dworkin jumped back down next to him. Something was tickling his senses and tugging at his attention.

"Okay, lets get back out there and help Darian," Dworkin said, already moving toward the other set of doors.

"No," Keslar whispered more to himself than anyone around, "he wouldn't."

Dworkin and Miramel stared at him. He held up a hand to stall their questions and moved back to the door they'd just barred. He rattled off the spell for magical sight and a soft purple glow covered the door.

"What is it?" Miramel growled, still gripping her borrowed bow.

Keslar gritted his teeth and bashed his hands against the door. "He's sealed the doors. I felt his power but assumed he was directing it at Clesum."

Dworkin and Miramel shared a knowing glance and set out for the back doors. Keslar followed at their heels, weaving through the crowd best he could, even though he already knew what they would find.

"Maybe he was just adding another layer of protection for the people," Dworkin yelled over his shoulder. "He wouldn't trick us like that."

Miramel grunted as they reached the other set of doors. "Darian not do what it takes to keep those he loves safe and face the evil alone? Do you even know him?"

"He's been through a lot lately." Dworkin shrugged but there was an edge of desperation to his voice. "Was hoping he'd learned a lesson."

Keslar pushed between the two as Miramel stared the Duke down. He pressed his hand to the wood and said the spell again. His heart dropped deep in his gut as the same purple glow appeared.

"He set this one even before the front. He never planned on us getting out of here to help him."

"I'm going to strangle him," Dworkin roared, kicking at a bit of rubble on the ground.

"We have to figure out how to actually keep him alive for that," Miramel snapped. "Is there any way for you to deactivate it, Keslar?"

He chewed his lip as he studied the glyphs and symbols in purple. It was actually a fairly simple spell, hastily thrown up, but everything read backwards like trying to read from the wrong side of a parchment.

"I might could, but I'd have to be on the outside."

Dworkin cursed as Miramel narrowed her cat like eyes. Keslar gripped his staff as his heart started to race. How much time had passed with the High Master facing that thing alone? The others hadn't seen his face after the encounter with the Leranti. Something wasn't right with the High Master and he definitely shouldn't be trying to do this without them.

He jumped a little as Miramel tapped him on the shoulder then pointed up.

"If we could get you up there, do you think you could squeeze through that hole in the rubble?"

He took a step back to get a better look at where she pointed. Above them was one of the areas that had been damaged in the first attack. Parts of the ceiling had fallen in to show the room above with only rafters in between. The rock of the wall had collapsed upon itself to create a mass of rubble but a small patch of brightening sky showed through a space at the top.

"I think so, but how?"

Miramel grinned and set down the bow then unstrapped the quiver from her back. She backed up a couple of steps and bounced on her toes for a second before running towards the opposite wall. With seemingly no more effort than walking, she ran up the wall then pushed off. Twisting in mid air, she stretched her arms out to grab the beam far above their heads and spun around it until she sat on top.

"Dworkin," she called down, "can you boost him up here?"

Dworkin reached up and arm as if testing the distance then pulled two chairs over. He motioned Keslar to one before climbing onto the other and turning to hold out his hands with fingers laced together.

"Put your foot here and just trust me."

Keslar took a deep breath and held it try and stop himself from shaking. Using Dworkin's shoulder for balanced, he forced himself to look up and keep his eyes on Miramel as he placed his foot in the Duke's hands. He could feel Dworkin's muscles shift under his hand and suddenly he was flying through the air.

He only had a second to panic before Miramel grabbed his wrist and pulled him up onto the beam next to her. They both sat there panting for a moment before she motioned to the pile of rubble.

"We are depending on you, Keslar. Once you get out, climb down and release the spell on the door."

He nodded, not trusting himself to talk. Quickly as he dared, he shimmied across the beam and up the rubble to squeeze out the small hole. The wind whipped his cloak around him as he clung to the wall, searching for a way down.

"No magic left?" Zarentle's voice cut through the night. "Or are you afraid to use it?"

Keslar shook his head. His fears had been right. Darian wasn't using magic against the creature. It didn't make any sense. He couldn't possibly hope to defeat it with just his staff.

With no hand holds in sight, he used a small spell to slowly float himself to the ground. He could hear Darian and the creature continue to yell at each other but couldn't catch what they were saying over the wind. Maybe Darian was yelling spells and his worries were for nothing.

Keslar ran to the doors and touched the spell again. He searched for a second and found the symbol that should unlock it. He pressed his hand to the symbol and said every release word he could think of.

Nothing happened.

He growled and shoved his hand in again, repeating the same list and throwing a few more in for good measure. After what felt like the hundredth try, the spell sent a spark of power through his hand and made him jerk back.

"Damn it, Darian," he muttered.

He could hear Miramel and Dworkin banging on the door but had no way of letting them know what was going on. He'd just have to apologize to them later or, better idea, get Darian to apologize.

He crouched low to the ground and crept around the edge of the building. He really wasn't sure what he was going to do. He doubted he would be much help to the High Master but maybe he could convince him to open the door.

Darian stood in the middle of the courtyard with his staff ready. His shirt was ripped and arm bleeding. The creature hovered just above him but Keslar couldn't feel any power gathering. What was the High Master doing?

"A shame," the voice was saying, "I had such high hopes for you, son."

What? Keslar shook his head. He couldn't have heard that right.

The creature dove. Darian's staff swirled so fast it was a blur of brown and sparkling gems. He bashed away each of the creature's attacks but was tiring quickly.

The creature saw it too. When it feinted left then pulled up sharply, Darian wasn't able to right himself as his staff met empty air. The High Master cried out as he fell to his knees, cloak pooling around him.

"Darian, look out," Keslar yelled as the creature angled its claws at the High Master's back.

The world seemed to freeze for a second. Both the High Master and the creature turned to look at him. Darian's face filled with terror as he screamed for Keslar to get out of there. The creature just grinned with way too many needle like teeth then shot towards him.

Keslar didn't make it three steps before the creature was upon him. Sharp claws dug into his ankle as he was hoisted into the air with blood rushing to his head.

"Well, well," the voice rumbled around them, "what do we have here? Looks like you left one of your toys out. How careless."

87

Darian used his staff to push to his feet. His knees ached from where he'd hit the stone and his arms felt like wet noodle from swinging his staff, but none of that mattered against the terror squeezing his heart.

"Put him down, Zarentle."

The beast flew over his head, keeping Keslar just out of reach. To his credit, Keslar didn't scream or blubber even though it would be perfectly understandable if he did. His dark eyes were wide and glued to Darian, brown skin flushed with blood and fear.

"I don't think so." Zarentle laughed. "But what should I do with him? Tear each limb off one by one? Squish him like a bug? Or maybe carry him up to the clouds and see if he leaves a dent when he falls? I'm sure you could come up with some ideas, my boy."

Darian gritted his teeth as his magic surged along with his fear and anger, begging for release. "I'm not like you."

"Are you sure?" Zarentle pulled far back into the sky, playing with poor Keslar. He tossed the boy in the air, catching him at the last moment by whatever limb was the closest. "Because sacrificing someone I claim to care about to protect myself is definitely something I would do."

Darian had quit listening. He snapped open the door quelling his magic and let it flood his system again. Fear of the darkness came with it but couldn't compete with the fear of losing Keslar. He couldn't have another body on his conscience. He would just have to deal with any consequences later.

And get his timing just right. He took a deep breath and rattled off both spells under his breath, holding them just at the ready in his mind. Purple light glowed around his right hand as a ball of pure energy gathered around the tip of his staff where he held it behind his back. He held his breath for as long as he could, letting the ball grow with each pound of his heart.

The next time the creature tossed Keslar into the air, he yelled the release word of that spell and stretched out his hand. The boy jerked out of the creature's grasp and floated towards him.

As soon as Kelsar was far enough away, he let the locks on the doors drop and fed that power into his staff. He could already barely hold Keslar up but this was going to take everything he had left.

The creature tried to go after Keslar but Darian whipped the staff out from behind his back and released the spell. It blazed into a bright purple column from the tip of the staff to smash into and wrap around the creature.

For a brief second he tasted the acrid touch of Zarentle's power, unsure if it came from the creature or inside him. He raised Keslar just a touch higher then pushed everything else he could down through his staff. With a great pop, the creature exploded in a flash of black and purple sparks. Meaty pieces rained from the sky to squelch against the stone and buildings.

"Darian!"

He didn't even have the strength to turn toward his brother's voice. Keslar was already dropping too fast as spots formed in his vision.

"Dworkin," he yelled over his shoulder, tossing his hand that direction with the last of his strength, "catch! Please!"

Zarentle's voice screamed along with Keslar's but it sounded further away and pained. "I am not done with you, Darian. You will pay for defying me."

Darian dropped to his knees, the world spinning and quickly fading to black. "You know where to find me."

Darian clung to the flag pole of the highest tower on Wizard's Isle and let the wind whip through his hair and cloak. He knew that he was deep within his own mindscape again but was hesitant to leave. Here, Ramleaj spread out below him as a perfect tapestry. Darsile was whole, the Great Forest wasn't sick, and Marslic wasn't in danger. Maybe if he just stayed here forever, that wouldn't change.

The scene below shifted and blurred until he was looking out over the sea where it touched the borders of Rosewood Forest. It was so odd to mourn ancestors that you didn't even know you had until just recently. Even more odd to think of how many hours he had spent playing on those beaches as a boy, never knowing that was where his father's, and therefore his, fate was sealed.

"I have to go back." He sighed but didn't move from his perch. Not yet.

"The work is far from done," a woman's voice whispered on the wind.

The scene shifted again. He knew what it would show even before things stopped spinning. Far to the North, even here in his mindscape, the tower made of darkness stood at the center of the circle of desolation it had created. Dark tendrils were growing from the tower and trying to reach out into the world. Or into his mind, he wasn't really sure.

"Maybe they'd be better off without me. What if I'm just a liability? What if I turn into him?"

"Can't we let them rest just a little longer?" A male voice spoke in his ear.

"They've already been through so much," a third voice said, female and almost familiar. "There is surely time for rest, and good food."

The first voice came again, warm and soft. "A little, but they must not delay too long. Things are set in motion that can not be undone."

"The prophecy?" the male voice whispered.

"All the pieces are on the board," continued the younger female.

"Yes, my children."

They didn't seem to be speaking to him, but to each other. There were no other presences in his mindscape, he would know if anyone had entered and he didn't think that he was hearing with his physical ears. Who were they, and how was he able to hear them? He tried to think of what prophecy they might be speaking of, but couldn't bring any to mind at the moment. To be honest, he'd never put much weight in them.

His eyes wrestled open to a gray twilight and the soft glow of candles. He blinked a couple of times to clear his vision and realized that he was in his own room in the top of the tower at Darsile, the cat Atreal a heavy weight where it snored on his legs. His arm was clean and bandaged but still ached like hell. His head was pounding and his throat so dry he coughed twice trying to clear it.

There was sudden movement in the corner of the room. A head jerked up as paperwork rustled and was pushed hastily aside. Before he could even cough again, Dworkin was at the edge of the bed with a cup of water held to his lips. He drank greedily before laying back against the pillows, the urge to sleep again still strong.

"You have got to stop scaring me like this." Dworkin growled as he set the cup down a little too hard.

"Keslar?"

Dworkin shook his head. "He's fine. A little bruised up and frightened but he's a strong kid."

"Yeah, he really is." Darian groaned and pressed a hand to his head to try and slow the general throb. "How long have I been out for?"

"Three days, Darian. You scared the life out of us. Again. Why would you try to fight that thing alone?"

He sat up so fast he nearly bashed into Dworkin. "Three days? Have there been attacks? What is Zarentle doing? Is everyone okay?"

"Everyone is fine." Dworkin pushed him back down with a firm hand and a dark glare. "There haven't been anymore attacks."

Darian let himself relax back into the pillow but couldn't stop the fear that clenched his heart. "There will be. We didn't stop him, just knocked him back a bit."

"Enough that you are going to stay right here and actually finish healing this time. Do you have any idea how exhausting it is thinking I've lost you over and over?"

He found a weak smile for his brother as the door creaked quietly open. Keslar backed into the room with a tray of food balanced on his hip. Darian's stomach growled violently in response to the rich smells that filled the room.

"The Lady Leslien asked me to bring this to you and insists that you eat every bite. She says you've been skipping too many meals and that it won't make the High Master wake up any quicker."

Darian winked at Dworkin before clearing his throat. "I hope you brought enough for two. That smells almost as good as old Marta's cooking."

The tray nearly slipped from Keslar's hand. Dworkin dove to grab it from the boy and set it on the bedside table as Keslar just stood there with his jaw open.

"High Master, you're..."

"Awake, yes, so it seems." He smiled and motioned the boy closer. "You didn't think old Clesum would be the thing to take me out, did you?"

Dworkin glanced between the two wizards for a second before nodding. He squeezed Darian's good shoulder then rose to his feet, trading places with Keslar in the small room.

"I'll go and find my own dinner, and let everyone know the patient is awake and obviously going to be fine if he can crack jokes."

Darian closed his eyes for a second as the door creaked open again then cleared his throat. "Brother?"

"Yeah?" Dworkin glanced over with eyebrows raised.

"Thanks, again, and I'm sorry."

Dworkin's lips pressed together and his eyes were more moist than Darian had expected. After a moment, he just nodded and slipped out the door. It closed firmly behind him, leaving Darian and Keslar alone.

Darian pushed himself up to sit against the pillows, wincing as the pressure made his arm scream in protest. Keslar hovered in the middle of the room, obviously unsure of what to do with himself.

"Have a seat, kid."

Keslar grabbed the chair and pulled it closer to the edge of the bed. Like Dworkin had said, he didn't seem to have any obvious injuries but there was a haunted look in his eyes Darian wasn't sure would ever go away.

"You shouldn't have been out there, kid. I put the locks on the doors for a reason."

Keslar sat a little straighter, eyes narrowing as his hands bunched in his blue cloak. "Stupid reasons."

"Excuse me?"

"Your pardon, High Master," the kid paused to clear his throat and for a second looked like he would chicken out then raised his chin again, "but you are friends with some of the most powerful people and best fighters in all of Ramleaj. Duke Marslic, the princess of the Wylthem, a Cregas warrior, even the King himself."

Darian cocked his head with a smirk. "And a very brave, though a bit impetuous, young wizard."

Color rushed to Keslar's cheeks but he wouldn't be distracted. "You spend all this time lecturing them of how they should trust each other and see each other's strengths, but then again and again you don't trust them to fight by your side."

Darian sighed as his shoulder's slumped. If only life were as straightforward as the young saw it. He remembered being that age and thinking that he knew everything and that the older generation just complicated things for the fun of it.

"It isn't that I don't trust them, or value them," he whispered. "I'm just trying to keep them safe."

Keslar raised an eyebrow. "And how are you going to do that if you're dead?"

Well, if that wasn't a punch to the gut then the way Keslar rose and grabbed the tray certainly was. He calmly moved it to the seat of the chair and brought both close enough that Darian could reach it without having to move much. Quietly, he stood back up and pulled his cloak tighter around himself.

"You've saved my life twice now, High Master, and for that I'm eternally grateful. I just hope you can figure out that as much as you love all of us, we love you in return and it nearly kills us watching you try to kill yourself. This Demon Lord guy? We might not be able to beat him without you, but I'm pretty certain you can't survive him without us either and the faster you realize that the sooner we can start making an actual plan."

He just sat, blinking at the kid with nothing to say. Of course his other friends had told him much the same over the years, but he'd never expected it from the young man. Something about it coming from someone so young and so emotional, made it hit different.

"You should eat and get more rest," Keslar said much quieter as he started for the door. "I'm sure everyone will be vying for your attention once they know that you are well."

He pursed his lips and closed his eyes for a second. He didn't want the kid to think he hadn't been listening, but there was something else that just couldn't wait.

"Keslar, about what you heard. What Zarentle said…"

The kid paused in the doorway before looking back at him, face completely blank. "I have no idea what you're talking about. Eat and rest so that we can finish this once and for all."

My travel notes

property of

Student
~~Apprentice~~ Keslar

Wizard and Healer Levels

- Recruit - gray - no stone
- Novice - black - ebony
- Apprentice - brown - amber
- Student - blue - sapphire
- Disciple - green - emerald
- Acolyte - yellow - citrine
- Master/Mother - red - ruby

Most children tested and taken in around age of 6 (I was 9. Don't know why I wasn't tested). Once taken in, you only visit family on holidays or special occasions. Never marry or have children so always put Ramleaj first. Many Masters say this means should have no ties and encourage you to distance yourself from even family.

Only Darian has passed Master to control amethyst and wear purple robe so they made the title High Master for him
 —(think anyone else will ever be able to? Certainly not me, but maybe someone)

Wizards show rank in robe colors and stones on our staffs
- (though most don't have a cloak made by the Wylthem! It's so nice!)

Healers all wear white for cleanliness but show colors in their necklace and belt, cloaks if traveling in cold weather

Wizard's Isle
- soaring towers
- huge library (my favorite place)
- lots of classrooms and dorms, masters get suites in outer towers
- magical barrier to keep anyone uninvited out

Healer's Mount
- smaller, squat buildings
- lots of gardens with healing herbs

Wylthem

- Ancient race of people who were the first to inhabit Ramleaj
- Live for thousands of years

(Miramel won't tell me exactly how old she is. Gave me a dirty look for asking.)

- Believe in Five gods but only one remains
    - Lord of Land ruled over all
    - Guard of Mountains
    - Spirit of Sea
    - Maiden of Meadow
    - Lady of Forest (lover to Lord of Land)
- Centuries ago, Dark God (Melteze) killed Lord of Land, weakening all the others. All but Lady of Forest faded away as their cities were abandoned
    - Said to be a prophecy to defeat Melteze and bring back Lord but no one seems to know anything other than it involves the Carseels
        - Carseels - four magical weapons that when brought together by right people could defeat Melteze. Even King Jarelt doesn't know where they are.

- Four types:

    - Forest born
        - Miramel and King Jarelt
        - love trees and animals
        - hair usually in browns, reds, and green or hazel eyes
        - most stealthy and adventurous
        - breed unicorns! Real, live unicorns!

    - Rock born
        - Queen Piala
        - sturdy and dependable
        - love mountains, rocks, and gems
            (like the Cregas, you'd think they'd get along)
        - used to live at base of Ykor Mountains

    - Water born
        - thinnest, most flamboyant
        - love rivers and lakes but mostly ocean
        - used to live in city of Femias along

coast south of Marslic

    - Meadow born
        - love open spaces, flowers, and farming
        - if like Leslien - always happy and gentle
        (such a good mom)
        - not sure yet where their city was

Words I've learned so far:

    - Carame - someone you care very deeply about, often romantic partner but not always
    - Inonym - direct translation 'of my blood', term of endearment for a beloved child
    - Enonym - term of endearment for a mother or father
    - Idilm - high rank in military/scouts
    (Miramel is this AND princess!!)
    - Laranti - a Wylthem who was twisted and turned evil by the dark god
        - thought just a myth by many but Miramel and I saw that one. She was like the

dark version of Miramel. Scary good at fighting too.

Cregas

- live in Ykor Mountains
  - mostly in Mother Mountain (we call it King's Peak, Wylthem call it 'rock that touches the sky')
  - short and small to fit in caves
  - very pale skin and sensitive eyes from not being out in sun much
    - wear layers and big hat when have to be out (Braslic hates his hat, wonder if we couldn't figure out something better for him)
  - mine the mountains for gems (that Wizards and Healers use! Jewelry makers too) and ore (to make tools, weapons, and tons other stuff)
  - Llamas!!
    - four legged pack animal
    - Braslic says more sure footed in rocks that horses or ponies
    - about size of pony but really long neck and pinched face
      - scream when frightened or angry
      - WARNING! Can bite and spit!!
      - super soft fur makes great yarn
  - "King" (called Gerent) chosen by prowess in

battle not heritage
      - anyone can challenge rule at any time
    - Aegis - leader of guard and military (Braslic! I know so many important people. It's crazy!)
    - tight knit community - everyone 'brother' or 'sister' or 'aunt' or 'uncle' if elder
    - worship Mother Mountain and ancestors

IMPORTANT PEOPLE I'VE MET

Dworkin

- Duke of Marslic

- foster brother of High Master Darian

- married to Leslien, father of two (adorable) kids

Bartol

- head of Dworkin's personal guard

- from Southern Isles like my dad!

Cantiem

- knight in Dworkin's service

Duntiel

- knight in Dworkin's service

Nemclis

- dragon raised by Darian

- not so bad, I guess

King Mathias

- king of all humans
- rules from Darsile

Queen Narlise
- queen of humans
- Southern Isle heritage
- mother to prince

Master Clesum
- King's Wizard

Lord Ranklus
- Duke Arnis' second son
- cocky and arrogant but good fighter
- I think he's good guy, deep down.

Maybe very deep

Marta
- street vendor in Darsile
- makes best fruit tarts!!

Brother Orin
- head of god twin's church

- doesn't like foreigners

- doesn't like wizards

- really doesn't like me

Zarentle

- aka Demon Lord

- super powerful

- what is his plan?

High Mother Quinta

- leader of the Healers

- kind old woman

Disciple Carly

- met at Healer's Mount

- told us about Wylthem healer

Selte and Raslan

- Sister and brother

- run the Golden Gryphon in Arnis

Jalden

- Wylthem healer living in Arnis

- water born

Miramel

- princess and Idilm

- close friend of Darian

Arilla

- Miramel's unicorn!

Idilm Larsle

- seems to be head of all guard

- close friend of Miramel

- doesn't like humans but especially Darian

King Jarelt

- Miramel father

- King of Wylthem

- powerful healer and kind leader

Queen Piala

- Miramel mom

- Queen of Wylthem, rock born

Braslic

   - Cregas

   - Aegis (head military guy) to his people

Leranti

   - Miramel says that's what she is, not her name

   - used to be Wylthem but got turned evil

   - scary good fighter

Guy in White

   - was that a dream? Still not certain...

Acknowledgments

I first met Darian over twenty years ago when I was only nineteen. I was obsessed with both Lord of the Rings and Star Wars, determined to create a world of my own that gave me the same feeling. Hopefully, it becomes somewhere just as exciting for you to visit, dear reader.

Obviously, a story that has been around for that long has had a lot of help. There are so many people to thank that I'm sure I will forget someone. If you are not listed here, I sincerely hope that you know who you are and just how much you mean to me.

My first reader and biggest fan has always been my dear mother. How I wish I could have reached this point soon enough for you to have seen it. I will forever be eternally grateful for the hours that you sat listening to me talk the story out, for caring about my characters with me, and for reading draft after draft. It was your encouragement and love that kept me going to this point.

To my husband and children- thank you for putting up with me. You deal with the laundry not being put away, with dishes still hanging out in the dishwasher, with Mom staring off into the distance as you try to tell her something. Thank you for loving me even when I'm crazy, for giving me the time I need to bring these characters to life, for listening to me babble over and over. May all your dreams come true the way you have helped mine to.

To my writing groups and friends- from Forward Motion Writers, to Bookdun, to the Threads community. There is nothing like being able to talk to other creatives who know what you're dealing with, who are willing to read your work and give honest critiques, to cheer you on when you succeed and commiserate when your down. As always, Mooseythehut, NeciaPheonix, and especially GlassQuill, you're the best friends that a writer girl could ever ask for and I hope you know just how much I appreciate and love you.

And of course, to you dear reader. Thank you for picking up this book and giving these characters a chance. I hope their world has been an escape for you, an enjoyable adventure to fulfill your fantasies as so many stories have been for me. Most of all, I hope you'll come back for the rest of the story.

About the Author

Robin Rhoden grew up in the beautiful Flathead Valley in Northwest Montana and now resides in Billings, Montana while dreaming of the sea. Diagnosed with ADHD in adulthood she is a proud advocate for the neurodivergent community

She is claimed by a husband who builds things, a daughter who wants to know everything about everything, and a son who loves puppies and video games. She is also the emotional support human for a pitbull/lab mix who just wants the world to love him as much as he loves them.

When not writing, she loves anything true crime, crochet, drawing, and getting outdoors. Be it hiking through the woods, camping by the lake, or a day on the beach, she'll be there with a camera and a notebook to capture the moment.

Robin writes in multiple genres but always with a magical twist, a touch of romance, and strong characters facing complex problems with no easy answer.

Printed in Great Britain
by Amazon

42443445R00238